# HOUSE OF CEDAR

## CHAD CORNISH

Acknowledgements:

For my parents, who supported this novel in countless ways.

And with gratitude to my editor, Dave Walker, who went above and beyond.

# PROLOGUE - *The Stranger*

*The man came at dusk. I had not expected him or anyone else as I finished the daily toils in my employer's vineyard, and I had first believed him to be a mirage through my sweat-stung eyes. In the far distance his form dissipated in the shadows beyond the field and I turned back to the line of weeds between the crops, vowing to drink a greater portion of water from the mended goatskin bag which hung on the post near the watchtower.*

*This was beautiful land, especially at sunset. A formation of rampart-like clouds had spread across the western horizon, varying in deep hues of red and rich purples – not unlike the dyes I've seen traded at the port markets along the shores of the Great Sea. The day's heat was subdued by a faint breeze which flowed throughout the acreage.*

*I spotted the stranger again as I glanced up from the moist soil. He approached from the west, seemingly advancing out of the setting sun as if he were an envoy of Ceres or Bacchus, the dual gods of farming and wine-making. I leaned against the shovel, raised a dirt-sullied hand to my brow and attempted to get a better look at my visitor. He appeared to be a tall man – nearly a half-head taller than I – and he sported a worn, gray cloak and boots distinctive of the mud-*

swallowed swamps of Germania. From his gait I could tell he was stately. Without doubt, he had served as a diplomat or soldier in some chapter of his life.

As the stranger stepped into the field, carefully avoiding the line of crops, I could finally make out his bronzed face, which was square-jawed and rigid. White locks of hair could be seen running from his high forehead as he neared.

The man raised his hand in greeting and said, "I come in peace, brother."

I squinted into the sunset at the figure and tightened my grip on the shovel. Though he didn't look the type, perhaps this was the bandit who would finally attempt to overtake my employer's vineyard. I took a deep breath and called out, "Traveler?"

"Of sorts," he replied in a deep voice. He sounded articulate and refined, proving my initial judgments true. The stranger spoke good Latin, but a faint accent shone through. There was an unusual tint in the pronunciation of the syllables and – despite my extensive travels – I could not place the origin. "I crave only a few sips of water if you're willing," he declared and stopped twenty paces from me. "But I'll leave rather hastily if you mean to assail me with your shovel. I'm nothing more than a tired vagabond looking for rest."

Embarrassed, I loosened my grip on the shovel. The stranger saw the change in my manner and walked closer, carefully stepping down the terraced slope to the level on which I had been working. He stopped in front of me and gave a nod. "My thanks, brother. On whose vineyard do I tread?"

I wanted to say that he was treading on my vineyard, but I answered in truth, "Junius Verus Apostello, noble statesman and servant to our emperor. Who is it who treads on his land, if I may ask?"

The stranger smiled when he heard my banter; the act softened his sharp features. His hair was very thick and pale in color, yet from the unapparent lines in his face I would not have placed his age at over forty. He was clean shaven and his eyes shone a bright blue. Though he professed to be a traveler, I saw no bag on his person. A diseased man, I thought immediately. Perhaps some form of leprosy or pigment disorder had assailed him and caused his hair to turn white. Perhaps he had looked upon the face of one of the gods. Diseased or not, if he was truly a traveler, he should have at least one bag or satchel.

"I am known as Siergo," he replied. "May I ask your name?"

"Marcus Athleo," I answered. A moment later I added, "A freedman from the Scaptia family from the city of Tarsus, in Cilicia. You must forgive my lack of hospitality. I rarely have visitors here. Follow me and I'll pull some more water from the well."

I led the stranger to the watchtower – which was not much more than a stone house with an accessible roof – and encouraged him to recline at the main table in its quarters. After gathering more water, I slung the goatskin over my shoulder and entered the watchtower. I poured water for the traveler into a glazed cup while I simply drank from the goatskin. When he had finished his first cupful I poured him another.

The watchtower's quarters were pleasant enough. In the center of the main room sat a circular wooden table with various pitchers and cups scattered atop it. A week old loaf of bread lay in the table's center, its surface covered in white growths. I hastily snatched it up while my visitor tilted his head back to finish the last of his second cup.

9

*After cleaning off the table, I retrieved two swollen wineskins which were hanging on the wall in the damp closet-space near the tool chest. I also retrieved another half-eaten loaf of bread – this one lacking mold – and placed it in front of my visitor with a plate of peppered oil. I carefully laid the wineskins next to the bread and sat across from him.*

*I poured us each a cup of wine from the first skin. The man nodded his thanks and took a drink; the edges of his lips curved into a faint smile when he received his first taste. The aged wine was very good and from Apostello's own reserve.*

*After my own taste, feeling the wine give a slight burn as it hit my stomach, I finally relaxed and smiled at my visitor. "Have you traveled far, friend?" I asked.*

*The stranger leaned back in the chair. "Yes, the gales from God have blown me through many lands."*

*I rubbed my muddied hands on the lower part of my tunic and asked, "Gales from God?"*

*He nodded. "Just like the weather, who can predict what God has planned for your day? The next year of your life? This very hour, even. Sometimes He chooses a calm, peaceful day. Other times He chooses a storm. The gales from God are ever-blowing. Not to say He doesn't listen to our pleas. With a single word He can silence a great storm or make it worse."*

*I raised my cup. "Ah, we've begun to delve into good discussion. But which god do you speak of? This is the true question, for there are many."*

*The man gave a rueful smile and shook his head. His white hair, in such contrast to his tan skin, swung gently against the chair's back. "This is something that I've always found curious about this* great, conquering empire: the belief in a copious amount of gods. Why do you feel you need so many divinities?"

I shrugged. "It wasn't my choice. It's just the culture I was born into. Things have always been this way, I imagine. There are gods for each aspect of life – for love, farming, warfare and wisdom; therefore, the gods encompass all paths to better help us as we serve them. They seem to have been replaced by luck in recent days. Destiny is a matter of chance, one might say. Or logical deduction."

"That is one way to view things," he said as if he was one who did not.

I looked outside through the open doorway and noticed that the evening had grown darker. The wall of clouds in the west had turned a shadowy purple. The faint breeze carried a shrill cry from some sort of nocturnal animal which had finally emerged from the woodland.

"I am a freedman," I said as I used flints to light two pale candles made of tallow. I placed them in the center of the table. "Though I am not yet thirty, I was once a servant for a family in Cicilia." I sighed and gave a humorless smile. "I always preferred the title of 'servant' as opposed to 'slave' though there is little difference. I am only a freedman because of your 'gales from God', you might say."

"As I said," Siergo replied. "They are ever blowing."

I reclined back and took another sip of wine. "I was born in the year of Rome's Great Fire. Not a good year to bear a child in Rome. At least my parents were not members of the sect he had punished."

Siergo's eyes narrowed. "I remember Nero lighting his gardens by setting followers of this sect on fire. He tortured them other ways as well. Prophets, scribes and missionaries. Entire

11

*families were fed to beasts in his foul Circus Maximus shows."*

*For the moment, my wine was forgotten. The Great Fire and its baleful after-effects were delicate matters to this man. He seemed to be passionate about this new faith which I only knew as a much disputed theology.*

*I shared his silence for a moment then took up the wineskin and refilled his cup. Once again, he nodded his thanks and allowed his soft smile to return. "I am passionate about many things," he said gently. "I've traveled far and witnessed much in this world. Such atrocities always grated on me like pottery against stone."*

*Siergo was then silent for a moment, looking down at his cup. After a few seconds of thought, he looked back up at me. "I'm in debt to you for your hospitality. I have nothing to offer you in return."*

*I waved my hand in dismissal. "A freedman needs little in compensation. This spirited discussion is payment enough, friend."*

*As if he remembered something of importance, Siergo's brow creased suddenly as he sipped his wine. "I once knew of another freedman," he said, putting his cup down. "A young man, much like yourself, who was freed from slavery's hold. His is an interesting tale of adventure and intrigue. It is also a story of sorrow and love. If you're not too tired, Marcus, I could offer this story as payment for your kindness. I warn you, though; it is all I have to give."*

*"I'll say once more," I replied, "I require no payment, but I am eager to hear your story. Is it fiction or a true account?"*

*"It is very true, brother. I will tell it to you as it was told to me, as I have remembered every word and incident. Many seasons have passed since this man told me his tale, yet I have retained it in its entirety. This is the tale of a thief."*

My eyebrows raised in confusion. "A thief?" I asked, wondering why such an allegedly epic narrative would stem from the life of a lowly criminal.

Siergo saw my disdain. "Even a thief can have a riveting story, Marcus. Not all heroes are soldiers and emperors."

Noticing my cup to be nearly empty, I reached for the wineskin. "Please begin this man's tale, Siergo," I requested. "I'll admit that I'm wary of his trade, but I also find myself gripped by your speech. We have much wine, by the grace of my employer, and the night has just begun. You have my full attention."

After a slow nod, Sergio rubbed his hairless chin for a moment then unfastened the knot at his neck and allowed his cloak to drape across the back of the bench. Under his fleece he wore a pale tunic which matched the color of his hair. A braided length of rope served as his belt, and on it he carried no knife, pouch, or bedding.

"As I have said," the traveler began, his cerulean eyes flickering in the candlelight, "this is the story of a thief. Most of his life was spent in occupied Judea. However, he told me his tale in a land far from there."

"What was his name?" I asked.

"His name," Siergo answered, "was Dismas... from the word for sunset. Those in his band called him Diz. Like yourself, he was a former slave, a servant of a Greek family who was very unkind. Like many, he was not born into the profession of thievery but the gales from God blow hard."

"Dismas," I said, repeating the man's name. "How old was he? Was he a murderer as well as a robber? Was his band-"

My speaker held up a sun-browned hand, silencing my throng

of questions. "In good time, brother, your questions will all be answered with my narrative. If you would only relax, keep your ears uncovered and your spirit open for any possible inspiration which may occur."

I stated my apologies and told him to continue.

After another nod, Siergo said, "I vividly remember when Dismas began his story for me. Though there was shame in his voice, he was unflinching in the oration of his tale, which started near the Jabbok River, in the cruel eastern wilderness that nearly claimed his life."

# JUDEA - 33 AD

# I - *Damned to Hell*

**O**f the multitudes I have stolen from or visited brutality upon [*the thief Dismas had imparted to Siergo*], one man stands out in my memory more than the others. You will come to understand later in my tale that my second meeting with this man – and his family – marked a turning point in the nature of my values. In truth, before this second encounter, my values were scarce and limited to the furthering of my own spiritual demise.

Moreover, my first encounter with the man was forgotten as soon as I left him bleeding in the mud.

\*\*\*

The rains had not yet begun on that evening, but the clouds churned overhead like a drunkard preparing himself to retch. Rain was imminent, and so was my greed.

I walked next to another from my band, Cyrus from Apollonia. He was a tall, skeletal man with a ritualistically shaved head and listless brown eyes. His shorn crown was too small for his body, nearly absurd in its deformity, and though he was diligent, he was not a smart man. We each carried a goatskin traveler's bag and leather belts wound around our tunics. Cyrus also carried a long walking stick which he used more for deception than for aid in travel. My dagger was hidden under my tunic beneath my belt, wrapped in an oiled cloth.

Brown sprouts of vegetation stemmed upwards from rock crevices and from the deeper fissures in the hills. The only true shade in this land was miles away along the Jabbok River, a dense oasis from which we had just come. The rest of our small band remained there, resting from our journey. Hours previously, we had spotted a small settlement to the south of our camp. Like a wolf smelling fresh meat, I couldn't pass up the prospect of a fast catch.

As we crested another hill, a single drop of rain hit my cheek. A second hit my forehead. I wiped my face and continued my stride as thunder rumbled in the distance.

"I see the settlement, Dismas," Cyrus said. His voice was deep and I was once again struck by the fact that he was the only one from our band, with the exception of our leader Obadiah, who used my proper name while all the others called me 'Diz'. Cyrus rubbed his bald head and said, "It looks shabby."

I squinted in the drizzle and regarded our destination – a grouping of raised mounds in the distance. "They make their homes out of dung," I said coldly. "What did you expect?"

This place was known by the Bedouin tribes as the Ehud Spring. They had chosen a favorable location for a temporary village at the edge of a small grove of palms which grew tall from the water below the sand. A line of smoke rose up from the settlement, likely from a kindled spit soon to be extinguished by the rain. Beyond the homes and past another large rocky hill, I saw a dark green line close to the horizon. This was the western edge of the oasis. Our band was further east, in its middle, less than an hour's walk away.

The nearest home, a mud-brick lodge surrounded by a slight fence of thin wood, caught my eye. It was furthest from the other homes and closest to us. I motioned to Cyrus and pointed in its direction. He grunted in approval.

As we neared, I noticed a figure at the home's side, near a livestock trough surrounded by goats. They were erecting a tent-shelter for the wall of bird cages that lined the home's wall. This person, a female with an unveiled head of long dark hair, looked in our direction and immediately ceased her struggle with the tent. She then hurriedly walked to the rear of the home, out of our sight, and after a moment's time emerged with a man who was no doubt her husband. The female quickly covered her head with a scarf as was their custom.

The couple waited near the trough as we neared. Cyrus and I vaulted over the property's small fence and I called out a salutation in Aramaic, "Greetings, friends! We have become lost from our caravan which is on its way to Jericho. Would you be willing to give a couple of lost pilgrims some water and perhaps a hint of direction?" I put a hand on Cyrus' shoulder and turned to him. "Such a hard journey from Antioch, my good Simon."

Cyrus, not one for the theater, remained silent and frowned.

The man whispered into the female's ear then walked towards us. The wolfish spirit inside of me grinned. The female also walked forward, though she remained in the man's shadow. Thunder rumbled overhead again.

"Surely, men," the man said when the thunder's echo subsided, "we are not ones to deny help to pilgrims." He stopped in front of us – a short bearded man nearly fifty years of age. His expression was one of kindness and generosity. This was a trusting man. Our fortune was good.

"I hoped this much," I replied and stepped towards him. I moved the wet hair out of my eyes and smiled warmly. He returned the smile just before I delivered a vicious kick to his left knee. He buckled, cried out in pain, and fell on his side. The female screamed and Cyrus ran to her, grabbing her roughly by the clustering of hair and fabric at her neck. His walking stick splashed in the mud at their feet. My partner's long, grimy fingers closed over the woman's mouth, silencing her cries. I kicked the man again as he writhed on the ground, this time in the back. He wailed and tried to crawl away from me. The drizzle had finally become a downpour and the man left an unruly trail in the mud and goat filth as he squirmed. I kicked him in his left knee again. He gasped for air and clutched his leg, curling into a quivering ball. I wondered if I had broken the joint in his knee. It had happened before.

I knelt over him quickly, not bothering to remove my dagger for further persuasion. "Your money," I said. He continued to shake in the mud and did not respond. I grabbed his hair and repeated my demand. After a moment's consideration, the man let go of his knee and slowly reached into his tunic. With a trembling hand, he withdrew a small, leather bag which was noticeably filled with coinage. The coins were likely silver *denarii* or copper *leptons*. This could buy our band enough food to last two weeks in places we could not steal, especially if some of the pieces were silver. It was a good catch.

I removed the bag from the man's trembling fingers. He then whispered something I could not discern – perhaps a prayer for strength in guttural Hebrew – and he looked up at me. Squinting in the rain, he said, "Thief... you are damned to Hell for this. Damned to *Sheol!*" His words were slow and he stuttered in fear as he spoke.

"You're misinformed, friend," I replied. "We are already in Hell." I struck him hard in the face with my fist and he lay sprawled in the mud, clutching his nose. His pale hands immediately filled with blood, which quickly mixed with the rain and mud. Cyrus released the female who wailed and knelt over her mate. A faint shine from under her tangled veil caught my attention and I ripped the necklace from her neck. As the man grasped his bloodied face, I saw a gold glimmer through the crimson-streaked fingers and I attempted to pull the ring from his swelling thumb. This was to no avail, though the man did not resist me. The ring was unique, forged into a braid like pattern, and it would have made a nice trophy. With a curse, I released his bloody hand, calmly placed my newly acquired money sack and necklace into my bag, and turned to Cyrus who stood behind the family with a grim look on his face. "We're finished here," I said.

"What about the home?" the tall thief said, nodding towards the man's humble mud dwelling. "They'll have more in there. We were lucky to have found anything on him at all."

I followed his gaze to the home and the buildings behind it. I saw at least two people in the distance attempting to cover their open windows with camel skins. We had already spent too much time with the couple as it was and I did not wish to alert the other villagers. I was a firm believer in ambushes and hasty retreats.

I ignored the whimpering of the couple at my feet and said, "These stingy desert people always carry their money on them. They don't even trust their children. You must better understand the different peoples in these lands, Cyrus." I glanced to the home and cages at its walls. "Be quick and grab some birds. We need food more than money right now."

Cyrus looked greedily to the home again then rubbed the top of his bald head. He cursed and quickly trotted to the cages of birds by the home. He pulled out two hens, snapped their necks and turned to leave, a twitching dead bird in each arm.

I gave the two mud-soaked people at my feet one last glance before leaving. The man had begun to retch in the mud from the pain. The female started to sob. Her moans were quickly swallowed by another rumbling of thunder.

We ran in the direction of the oasis and the man's face, as well as his wife's sorrow, was forgotten as soon as my sandaled feet cleared their fence.

\*\*\*

In those days, I hated the gods with great passion. The winds of fate blew hard during that season of my twentieth year. Perhaps not fate, for such a word gave allusions to the silent divinities that I believed to be either dead or not concerned with my life. Cruel chance seemed a more fitting title. Whatever name one bestowed upon this force, it drug me around like a child's toy in the mouth of a stray hound.

On the afternoon our band reached the desert oasis, hours before my encounter with the family at the settlement, I watched the storm build in the west. It swallowed the parched desert like an evil specter. The shadowy view was bizarre, as if a gathering of the *Manes* – the divine dead of Roman lore – had risen up from the abyssal underworld to at last claim the earth. The season of rain had been hammering the land for over a month and this fresh storm would be over our heads before nightfall.

The last forty days had been tiresome for our band. During the year's second month, *Ianuarius,* we traveled south from the ports of Caesarea Maritima, then east nearly to the settlement of Amathus. Midway through the coastal plains our band made a turn for the furthest edge of eastern Judea where we would suckle from the line of roads and villages that were clustered near the Jordan River. We avoided the main Roman roads, for Herod Antipas – in his twenty-first year of governing – was still wary of the thieves that plagued his emperor's eastern territory.

Rome permitted and oversaw the flow of commerce throughout these lands, but only through her own highway system, which stretched across the whole kingdom. These "Roman Roads" all stretched from the capital city and were maintained by slave labor.

Herod loathed thieves and had dispatched his private army of outriders to arrest – or execute on sight – all bandits and clean up his cherished Roman roads. These soldiers would routinely clash with the larger groups of marauding brigands and local zealot groups such as the *Sicarii,* but the smaller, quieter bands – such as ours – remained hidden during the numerous holiday seasons as we stuck to the smaller roads not patrolled by outriders.

During Passover, Rome gave the locals more security and both sides made money. Those who dared to speak in honesty could tell you that these times were about money as much as they were about worship. And where there was money, there were thieves.

\*\*\*

Our band's leader, a brusque but wise man we called *Protos-*Obadiah, had told us of the oasis months ago. Obadiah had been given the title of chief, or *Protos*, because he was the eldest of our group by at

22

least twenty years and it was a sardonic contrast to his Hebrew name, which his mother had given him after one of their faith's prophets. As one could easily discern, he was no longer a practicing Jew, but he was our strict leader – the fastening which held our band of deserters together. He gave orders and we obeyed, this being one of our only unified decrees. If you disobeyed, you were exiled from the band and would have to survive alone. As any fool could tell you, it is much easier to survive in numbers in this province; laggards were consumed by the hate this region is so good at dispersing.

Our trek along the Jabbok River to the oasis had been long. The barren land was a mountainous vista of rock, sand and pointed desert ferns which often grew as high as a man's waist. The Jabbok River flowed heavily, its channel cutting deep into the hills and its vegetation growing fast at its banks, flourishing by the waterway. After a two day journey east of the Jordan, we saw the river arch around a valley at the base of a great hill. This valley was filled with green plants, palms, and dense forest. The oasis stretched for miles. This place was lush and green, such a change from the brown landscape around it. A grouping of rocks within the oasis rose from the earth and curved outward, exposing a series of small caves which would serve as our shelter during the cold nights.

*** 

Hours later, after Cyrus and I returned to the band's camp from our thievery in the settlement, *Protos*-Obadiah called me aside and we spoke privately under a small rock ledge in the oasis. The stone ridge gave us shelter from the pouring rain.

Obadiah knelt and rubbed his mud-spattered calves. His lengthy gray hair was pulled back and bound tightly by a leather cord, but a few wet strands brushed across his face. He had slung his sandals by the ties over his shoulder and I heard his back creak in a chorus of 'pops' as he worked on his legs. I saw the shine of brass under his dark cloak – the hilt of his Roman short sword, stolen decades ago.

"I'm old, Dismas," he finally said. "Too old for such a life, I sometimes think." He continued to rub his feet then looked at me after the silence. "You were supposed to argue, young scion."

I smiled and said, "You tire much of the band with your energy, *Protos*. You'll still be driving us like oxen when you're over a hundred years old. You know this. You don't need an argument except to ignite your pride."

Obadiah gave his own grin and sat down on one of the boulders. I sat next to him and watched his faint smile turn into a frown under his hawk's nose as he looked at the greenery outside the stone alcove. A desert hawk gave a shriek somewhere in the foliage before fluttering off towards the river to seek shelter elsewhere. Obadiah listened for a moment, then sighed and said, "By the sun, I pray I don't live to be that old. I've lived long enough already." The frown relaxed. "How was your own little jaunt?"

I held out my right fist which was bruised and slightly swollen from punching the man I had robbed in the settlement.

"How much?" Obadiah asked.

I tossed him the small sack of money. "Coins and a necklace. The jewelry is cheap, but Cyrus also took two hens. He's at the stream, readying them now."

Shaking the purse to hear its contents, Obadiah smiled and tossed it back. "Well done, Dismas. I figure we can hole up here for a few weeks, or a few months, depending on what the desert winds blow us. Do not forget, our *Sicarii* contact will be back in Jericho in but a season."

"The lunatic?" I asked.

"As crazy as a three-legged hen, but his schemes may lead us to our *eschatos kleros*."

Obadiah had been toying with the wistful idea of the *eschatos kleros* – our "final catch" – for as long as I'd been with his band. This contact he knew from the *Sicarii* was too crazy for even the rebel sect, but Obadiah seemed to believe that this man had a genuinely solid scheme that would afford our band enough money to leave the Judean Province and perhaps even retire somewhere along the coast of the Great Sea. This contact was supposed to meet with Obadiah in two months, in the city of Jericho, just west of the Jordan River.

"I follow where you go, *Protos*," I said, "but many in Jericho will recognize our faces from last time. It is a great risk."

Obadiah looked at me for a moment and looked away. "A risk worth taking." He stood up and nodded towards the deeper oasis where the rest of the band was. "In the morning," he said quietly, "we will let Gaius go. We've waited long enough."

I nodded. "Far too long."

This was the true meaning for his private discussion – necessary culling within the band. If you steal from a fellow brother inside our group, you must face the reproofs. We were criminals but not fools. Gaius had been foolish.

Obadiah nodded back, implying the conversation was done. I stepped into the rain and descended from the outcropping, meeting my good friend Titus near the stream. He sat alone under a large tree, trying to start a fire with flints. The other five members of the band were spread out under other trees or palm leaves, some sleeping and some helping to ready the chickens for dinner.

Titus was short, stocky and fairly rotund. His face was pock-marked but warm. He was one of the more powerful men in our group but also somewhat ungraceful. He was trustworthy though, and I was proud to call him my friend. *Adelphos* in life. *Adelphos* in death. This was our recent maxim – brothers through life's every twist and curve.

"You're doing it wrong," I told him as I sat across from him.

He smiled. "You always say that, yet the fire always gets made. The gods favor me, Diz. They always have. Roma, our kingdom's great spirit, looks after all who embrace her. You must learn to embody the gods and be happier."

I raised my hands in feigned admiration. "Ah, honeyed words from Titus the sage. Well, death to Roma and curses on the gods. I will watch over myself and my band."

Titus winced at my mockery. "Roma can't die."

"I don't think it was ever alive."

"She."

With a snort, I spit onto his smoking kindling and he cursed at me.

I turned away from him and found a good sized palm leave that had been turned over and was half full of rain water. I gingerly drug it into the shelter of the tree and bent down to take a sip from it. Though the oasis was growing darker by the minute, I caught a glimpse of my reflection in the water. I regarded my tanned, sharp face – softened by three weeks worth of beard – and thought, for a brief moment, that I was looking at the face of a stranger trapped beneath the water. This was not the young servant from Sychar who had once thought of becoming an actual Roman "citizen" and toiling as a scribe or runner in the games. My black hair had grown long and was constantly falling into my eyes. Over my wiry body, my gray tunic was worn and fraying at its every edge.

I regarded this dark man for a moment then splashed the reflection away, suddenly sad. I drank from the leaf and pushed away thoughts of my past.

"And what of Gaius?" Titus whispered. His cheerful mood had turned somber.

"What do you think?" I replied without looking at him.

Titus grunted. Though he was a thief, Titus did not like to dwell on the darker acts of our trade. He would have to learn – and hopefully in a gentle form – that this was the path he had chosen and its roads were usually dark. These lands were grim and unforgiving; one had to match this gloom or be swallowed by it.

After bending for another drink, I splashed water into my face and pulled my hair back out of my eyes. An itch on my upper right arm grabbed my attention and as I reached into the sleeve of my tunic to scratch it, I felt the upraised scar tissue of my branding. My frown deepened as it always did when I felt the cruel letters seared onto my flesh, but I did not raise my sleeve to look at them.

Rubbing my hands on my tunic, I stared for a moment at the silver linked bracelet on my right wrist. One half of it was a brown leather band, while the other half was formed of thin clasps of solid silver. Like the brand on my arm and the prized Damascene dagger within my belt, the bracelet was a vestige of my forsaken life in Sychar.

The woe came back quickly and I withheld a deep sigh as I gathered myself and my thoughts. And above, the gods that Titus believed in so fervently continued their sodden assault from the heavens.

## I I - *A New Cloak*

The storm's intensity wavered throughout the night. Most of the band slept in the small caves in the rock outcropping, avoiding the rain and wind and using their cloaks for padding on the hard surface. I also attempted sleep among the rocks, under a curving arch of stone which served as a shelter against the weather. My goatskin bag served as my cushion, but I had no cloak to keep me warm. I loosened my belt and drew my knees against my chest under the tunic and pressed further into the earth. My trembling eventually subsided, though my right hand still throbbed with a slight pain in the knuckles.

Despite my exhaustion and relative dryness, sleep did not come quickly. I found myself regarding the others around me, spread out in different outlets among the rocks.

Titus snored loudly in the alcove next to mine, proving his claim that he was able to sleep through anything. He had originally come from the island of Crete where he had been a young thief in the city of Phoenix. Pock-marked Titus had been a sailor, the only seaman among us. He had traveled throughout the empire by ship to nearly every costal town and province around the Great Sea. In every city he stole, of course, and in every city he was chased by prominent merchants and the Roman Urban Cohort street soldiers. Titus was the most famous in our band, known by every faction of merchants along the shores of the Great Sea. He boasted of this regularly.

Near my feet, in the cleft below me, I saw Festus-Naevius, a dark man who was nicknamed Charon, after the skull faced ferryman of the River Styx. He, too, was awake and he squinted up at the storm. He was of average build, like myself, but slightly taller and his hair was closely cropped as was his dark beard. Charon's gaze was always tightly drawn in contemplation, or in anger, it often seemed. Many times we jokingly wondered if he really had eyes or if he had been granted sight by invisible powers from the underworld. He rarely spoke, but when he did the words were astute and worthwhile, and everyone listened with a fervent ear. His senses were acute – more so than any other man I had ever known. Under his cloak, Charon wore a thick belt which sheathed nine bronze hunting darts. With these darts, I had seen him kill fleeing goats, boars and even a hawk in mid-flight. In his dark gaze you could see the spirit of a cunning animal – silent and vigilant.

Despite Charon being an obviously dangerous man, for the last two years Titus had been on the leery mission to make the dark hunter smile. He usually made a fool of himself with his efforts.

Lying in a cleft next to Charon, Mercius-Porsis stole sips from a wineskin and spit purple globs of snot into the wet foliage around him. Mercius had been with Obadiah the longest and had made stealing wine his greatest priority among all of our catches. I had even seen him shake uncontrollably after going a single day without the fermented drink after his wineskin burst open during a long trek through the northern wilderness. This ailment was remedied after we happened across a traveling scribe on a pilgrimage to Damascus who had a half-full wineskin among his belongings. Mercius, a dependable – yet usually drunk – thief, had drank the pilfered wine in one fast sitting. His shaking stopped a few minutes later. Since then, he has always made sure to have at least one wineskin in reserve during our more arduous journeys.

Deeper in the oasis, Jaximo-Marius, a burly stone-worker-turned-criminal from the city of Sidon, had erected a shelter out of palm leaves and branches. Jax was an arrogant man and he let this pride rule him, much like the fermented grape ruled Mercius. The large thief had once helped build monuments and sculptures with shale and marble, so the prospect of a modest shelter had likely seemed effortless to him. His tools and materials were still in Damascus, however, along with a reputation tarnished by fraud and allegations of murder.

Jax was a hard man to get along with, and his anger tended to turn even the most mundane acts of thievery into overly violent encounters which led to unwanted attention. His nose had been broken several times in fights and falls, and was crooked in one direction. His thick wrists were banded with leather bracelets and his stubbly face was wide under curly black hair.

For a reason unknown to me, Jaximo had always disliked me. I had often thought that this was some fashion of jealousy, for the burly thief had always thought of himself as *Protos*-Obadiah's most elite bandit, while Obadiah seemed to favor me more.

I usually ignored Jax's insults and tried not to add kindling to his occasional tirades, for a man such as he could easily strangle a grown man in his sleep.

I peered out from the cave and looked up at the raging storm for a moment. The rain had stopped but the winds continued to howl through the oasis. The tops of the trees swayed and bent under the dark sky.

I remembered my conversation earlier in the evening with Obadiah and realized that this was Gaius' last night to sleep within our numbers. The young, scrawny thief from Jericho was curled into a ball under his cloak, close to small-headed Cyrus, in the cave above me. Between the stronger gusts of wind, I could hear Gaius' teeth chattering. While awake, he was a loud person, vulgar and unduly proud for reasons we could not see. We had picked him up in Jericho as we observed him stealing clumsily in the markets, bringing attention to himself and to all the thieves in the area. Obadiah, in one of his more charitable moments, had believed we could forge him into a better thief and allowed him to travel with us to the port city of Joppa, along the western coast of Judea. Though he picked up on the art of thievery quickly, Gaius' personality never fully meshed with the group. The young thief made rash statements, started fights, and had obviously withheld funds from the band on numerous occasions.

For his more recent acts of iniquity within our numbers, he would be exiled from our band upon the morning. If he refused to leave the oasis, or if he pleaded longer than the time it took for Obadiah to remove his sword, Gaius would be killed.

Our leader slept in the furthest recesses of the cave. I could not see him but I knew he was sleeping on his side, under his dark cloak, with his right hand gripped tightly around the handle of his sword. This was how he always slept, and from what little I knew of his fierce past, he apparently had good reason to do so. One might call him "Scar" if they thought to dishonor him, for much of his body was covered in purple and brown scar tissue. It was as if his flesh had been used for practice in a Praetorian training camp.

I turned from the calloused group of men and forced my eyes closed, willing sleep to overtake me. It eventually did, despite the shrieking wind and the sound of chattering teeth above me.

***

With the morning came an unexpected surprise: the sun. For nearly an hour's time, the thick clouds above us broke up and allowed the sun to shine down upon the oasis. I was sore from the uncomfortable sleep, but upon seeing the rays of light filtering through the canopy above, I quickly rose from my den and ran out of the oasis, through the wet foliage, and into the sand hills to feel the warmth. Titus and Mercius joined me, and we all stared up into the blinding light, letting the rays soak into our chilled skin.

I was a lover of the sun – not a worshiper like some – but a devoted admirer. In my mind, it held no spiritual power, but I missed its warmth greatly in this season of rain.

Titus and Mercius soon grew tired of standing on the hill and eventually went back down into the oasis where Obadiah had started making a breakfast of soup from the remnants of the previous night's meat. I stayed a few minutes longer, letting the sun perform its magic on my face.

Once back at the camp, we sat around the fire pit that Titus had created and took turns sharing soup from a hot clay basin. Titus divided a few pieces of stale bread from his bag. We all drank water from the stream except for red-eyed Mercius, who sipped from his wineskin, which never seemed to empty. Charon leaned against a palm tree a few paces from our group, eating his own portion in silence.

The sun occasionally peeked through the leafy canopy above us, giving enough light to warm our bodies but not enough to dry the sodden oasis. I wondered how long the rainy season would last. We kept no record of time or days in a calendar because we did not possess one. Obadiah seemed to always know the month and days, as did Charon, but the rest of us simply did not care. Thieves did not usually keep a scheduled docket. Sometimes Obadiah would tell us that the merchants would be traveling more in one month or another, or that priests and scribes would have more money than usual because of different Jewish holidays. We trusted in his word and followed his commands.

Towards the end of our humble meal, Gaius tried to take more bread than was his share. I was surprised when Obadiah ignored this act, simply letting the young thief eat another mouthful of the scarce food. Gaius stopped chewing for a moment and looked around at the other thieves, no doubt wondering why he had not been reprimanded by anyone. He shrugged his thin shoulders and swallowed. Jaximo gave a dark chuckle, stood up, and walked away. Titus gave me a sad look. I shook my head and worked on my own portion.

"We can expect several big storms a week," Obadiah said as he reclined against a tree after eating. "We could work on some better shelter for when it rains, but I think this place could serve us well. At least for a while until things cool down a bit west of the Jordan. A well-traveled merchant road is less than an hour north of here. What do you think, scions?"

"Only if we make a better shelter," Mercius said. "I slept badly last night, and when I did sleep I dreamt about being cold and wet."

"Is there enough game to hunt around here?" Titus asked.

"Charon?" Obadiah inquired.

The dark thief didn't move his squinted gaze from the deeper part of the oasis, but gave a slight nod.

"Better than sleeping in alleys," Cyrus said slowly, his mouth full of bread. He swallowed and looked around. "In the cities, I mean. Trash heaped on you from the window – dogs and rats around you. This is much better."

"We are kings of this oasis," I agreed. "Caesar is not here and neither are his soldiers. We don't have to hide in the shadows. And I agree that if we can make a good shelter then it's better than sleeping in an alley. I wouldn't want to stay here forever but I think we should see how profitable it is."

Looking up from his second portion of bread, Gaius rolled his eyes. "But there's nobody else here," he protested. "I don't like seeing the same ugly faces. I wanted to see Caesarea Maritima and Egypt. We're traveling robbers, not women looking to make a pretty home."

Mercius leered and replied, "All doubt aside, you *will* make a travel, boy."

Gaius spit into the smoking fire pit. "One day, Mercius, I will have even more wine than you. It will be good wine, too – not the sludge you drink. And after my days of thieving are over, I'll build a villa along the coast near Rome, and I will have a wife more beautiful than Aphrodite. Just wait, drunkard. You'll see."

His smile large, Mercius raised his hands in mock surrender. "I'll see," he said with a short laugh. "I'll see it sooner than later, I imagine." He laughed again and shook his head.

"Why just one wife," Obadiah asked, playing along with Gaius' ranting. "I would rather have many."

"Too many harpies nagging," the young thief replied. He stood and declared that he needed to relieve himself and that he would do it in Mercius' wineskin. We watched as he walked from the oasis into the hills to do his private duty.

I turned to Obadiah. "When?"

"Why not now?" he answered. "I say we let the boy have one more fine moment as he does his business in the hills. You gather the rest, and we'll meet him as he walks back to the oasis. Good enough?"

I nodded briskly and stood.

Obadiah remained sitting and his eyes narrowed. "Titus?"

"I'm fine, *Protos*," he answered. "I just wish we could release him closer to the cities – maybe around the Jordan. I'm a thief, not a killer."

Obadiah grunted as he stood up, his joints popping. "If we don't let him go now, scion, the others *will* kill him. Do you truly think you can control Jaximo's rage? Or the anger of the others? I'm saving his life, not ending it. It's his decision, not ours."

"At least give him some water."

"The Jabbok has enough to spare, I think."

"A cloak to keep him warm, at least. If he journeys back west, or even north to the Decapolis, he'll be walking for days. The nights will kill him."

"His cloak is mine," I declared.

Titus turned to our leader. "Why not just kill him quickly and save him the desert's suffering." His last statement was of jest, but you could see the frustration in his eyes.

Obadiah nodded briskly and moved his cloak, revealing the worn handle of his short sword. "I favor such an idea, Titus. Spare him the desert and kill him quickly." Our leader then marched from the fire pit towards the hills – towards Gaius.

Cyrus stood quickly. I turned from the fire, as well, leaving my last bite of bread uneaten on the log I had been using as a table. I whistled to Charon, Jaximo and the rest of the band, a signal that it was time. My eyes searched the upper alcove of the caves where Gaius had slept and I saw his shepherd's bag drooped over one of the boulders. His cloak was in there, as was his rusted dagger and whatever miscellanies he had stolen from the band. He would be unarmed. Titus cursed loudly and followed us to the border of the oasis where Obadiah had stopped.

We waited in silence in a line behind Obadiah. The familiar anticipation of potential violence made the center of my palms tingle. It was a feeling I enjoyed.

After a few moments, we spotted Gaius walking back from a string of ferns at the base of a hill. He was looking at his sandaled feet as he walked, humming a song that was mostly lost in the breeze. Suddenly, when he was almost ten paces away, Gaius swung his gaze upwards, saw us, and halted. He stared for a moment, taking the scene in. I saw his eyes narrow and his lips puff outward as if he had just been caught in one of his misdeeds.

Silence reigned for a few seconds, and he then asked, "What's going on, Obadiah?" There was a slight tremor in his voice. He knew.

"Call him *Protos!*" Mercius called out. "Detestable half-breed!" Jaximo and Cyrus yelled in approval. I remained silent with Charon and Titus, eager to see what would happen.

"You're out," our leader said calmly. "We have but a small handful of rules in this band, and you somehow manage to break them all – nearly daily."

Gaius mewled, "But, I…"

"Think of this as a blessing, Gaius," Obadiah said, interrupting him. "I don't have enough fingers to count the times I've convinced several members of our band not to kill you." He pointed at the young thief. "More words are not needed. You are exiled. Leave the oasis and go back to Jericho or Hebron. You've learned much from us and will no doubt do fine. Drink from the Jabbok until you reach the cities. If you happen to see us again, though, I recommend going in the other direction."

Looking to all of us, Gaius raised his arms in bewilderment and I saw his fingers trembling. "But *why*? What have I done? You pigs… you need me!"

Obadiah walked forward and stopped a single pace away from the sniveling thief. "You stole from us, Gaius," he said softly. "Like I said before, I can't even profess how many times I've spared you from death by those in my band you've undermined. This is not a matter for argument. Make more of an issue with this and you'll find yourself swimming the current of the Styx."

Gaius stood there with his mouth hanging open in silence. Obadiah abruptly turned away from him, showing him his back. Everyone waited in silence.

The young thief stood there trembling, angry tears in his eyes. From Obadiah's belt, I saw the brass hilt of his short sword gleam in the sunlight. The handle faced Gaius, only an arm's length away. I almost called out a warning and then saw Obadiah's eyes flicker to Charon, and I suddenly knew what had been planned. Beside me, with the pace of a snail, the dark hunter slowly shifted his stance.

Everyone stayed very still. The breeze ruffled our tunics and cloaks – the only noise at that moment, save Gaius' sniffling.

Gaius' eyes narrowed as he stared at the sword's handle. Holding my breath, I watched as his gaping mouth closed. Twin tears broke free from his eyes and ran down his cheeks. His eyes rose briefly to us and then focused back on the sword.

Obadiah slowly lowered his head. His hands were down at his side.

With a sudden grunt, Gaius went for the sword. His thin fingers gripped the handle and pulled the blade quickly from its sheath. He hollered as it came free.

The bronze dart made a hissing noise – like an angry snake – as it flew straight and sunk deep into Gaius' neck just under his chin. It had been thrown so fast that I had not even felt Charon move at my side.

Obadiah calmly turned around as Gaius dropped the sword and fell to his knees. He clutched madly at the dart's shaft but it had driven too deeply for him to get any sort of purchase on it. He gurgled, looking up at Obadiah with pleading eyes. A second dart hit him in the chest right under his grappling hands and then a third right next to it.

With a wet sigh, Gaius finally fell forward to the ground. He gave a single spasm and lay still.

Calmly, as if he had just been practicing on a wooden target, Charon walked forward and stood over Gaius' body. Blood collected under it, spread quickly around the rocks and settled in the wet sand. Charon kicked the body over so that the dead thief lay on his back. The hunter then knelt and pulled the darts from the body, wiping each one on Gaius' tunic before placing them back into the notches on his thick belt.

Many a breath was finally exhaled.

Charon did not, as his nicknamed implied, look to remove a coin from the dead man's bloody mouth. Gaius would not have a toll to cross the River Styx.

"You're a demon with those things, ferryman," Jaximo said in admiration.

The hunter remained silent, glanced to Obadiah, then walked back towards the oasis.

Our leader stooped to pick up his sword and proclaimed, "Gaius made his choice, men. Follow the meager laws we have within the band. While we are indeed thieves, we do not steal from our own brethren." He turned to Titus as he finished. "He could be on his way west right now, but he made his choice."

He then bent to clean the mud from his sword.

Mercius gave a wavering laugh, and Jaximo slapped him on the back. They had enjoyed the little show.

I turned to Titus, whose face was somber. "His choice," I said softly to my friend. "He had it in mind to kill *Protos*. You saw it, Titus. We all did."

Titus looked to the dead thief. Gaius's shocked expression faced upward, half covered in red sand. My friend sighed and said, "I don't think he ever had a choice. He stole from me, too, but I hate watching people die, Diz. I've seen it too much in my life, I think."

"Such *is* life, brother," I said and gripped Titus' shoulder. He sighed and walked back into the oasis.

"What about the body?" Mercius asked.

"Burn it," Jaximo declared with a grin. "I'll gather kindling."

The deep voice came from behind me: "Bait."

I turned and saw Charon in the shadow of the foliage, leaning against the one of palms. He had spoken. None of us had actually seen it, but it had surely happened.

Obadiah was silent for a moment, dwelling on the grim idea. "For the Jackals and birds," he finally said in agreement. "We will have a good hunt tonight." He turned to Jaximo and Mercius. "See to it."

I thought about helping them, but the prospect of fiddling with the bloody body of a man I had just spoken with during our morning meal seemed a bit too ghoulish, even for me. I followed Titus back into the oasis. Stopping at the caves, I climbed into Gaius' alcove and took the cloak from his bag. The rest of the band could sort through his other possessions. Perhaps now I would be warm during the night.

With the cloak draped over my shoulder, I walked back to the burn pit to finish my bread.

# III - *Night Hunt*

The next three days were spent hunting, resting, and making our section of the oasis more livable. The rains came again on the second night, a slight drizzle this time, but under Jaximo's haughty instruction we erected a shelter at the base of the rock outcropping. We stayed dry and my newly acquired cloak served me well.

Jaximo and Mercius had placed Gaius' body in a small ravine about sixty paces from the northern tree line of the oasis, which was far enough away that the smell did not reach our shelter but was still close enough to use the body for bait during hunts. We could hide in the northern cover of the oasis, within the dense ferns, and watch the ravine, for we knew that any wandering desert creatures would be attracted to the decaying meat. On the last two nights, we had listened to the far away cries of desert jackals as they, too, seemed frustrated by the storms. A rainless evening would give us a fruitful hunt.

During the day, we had already killed three vultures and two other strange black desert birds with our stiffening bait, but had failed as yet to catch anything larger. The meat from these birds was scarce and hard to chew. The third night would be more promising, for the jackals had grown louder on each previous night, expanding their territory as they searched for food.

We had made long spears from tree branches, and our plan was to descend quickly upon the feasting jackals in the ravine, spearing as many as we could from our elevated position. Charon would also use his darts. Most would surely escape, but we would get at least one. Despite the loss of one or more of their numbers, they would return, as such creatures always did. It was not just animal stupidity, but was simply their way – constantly driven by hunger and instinct, not unlike thieves.

The band had nicknamed me 'the hare', as I was known for my speed and agility. In the days of my youth, I had been called "*tachu soma*", which meant "speeding slave". Being quick was always a great asset for a thief. I had never been caught, and I had never met anyone faster than I. Besides, the soldiers were usually too weighed down with armor while the merchants were too weighed down with robes, jewelry, and fat.

Because of my speed, I would probably be first among the jackals – if they came – so I practiced spearing palms as I ran through the oasis during the day. My skill grew with the homemade spear as did my confidence. I was ready for the beasts.

***

Before our evening hunt, I met with Obadiah at the top of the outcropping above our shelter as he looked westward towards the hills. His thoughts were even further west, I imagined, somewhere in Judea or closer to the Great Sea. We were nearly as high as the tallest palms, and one could see past the oasis in all directions.

"What vexes you?" I asked him. I sat next to him and pulled out my dagger to sharpen my spear. The hunt was to begin in but a few

43

moments.  The colorful hues of the setting sun cast an enchanting gleam upon the unique ladder-like pattern on my blade.  This dagger, I often thought, was fit for a king, not a thief.

Obadiah took a sip of wine from a small wineskin and continued to stare out into the desert.  "The past," he said.  After a moment he added, "The present, and the future… they all vex me, Dismas."

"All of our pasts are dark, *Protos*," I said.  "If you're referring to Gaius, then-"

"I don't care about that fool," he said quickly.  "While I agree with Titus that too much death can summon bad omens, I don't lament the loss of someone like Gaius, nor do I mind the blood on my hands.  Though it was Charon himself who did the deed, it was from my own command.  I have tried not to kill the ones we steal from, but I have never had a problem killing other thieves."  He shook his head and smiled.  "I guess I loathe my own profession."

"What else would you do?" I asked, not understanding the full meaning of his words.

"There is nothing else for me.  Long ago, I had wanted to be a philosopher of sorts, as well as a seasoned traveler.  Yes, I have traveled much, but the philosophy… well, that seems to avoid ones such as us."

"You are very wise, *Protos*.  Most of us would have been arrested or executed had it not been for your wisdom.  You have taught us much.  Not just of thievery, but of the world and its ways – the history of these lands, and the way of many cultures.  No other band of thieves is as lucky."

"And why, young scion?  To what end?"

I shrugged. "A smart thief stays alive. A wise thief will not find himself missing a hand after capture."

Obadiah adjusted his position on the rock and looked at me. "And how long do you plan on being a thief?"

The question confused me. Like everyone else in the band, I had not ever planned on being a thief. Most children do not hope they grow up to be criminals – hated by all others in the land. But when you fall into a fast moving river, it is nearly impossible to crawl out. Swimming against its current is harder still. You follow the current and see where it takes you. I did not state this as I pondered Obadiah's question, but looked away, into the desert outside the oasis. "I haven't given it much thought," I finally said, resuming my work on the spear point.

He grunted and looked away. "Thirty years ago, when traveling and musing did not bring food to my lips, I found myself stealing to survive. I quickly forgot that there was a line between good and evil. Once that line was crossed a few times, due to hunger or whatever reason I proclaimed, the line just sort of disappeared. I think about that line now."

"We do what we have to so that we can survive," I said, working at my spear quickly. Such talk unnerved me. "There is no line when it comes to survival."

"And you plan on surviving in such a way when you are my age?"

I lowered my knife and looked at him. "Like I said, *Protos*, I haven't given it much thought. My thoughts are of today. Tomorrow, my thoughts will be of that day."

He returned my stare for a moment and looked away. Looking

at the darkening horizon, he took another sip from the wineskin and said, "We will all have to answer to the bearer of that line I speak of, young scion. Even you, a seasoned hater of the gods, must admit to the difference between good and evil, and the inkling to tell them apart and act accordingly. The gods, or whatever powers you believe in, are set in punishing those who do evil. Those like us. We cannot escape it." He turned back to me. "I've killed many men in my life, Dismas. Most of those times I was forced into such acts, but other times it was simply for my own fleeting gain. In turn, the gods have thrown much at my own flesh, scarring me with blades, arrows, fire, and rope. Whether it be Hades or his wife Persephone, someone in the underworld doesn't want me yet, but as I attempt to muse as I did so long ago, I feel that I am nearly ready for them."

"Don't say such things," I said firmly. My spear-point was sharp and much shorter than it had been before this conversation. I set it aside and placed my dagger in my belt. "You are not ready for death, but have just drunk too much wine. Too much musing is not a good thing. We do what we do to survive, *Protos*. We have no other choice but to die, and that is not a fine decision, at least not for me – not yet. We will never be honest citizens. We are too far along in life to start fiddling in a new trade and no one would have us for hirelings. We live as thieves and we will die as thieves – but not today and not anytime soon."

Obadiah sighed. "You're still young, Dismas. Full of vigor and anger. When you reach my age you may finally see the mistakes of your life, as I have seen mine. Such insight eludes us until we're far along in years and our hair is gray like iron. Then we see our sins. I tell you, scion, they are many."

"As are mine, but what else do we do? There are no other paths for us."

"To settle somewhere, I think. I find myself dwelling on our upcoming meeting with the dissenter in Jericho. Sometimes, I find myself unable to think of anything else."

I looked to the horizon which was starting to turn red as the sun settled downwards. "You really believe in that man's plan? You think it's possible to make a single catch so large that one could retire and never have to steal or work again?"

"I guess we will see. I like to think it is. I've heard of such a feat being accomplished before. If those are just fanciful tales, though, perhaps we will be the first."

I thought for a moment about living in my own home and buying things rather than stealing them. Though I had lived in a home in the years of my childhood, such comforts seemed far beyond me now. "Let us hope," I said, "that this man isn't as crazy as his reputation."

Obadiah smiled. "Or let us hope he is just crazy enough."

Gripping my spear, I stood. The clouds were a deep shade of purple; the jackals would be emerging soon and we would need to be in position. I looked down at my leader and said, "Let's forget about the past and the future and enjoy a good hunt in the present."

Obadiah nodded and fastened the wineskin's thin cord. "Perhaps it *is* the wine after all, Dismas." He laughed and stood. "Don't tell the others of this discussion. I may have some greedy heirs looking to stab me in the back if they heard about my inner discord. Now, let us hunt the ugliest creature in this desert – the demon-faced jackal, a beast even uglier than any of us."

A breeze moved through the oasis with a faint whistle. The plants gently swayed around us as we stared into the shadows of the hills. Our eyes were focused on a thin, dark line sixty paces from us – the ravine, nearly as deep as a man was high. We could not see the body within the shallow gully, but we could smell its sickly sweet odor. I had looked at the carcass earlier in the afternoon, before my talk with Obadiah, and Gaius' body had turned a pale green, much like the inside of an olive. We had stripped the body of its tunic so that it lay naked in the ravine, facing upwards. One of the eyes had been eaten by a bird while the other had been spared, its wide stare seemingly fixed upon the slowly moving clouds in the sky above. To prevent the bait from being totally ravaged by the desert birds, we had posted one of us to watch the ravine at all times, taking turns as we grew bored.

When night was fully upon the desert we heard the first cry of the jackals. The sounds were far in the distance, but we knew they would come closer, as they had the last two nights. Our bait smelled horrible now, and though it was unpleasant for us, it was good for the hunt.

I was sitting under one of the stumpy palm trees, its thick leaves stretched over me offering good cover from my vantage. My spear rested next to me and I felt the weight of my dagger within my belt, wrapped in the oiled cloth. The rest of the band was spread out around me, hidden in the deep foliage at the northern edge of the oasis, staring out into the desert as they also watched the dark line of the ravine.

And we waited. One hour passed slowly. I heard one of the thieves whisper a curse after the second hour and Obadiah, in turn, cursed at him to be silent.

It was starting to get cold, but thankfully, I had brought Gaius' cloak with me. I quietly wrapped it around my body and continued my vigil of the shadows. Thick clouds moved overhead, and in between them, the stars could be seen shining brightly, giving the hills a small taste of light. The metallic smell of coming rain wafted from the hills and marked the imminent arrival of another storm.

It was during one of these breaks in the clouds, when the starlight shone upon the hills, that I saw a swiftly moving shadow curve around the base of one of the distant mounds and stop next to a string of ferns. The animal was nearly two hundred paces away. Above, the clouds shifted, and the shadowy form disappeared in the darkness of the night. I took my spear and slowly pointed it towards Titus, who was perched under the ferns next to me. I gently prodded him, and he gasped in fright. I winced at the noise, pointed towards the desert, and held up one finger to explain what I had seen. He gave a mortified nod and passed the message on to the rest of the band.

As I stared into the darkness, the clouds broke again, and I saw three shadows loping towards the ravine. They were the size of hounds, and the faint sound of yelping reached our ears as they neared. They had picked up the body's scent, and their shrill cries were of eagerness. I did not reach out to signal Titus for I had no doubt that the rest of the band saw them now as I did.

"Wait until they get in the ravine," Obadiah whispered. "Give them a moment to begin eating and then we'll move. Fast and silent. Dismas, you move first when you're ready and we'll follow. Cyrus, stay behind, and when you hear my yell, light your torch and follow. If more of these beasts come, I don't want to fight them off without some light. We must hurry for the storms are coming again. I can smell it in

1

the air."

I nodded and kept watching the pack. There were now five shadows nearing the gully and I thought I could actually smell them – a deep, musky animal scent mixing with the putrid aroma of Gaius body. I started to shake with anticipation, much like I did before a robbery. I gripped my spear tightly and in the shadows, its point trembled. This shaking was not of fear, but from that special physical essence that made men strong and gave them courage.

The creatures hesitated for a moment at the base of the ravine. They sniffed the air, stared into its darkness, and then descended with great fury, each beast growling and snapping, trying to get at the meat.

I waited nearly a half-minute as the sound of feeding carried to our ears. Just as I was about to rise I saw one of the jackals suddenly emerge from the ravine and remain still as it looked to the east. Another beast rose from the ravine with something dark hanging from its jaws. This animal joined the first in its vigil of the east, though it lay down and chewed on whatever it had pulled from the gulch. The first jackal raised its head as if it were sniffing the air as it focused on some unseen distraction to the east.

"*Protos*," Charon whispered in his abrasive voice. I turned around to look at him. "I hear voices," he said calmly. "Coming closer. From the east, along the tree-line. Camels and oxen too, I think."

I heard nothing but the breeze whistling through the oasis, but my heart started pounding even faster than it had as I was readying myself to attack the jackals.

"Everyone move back," Obadiah whispered. "We may have a larger prey on this hunt than we thought."

As silently as possible, we withdrew deeper into the oasis to wait and see what the night winds had brought us. We did this not knowing that by the end of that night one of us would be dead, one of us would be captured, and that the "bearer of the line" Obadiah had spoken of would strike out at all of us like a startled desert viper.

# I V - *Oasis Demons*

**I**t was odd, I later thought, that a caravan would be traveling at night, through the desert hills miles from the merchant road, no less, where jackals and thieves were known to prowl. It was not prudent. These curiosities were remembered later, after that night and after the storm. As I have said before, the winds of fate blow hard and one cannot escape them. Sometimes, you just find yourself stuck, like a young sheep in a muddy creek bottom, waiting for the shepherd. Or waiting for wolves.

In my life, it seemed, I had fallen in the mud and there was no devoted shepherd, and the wolves were definitely circling in ever-shrinking loops with long teeth bared and yellow eyes locked on my jugular. This night in the desert was no different.

***

It was, as Charon had deduced from his keen sense of hearing, a large caravan from the east. Two men, scouts, came into our view first, each carrying a walking stick, a bag and a curved sword on their belts. Lightning erupted across the western horizon and in this brief light I could see the jackals flee the ravine. Two hundred paces away from the gulch, the two men stopped and watched the beasts' retreat. The scouts had spiraled headdresses and long tunics under their cloaks. They neared the ravine and pointed to the hills in the north, talking loudly, but I could not understand their words from my vantage for the wind had strengthened. Most likely, the men were commenting on the jackals in the distance. The beasts had been scared off but remained on the horizon, not wanting to fully abandon their plunder in the ravine. The scouts were about to find out why.

I felt a few sprinkles on my brow, falling from between the palms above me. The night rains were beginning anew.

"Bedouins?" Mercius whispered.

"They're from Gilead," Obadiah said. "Jabesh-Gilead, I think. A caravan probably looking for the Ehud Spring with hired Bedouin scouts. They're fools, all of them, to travel at night in this season."

The two men finally reached the ravine, looked inside and babbled swiftly to each other. One raised a curved ram's horn to his lips and sent a low tone to the rest of the caravan that was still along the far northeastern side of the oasis, out of our view. Another three men hustled into sight and met with the first two at the ravine. They were dark men, tall forms moving through the shadowy hills, and the winds, now strong, made their cloaks flutter and the cloth on their heads unfurl. They pointed into the ravine and spoke rapidly. One of the men kept motioning to the sky, signaling the coming rains.

"They speak Aramaic tinted with Hebrew," Obadiah whispered. "I think they're quarreling on whether or not to stop at the oasis. One says 'yes', because of the weather; another 'no', because of the body, as it is an omen."

Cyrus stirred in his hiding place and said, "We might have to leave our shelter?"

Obadiah nodded and looked back at the shadowy group standing over the ravine.

One of the men was the family head or caravan leader; this was a judgment formed by his gait and directives. He was tall, a large man in girth and height, and louder than the rest as he pointed commands at the others. Lightning flashed in the distance. This man was older, with a long beard, while the others were much younger with thin dark beards. We crouched lower as the older man pointed in our direction – at the oasis. The man with the ram's horn gave another two blows, fighting with the wind's timbre. We heard more voices and sounds. The caravan was coming around the tree line. The rain had picked up and was starting to come down in heavy drops. Soon, it would hammer us in sheets.

"Let's move back to the shelter and gather our things," Obadiah whispered warily. "We'll have them ready in case we need to flee in the night, but we should be able to hide further in the oasis, at least for the night." He paused for a moment and stared at the men in the hills. He then hissed a curse and said, "Let's go."

Our leader was obviously disappointed, as was I, and we followed him deeper into the dark thicket and curved back around the tree line to the outcropping and our shelter. I grabbed my bag, bent over to retie my sandals and whispered my own curses. This oasis was ours, I brooded. Our kingdom. Yet we were being pushed away by some stuffy band of merchants too foolish to know not to travel off of the main roads at night. What fools! We had spent nearly a full day's time working on our shelter and had finally found comfort in the oasis. Even though we had no beds or true accommodations, this was *our* place.

I stuck my spear into the soft ground and marched to where Obadiah was gathering his own belongings and speaking with Jaximo. I stated my concerns to them.

"You're a foolish boy," Jax said, flicking a drop of water from the tip of his crooked nose. "We have no other choice but to flee. They are too many and are no doubt wary of thieves after finding that rat's body. You can stay here for all I care, Dismas, but you'll just end up like Gaius. These merchants from the east are strange. I've heard they'll do worse things to you than kill you."

"All your strength," I said to him, "but no courage." I turned to Obadiah. "I say we stay close to them, find out what they have and if it's possible to make a catch of this."

Jax growled down at me, "You're a fool. We don't have the numbers if something goes wrong. And if you call me a coward again you won't even have the chance to be captured by them."

Though I couldn't see it in the shadows, I knew the large thief's face was red with anger.

He was always at odds with me. While I had not actually called him a coward, I knew that I could have been more tactful with him, just to avoid his great rage, but I had grown tired of his insults and threats over the years.

I chose to ignore him and turned once again to Obadiah. "What do you think, *Protos*? Leave now, cold and pitiful, or stay close to them and see what they do? They probably have strongboxes in the wagons. We can wait and see, at least."

Our leader rubbed his bearded chin as he considered my words.

"This could be big, *Protos*," I said. "Maybe not quite the *eschatos kleros* we've spoken of, but still big. And we know this part of this oasis while they don't. Besides, if we had to run, they surely wouldn't chase us into the desert. Not in this storm."

Jaximo huffed again and said, "How can you even consider this rubbish, *Protos*? The words of an imbecile!"

"Keep your voice down," I told him. "Or else we might not be given a choice in the matter."

Jaximo stalked over towards me and stopped a handbreadth away from my face. He stared down at me, water dripping from his aslant nose. "Samaritan dogs like you don't give me orders, Dismas. You would do well to remember this."

I grinned up at him, my face sprinkled with raindrops. "You would do well to not eat animal dung, for your breath smells like it. Or perhaps you ate your own filth. Either way, it-"

He pushed me and I fell backwards into the wet ferns. Obadiah grabbed Jax's arm and ordered him to calm himself. Titus looked to the dark sky above in exasperation, slung his bag over his shoulder, and helped me up. Once on my feet, I lunged for the large, fuming thief but was held back by Titus and Mercius. Jax and I hissed curses at each other for a few moments and then Obadiah walked over to me, slapped me hard across the mouth, then went to Jax and did the same to him. After this, we were silent, but still breathed hard and made threats with our eyes.

"No more of this," Obadiah hissed. "You're both fools and you both stink of dung, so no more arguing and being loud. I'm surprised they haven't heard us already. By all that is under the sun, you two will get us all killed. Behave, both of you, or I'll gut you myself."

We were released and led in different directions. I went with Titus, deeper into the oasis, but not before turning and giving Jax another glare as he mouthed the word *"dead"*. He held one of his meaty hands up in front of his face, curled it into a fist, and then pretended to blow out imaginary dust as he opened it. The dust of my crushed bones, I suppose.

Titus and I stopped under one of the palms, where the rain could not hit us. The darkness was absolute in the oasis, but every couple of minutes, lightning would flash, sending a brilliant light dancing throughout the grove. In the north, where the caravan was, I heard a dog barking at the storm.

Titus stooped and sorted through his bag. "Why do you always fight with him, Diz?" he asked. "You two behave like a couple of rowdy children."

"When have you ever seen me start it, Titus?" I replied. "He has hated me since the first day I entered the band, when *Protos* took me in. He is jealous, just like a scorned woman. He thinks I am favored over him, as well I should be, but *Protos* sees us all as equals. Jax is blind to this. He has to fret and be angry about something, or he can't be happy. He has chosen me as his mark to belittle, and I will not cower from him."

Titus stood and looked up at the palms. Water dribbled onto his cloak and he shifted his position. "Such pride, friend, will kill you both. I just hope it gets him first."

I gave a tense smile. "Either way, I'm tired of being his whipping post." I looked down at my hands and felt them tremble in anticipation of the hunt that we had not finished, and from the fight that had not happened. In truth, part of me was glad the others had pulled us apart. At more than twice my size, Jaximo would have thrown me around the dark oasis like a toy, and I would have been forced to pull my dagger, which would have led to a whole assortment of trouble within the band.

Obadiah walked over to us, leaving Jaximo with Cyrus and Mercius. Charon had disappeared. I wagered he was probably hidden closer to the caravan, cloaked in the wet ferns, observing the group of travelers.

"We leave," Obadiah said briskly as he stopped in front of me. "Now, to the far eastern part of the oasis. I don't want to risk our lives for foolish merchants, or their money. We'll hide out until the storm clears then journey back here to see if it's safe. If not, then we'll travel to the Decapolis or try our fortune back in Judea, where the desert can't taunt us. I want to be near Jericho in these coming months."

I shook my head in disapproval. "But if we could just-"

"This discussion is over," he declared. "We're leaving now and there will be no more fighting tonight. You two pig-headed fools can fight all you want when we're closer to the Jordan and away from this caravan. Something about these travelers, and this night, vexes me and I think it would be wise to leave before I find out why."

While I thought of many words to give in contention, I simply nodded, then walked back to retrieve my protruding spear from the ground, ignoring Jax's baleful glare. Charon suddenly emerged from the shadows and walked quickly to Obadiah. They conversed quietly in the dark. I plucked the spear from the mud and waited, watching the dark hunter talk with our leader. Jax finally looked away from me and also stared at the talking pair. Cyrus was next to me, squatting in the rain, and he asked, "Are we still leaving?"

"Perhaps not," I whispered, as Obadiah and Charon walked over to us. Titus also bounded over to hear what was to be said.

10

Our leader ran his hands over his wet face and flicked the water to the undergrowth. He sighed and said, "Charon says they've set up camp outside the oasis, with tents and coverings. Four packing camels in the rear and two oxen on each of the two carts. The travelers, twenty or thirty of them are setting up tents. They appear to be a merchant caravan from Gilead, as I said before, but they're guided by two Bedouin scouts. Fools, all of them. No one makes such a journey in the rain, this far from the main road. Charon said their leader, the big man, didn't want to stop moving, but was forced to by the scouts. They refused to go any further on this night." He paused and looked back to the north, where the unseen caravan had settled. "They're in a great hurry for some reason and will be gone upon the sun's arrival. And here's the part that concerns us: they've placed their two covered carts against the tree line as a shelter of sorts. There are many boxes in the wagons, and many bags, as well. A single guard is in the first cart, already nearly asleep in his cloak. The rest are in the hills, in their tents along the line of palms. The second cart is closer to the tents. Either way, much of their goods are in the first wagon which is bunched up against the oasis, close enough to touch."

"So they've hidden the merchandise against the trees," Mercius asked, "to protect it from the storm? Gaius' body didn't make them suspicious?"

Obadiah looked to Charon and the hunter nodded. "The Bedouins," Obadiah said, "think demons hiding in the oasis killed the man," the hunter said. "The merchant wasn't afraid of demons but insisted the goods be sheltered under the palms if they had to stop."

Lightning flashed and all the shadows in the grove frolicked for a moment in the sudden illumination. We all stood in the rain, silently

11

pondering what we should do. My mind was already made up. I wanted to develop a plan and try for it, as was my nature. These foreign traders from the eastern regions were probably carting fine linens, pottery, metals, and other luxury goods – as well as various moneys. Their trade was usually for the rich and we could sell such items in any market in the ten cities of the Decapolis. If we could quietly subdue the lone guard, we could take our time and fill our travel bags with as much merchandise as possible, flee into the oasis and head south, then back west to the Jordan. It was possible that they even had great amounts of precious stones in these boxes that Charon spoke of.

My greed swelled, and I am sure that such feelings were mutual between all members of our band. While some of us suffered from pride and stubbornness, greed was commonplace for all thieves, in any land.

"What do you think, scions?" Obadiah asked. "Try it or leave? It is risky, but the rewards could be very great, I think. But I will not lie to you, men... it would be most prudent to leave now, with our meager possessions and our lives. This would be prudent, no?"

"When have we ever been prudent?" Mercius replied. We all laughed quietly as we stood in the rain, water dripping from our bearded chins. The winds covered the sound of our joviality.

"Let us think of a plan," I said, glancing at Jaximo, who was looking downward in thought. "We can do this. We've done things much more dangerous and much more foolish than this."

"Titus?" Obadiah implored. "Cyrus? Jaximo?"

Titus was silent for a moment, nodded, then said, "The gods have smiled upon us on this night, it seems. Such blessings should not go wasted. We should try it. We can always flee into the oasis and lose them if they follow. What if they're traveling off the roads to *avoid* thieves and patrolling soldiers because their cargo is so precious?"

Cyrus grunted in approval and nodded with his small head. Jaximo, obviously still uneasy about the engagement, stated his approval, not wanting to seem the coward. He gave me another glare then spit into the sodden greenery at his feet.

As lightning flashed again overhead, Obadiah presented a wolfish grin, his teeth gleaming white and I knew that despite our earlier talk he could never leave this life. Thunder followed, and as it died, he said, "We're all in agreement then, scions. The only thing we have to lose is our lives, and they are worth nothing anyway."

His lupine smile was contagious as we gathered closer to discuss our plan.

## V - *Man of Shadow*

The rain was to our advantage. It had grown loud, pounding through the desert palms. The storm's gusts howled through the plants and over the hills, covering any sound of my movement. I slid under the ferns, in the mud, crawling up the slope like some pale form of large vermin. My tunic was drenched, covered in mud and I smelled the earth: a deep, natural smell reeking of plant life and soil. My hair was matted and thick with mud, heavy against my face and eyes.

For what seemed to be an eternity, I crawled through the undergrowth, pausing only twice to peer out from the foliage. My slithering continued and finally the slope leveled and after crawling between two large palms, the rain suddenly stopped hammering over me and I found myself in a darker space, drier and still. I was finally under the cart. The merchant guard, not one of the hardened paladins, but one of the actual travelers, would be just above me sleeping fitfully in the wagon. I wondered if he shared in his leader's thoughts about there being no demons in the oasis or if he shared in the superstitions of the Bedouin scouts. Whatever his temperament, he remained silent as the storm raged around the cart. Before my crawl, as we surveyed him from within the foliage, we had watched him stir long enough to light a small oil lamp and place it on one of the boxes. He had then drawn a blanket over himself and had settled amid the crates and sailcloth bags. He was evidently afraid of the dark, but the oasis didn't scare him enough to flee his duties.

The second cart was further away, also along the tree line. It was larger, covered with planks of wood sealed by tar, and we had seen a faint light from the fluttering camel skin door at its rear. There were people inside this one, but Charon had not seen inside it and its contents were a mystery. We would have to be content with the smaller covered cart and its freight.

I twisted around and slowly rose on my elbows. The wide shadow above me was dark but from several cracks in the wood – between the two iron wheels – I could see slivers of lamplight. Towards the front of the wagon, I saw the thick black legs of two oxen, inert from fatigue. The animals mewled in the rain but remained still. The beasts were still bound by two large horn yokes.

I wiped the grime from my face and hands, and allowed myself a moment's rest to slow my heart. The Bedouin scouts were likely camped near the others on the hill, little more than a stone's throw away. Their curved scimitar was to be feared and I had been told stories of how these paladins trained daily with their blades. I had heard tales about them even sleeping with them, cherishing the swords as if they were women.

The rest of the band was still in the oasis, waiting for my signal. Slowly, I crawled to the rear of the wagon, which still faced the palms, and removed my dagger. I cleaned the dirtied blade and wove it front of me, just outside of the cart's billet, hoping to catch a gleam of light from the lamp.

I replaced my dagger and waited. After what seemed like an eternity, a dark form silently crawled from the ferns in front of me and emerged under the cart. Charon rose on his elbows, as I had done, and wiped the mud and wetness from his face. He nodded to me, and he rested for a moment, stretching his arms and legs.

Our plan was simple and had been mostly devised by Obadiah. Two of us would crawl under the foliage to the cart and dispatch of the guard. This would have to be accomplished as quietly as possible, using the raging storm to our advantage. We could not risk alerting the paid scouts or the travelers themselves, for their numbers were far greater than our own. They had erected two large goat-hair tents along the line of palms at the edge of the grove and they swayed and fluttered madly, but stayed intact. The thick hide of desert goats was waterproof and if sewn correctly, could be constructed into a large tent capable of sheltering an entire family from such a storm. The dark skins flapped and trembled in the wind and I imagined the occupants to be nearly deaf from the noise, but we would still need to be careful.

Once the lone guard was subdued, we would give another signal to the band and two more would come up the slope on foot, not crawling as Charon and I had. Then each of us would load up as many valuables as our bags and hands could carry and we'd journey back through the oasis and flee south. We would stay away from the Ehud Spring because they were probably still wary of the thieves that had struck their settlement several nights ago. We would journey well south of the Jabbok and head west to the larger cities near the Jordan River, where we would finally rest and take good stock of our catch. There, we would barter and sell our spoils. My first purchase would be better sandals. The ones on my feet were worn and nearly falling apart.

Charon looked at me in the shadows and gave a slight nod to show he was ready. I nodded back and whispered in his ear, "Whatever is fast and quiet. If you feel you can just knock him unconscious, then do so. The less blood we spill, the less inking they'll have to follow us upon morning."

We stealthily rose from beneath the cart and peered into its space, squinting in the rain. The man was sleeping in the front of the cart, lying on his side and facing away from us. The lamp still burned brightly and we saw the man had a short sword attached to his belt in a thin leather sheath. The wagon rocked in the wind and the guard stirred with a snore. Crouching next to the opening, we waited.

After another minute or so, lightning crashed throughout the hills and we leapt quickly into the covered cart. I reached the man before Charon and saw the guard's eyes suddenly open as he registered the shifting weight in the wagon. My muddy hands quickly wrapped around his mouth to silence him while Charon struck him several times in chest. The man stopped struggling and his tunic swiftly turned red. We let the body slide quietly down in between two of the crates and I realized that Charon had been stabbing him with one of his darts. The act had been so fast I had not even seen the iron in his hands.

I made my way to the back of the cart and waved my dagger in the lamp light, signaling the others. Two shadows surfaced from the herbage and loped silently up to the rear of the wagon. It was Titus and Jaximo, and they stopped at the back of the cart, crouching low as they tried to blend in with the weeds. Charon hurriedly moved the lamp off of the first strongbox and pried it open with his dart. To our good fortune, we found that the boxes were nailed shut; these merchants were too stingy to buy good locks, it seemed. After tonight, no doubt, they would spend the extra money for better safeguards.

The first box held linens, purple and gold, and lined with twinkling sequins. I removed an armful of the cloth and handed them to Jaximo, our dispute forgotten for the moment. His wet face was no longer red with anger, but was drawn tight with business and silent execution. He took the linens and placed them in one of his bags, quickly so they would not be ruined by the rain, and I saw that he had several more bags draped over his wide shoulders, as did Titus. We were going to make a splendid haul.

At our feet, the murdered guard twitched as if alive. We ignored this and continued our pilfering as thunder echoed above us.

The next box held more linens; this time a costly white material known in the markets as *byssus*. The next two boxes were filled with containers of fine spices and peppers such as cinnamon, cassia and frankincense. There were also glass bottles of perfume, which we wrapped quickly but carefully in the fabrics and placed them in the bags.

The first load of bags went down the slope with the two burly thieves and they disappeared in the dark grove, handed the goods off, then returned swiftly back up the slope. Charon and I handed them the unfastened bags which hung above the strong boxes, not even bothering to see what form of merchandise was inside them. I moved the lamp to the rear of the cart to give my brothers more light. Mercius ran up the slope to help. He winked at me in the rain and whispered, "This was a grand idea, no?"

I nodded and handed him a bag which he slung it over his shoulder. He looked about the covered cart. He stared at the guard's body and his eyes lit up. "There," he pointed with his free hand. "A

18

small box under the body."

Charon followed Mercius' stare, found the small box and retrieved it from under the body. It was a small chest, as wide as a man's foot. Jaximo returned for another load, as did Titus. Charon inspected the bloody chest, shook it and we all heard the distinct, muffled sound of shifting coins. This small box, unlike the others, was actually fastened by a small iron lock. Charon handed it to me, and I then handed it to Mercius who stood silently in the rain with a passionate look of discovery in his eye. He cradled the small box in his right arm, evidently deciding to release the sodden bag to further examine the box.

"Just take them both," I whispered to him. "Be quick, Mercius."

He ignored me and wiggled the heavy bag off of his shoulder, and heaved it back into the cart. There was a sharp crunch. Before I could wince at the sound, orange light and a fierce heat suddenly filled the wagon, and as I fell backwards, striking the inside of the cart, I realized it was not a lightning strike. The clay lamp, which had been full, had exploded under the weight of the bag, sending liquid fire into the cart and onto Charon. For a brief moment, as I lay stunned on the floor of the wagon, I had a glimpse of a fiery nightmare. Charon's cloaked body was covered in blue liquid fire which swarmed like hissing snakes. These flames rose and turned orange and yellow, spreading onto the cart's roof and billowing into the rain. Without a cry, amazingly, Charon surged out of the cart and as he passed me, the fire grazed my eyes, singed my beard and I was momentarily blinded. The heat shot into my mouth and I gagged as my throat was scorched.

For some curious reason, as I lay sprawled in the cart nearly choking, I thought of how I would commend Charon for not screaming and immediately giving us away. The cart raised up as Charon's weight left it. Still momentarily blinded, I wiggled over the remaining sacks and boxes, flopping out of the wagon into the wet ferns and into the rain. My hands found cool mud and I rubbed it in my eyes to cool them as I started crawling towards the slope to escape the onslaught that would soon be upon us. With great heaves I tried to take in air, but couldn't find my breath amid the rain and smoke. In my confusion and blindness, I crawled the wrong way, and my head struck one of the iron tires of the wagon.

Voices filled the night… cries of anger and confusion. I held my eyes open with my fingers and took in my direction. Through the rain I saw men pouring out of the two tents like disturbed hornets from a nest, but it was one of the Bedouin scouts who arrived first. He leapt over me, perhaps not even realizing the piteous form beneath him was alive and swung his gleaming scimitar at someone behind me. The sound of steel against bone echoed over the downpour and lightning flashed overhead. In the light of the now blazing wagon, I saw the scimitar swing again and a red mist erupted from one of the figures and mixed with the falling rain. This figure tumbled down the slope, his pale face fixed in agony. Was it Mercius? Titus? I could not tell through my stinging eyes. Other blurred figures wrestled like demons in the firelight.

In no condition to stand and run, I decided to squirm under the cart. My lungs burned and I could hardly breathe, making the simple act of crawling difficult. At the wagon's front, the oxen were bellowing their confusion. Their legs stamped heavily in the mud. Once fully under the cart, I pressed myself into the ferns and looked out from between the spokes of the iron wheel at the continuing brawl at the wagon's rear. A large shape, Jaximo I think, was struggling with the scout, the curved sword wavering between them. Jax shoved the man to the ground and wrestled the sword from his grip. The large thief started swinging the blade at the howling figure on the ground, hacking and hacking, until the screaming stopped. Lightning flashed again and I saw bright red blood dripping from his angry face, the rain turning it thin and watery. Several other men threw themselves upon Jaximo, coming from his side. He bellowed like on ox and started swinging the sword at them.

Where were the others? Had they escaped? My thoughts were a blur and as the cart above me moved a few feet when the oxen tried to get away from the smoking cart behind them, I knew I had to find the strength to make it the ten paces to the oasis.

Over the hollering and curses, I felt someone strike the wagon as if they had been thrown into it. The oxen cried their distress and pulled the cart nearly the full length of a man. My face suddenly felt the rain and I slithered back under the cart, hoping it would not be pulled further from the oasis. I turned back to look to the trees and saw a man laying no more than a few paces from me, his forehead bleeding and eyes closed. Behind him, Jaximo's large figure could be seen rising from the ferns. He looked past the fallen traveler, and stared directly at me for the briefest of moments. He gave me a bloody grin and ran into the oasis; the dense foliage swallowed him like a black sea. And from this blackness, another figure emerged. Obadiah. His eyes looked over the carnage and they finally settled on me. He made to move up the slope but halted suddenly. From behind me, I heard the sound of shouting as yet more men neared. Obadiah's eyes focused on these men then turned back to me. He gave me a sorrowful look – a pleading look, as if asking for forgiveness, and he, too, disappeared into the oasis.

Before I could pull myself out from under the cart to try and follow, I saw the legs of nearly a dozen men swarm all around the cart. A number of them bounded into the palms to pursue the thieves, yelling in coarse Hebrew. Through the smoke and rain, I saw that there were several figures sprawled out in the mud at the base of the cart. These figures were still and their only movement came from rain drops hitting their tunics.

My breathing came in ragged gasps and I tried to be quiet, but was forced to repeatedly draw greater, louder breaths to get air. I wheezed like a dying old man.

The men who had remained by the cart were yelling, battling to be heard over the fury of the rain. Their tunics and cloaks were pulled by the wind and they bent towards the storm, holding their hands to their faces as they surveyed the scene. Some of these men knelt by their fallen comrades. Under the cart, I remained as still as possible. My lungs were throbbing and my heart pounded so loudly that I wondered if they could hear its beat over the storm, drowning out all other noises save my grated attempts at breathing.

Some of the men had brought covered lamps, while others carried swords and shepherd's staffs. Through this new dim light I saw a figure laying at the base of the oasis, midway down the slope. It was Mercius. He lay in the mud, alive and gasping in pain. His face was covered in sludge and I saw he had been cut badly across his stomach; his bloodied hands held tightly to a mass of redness in his tunic as if it were his soul. Through the rain I saw his eyes move feverously about the men around him. He raised his head to speak and a staff struck him in the face. His head fell backwards and he was still.

Fear gripped me and I continued to try to slow my loud breathing. The travelers knelt by the other fallen men – the Bedouin and the other travelers – and attempted to revive them. I saw the Bedouin's hacked form and knew he would not be awakened. Another man had been struck in the side of the head with the scimitar and he also lay still in the rain. I could see the gleaming whiteness of his skull through the great wound at his temple.

Others tended to the unconscious man next to the cart. They were close, loud and speaking quickly in their guttural language. I was able to pick out several words over the rain, both curses and prayers. If they only peered deeper into the shadows under the wagon, they would have seen me hiding. I tried to hold my breath again but was granted more fiery pain as my lungs constricted with the effort. A sudden movement in the mud in front of me caught my attention: a four legged shadow, moving swiftly through the rain and sniffing around the carnage. For a crazed moment I wondered if one of the jackals had been bold enough to actually venture into the camp during this chaos, but I saw the speckled hide of the hound and realized it was nothing more than an ugly sheep dog. It loped to the cart and barked at the smoke. My heart stopped and I remained as still as possible, my wet fingers tightening on my dagger. It sniffed under the cart, licked the ferns in front of me and also licked the face of the wounded man at the cart's base. The hound was quickly shoved away by the other men and it ran off into the rain.

Over the wind and rain I heard a low groan in front of me and saw that the unconscious man was stirring. His face was smeared with watery blood. His eyes slowly opened and focused in front of him… directly on me. I remained deathly still, trying to blend in with the mud and ferns. He blinked in the rain, confused and in pain. His companions started to roll him over and sit him up, and he complied, not sure of where he was or what had occurred. I slowly squirmed backwards, to the front of the cart. I would make my way between the oxen and just run. Maybe in the confusion they wouldn't see me.

Suddenly the injured man lay back down and his tired eyes found me once more. Then he pointed and coughed a flurry of Hebrew. One of these words I recognized as "thief". He was swiftly pulled away and other dark, wet faces bent down and peered under the cart.

I turned and threw myself between one of the cart's wheels and the stomping legs of the oxen. The rain nearly blinded me and before I could fully stand, hands grabbed my tunic and I was shoved back to the ground. My dagger was roughly pulled from my hand. They struck me as I lay there, with their fists and staffs. My lungs heaved and I felt as if I was choking on blood and rain. And suddenly a loud command echoed over the storm's din, and the beating stopped.

I squinted up into hate-filled faces and saw that one of the men had a sword raised high, waiting for a command to finish me off. All of them were breathing heavy and the one with the sword smiled down at me. His black hair was long, fluttering violently in the wind, and his features were as sharp as his blade. My confiscated dagger was tucked into his belt, useless and mocking.

"I was their captive," I rasped in Aramaic, not knowing where the words came from or what weight they could possibly hold. One last gambit at survival.

From behind them, another man neared, one hand held out to

24

block the rain from his broad face. I could tell instantly that it was their leader; a bulky man with a flowing gray beard and dense robes now heavy with rain. He stopped next to the sinister looking man with the upraised sword. Their leader also had a sword, and as lightning flashed again, I could make out Hebrew lettering that had been etched onto the flat of the blade.

This bearded man looked down at me, still holding one hand to his brow to block the stinging rain. In his eyes I saw a mixture of emotions, but sadness dominated his look.

"I was their captive," I repeated hoarsely, trying to be heard over the storm.

The large man's eyes narrowed and he suddenly turned from me, yelling a command over his shoulder. Several pairs of hands gripped my tunic and hoisted me up. They started dragging me towards their line of tents. Through the rain, I saw many dark figures moving frantically throughout the camp. At the second covered wagon, a lone woman stood watching me. She was robed, and as I watched, the storm ripped the veil from her head. She was beautiful, with black hair flowing wildly in the wind. A desert flower, I thought, and when she saw my stare, her lovely features turned into a scowl.

Behind her, beyond the curve of the palms, far in the hills, another figure seized my attention. It was a cloaked man, standing tall as he watched the grisly scene next to the oasis. In the darkness he seemed more phantom than man, and as lightning lit the hills, I saw that his cloak was long and black, billowing behind him like a pair of huge wings. Though he was far away, I saw his radiant eyes and felt their stare. His hair was sable, very long and fluttering behind him in unison with his cloak. His face was sharp and his black beard was trimmed thin.

This man was a stranger to this land and was not one of the travelers. However, he was no stranger to me. I had seen him several times throughout my childhood, though not in many years. I tried to remember the name I had given him back in those days, but it flirted on the tip of my tongue.

Before I could reflect further into my past, those who were dragging me reached the first tent and there was another shouted command from behind me. Then a hard blow to the back of my head with something steel. As pain and total darkness engulfed me, I sputtered, "Man of Shadow…" and fell to the ground.

# FIRST INTERLUDE

*A smile of embarrassment came across my face when I saw the whiteness of my knuckles on the hand clenching my cup. After relaxing my grip, I massaged the fingers and said, "A brutal story, indeed."*

*The orator Siergo nodded.*

*Shaking my head, I remarked, "This Dismas is not a good man. So violent and crude. And his band... all savages."*

*Siergo smiled and held up his cup of wine. "Well, what did you expect, brother? They are thieves. This is not a tale for children."*

*This was true. I did not fancy a tale fit for children, but I favored characters more deserving of attention. "How can you expect me to follow this man as the hero of this tale?" I asked. "One is supposed to love the main role in such epics. Witness Odysseus. Or Septus from the Stand in Armenia. The Spartans in Thermopylae. These were good men. You could identify with them and you wished them well in their adventures. This is why many cry during the epic tragedies in the theater. We are moved when good people are killed or befallen with ill circumstance. Heroes should be worthy of narration."*

*"He was not always like this," Siergo countered. "You must hear the full story. At this time in his life his spirit seems certainly*

27

*unsalvageable. But nothing, Marcus, is impossible if heaven's eyes see something more of you than what you are."*

*A strange answer from a strange man, I thought. I was beginning to expect nothing less from him. Regardless, my interest was still kindled and I had another inquiry for him that would hopefully be granted with a more straight forward answer. "Who was this 'Man of Shadow' he spoke of?" I asked. "He sounds like one of the gods incarnate in human form. Perhaps Apollo."*

*Siergo gave a smile. "This question plagued Dismas for much of his life. He had to wait years before discovering the truth. You, Marcus, will need to wait as well, but not nearly as long."*

*I shrugged. "Fair enough, friend. But it sounds like his life is about to end rather quickly though, unless he spends the rest of his days held captive."*

*"Do not forget about the gales from God," Siergo said with a wink. "For they are ever-blowing..."*

# V I - *Song of the Zither*


They did not kill me during that first night [*Dismas had imparted to Siergo*], but after the first day, I had started to wish that they had. The caravan's form of torture was simple and effective: neglect. They did not, as I have been told in fables meant to unnerve listeners, cut a slit in my stomach and let loose a desert viper into my bowels. Nor did they fasten a wicker basket onto my head and release a brood of angry, starved rats through its top opening. I was not further burned, cut, beaten or whipped with catgut. Their most effective method of torture was denial. For an unknown amount of time, long hours or possibly even days, I was trapped inside a rough sackcloth bag, my wrists bound together behind me with rope. I was denied food, water, sunlight and at times, it seemed, even air. From the jostling noises of travel and the turbulent movement it was evident that I had been placed in one of the wagons and the caravan was on the move again.

The bag which served as my cell was coarse and smelled strongly of spoiled grain. I was lying on my side with my knees curled upwards towards my stomach, for the bag's length would not permit me to stretch out fully. The muscles in my legs had ceased their burning long ago with this set posture. But had this been hours ago or days ago? Bouts of panic swept over me every few minutes during my times of consciousness. It was unbearably hot and my own putrid stench quickly merged with that of the bag. Sharp pains assaulted my stomach and I remembered the words of a spindly thief from the south I had once met; he had been a rugged man who said that starvation was the cruelest form of all deaths. *Your stomach will turn on itself,* he had blubbered with only half a tongue in his mouth. *It will devour its own lining in attempt to find nourishment.*

There were numerous small holes in the bag and fragments of sunlight occasionally shone through. My breathing was still labored from the explosion of the oil lamp and its heat down my throat.

After that stormy night, when I had finally woke, I was already bound and inside the bag. The weight of someone's sandaled foot rested heavily upon my hip. Grim imagery from the previous night came to me. The storm's fierceness. The fiery explosion in the wagon. Obadiah's look of sorrow. The beautiful woman and her scowl. And, of course, the stranger in the hills whom I had not seen in many years… his silent gaze meant to give me courage. Many emotions ran through my head during this agony inside the sack, but anything resembling courage was not to be found.

My head pounded from the beating I had endured upon my capture. Occasionally, when I would thrash about in the bag in panic, an unseen person would throw another cloth over the bag, giving me total darkness and even less air. When I stopped my flaying about, the cloth would be removed. This occurred too many times to keep count.

My only comfort in this suffocating misery was the feeling of the thin bracelet on my wrist… a parting gift from my mother, long ago. My captors had evidently not noticed it before placing me in the bag.

Hours in my own filth. Days. Years. I could not tell. It seemed the gods had finally surfaced from their silent lull to punish me for my misdeeds. The crossed line that Obadiah had spoke of came to my thoughts. Not knowing whether it was night or day, I screamed through my seared throat, but the guard above me – who used my backside as his footstool – remained silent.

My curses, once directed towards the gods, were turned upon myself and I attempted several feeble prayers to several different gods under Jupiter, the watchman of Mount Olympus. The agony continued, and eventually, so did the curses aimed at the worthless divinities. I thought of the Jewish man and woman I had robbed at the Ehud Spring. His vex had finally found me, it seemed.

*"Thief... You are damned to hell."*

I cursed the God of the Jews and screamed again. The guard above me flung the heavy blanket over me once more.

\*\*\*

The sound of fabric being torn woke me. Sunlight – once welcomed but now painful – hit my eyes, and I turned away with a moan, burying my battered face deeper into the burlap sack. With the sudden movement, dry heaves racked my body, but I had long since purged myself of all fluids and waste into the bag and my tunic. I heard several voices curse as the smell reached them.

A sharp blow struck me in the shoulder as I was forced off the wagon's edge and I hit the earth. I lay there, dazed and aching, my eyes open yet seeing only dancing pinpricks of light.

"Look at the fool," a male voice said in Aramaic.

31

"Waste of a man," someone else said. "Why we don't just kill him like his rat-faced friend is a mystery to me."

Other voices concurred, some in Hebrew. "Crawl out of there," one ordered, "and have yourself a look at your friend." The others laughed.

Why I was still alive was a mystery to me as well. I attempted to move but gasped in pain and remained still. A foot prodded my temple. Someone then placed a walking staff under my bound arm and pulled me halfway out of the bag. As my legs uncurled, the joints popped and came alive with a hot pain. I rolled away from the bag and moaned. After a moment, my vision slowly adjusted to the bright sun and I could make out several shapes standing over me.

"Stand up."

If I knew the act of laughing would not hurt so much, I would have done so. I could hardly move, let alone stand on my own. If my captors thought differently, then *they* were to be called fools.

One of them knelt over me, grabbed the edge of fabric around my neck and hauled me into a sitting position. "I hate thieves," he said. "I have wondered if it is laziness that makes one a thief or simply inbreeding." His blurry face sneered at me. "I would wager that your mother was a whore and you never knew your father. That's it, isn't it? Your mother probably drew lots to see who she'd claim as your father."

As I stared back at his blurry face a line of spittle ran down my chin. I made a sputtering sound.

"What's that?" the man asked. "You have a reply, thief?"

"I…" My voice was hoarse, but I had to speak. "I… I'm trying to spit on you."

One of the shapes behind him gave a laugh. The man who held

me scowled and dropped me to the sand. He then spit on my chest and said, "That's how it is done, friend." He spit on me again and the other men joined in. I felt several globs and droplets hit my face, and in truth, it actually felt good on my parched skin.

"Stop this," a deep voice said, coming up from behind them. The men obeyed at once. The voice had sounded familiar. Had I heard it on the night of my capture?

"We're not going to act like heathens," the voice said. "Are we not better than these thieves? Stand him up."

"We tried, Aaron, but he won't."

"Can't," I corrected them with a cough. There was still a fire in my legs, but my vision had cleared. I recognized the enraged man above me as the one who had stood over me with the sword on the night of the storm. He was dark skinned and wore a long gray tunic with a matching turban-like headdress. Above his black beard, his eyes were still afire with disdain and his breathing was heavy.

"Come, Jaspe," a large, gray-bearded man I recognized as the caravan's leader said. "Pick him up and rest him against the palm." He pointed and the men obeyed. I was hauled to my feet and dragged backwards. The solidness of wood touched my back and I rested against it, but the men on either side of me still had to hold me up.

"Here," one of them said, brandishing a long strap of leather I recognized as a tether for goats. They stretched it across my chest and fixed me in an upright position against the tree, tying the leather in back. They released me and I slumped forward but remained in a standing position. The leather cut into my ribs but I was still able to give shallow breaths.

My vision had slowly grown better and I looked around at my

surroundings. Directly in front of me a line of mountains rose from the desert wilderness. The Jabbok River was gone and I wagered the caravan had traveled back east towards the Azurie-Geho Mountains, which was a day's journey east of the desert city of Gerasa, and nearly three days journey from the Jordan River. The sun was high in the sky and only a few clouds could be found drifting over the mountaintops.

The caravan's leader, Aaron, stood before me. He was tall and very wide in girth. His long beard was fully gray and it fell over the tie of his coat and onto his broad chest. On his head he wore a headdress, held by a band of woven goat hair. He had a purple linen scarf around his neck and a purple dyed sash over his shoulder. Behind him I saw other members of the caravan setting up a large, goatskin tent, unpacking their bags and tending to the oxen. Two young men were constructing a fire pit and had erected two forked sticks to hold either roasted game or stew over the flames. The caravan's four packing camels rested and mewled near another grouping of palms.

A young man near the fire pit, perhaps eleven or twelve years of age, was playing a stringed instrument I recognized as a zither. His song was sad but rich in notes. He played the instrument well.

Most of the people near the tent were women and the younger members of the caravan, while the men had circled around me. I thought of the beautiful woman I had seen the previous night, but I did not see her toiling under the sun with the others.

In the Hebrew language, Aaron spoke to Jaspe, motioned to me, then to the ground and to the others behind him. The sun was bright and made my head pound even more.

Aaron stepped closer to me and gave me a good look over. His large nose wrinkled as he smelled my filth. "You smell like a pig's trough," he said to me in Aramaic. He sighed. "We have a law among our family. *The* Law. Perfect and holy under the Lord and we have exacted His good justice upon your friend. Now look." He motioned to the ground to my left. When I refused to look, he grabbed my chin and jarred my head towards the good justice he had spoken of.

When a body is torn apart, it is not, as one would imagine, just a red bloody mess. Indeed, it is bloody, but one can see many other colors inside a rent corpse for the inner workings of man are multihued. Deep shades of purple, yellow, orange, and blue, like the many dyes extracted from the affluent fishes in the Great Sea.

"You will share the same fate," Aaron said softly.

His voice was lost to me as I stared at Mercius. Once a jovial friend who strove for nothing but good humor among our band – and a light temperament from wine drinking – his face was now gray and swollen as it faced upwards towards the sun. He had been pulled in half. Colorful organs were displayed for all to see though he was still partially hidden within a burlap sack, not unlike the one that had held me.

One of the men moved the bag away from the thief's body and more of the gore was displayed. Mercius' intestines had been gathered and bunched up under him; they were yellowish and pink, a heap of pallid loops. The spongy layer of yellow fat tissue at the hewed torso could also be seen, just over the paleness of the ribs.

Another series of dry heaves racked my stomach and throat, but nothing came from my mouth save a low moan. Had they used the oxen to pull him apart? Swords? Mercius had been a friend and their plan of terrorization was working. I closed my eyes and Aaron released my head.

"If you'd only taken our money or stock, and not lives," Aaron said, "we would have simply taken one of your hands, that you might not reach for property not belonging to you."

My eyes were closed, but I still saw the ravaged body of my friend as if the image had been burned onto the inside of my eyelids.

"Mercy," I whispered. "I did not kill anyone. I beg of your mercy."

"Mercy?" The man asked coldly. "Why should I spare your life, thief? Were you not being held captive by these thieves like you told us last night?"

Had I said that? Much of last night, especially my capture after the lamp's explosion, was a blur. If I had told them that I was a captive, then perhaps this was why they had not killed me yet.

"I met these men less than a month ago," I lied. "In Jericho. They told me they would help me find work in the east. I did not know they were thieves. When they saw your caravan near the oasis, they told me to help them rob your wagon or they would kill me."

"Liar!" the man named Jaspe yelled. "He has been a thief since birth. Look at his pagan eyes! You can see the greed and sin."

"That's not true!" I managed to cry out. "I have never stolen anything before last night. I am no thief!"

Jaspe bent to the ground and scooped up a handful of sand which he threw in my face. I winced and tried to turn away from him. "Just a murderer then?" he mocked.

"No," I said, spitting out sand. "No murderer. Ask all around you. I was hiding under the wagon the whole time. There was a big thief… the one who killed your men. It was not me and they know it."

Aaron gave a grunt. "Then why was your tunic burned?" He

36

asked, regarding me with a wary eye. "Part of your hair as well. The fire was inside the wagon. Not under it. And your voice sounds as if you've been swallowing hot coals."

I shook my head. "There was so much confusion, I do not remember. At one point I tried to flee and must have inhaled smoke. But ask everyone else. Did anyone see me steal or murder anyone?"

Jaspe bent to the ground for more sand but Aaron raised a hand to still him. Turning back to me, he asked, "What is your name?"

"Dismas," I said. "A former slave of the Menenia family near Sychar."

"A Samaritan as well as a thief!" Jaspe hollered.

"Good people," I sputtered. "Please... I..."

Aaron stepped closer to me, just a handbreadth away. "Why do you call us 'good people'? You know nothing about us. What could a Greek pagan know about our people?"

I looked up at him. "You would be surprised what I know. I have been taught much about many cultures." I thought back to the last few years with Obadiah and his lessons about all of the different cultures that inhabited these occupied lands. Obadiah had been a Jew, and while he despised his old traditions, as he despised all formal traditions, he had still told us many tales of Old Israel.

Aaron turned and looked at his people. Several shouted condemnations while most remained silent. Jaspe was still, glaring at me with a handful of sand running between his fingers. Aaron turned back to me and said, "I'd be surprised at what you know, huh?"

I looked to him and nodded.

"I would like a display of this knowledge then. For the price of one day. I will ask you a question about our faith. Answer it correctly and we will spare you today, but you will come with us back to our settlement in Gilead, where you will remain imprisoned until I think of a better fate for you. Answer correctly and you earn *today*. Tomorrow is uncertain."

Jaspe dropped the rest of the sand he had been holding and said, "Aaron, we-"

Without turning, Aaron said, "You believe in this pagan's claim, Jaspe?"

Looking at Aaron's back for a moment, his glare never softening, Jaspe said, "Of course not, but we have a right under the Law to punish him for his crimes."

Aaron nodded and gave me an insincere smile. "Well, Dismas," he said. "Do you think you're up to my test?"

I took a deep breath and nodded. "I don't think I have much choice in the matter. But truly I am just a traveler who-"

His large open hand slapped me across the face and I nearly blacked out again. My head throbbed anew and I saw dancing lights in front of me. When my vision cleared, the first thing I saw was Mercius' rent body laying on the ground. My ear was ringing on the side he had struck me on. The sad melody of the young man's zither continued without missing a note.

"Your explanations won't bring back the men who were killed," Aaron said. "Nor will they silence the cries of their wives."

My eyes focused on his face and with a painful effort I nodded again.

"Ready a blade, Jaspe," he said, and the dark traveler did as instructed, pulling my own seized dagger from his tunic and clenching it tightly.

Aaron rubbed his huge hands together in thought, and after a moment his bushy eyebrows raised. "As for your test," he said, "our father Moses, the deliverer of our people from Pharaoh's Egypt, wandered in the wilderness as the Lord prepared our promised land for them. This land was all of Judea, from Gilead to Dan." He looked to his hands, then back to me. "How long did Moses wander with the people before he finally entered into the land our Lord had promised him?"

*Forty years.* I had heard the old tales of the Jewish exodus from Obadiah several times. I nearly smiled with relief, but refrained myself. I let my head clear for a moment, as this question's stakes deserved more than a second's thought. After a few breaths, I opened my mouth to speak... but something stopped me.

Aaron glowered down at me and said, "Well?"

His question had been one of trickery and I had almost found myself dead with a hasty answer. This story had been told to me several times, not because of God's mercy, Obadiah had declared, but because of the apparent spite He had shown Moses.

"His people wandered for forty years," I answered carefully, "but Moses, himself, never touched the promised land. God let him see it from a mountaintop on the other side of the Jordan, but he was not allowed to enter it."

Aaron's eyes widened in disbelief, as did the eyes of several of those gathered behind him. Jaspe gave a curse in Hebrew and stalked away.

Aaron was silent for a moment and the only sound after Jaspe's departure was the song of the zither. The breeze continued to gently ruffle my captor's beard and after a few more notes of sad music, he quietly said, "Mount Nebo, yes." He shook his head and looked to the ground between us.

Suddenly, his eyes rose to mine and his look of bewilderment turned into one of fury. His hand came up to strike me again, this time with a closed fist, and the darkness returned.

# V I I - *Cup of Mercy*

**My** eyelids fluttered open and my vision slowly came to focus on a black monster. Its shiny maw twitched a few times and it moved closer to me, scuttling on myriad legs. I blinked several times and found that the monster was only a large desert beetle cavorting on the dirt next to my face. With a groan, I rolled away from it and stared upward. There was no sky, only more hard packed dirt between heavy cedar beams. I lay there for a while, staring up at this dark ceiling. Dust and sand could be tasted on my tongue and I tried to spit but found I had no saliva. Never had my mouth felt so parched.

There was no longer a rope binding my wrists together and I slowly curled my arms to my chest and felt for my bracelet. It was still attached to my right wrist. I gave a faint smile at this small blessing and sat up slowly, wincing at the pain in my head. After wiping the sand from my lips, I regarded my new cell: an underground room divided in the center by a wall of rusted iron bars. On the room's opposite side, a collection of colorful glazed pots were grouped neatly in one corner. To the left of the pots was an arched entryway with a camel skin covering serving as a door. The pots looked empty but I smelled grain and a small hint of raisins or dates in the musty air. Two clay lamps had been placed on the pots, but only one was lit. Shadows from the pots and the line of bars danced across the dirt walls and over the floor. A small section of the bars, near the wall on the right, was cut and hinged to provide a door. An iron box touched both the heavy cedar beam at the bars' threshold and this door. The lock, I wagered, and I immediately thought of the key, where it would be and who possessed it.

I cursed at the pots. Aaron most likely had the key, I thought. Or perhaps the teeth-gnashing Jaspe, and they were both likely plotting a suitable death for me as I sat there. Or another trick question about their faith, perhaps. My wits had spared me twice now, and I gathered that I was probably out of luck.

Trying to push the prospect of an impending death away, my thoughts transferred to escape. Slowly, I moved to my knees and stood, holding the bars for support. Darkness began to close in around my vision, but I held tightly to the cool steel and it eventually passed. I blinked and gave the bars a shake. They felt firm, but dust floated down from the wood-beamed ceiling and settled in my already dirty hair. With slow effort, I shuffled towards the barred door and placed a hand between the bars and felt the lock. The key hole was smaller than I would have guessed and the lock seemed surprisingly sturdy for a makeshift desert prison cell. I shook the door and was granted with nothing more than another descending cloud of dust.

I slowly turned and regarded my half of the room more closely. In one of its dark corners, I saw the outline of a sackcloth bag, and for a dreadful moment, I wondered if Mercius' body had been placed in the room with me. A second, more discerning glance told me the bag was empty and just bunched up with its own folds. A small pit had been dug next to the bag; this was a hole of unknown depth that would carry my waste into the earth.

As my senses continued to clear, I noticed the vile smell of my tunic, which had been soiled with sweat, dirt and my own filth. Part of me felt ashamed to be in such a garb, but I had no other choice but to parade naked around the cell.

My face crinkled as a hunger pain hit my stomach. I sighed and glanced down at the earthen floor of my cell, looking for the beetle. It was at my feet. Energy, Obadiah had taught us, can be found in places that most would not want to look. Thinking of those words, I bent and scooped up the beetle. I blew the dust from its body, regarded it for a thoughtful moment and then placed it on my dusty tongue. I chewed only once and swallowed. With my senses dulled and mouth still dusty, the beetle had no taste, though I did not enjoy the frantic moving of the small legs as it passed down my throat.

For a few minutes, I waited at the bars, staring at the designs on the clay pots. Eventually, I lay back on the ground. My thoughts were of food, death and escape, but only one seemed likely.

***

As I slept in the dust I dreamt of a storm. The rain felt good and I realized that I was back in the oasis. I sat at the top of the rock outcropping with Obadiah, Titus and Mercius, and though it rained, the sun also shone down on us. Eventually, the storm grew so strong – the sheets of rain so dense – that it began to feel more like coarse fabric. I suddenly found myself back in the sackcloth bag. Yet this nightmare storm continued and I felt the bag filling quickly with black desert beetles. I tried to scream but the only thing that came from my mouth was more beetles.

"Wake up, pagan." The voice was deep and loud, finding its way through the bag and through the mass of squirming insects.

As I became fully awake, the sack thankfully disappeared and the beetles faded away. I coughed and rolled over to stare at the bars on the other end of my cell. The second lamp was now lit and I saw a figure sitting on one of the pots, staring at me. My eyes adjusted to the brighter light and I saw it was the caravan leader, Aaron.

"How was your rest?" he asked. In his hand he held a cup of wine, which I instantly smelled. Deprived of food and drink for so long, my senses had become attuned to even the distant odors of sustenance. I swallowed and my tongue fastened itself to the top of my dry mouth.

I cleared my throat and said, "Bad dreams."

"Do you believe you deserve good dreams?" Aaron replied.

I gave a slight shrug. "As I am not a thief or a murderer, I would have hoped for better."

He grunted and leaned forward on the pot. His eyes flickered in the lamplight and in them I saw a combination of amusement and anger. "Some of my people actually believe your lies. In truth, you are good at it. I would imagine most thieves are. However, I know for certain you are lying."

I rose to a sitting position and stretched my neck. "You're wrong about me, good sir. As I told you, I-"

"You talk in your sleep."

I stopped talking and stared at him.

"I take it *Protos* is the leader of your band of thieves?"

I shook my head, trying to think quickly. "No, he was just a-"

"And it seems you're quite distressed that he did not save you from capture." Aaron leaned back and took a sip of his wine. "Your friends had something big planned back in Judea it sounds like. Something you very much want to be a part of."

My mouth was open but as my thoughts tried to catch up to his words, I could think of nothing prudent to say. Knowing silence was damning, I muttered, "You're wrong. I had heard them speak about big plans they had after they were done in the oasis."

Aaron frowned at me. "So this was before they forced you to terrorize my people?"

"Right before, I think," I said quickly. "I heard mention of it from some of them when they had blades drawn on me."

"And why is it you lament over the death of Mercius? And why do you feel that the oasis is yours? Your kingdom even?"

Slowly, as to not blur my concentration, I stood and regarded my captor. "Perhaps the beating to my head and the lack of food or water has turned my dreams crazy. You would judge a man on the ramblings he has during feverous nightmares?"

He stared at me a moment and suddenly smiled. "Well, perhaps your head may indeed need cleared," he said, "so that your future ramblings won't be so hazy." He took a sip of wine and adjusted his position on the pot. I noticed another cup, next to one of the lamps, sitting atop a heavy parchment that had not been there the last time I had been awake. Aaron saw my gaze. He looked to the cup then back to me. "I'm not totally heartless, Dismas. This is good, aged wine from my own stock. You may have half a cup so that your thoughts might not be so feverous. A cup of mercy, I suppose." He looked behind him quickly, as if suspicious of witnesses. His eyes turned back to me. "You must drink this very quickly for others in my village will disagree with such charity. Do you understand?"

With a vigorous nod, I walked to the bars and leaned against them. Despite the dust, my mouth still watered at the prospect of a quick gulp of wine. Aaron stood with the second cup held behind him. He gave a furtive look to the doorway again then stuck the cup between the bars near my head. "Quickly," he whispered.

I took the cup, and as I had been directed, raised it to my mouth and closed my eyes in zeal as I quickly poured its contents into my mouth. My eyes shot open as sand flowed over my tongue, around my teeth and partway down my throat.

With a roar of laughter, Aaron stepped away from the bars as I retched the sand from my mouth. "You're a gullible fool," he said. "Next time, look in the cup before you drink. Much like the trade you've chosen. Reap what you sow, boy."

I continued to cough and spit for a few moments, the sounds echoing off the dirt walls. "Is this the mercy of your faith's god?" I sputtered. "Torture and games?" I spit at the floor and saw where I had dropped the cup. I bent slowly and picked it up. I glared at my captor.

Aaron muttered something in Hebrew under his breath then said, "Better than being pulled apart by beasts of burden, no?" He raised his own cup to me in salute and took a swallow.

I spit a few more grains of sand onto the floor, cleared my throat and said, "Let's get to it, then. Other than your god directing you towards cruelty, what do you have in store for me?"

Aaron gave me a thoughtful look. "Don't mistake my own anger for the Lord's will," he said. "Not all of my bidding is directed by Him." He paused for a moment. "But to show you the compunction

He gives me towards mercy…" Aaron held his own cup out to me. "Let us trade."

Naturally, I hesitated this time, but then slowly held out the empty cup between the bars. He reached out, plucked it from my hand and held his own out to me. Slowly, fearing some new sort of test or affliction, I reached between the iron bars and accepted it. My eyes moved from his face to the cup and I saw the darkness of a red liquid inside. I looked back to Aaron and he nodded his approval. In three gulps I finished the wine and handed the cup back to him. He looked at me expectantly. After a moment's thought, I said, "Thank you." My stomach rumbled in pain again, but my mouth and throat already felt scores better.

"I'll say again," he declared, "the wine is from the Lord, not from my own generosity, or from that of my people. Don't mistake it as such." He stared down at me between the bars, his face dark with shadow. "Now to get to it, as you say. How shall we kill you?" he asked.

My laugh was weak. "Nothing comes to mind in that regard," I said. "But I can make a few suggestions about the goodness of continued mercy."

Aaron gave a snort. "You shouldn't be laughing, thief. You should know that a meeting was held this morning concerning you."

"About letting me go?" I said with a small measure of jest. I stepped to the bars and gripped one with my right hand.

He shook his head. "Hardly. During this season, our food is more scarce than usual, so the idea of keeping you imprisoned for any length of time, before handing you over to any outriders who come this way, seems out of the question. Carting you to one of the far eastern tribunals for punishment takes it out of our hands and it puts it into the hands of other pagans, as well. However, their punishments would be no different than our own." He gave a nod towards my hand on the bar. "Most want you killed slowly, while others want your hands lopped off before leaving you to wander the desert." He smiled. "We'll be kind enough to cauterize the stumps, of course."

My eyes moved from his face to my hand on the bar. I slowly withdrew it and said, "And what is your verdict, Aaron?"

"I hate nothing more than thieves," he growled. "I've worked hard for the position I've attained. I've enough wealth and influence to make grand transactions in the markets during our travels west. I did not attain this by stealing." He moved closer to the bars, his beard nearly touching the iron. "Over the years, we have dealt with your kind before. In truth, the only reason you're still alive is that you intrigue me a bit."

My eyebrows raised and I waited for him to continue.

He sighed and said, "You're unlike those I've encountered in the past. Despite all your lying, you obviously haven't been a thief your whole life. You're somewhat learned. I can tell this not just from the question you answered correctly about Moses, but simply from the way you talk."

"My accent?" I asked.

He shook his head. "Your words. Even the lies have an edge of refinement to them. You are learned in both Greek and Aramaic, and even seem to know some of our old language. Tell me, pagan, can you read the writings of the west?"

"Latin," I said. "Yes, I can."

He nodded once more and then pointed at my body. "Tell me

about the brand on your arm. Not a common slave brand, no?"

I took a step away from the bars and felt the upraised letters on my arm. I traced their shape, as I had so many times in the past. NON-FID. After a moment's silence, I said, "It means 'unfaithful'."

"I know what it means. I, too, am learned in many tongues. Why was this put on your arm?"

Still touching the scars, I said, "It was a parting gift from my ex-master. A prideful Roman who lived with his family in a villa outside of Sychar." My eyes turned narrow at the memory. "I did something he did not approve of."

"Thievery?"

I grimaced. "No. This was before I…" I paused, trying to not give too much away about my younger years, or the darker ones after. "I participated in an acclaimed foot race with other youths in that region and he punished me for it." The worst day of my life, I thought. The hatred I still felt for my ex-master was matched only by my hatred for the gods.

Aaron stared at me and I could tell he saw this hatred in my eyes. "Did it hurt?" he asked.

"Very much so."

"Why did this race trouble him so much?"

I sighed and said, "It is a long story about a very bad day. I was freed on that day but part of me was also killed." I looked away from him. Why was I telling this to him? Would a haughty desert merchant even care? Would he spare me another day if I further delved into the horrors of my past? I was a hard person – a bad person even – but when I thought of those days, and of my mother, I felt weak.

"With death comes freedom," Aaron said. He pointed to my

right hand. "And what of this bracelet you're so intent on keeping on your arm? It is not even attractive, but even in unconsciousness you held on to it as if it were your life."

I gave another long sigh. "The bracelet is also a part of the lengthy story about that awful day. To be truthful, I do not know if I possess the energy to tell it without food or water."

A faint breeze caused the camel skin door covering behind him to flutter. Somebody was coming from the passage. Aaron raised his head as the sound of footfalls echoed into the chamber. "Ah," he said. "Perhaps someone with another idea of how to dispatch of you."

I remained silent and stared past him at the entryway.

The camel skin was pushed roughly aside as a man walked into the room. The lamp light skirted around his face, but I knew who it was from his gait and angered breathing. Jaspe stopped next to Aaron and stared at me. His eyes were hidden in Aaron's large shadow but I still felt the hatred radiating in them.

Jaspe started to say something to me, then stopped and turned to Aaron. In Hebrew, he asked something to effect of how long until "the rat" was killed. There was also some mention of a man named Abuid and his family.

Aaron did not look at Jaspe or answer him at first, but continued to look at me through the bars. After a moment, as he still stared at me, he asked him in Aramaic, "How is Nahum?"

Jaspe scowled at him, but answered, "He's not well. He needs his father. He's not well at all. That's why I will ask again: how long until this man is-"

"Until I say so," Aaron said loudly, his voice swelling against the chamber's walls. "I wait for the Lord's verdict regarding this matter." He turned to Jaspe. "Now leave us, brother, and help the others with the preparations for the Feast of Ester. I want *Purim* to be grand this month, to thank God for all He has blessed us with, even in this time of tragedy."

Jaspe was silent for a moment, his breathing fast. He gave a slow nod to Aaron then turned to the bars and glared at me. He leaned in close, the dark point of his nose nearly touching the bars. "You'll die screaming, thief," he whispered. "Just like your friend. He screamed like a young girl when he died, and I imagine that your own screams will be even more pathetic."

"That's enough," Aaron commanded. "Leave us, brother, and we'll discuss this issue later."

Jaspe remained against the bars for a moment. There was just enough saliva now in my mouth, purple from the wine probably, to spit in his face. He was certainly close enough, but I knew that I was already treading on the thin ice of the Black River. Such an act would instantly damn me. With a measure of effort, I simply looked to the floor and remained silent.

He snorted at my silence, turned and stalked out of the room without another word to me or to Aaron. The camel skin fluttered in his wake.

After an uncomfortable silence, I asked, "How old is Nahum?"

Aaron stepped away from the bars. The light caught his face and I saw that the anger had returned. He shook his head and said, "You're about as obstinate as my daughter in some regards, pagan. You need to learn when to talk and when to keep your mouth shut. At least you held your teeth together when Jaspe was in here." He walked back to the lamps and gathered them. He then bent to the ground and picked up the heavy looking parchment. "It would be wise," he said, "not to mention that boy's name again."

"I won't," I promised.

Holding both lamps, he walked to the bars again. He placed one of the lamps on the ground, just out of my reach. He then stuck the parchment through the bars and held it out to me. "Here," he said.

Once again expecting some sort of test, I slowly reached out and accepted the bundle of paper. It was thick, crudely bound and contained countless pages of yellowed papyrus. "Do you ever hear her voice, Dismas?" he then asked softly.

I looked from the heavy parchment to him. "Whose voice?"

"It calls aloud in the street," he said softly. "'She raises her voice in the public squares; at the head of the noisy streets she cries out, in the gateways of the city she makes her speech…'"

He then turned and walked towards the entryway.

"Aaron, wait," I pleaded to his back. "If your God gives you compunction to spare me this day, I will need food and water. I am already dying of starvation, I think. Have mercy, please."

He did not answer as moved through the camel skin and disappeared. I heard footfalls on steps and then silence.

After a sigh of dejection, I regarded the manuscript in my hand, and after dropping the empty clay cup to the ground, I thumbed through the brown pages. It was in Latin, surprisingly. I studied the words slowly, as my skill at writing wasn't quite as refined as my speech. After a few minutes of squinted examination, I found that what I held appeared to be the books of history and laws of the Jewish people. The story of their past and prophets. It had been translated into Latin, with old Hebrew scrawl accompanying the letters of the west.

With a curse, I sat down in the dirt, flipping through a few more sections of the papyrus. I cursed again and looked upwards, towards the wooden beams above. Starvation would be their means, I mused.

With a violent flick of my wrist, I flung the manuscript to the corner of the cell and watched it spin in the dust. To my dismay, it remained intact.

# V I I I - *Desert Flower*


The bound manuscript made for a lousy pillow, but I was not about to use the soiled burlap sack that covered my waste hole. Sleep did not come to me and I found myself grudgingly flipping through the manuscript I had been given. I was a good reader – from my lessons with my Roman family in Sychar – but the language in the manuscript was slow, though Latin, and I found myself bored and anxious.

Skimming through the thick pages, I found one with color on it. Someone, perhaps Aaron, had taken either blood or reddish-brown ink and had circled a passage from one of the books of the Law, which read: '*Hear, O Israel: The Lord our God, the Lord is one, the Lord alone. Love the Lord your God with all your heart and with all your soul and with all your strength. These commandments that I give you today are to be upon your hearts. Impress them upon your children. Talk about them when you sit at home and when you walk along the road, when you lie down and when you get up. Tie them as symbols on your hands and bind them on your foreheads. Write them on the doorframes of your houses and on your gates.*' This passage seemed familiar and I wondered if I had heard it from Obadiah. The unknown writer had written: '*The Shema - Simple Law*' above the circled passage. This markedly summed up the entire law of the Jewish god. Love Him entirely and dwell upon Him fully. Why couldn't they just say that instead of having so many different, droning passages on the matter? I wondered. At least the Romans were more curt to fit the speedy nature of men. I had even seen Jews in the cities strap small boxes to their foreheads with the bound *Shema* inside, acting out a more literal translation of the scripture. Such practice was serious to them but had always been rather comical to me and to other Romans.

After reading the section which spoke of '*the holy ten commandments'*, I finally fell asleep as I tried to count how many of their laws I had broken. In my slumber I still felt the pain in my withered stomach.

My sleep was short-lived as I heard noises in the passageway behind the camel skin. I rolled from my side, sat up and gathered the dusty manuscript in my hands. Near total darkness had claimed the chamber as the lamp had burnt out during my slumber, but a faint amount of sunlight peeked out from under the camel skin. This dim light wavered as someone neared. The sound of footfalls grew louder and I stood. I backed up into the furthest shadows of my cell, near the sackcloth bag which covered my waste hole, unsure of what to expect.

A figure entered the room with a lamp in one hand and some sort of bundle in the other. When my eyes adjusted to the light, I saw it was a veiled woman. From the gleam of her golden eyes, which sparkled brilliantly in the lamplight, I instantly recognized her as the women I had briefly glimpsed during my capture. She wore a long pale tunic which nearly brushed the ground. Her veil was blue with a circular pattern of sequins and her hair was pulled up under it, but I remembered how long it was, and how it fluttered in the high winds of the storm.

Behind the woman, a speckled hound also entered the room, slipping under the camel skin and immediately moved for the bars to smell the captive behind them. The woman kicked at its rump and gave a sharp Hebrew command, calling the dog "Mathias". The dog left the bars and slumped down under the camel skin covering, breathing heavy as if it had just been running. The hound's pink tongue hung out of its mouth as the animal stared at me. I then remembered that this was the speckled hound from the storm that had seen me under the cart.

I remained silent as the woman placed her lamp on one of the covered pots. She then turned to me, regarded me with her shining eyes for a moment, and I saw the same fiery anger there; this was the same scorn I had seen the night of my capture.

After the moment's uncomfortable silence, I looked from her eyes to the bundle in her hand. While I hoped food was inside it, I couldn't help but worry if she had brought scorpions or desert asps to release into my cell. Or if it was food, had it been poisoned?

In the distance, outside of my stone cell, I heard the faded tune of a zither, and I wondered if it was the same boy who I had seen playing it days previous. It was a different song, fast-paced and not as sorrowful.

The woman continued to glare at me for a moment then walked to the bars. The light was behind her, so I could no longer see the gold in her eyes. Though she was veiled, I recalled the beauty of her face. She was short – not at all like the tall, Athenian women that were so well regarded in Rome, but her demeanor was strangely similar. Her gait, as well as the vigor in her eyes, held a certain measure of authority and confidence. This sort of poise for a woman, even in front of a prisoner, was a trespass for the Jewish culture and I found myself intrigued by her obstinacy. It was something we shared in common, though probably the only thing.

"From my father's own plate," she said in a soft but spiteful voice, her Aramaic accented with the Hebrew tongue. She thrust the bundle through the bars to me. This, no doubt, was the stubborn daughter whom Aaron had briefly mentioned. As I walked to the bars to accept her package, I thought that her voice had the potential to be beautiful if it was not so tainted with scorn for me. It was a singer's voice, I thought, so different from her father's deep pitch.

When I neared the bars, she dropped the bundle to the ground and took two steps backward as if afraid I would grab her from between the bars. Behind her, the hound looked up for a moment, then gave a mighty yawn and rested its head on its front paws.

After reaching the bars, I slowly bent down and picked up the bundle. Without opening it, I just stood at the bars and stared at her. Even through the nearly translucent veil, one could see that she was beautiful. Her cheekbones were high and I liked the way the faint lamp light danced off the bronzed skin around her eyes. I would have guessed her age at close to twenty.

Obviously uncomfortable with my scrutiny, having lingered for a reason unknown to me, she turned to leave.

I called after her, "Tell your father he has my thanks, once again. And tell him I've been reading the Law."

The woman whipped around to face me and the veil slid to her neck. Her face, though beautiful, was masked in detestation. "My father cares not for your thanks, thief," she hissed, taking a step closer to the bars. "No one knows why he has kept you alive this long. They should have killed you that very night."

"Mercy," I said. "Your father isn't a barbarian like the ones who pulled the other man apart. Perhaps he doesn't want to drown himself in bloodlust like some of the others in your village."

She laughed at me. It was a beautiful laugh, and I wish it had not been directed at me in disdain. "You have no idea what you pagans ruined that night," she said, a measure of sadness mixing in with the anger. "There was a reason we were traveling so late during the season of storms. But a lowly thief would not care. You care for nothing but greed and blood. *Nothing*."

With a sigh, I said, "I am not nearly as terrible as you think." A lie, I thought, but I wanted to keep her here in the chamber. My body had seemingly grown used to its lack of sustenance and I was nearly as hungry for company as I was for food. "Horrible things happened on that night," I said, "but they were not my doing. I killed no one. I have never killed anyone."

She sneered and the loveliness faded for a moment. "You're as wretched as your lies."

I was silent for a few seconds, thinking of something to say to prevent her from leaving. "What is your name?" I asked softly.

"You must be joking. I'll never tell you."

"Why not? I know your father's name. And Jaspe's name. I know about Abuid and his son Nahum. I even know that your dog is named Mathias." The hound's ears perked up at the mention of his name. "My name is Dismas. My family used to call me Diz." I was trying to personalize myself to her, hoping she'd see me as a person and not just a creature in a cell.

Her eyes narrowed. "Names do not matter. You are already

58

dead in my eyes."

"Why bring a dead man food, then?"

Her mouth opened but she was silent for a moment. She then shook her head in frustration and said, "Because I am usually obedient."

"But not always?"

She sniffed the air and her nose wrinkled. "You smell like what you are." She turned and began walking towards her lamp. Mathias suddenly stood and wagged his tail.

"Wait!" I called out. "Why were you traveling at night in the storm?"

"My father can make me bring you food, but he can't make me speak to you," she answered without turning around. She picked up her lamp and walked to the entryway.

"Please don't leave," I begged, my voice taking on a pleading tone I did not like but could not help.

She turned and gave another scowl. "Dead men go unheard," she said.

Light footsteps slapped against the dirt in the passageway and Aaron's daughter quickly fiddled with her veil to cover her face. A young girl entered the room. She was perhaps five years of age and, like the hound, was breathing heavily. "Jael, I…" she began, but was suddenly quiet when she saw me behind the bars.

The woman looked down at her and said, "You should not be in here, Sarah."

The girl continued to stare at me with a mixture of fear and curiosity, but said, "We was looking for Matty."

"Here he is, young one," Jael said and ushered the girl and the hound through the skin covering. "Now let's get out of here."

"Jael?" I said to her back. "A beautiful name."

She turned around, gave me a tight frown, and fled the room with the lamp, leaving me in darkness. As my eyes adjusted, I saw that a bit more sunlight than before was peeking out from under the camel skin. Evidently there was another doorway at the top of this cellar's stairs and it had been left uncovered.

With a dejected sigh, I sat down on the dirt floor and untied the bundle. Inside it I found a slice a red meat which was cooked nearly black, a section of unleavened bread and a small water-skin. I suddenly started to shake with hunger. Not caring if it was poisoned, I ate quickly, thinking of Jael and my brief words with her. The food was not warm, but it tasted wonderful; it was a simple meal, yet it seemed an extravagant feast for my shrunken stomach.

***

Hours later, after the faint light along the floor crawled closer to the bars, I read more of the manuscript, flipping to random pages and skimming through different sections. As I lay in the dirt, holding the scripture low as to catch the light, I thought I heard a faint noise in the passageway behind the camel skin. I watched part of the covering bend, as if someone behind it were moving it to gain a better vantage of me as they spied. I pretended not to notice, and continued to read about the history of the Israelites.

After an hour or so, I found the name Jael in one of the stories and I read this part diligently.

*'But Jael, Heber's wife, picked up a tent peg and a hammer and went quietly to him while he lay fast asleep, exhausted. She drove the peg through his temple into the ground, and he died.'*

She had been given a fitting name, I thought with a smile. Beautiful, yet dangerous. A desert flower with thorns.

The camel skin fluttered again and I thought I heard the faint breathing of a child. After a few minutes, the sound of bare feet hitting dirt was heard as someone ran up the steps.

Eventually, my single ray of light thinned to a sharp edge and then disappeared completely, leaving me alone in the darkness again.

## I X - Unfamiliar Emotion

**The** sound of heavy breathing woke me. I rolled to face the bars and saw that the room was once again partially lit by a faint light from underneath the camel skin. Another dark night had passed. The heavy breathing continued and as my eyes further adjusted to the dim light, I saw the hound, Mathias, next to the bars, staring at me and wagging his tail. The gaunt animal's pink tongue was hanging out of his mouth and he looked both pleased and mystified by the foul smelling thief behind the bars.

After stretching my legs and back I sat next to the bars and stuck my hands through the iron bars to pet the hound. Mathias nuzzled my hands with his wet nose and gave a low growl of pleasure as I scratched behind his ears. At least somebody here liked me, I thought as the animal licked my fingers. He then lay down next to the bars and rested his head on the dirt. His bony tail continued to wag in the dust.

The sound of hushed whispering could be heard in the passageway behind the camel skin. It sounded like children, unsure and in some sort of debate – probably over whether they should enter to retrieve their hound.    The sounds of stringed instruments and tambourines were also heard, further in the distance, along with shouts and laughing.  For Aaron's village, the Feast of Ester had begun on this morning, it seemed.

"You can get your hound," I said loudly in Aramaic.

The whispering stopped and there was only silence.

"I won't hurt you."

After another minute, the whispering resumed and I heard one child prodding another.  Suddenly, the camel skin was pushed aside and a young child was jostled through.  I caught a glimpse of two other children behind the covering.  The one who had been pushed through, a boy no older than five, stared at me in horror and distrust.  Mathias raised his head to look at the boy, then rested it again, content in the dust of the floor.

Very slowly, as to not scare the child, I stood and took a step away from the bars.  "You can get your hound, boy," I said softly. "These bars are probably strong enough to hold me."  I said this in jest, but the child's eyes widened.  He stood there, gaping at me like a frightened animal.  His black hair nearly hung into his wide-staring eyes.  I noticed he was shaking.

After a few moments, one of the other children whispered, "Be quick, Nahum.  Grab him!"

This time, my own eyes widened.  This was the boy whose father had been among those slain by Jaximo during the storm.  He looked sad even now and I saw the hurt and confusion in his red-rimmed eyes.  No doubt, he did not fully understand yet what had happened to his father, but had been told about me, and how it was my doing.  His friends were cruel to goad him into this, I thought.  They were making him face the worst of monsters.

The boy continued to stare at me and I sensed a familiar anger building in his eyes. While the village seemed to place all the blame on me, it was, in truth, at least partially my fault that his father was dead. Surely, if I had escaped on that night, I would have not cared in the least about Nahum or his father. But something about the boy's face gave me great pause. There was an immense mystification in his sad eyes as he still tried to process the fact that he would never see his father again, and the man he thought responsible stood only a few paces away. As I had not known my own father for most of my life, I realized that my actions had helped lead this boy into a similar sorrow. The grief of the fatherless.

For the first time in years, a particular emotion came to me that I had thought abandoned long ago; its growing sting worked through me slowly like a concocted poison. Regret crept through me and though it felt foreign, it continued its crawl throughout my mind. I thought of my childhood. As I looked into this boy's eyes, knowing he would have the particularly brutal derision of having no father, the regret made way for another unfamiliar emotion: pity.

"It wasn't me," I told him softly. "But I am sorry."

The boy looked away to the shadows and his lower lip began to tremble. He then turned and ran to the entryway. The camel skin was slapped away and I heard several sets of feet running up the dirt steps. Mathias remained, nearly asleep and oblivious to the drama that had unfolded.

A few minutes later, I heard somebody much heavier walking slowly down the steps. Aaron emerged with a lamp and stared at me in contempt for a moment. His eyes then lowered to the hound and he slapped his leg as he commanded the hound to leave the room. Mathias obeyed with haste, tail curved down between his legs as he left the chamber.

"You try my patience," Aaron said, looking back to me.

With the boy's sad eyes no longer on me, the lament transformed back into my usual cold deceit. My words with this man had to be careful. "I told that boy the truth," I answered. "What else should I have said?"

"Silence would have been better. One can never do wrong with silence." Aaron walked to the wall and leaned against it. He wore a purple robe and his headdress was loosened in casual wear. I could smell freshly baked bread on his clothes and honey on his breath.

"Perhaps you should be angry at his foolish friends for pushing him in here," I countered.

His bushy eyebrows rose for a moment. He then he said, "It will be addressed."

"What I told him was true, Aaron," I said, attempting to put a mask of contrition on my face. Surprisingly, it took no effort for this as thoughts of the boy's eyes came back to me. "Though I did not kill his father, I am sorry about that night."

"You think apologies matter?" Aaron asked, still leaning against the wall.

"I've read much of your manuscript. Your law and history. Apologies seem to matter to your God."

He gave me a cold smile. "Your words are like honey without taste. Thorns without flowers."

I thought back to my reading of the manuscript and asked, "Who said that? Moses? Abraham?"

"I did."

I gave my own smile. "Either way, you have my sincere gratitude for the food. Was it really from your own plate?"

He moved away from the wall and looked at the manuscript behind me. He stood in silence for a moment then said, "Regarding thieves, King David declared, '*The wicked boast of their greed; these robbers curse and scorn the Lord... They wait in ambush near towns; their eyes watch for the helpless, to murder the innocent in secret. They lurk in ambush like lions in a thicket... Rise up, Lord God! Raise your arm... Break the arms of the wicked and depraved; make them account for their crimes; let none of them survive.'*"

I tried to think of something pithy to say that wasn't disrespectful. Nothing came to mind but after my own glance to the manuscript, I answered, "'*Though your sins are like scarlet, they shall be as white as snow; though they are red as crimson, they shall be like wool.*'"

Within his immense beard, his mouth opened but he was silent.

"I've read much about mercy within those pages, Aaron," I said. "It is not all about strict laws and punishment."

My captor's eyes narrowed. "Do not ever lecture me on what is in those pages, pagan."

Above, the faint sound of merriment continued and Aaron seemed to gather himself as if he had forgotten there was a festival above us and he was wasting his time talking to a prisoner. "I'll leave you to your reading," he said brusquely and left through the camel skin.

I stood at the bars in silence, listening to the festival above. After a while, the sounds grew louder and I heard people laughing right above my chamber. Their dancing echoed in my cell and dust floated down from the ceiling. The dancing eventually moved away and the sounds of cheerfulness drifted to another location in the village, further from their captive.

# X  -  *Tale of a Thief*

**T**wenty days passed without them killing me.  Twenty days of loneliness, fear and intense hunger.  Eventually, the fear turned into apathy, as the neglect of my captors wore on my mind and body. Nearly every night, Aaron would enter the chamber, stare at me as if he were dwelling upon some huge quandary, then declare, "Enjoy this night, Dismas."  My calls for continued discussion went unheeded. Initially, I would be filled with a great apprehension for what the night would bring, but as the nights passed by without incident, his words lost their effect.

Once a day, usually in the evening, either Aaron or his daughter Jael would bring in a small bundle of food and water.  They would also collect the empty bundles from the previous day.  Aaron would usually remain silent during this process, while his daughter would sometimes offer a curse after my attempts to engage her in conversation.

In this span of days, there were at least three instances when I awoke in the total darkness of night, with no light from the doorway, and felt someone in the room with me.  The hatred almost gave the room a glow, and I knew that Jaspe was in the room with me, loathing me and wanting my death. Because of these occurrences, I took to sleeping in one of my cell's corners, as far from the bars as possible.

During the day, a faint amount of sunlight came in through the passage under the camel skin, giving me just enough light to read. On the days the storms came, I would simply sit in the darkness and dwell on my own dark thoughts. I came to long for this daily light, and in turn, came to long for my reading of the scripture. This was not because I had any interest in the history of the Jews, but because there was nothing else. In my readings, I quickly discovered some adventures of a near Homeric stature. My favorite was the story of King David, son of Jesse, and his exploits. Some of the stories were outlandish, but over time and after much rereading, I found myself captivated by them as I had been by the epic poems of my youth. The psalms of David, as well as the insightful words of his son Solomon were also enjoyed, especially some of the parts whose authors lamented about captivity.

Despite the occasional readings of encouragement and redemption, my own hope eventually died as the days continued to mount.

During the first seven days or so, I spent much time contemplating escape. There were deep bruises on my shoulders from ramming my body against the bars, hoping to loosen them from their base. My fingers were cut and scarred from jamming my finger into the lock's key hole in attempt at unlocking it. Digging was futile in the hard packed walls and the cedar beams were incredibly sturdy, offering no movement at all.

These twenty days passed slowly, and the days of captivity continued past this, though I no longer counted. There was only dust, darkness and scripture.

***

In recent nights, the distinct sound of arguing voices reached my cell. These came from above and mostly in the distance; how far away, I could never tell. Though I could rarely pick out any specific words, I could hear Aaron's voice, loud and in obvious contention with other male voices. As I strained against the bars during these times trying to hear more, I gathered that the debated matters were not usually about me, though the word "thief" reached my ears on several occasions. They seemed to be arguing about politics within the village. There were also a few times when Jael brought me my food at night and I noticed tears in her eyes. As always, she would only grant my concerned questions with red eyed glares from above her veil.

There was obvious strife in the village, and I didn't know if this was good or bad for my situation.

Often, I thought of *Protos*–Obadiah and the rest of the band, and I wondered where they were and how they were doing. Had Obadiah already forgotten about me, or did he think me dead? No doubt, Jaximo had been happy that I had been taken captive. They had gotten away with a great deal of wealth and were probably back in one of the cities of Judea, buying, selling and stealing. They were no doubt having a grand time while I remained imprisoned in this earthen cell, constantly afraid of death while using any available light to read the Jewish scripture.

As the days continued to drift by, my beard grew longer as did my hair. My body became even weaker and my frayed tunic hung loosely on my frame. The man who once prided himself on his speed and cold-hearted spirit was dead. Only a withered husk remained, spiritless but knowledgeable in the writings of the Jews.

***

Suddenly, a change. The light disappeared on that day as it always did, and I found myself flipping through the heavy pages of the manuscript in the dark, counting them and running my fingers over passages I liked, much like a blind man would do. Jael had come earlier in the afternoon with my meager food bundle, while daylight still reached the chamber, and I had remained silent during this routine encounter.

The days of my captivity numbered somewhere near forty, though I could not be sure, and on this night, I heard heavy footsteps nearing the chamber. I recognized them as Aaron's. Sensing something was wrong – as my food had already been delivered – I scrambled to my feet and pressed myself into one of the rear corners of my cell. Lamplight filled the chamber as Aaron entered through the camel skin. He carried two cups of wine and had his oil lamp in the crook of his arm. I just stared at him blankly as I stood in the corner. My tunic was pulled down to my waist, exposing my bare torso, and my hair hung into my eyes.

"Some wine, Dismas?" Aaron said as he stood at the bars, holding up one of the cups.

I said nothing and continued to stare at his lamplight.

"Fine," Aaron said, "more for me then." He moved away from the bars and sat on one of the pots. It seemed as if he desired the company of his wilted prisoner for some reason.

"Not sand?" I asked quietly. The sound of my voice seemed foreign                    to                    my                    ears.

Aaron sighed, stood up with a grunt and walked to the bars

71

again. He held the cup through. Slowly, I walked to the bars and accepted the cup, which was full with dark wine. The smell hit me hard and I nearly felt loosened already. With a nod, Aaron moved back to the pot and sat down. He took a swallow from his own cup and said, "You don't look well, Dismas. Perhaps you need another forty days to wander. Or perhaps you should have chosen a different trade, no?"

I took a small sip of wine. There was an immediate burn in my stomach, but it felt good and I took another drink. Cradling the cup in both hands as if it were an infant, I sat down at the bars and asked, "Forty days? This is how long I've been here?"

Aaron nodded. "Much like Moses, as you said when we first spoke."

My eyebrows rose as I considered the implications of what he was saying. "So is my time in here coming to an end?"

"As I said, pagan… you are like Moses in a sense. You've wandered for forty days but will never see the promised land." He raised his head and laughed. It was then that I noticed his brow creased in disconcert, despite his feigned jest. His eyes appeared red from fatigue. While still a man of large stature, he now appeared much thinner.

He lowered his head and saw my stare. I looked back down to the dust. Slowly, I raised my cup for another drink.

"These are trying times," he said. "I've been without sleep for many nights now."

"Is this my fault?"

"I've wanted to blame you for a long time, but this began long before you graced our village with your presence. You're just an excuse for some."

"So there is a rift among your people?"

He shook his head in frustration, as if wondering why he was discussing this with a prisoner. "It's a mystery to me that so many can focus only on death while forgetting about the glories of life. And honest work has seemed to have fled the hearts of some."

I looked from my wine to him and said, *"Sheol and Abaddon are never satisfied, and neither are the eyes of man."* It was a quote from King Solomon. I had long since memorized many of the passages that I found of interest.

Aaron's eyebrows raised in surprise. "Reciting scripture now, are we? Do not forget: *'Like a thorn-bush in a drunkard's hand is a proverb in the mouth of a fool.'*"

Thinking back to my forty days of suffering and reading, I realized that I could play his game. *"'A ruler,'"* I said, quoting another proverb, *"'who oppresses the poor is like a driving rain that leaves no crops.'"*

"Well, you've turned into quite the scribe," he said, his eyes narrowing. "You may know a few bits of scripture, thief, but it won't matter to Jaspe and Abijah, and the others who demand your execution. My word will not always be enough to spare you." He paused and shook his head once again. "Either way, the affairs of this village are not your concern."

"It was not I who brought them up."

He grunted. "True." He was quiet a moment then said, "There are some who believe more in the old ways of our faith, while there is this... man along the Jordan who speaks of a change. It has caused some trouble for us and they've insisted that I chose a side."

"Someone in your village?"

"No. A rabbi further west, near Galilee. Some teacher who talks of Jewish tradition and how a time of change is at hand. A Nazarene, no less. He is apparently a healer as well."

"What is his name?"

"It doesn't matter," Aaron said briskly. He took another sip of wine. "Most likely, he is a fool or a lunatic, stretching out his neck for Rome's sword. Caesar wants tranquility in the Jewish sects, and this man has everyone stirred up in Judea. A fool who will soon learn the Emperor's fury, or that of the high priest of Jerusalem."

There had been many claims by men who said they were great healers, prophets or fabled messiahs from the Jewish tradition. One had to wonder if the true messiah, if one ever existed, had already been persecuted and killed by the locals. The thought of such brutal irony made me smile.

"What is my own fate?" I asked.

Aaron gave me an odd look. "No more begging or pleading? You are ready to accept justice?"

"*'In the place of judgment - wickedness was there, in the place of justice - wickedness was there.'*" Another quote from Solomon.

"Stop this!" Aaron bellowed, and stood up. Wine sloshed from his cup and hit the dirt floor. His face was suddenly red and his beard seemed to tremble as he shook with anger. "You know nothing of justice, thief. You've only lived this long because I've decided to spare you these days – not for your wit or humor, but because I simply did not feel like letting my people enjoy more bloodshed." He shook his head and sat down again. "Your time is nearly over, Dismas. It will soon be out of my hands."

"Perhaps your people do need a change, Aaron," I said.

"Maybe you need to make a trip and find this rabbi who teaches of a change."

"We tried," Aaron said, the anger still in his voice. "My daughter had some grand idea of how we could travel to see him, quickly during the rainy season, and stay near Jerusalem for Passover, to get a head start on the other merchants. Her friend Gideon, a young man crippled since birth, had fallen very ill and would come with us to see if this man truly was a miracle worker. Two Bedouins were hired to guide us along the Jabbok, during the storms." Aaron looked directly at me and he shook his head once more. "You know how that plan ended."

I finally understood much of what had confused me for over forty days. The caravan traveling at night. Jael's particularly intense hatred. "You were traveling at night, during the storms to see if you could reach this rabbi. You wanted to see if he could heal the boy. Did you ever make it?"

Aaron remained silent for a moment, staring at his wine. After a moment he said, "No. We returned to our village in Rammoth Gilead and counted our losses. Some of us eventually made the trip for the Passover, but by then, Gideon was far too ill to travel. He died nearly a month ago." He looked up at me. "It was a foolish idea. Ruined by your band of despicable bandits, but still a foolish idea."

This sick boy, Gideon, had been in the second wagon with Jael, as they traveled. This tribe attributed his death to me, as well as the others. It was no surprise now that Jael seemed to hate me nearly as much as Jaspe did. In her mind, I had indirectly killed her friend Gideon.

"I am sorry," I finally said. My words were sincere, not for the settlement as a whole, but for Jael's loss.

Aaron looked at me for a moment then nodded. "Perhaps God has forgiven you, Dismas." He opened his mouth to say more, but closed it and remained silent.

We drank our wine in silence for a while.

"Tell me," he said, leaning back on the pot, "you are from Sychar, no?"

"Yes. The family that I was a servant to lived in a villa just outside of town."

"Is this where you became a thief?"

I shook my head. "I was never a thief there, though mine is not a happy tale."

"Do you think you could tell it to me? Your tale, I mean."

"Are you hoping it will put you to sleep?"

Aaron laughed. "Is it that boring?"

"I wish it were more boring, to be honest." I looked away from him, towards the lamp at his feet. Never, with the exception of Obadiah, had I told anyone of my past. And even he did not know the whole truth, as I had omitted much from my first telling. In truth, no one had ever asked of my history. I had always assumed people, even those in my band, were too caught up in the worries of their own lives to care about mine.

"I want to hear about your brand," he said, pointing to my arm, "and about this beautiful dagger of yours you said was a token for participating in a race. Tell me your tale, Dismas. I will not be sleeping tonight, this I am sure of, and I would be a rapt listener."

I looked up. "My tale would be wasted on you. Why should I tell it to you?"

"Because," Aaron answered, holding up his wine cup as if it held the answer, "I have given you wine. And because I gave you the gift of forty days."

"I thank you for the wine, but I hardly consider the last forty days a gift."

"I assure you they were, especially when compared to the proposals of nearly everyone else. I have spared you, fed you from my own plate, and have answered many of your own questions tonight. This is why I deserve to hear your story."

There was no doubt in my mind that he had fought for my life's prolongation, day by day, as such an act had only helped tear him further away from his family and tribe. Would it be so hard to grant him the bitter tale of how I was finally freed as a youth?

After another swallow of wine, I said, "Very well, Aaron. If it pleases you."

"It would," he answered with a smile nearly hidden in his gray beard.

It was at that moment, as Aaron stared at me waiting for the tale to begin, that I felt the burden of my history. It suddenly felt like such a hefty weight, and I became eager to tell it to a listening ear.

As I was about to begin, just as my mouth opened for the first word, my eyes caught a glimmer in the passageway as a faint draft ruffled the camel skin covering. For a moment my heart seized as I imagined it to be the flash of steel from my own dagger, no doubt in Jaspe's long fingers. The covering wavered again and I saw the reflection of lamplight in gold-brown eyes above a sequined veil, then the covering moved back into place and the image was gone.

After a long sigh, and an even longer swallow of wine, I began the dark tale of my past – both for Aaron and for the spying beauty in the shadows of the passageway.

# X I - *Home in Sychar*

**B**efore my immersion into thievery, I had been a common slave boy, a servant to a wealthy Roman family in the city of Sychar, the capital of the Samaritan region, under the appointed ruler Herod. Samaria was a land filled with fertile plains and rich farmland. Nestled in the valley at the base of Mount Ebal was the city of Sychar, which had a steady population of nearly nine thousand people. "Jacob's well", a much-used water spring for the Jewish community, was a small walk south from the city's heart.

The homes in Sychar were crowded together and crooked unpaved lanes wove between them like unfurled ropes. These streets grew horribly dusty in the dry season, while the rainy season made them little more useful for traffic than mud trenches. Many had built their homes upon the ancient foundations of old buildings, these structures dating back to the warring days of Jeroboam and Rehoboam, almost eight hundred years ago. These remnants of the Jew's archaic history were thought of only as simple stone to be used and nothing more.

Samaria was thirty-five miles north of Jerusalem and the paved road between was greatly used and kept up by Rome, in order to increase commerce… thus increasing taxes for the emperor. There was, however, a great partition between Samaritans and the other Jewish peoples of Judea. This stemmed from the Samaritan's approved practice of mixed marriages and other cultural differences thought to be atrocious to the strict Jews in greater Judea. The Romans in this province did not care about such grievances, as long as the locals remembered their tax obligations.

Fifty years before my birth, Herod the Great had been appointed king of Judea by Caesar. He was known as "the great builder", not by his own hands, of course, but by his will and instruction in his extensive reconstruction in Samaria. He even renamed the entire region of Samaria to *Sebaste*, which was Greek for "the revered one". Herod harbored many of the late Gabinius' ideas and finished them, giving Samaria an expansive stadium, the great temple to Augustus and the round towers of the west gate.

Due to this influx of Greek culture, and Caesar's desire to spread the Roman culture into Judea and all the eastern lands, there were many Roman nobles who chose to move their families to the fertile plains of Samaria, to build sweeping villas and partake in Herod's innovations.

One of these nobles, a wealthy Plebeian named Quintus Flavius MEN, of the Roman Menenia tribe, had left the turbulent western regions to be one of Herod's advisors in Samaria. From the westernmost territory of Hispania, he brought his wife Cornelia, infant son Tarius Cladius, and numerous servants. Among these servants was a native woman from Hispania named Lucilla. She was only twenty at that time and shortly after the move to Samaria she gave birth to an infant son whose servant father had purportedly died of the prevalent fever in that region only days before the child's birth.

I was that son, born into servitude. My mother Lucilla remained strong for me, despite the death of my father, who remained nameless to me for my entire youth.

***

Life as a servant in Sychar was not altogether bad. My days were governed by routine and chores took precedence over everything. My mother and I lived in separate quarters in the rear of the family villa with the other slaves, Mesick and Frenda, who were an older married couple from Italia, and another servant woman named Shara, who was from Gardenia and was my mother's good friend. Old Mesick, while not tending to the property's landscape as he had been charged, would often joke with me and tell me stories of his youth and the events he had witnessed as he had been a naval squire for a Roman admiral during the marauder battles near the island of Sicilia. To this day, I believe he had made up most of his stories, but my youth was better for it.

My mother Lucilla was strict, if only to spare me the occasional wrath of our master Quintus, but she still managed to be loving and would always offer a shoulder to cry on when I became distressed or hurt in my younger days. She was everything to me: mother, counselor, friend and healer. It pained me as I grew older to see that she was considered to be in a much lower class than the other "free" Roman women, such as Cornelia and her pasty-faced friends. Regardless of my mother's banal stature, she was a goddess in my eyes, full of wisdom, encouragement and beauty. She did, however, maintain an upraised hand to swat my backside if I fooled around too much.

Despite her warnings, I did fool about, mainly with the family's son, Tarius. He, of course, was not bound to servitude as he was born the son of a proud noble, but in our youth such status meant nothing save the occasional jest or insult. We were best friends and our make believe adventures spanned the entire stretch of hills around Sychar, including Mount Ebal and Cometh.

These fantasies slowly withdrew into the recesses of memory as our years numbered eleven and twelve, Tarius being one year older. In my recollection, it was him who first turned from a warrior to a worrier. The burden of daily labor weighed upon me, while Tarius was engaged in tutoring from both hired teachers and Mesick, who was an expert in the empire's history. Many times, I wondered if Tarius' lessons were tainted by Mesick's fabled recollections of fictional adventures and decided that, like myself, my friend would be better for it. Most of my own teaching came from either Mesick or Tarius, who would divulge much of his lessons to me as we played in the hills.

There were other neighbor children, both servants and youths of Roman families – as well as Jewish youths – and many a gang was formed and many a fight was had. Most of the Roman youths saw themselves as bold Spartan soldiers, whereas all Jewish youths saw themselves as King David's "Mighty Men", warriors of their old scriptural lore. These "Mighty Men" were usually careful enough not to hurt any "Spartan" youth as the consequences could be dire for the Jewish family.

After any particularly rowdy skirmish, Tarius would usually escape his father's leather whip, whereas I had felt the thin length of hide across my backside many times. Quintus would strike until I sobbed and would leave me on the ground for my mother to tend to my welts.    During these scourges, which occurred outside the slave quarters, my mother would stand there with a bowed head and listen to the whistle of the leather through the air and the "crack" across my backside.    She would say nothing, and in my younger days I resented her for this.    Many years later, however, I understood that her intervention would have simply brought more ire towards the both of us.

By and large, life was tedious but good.    Everything changed with the Race.

* * *

On our choice hill, a lone fig tree stood atop the great mound like a tall crucifixion post.    We had pretended that it was such many times, feigning capture and execution for various imaginings.    It was late afternoon and the spring sun began its arch towards the western horizon.    A breeze from the south ruffled the small, budding leaves of the fig tree.    At the hill's western slope, a lone sheep wandered at the terraced mound, looking for a patch of green to eat, while its shepherd, unseen but surely somewhere among the hills, searched for the straggler.

Tarius was sitting on one of the tree's branches, swinging his legs in harmony with a favorite Greek ballad he hummed.    He had just turned fourteen and his father had sat him down, after the banquet and gift-giving, and told him of his new responsibilities as a man - as a wealthy Plebian under Caesar.    Tarius had stated he understood and had agreed not to behave like a reckless youth any longer.    Later that day, however, he found himself hanging from a tree limb like an animal, very unlike a future noble statesman.

After my daily chores, I joined Tarius in the tree.    My usual perch was higher than his, and I stood atop the branch, leaning against another limb as I gazed towards the western wilderness. I stared away from Sychar, as I usually did.

"I don't feel any different," Tarius said after his ballad was finished.

I continued my stare at the western horizon and said, "Were you supposed to?"

"I don't know. My father thinks so, I guess. When he was fourteen, he had already amassed holdings for himself in Hispania and had become an investor. I rather like the idea of earning money and having it grow without doing anything, don't you?"

"So you're going to be an investor then? A statesman."

"Maybe. I don't know, Diz, but it wouldn't be bad, I think. I know it's not exciting, but with my father's help, I could inherit some holdings of my own and quickly make a name for myself. Maybe even go to Rome. Who knows? Wouldn't you like to meet Caesar one day, if you had the chance? Or the Senate?"

"You *have* changed."

"How do you mean?"

"Whatever happened to traveling to new lands? Seeing the unconquered world?"

"I could be a statesman and still travel. It would work out better that way, even. I could stay in villas instead of tents." He looked up at me. "You could come with me. We'll still travel to Egypt, to the Nile and hunt crocodiles and gazelle, just like we planned. Nothing has to change that much. It's just that we need to bring our heads out from the heavens for a bit to think a little more realistically. Such is the way of the world."

I scoffed. "Sure, Tarius. I'll just wait here in Sychar until I'm forty years old, doing chores for your father, and probably for your own house at some point, and then, when my hair is gray and you have your own kids, we'll make a trip. I can hardly wait, friend."

"There are dues to pay," he said with a serious face. "It won't be that long, surely, but to enjoy life you need to work."

"And be free."

The breeze seemed to grow louder as it ran its course through the leaves of the fig tree. Suddenly I realized it was the silence, and not the wind, that had grown more noticeable. My friend and I were destined for vastly different futures, and over the last year we had finally started to see this. We had reveled in the ignorance of childhood for so long that the inevitable split between us made my spirit already ache.

Tarius shifted his position in the tree and stared up at me. He smiled and said, "Let's forget this talk of work and speak of play. My father also mentioned the Race today. He's excited about it and thinks his son can win. My training starts tomorrow and he wants you there, by my side, pushing me and training me with Mesick."

I stared down at him. "What about my chores?"

His grin widened. "I told my father you were faster than even I and that for me to win I would need your instruction. He has pardoned you from the morning chores so that we may train. So that we may win."

The earlier talk of growing up and the future was forgotten. Beaming, I said, "But the Race isn't until next month. He really said... wait. If I don't have to do chores, who's going to wipe your rear?"

"Very funny. I'm not lying, though. No morning chores for a

month. So you're in debt to me, friend, and I want you to help me win this race. The prize has not yet been set but Publius Gracus is said to be there to host the event. Every fast Roman youth in Samaria, and from all over Judea, will be there."

The Great Race had been under discussion already for months previous. It was a youth's event, and Roman boys between twelve and sixteen would run an extended sprint outside of the west towers. This length would be nearly three *stadiums* – just under a quarter of a mile. For the Roman nobles and governor, this large event would precede many political meetings and league changes. Publius Gracus was a renowned senator who often spoke with Caesar himself over issues. Publius had a fascination with the eastern lands, as well as the dark-skinned peoples of the far south. Often, he had spoken on issues to help preserve, as well as strengthen, the desert lands along the Jordan River through further construction and compulsory influx of Roman culture. He was also a great supporter of the Games, and hosted many large festivals for runners and other athletes. Much like the esteemed writer Cicero, Publius condemned harsh treatment against slaves and treated his own freed servants like family. The senator was a frequent visitor to Sychar and the Menenia family had hosted a banquet for him at our villa years ago, when I had been just five years old. Quintus, while not a senator, always strove to grapple a few rungs higher on the political ladder, keeping in seasonal contact with Publius and his scribes.

It was evident to me, and I could see it in his covetous eyes when Quintus first told his son about the Great Race, that he saw Tarius as another rung on this ladder, and if he were to actually win the race, Quintus would be further injected into Publius' more esteemed world.

SPQR - the Senate and the People of Rome – held Quintus' every thought. At forty years of age, Quintus was ten years older than most campaigning hopefuls, but he potentially had the holdings to succeed. The only thing he lacked was the influence with other statesmen. This race could be crucial for his political stratagems.

I had always disliked Quintus for the sometimes cruel and always dismissive treatment of his servants – my mother most of all – but after the event's of the Great Race, I would forever hate him.

"How many boys will attend?" I asked Tarius after pushing away thoughts of his father. The western sky had turned red and the step-like formation of purple clouds above us mirrored the terraced slopes along the hill's backside, as if the hills continued into the sky. The lone, wandering sheep had disappeared.

"Twenty," he said, "and any free youth may enter the qualifications." He smiled. "The qualifications are in nine days, Diz, and I wager there will be nearly a hundred or more that will try out. I will have to be in the top twenty." With a sigh, he leaned back against the trunk and closed his eyes, no doubt thinking of his odds. "The prize is unknown, but it will be fantastic, I'm sure. In the last race Publius hosted, in Italia, the prize was a year's stay in Rome at his own villa, to be tutored by the best teachers and philosophers in the empire. What a prize!"

I grunted and said, "I'd rather have gold."

Tarius laughed. "There are things more important than money, friend, such as an education, and the experience of Rome."

"Yes, but you have to have money to do these things. It takes money to get an education. It takes money to travel. Money to live, Tarius. With gold... one can do anything. Such is the way of the world. You said this yourself."

Tarius frowned and looked to the sunset. "Perhaps the prize will be gold, but I doubt it. Gold may get you a lot, but it's not refined, nor inventive. I'd rather have the journey to Rome."

In truth, I did not fancy gold as I led on. As a servant, I tended to enjoy simple things which cost nothing, such as adventures with Tarius in the wilderness, listening to Mesick's tales, chasing deer and hounds in the hills, and making wooden swords out of lumber given to us by the city's more generous carpenters.

"The training begins tomorrow at dawn," Tarius said as he swung himself off the branch and dropped down to the ground. "We'll run up the terraces and maybe to Old Jahair's farm without stopping. That would be good training, I think."

I nodded and climbed down the tree. "It would be a good run to Jahair's if we didn't stop, but we can't dawdle and run slow. It needs to be a good pace to do any good. And we should swim the southern pond every day, as well."

As I dropped next to him, Tarius gave me a confused look. "Why swim? We need to stretch our legs, not our arms."

"Yes, but swimming can help build up endurance of the heart, which is what wins a race. It's endurance that will get you your trip to Rome."

"My father won't like us swimming."

I scoffed. "Your father can take a fall in the Styx, Tarius. If he wants you trained, he needs to loosen the reigns a bit, don't you think?"

Tarius smiled. "Your words are colorful, but I'd like to see you talk like that to his face."

"Not a chance. And now our training begins early, for we race home!" With a bound away from the tree shaped like a cross, I started running. Tarius gave a yell and followed.

*** 

The winged *villa rustica* was very large and the view of the northern hills and Mt. Ebal was fantastic in the setting sun. Mesick waved at us from the garden and gave a near toothless smile as we neared the villa. We yelled a winded greeting as we passed by him and continued between the stone property markers. The family's garden was expansive, and at its rear, a small pond had been constructed with a raised island in its center. In the island's middle was a slender statue of Matuta, the goddess of dawn, who we worshiped in June during the festival.

The aroma of spiced cabbage and sausage with *garum* sauce drifted from the home as my mother and Frenda prepared dinner. I knew that the other servant, Shara, was probably in the home helping Cornelia with her hair dressing before dinner.

Another figure stepped out from the rear of the villa and as I saw it to be Quintus, I slowed my pace and let Tarius shoot ahead of me. Quintus looked up as we neared and was about to yell a reprimand, but stopped when he realized we were probably running in training, and that his son was ahead of the servant.

Tarius stopped near his father and bent over to suck in great heaps of air. I also stopped but did not heave for breaths as heavily as Tarius. Quintus stared at his son and said, "You'll need to work on your endurance, Tarius Flavius. Perhaps I may find a trainer for you somewhere in Samaria – a Jewish runner, perhaps, or maybe even a Roman if we're lucky." As the day was nice, he had chosen to forsake his more formal toga, which did not yet display the broad purple stripe of the Senate. He wore a short-sleeved tunic with a soft belt. His graying hair was cut short to show his dignity and he insisted that Tarius' hair be cut in similar fashion.

Tarius shook his head and tried to slow his breathing. "I don't," he said between breaths, "need anyone else. We can train... ourselves."

Quintus looked from his son to me, then back to Tarius. "Very well, but no more running about in the garden. It's not civilized. Don't forget your prayers to the gods, that they might help you in training. Understood?"

Tarius nodded. "Yes, father. Hermes for speed and Zeus for power."

"And Mercury for wisdom, my son, for there are certain stratagems for winning a race." Quintus then looked over our heads to ensure Mesick was still toiling in the garden and turned to go inside. After Tarius and I rolled our eyes at each other, we followed him.

My mother was in the kitchen area with Freda, and the older slave woman gave me a wink as I entered the room. I returned the wink and went to help my mother with the bowls of vegetables she was preparing to carry outside to the garden table. The family would eat dinner there while the servants would eat quietly inside as we continued to serve them.

"You need a bath," my mother said with a smile. "Was yours a good day, Diz?"

I matched her smile. "Yes. We started our training for the Race. Did you hear? I've been charged by Master Quintus to aid in Tarius' training."

She nodded. "No morning chores for a month. More work for

your mother." She ruffled my hair and said, "Just have fun, young one. Enjoy these days while you're free from work, and don't forget your dear mother while you're having so much fun." She handed me one of the clay bowls and I noticed her silver clasped leather bracelet was wrapped with a cloth to prevent tarnishing, as it usually was when she labored in the kitchen. For as long as I could remember, she had worn that bracelet, which was made of a combination of silver links and leather. My suspicion was that this meager piece of jewelry had something to do with my father but I knew she would never tell me the truth about it. Talk of my father grieved her terribly.

"I won't forget," I promised, hefting the bowl in my right arm and signaling her to give me something for my left. She handed me a second bowl with spiced porridge and cooked snails, and told me to be careful.

"Drop those," Freda said as she finished preparing another tray of food, "and I'll whip your hide worse than Quintus ever could."

"You ladies worry too much," I said and walked outside where Shara was preparing the stone table for the meal. I set the bowls down and greeted her. She smelled like perfume and seemed slightly stressed, as she always did after helping Cornelia ready herself. As I walked back to the villa for more food, I saw Quintus emerge with the tall figure of Cornelia, her hair done high and makeup profuse. She was laughing and wielded her cup of wine as if it were a royal scepter.

Tarius entered the garden with a clean tunic and washed face. He sat down with his parents and his father commenced to giving a hurried prayer to their ancestors of the Menenia Tribe. When the prayer was finished, my mother and I brought out the rest of the food and drink.

Instead of eating inside with my mother and the other servants, I walked to the furthest corner of the acreage, past the home's eastern wing, where no one would see me. There, as I leaned against one of the property stones, I gave my own prayer, not to any of the gods, but to the father I had never known. His name was a mystery to me, as my mother refused to speak of him and I hadn't the fortitude to ask Quintus. Mesick and Freda had also been directed by my mother to stifle the issue upon my prying.

My prayer was simple: a request to my father that he might watch over my mother and I and that freedom might one day find us. As many fatherless youths do, I conjured a greatly exalted image of my unknown father; a guise of strength, courage and wisdom, much like the greater male gods of Roma. For all I knew, my father might have been some sort of invalid... a lowly cripple or blind man who lacked honor and begged on the street corners in Hispania. I pushed such thoughts from my mind, however, and took in the more enviable likeness of the tall, regal man I had always envisioned.

When I opened my eyes after the prayer, I looked towards the western tree line, which was awash in red sunset, and saw a figure standing motionless atop one of the hills outside the estate's land. Even from such a great distance, through squinted eyes, I could distinguish the sable cloak and long black hair. As a young child, I had named this strange entity the "Man of Shadow". Not a god. Not the wraith of my long dead father. Something else, entirely. Always in the distance watching me as if a hired guard. Somehow, through divine erudition perhaps, I knew this figure was not evil, but seeing him always caused feelings of misgiving.

Suddenly uneasy, I turned away from the hills – away from the ominous stranger – and closed my eyes. The redness of the sunset continued to fill my vision even as my eyelids were closed and small dots of light danced across this wall of scarlet. After nearly a minute, I opened my eyes and fixed my squinted gaze back upon the tree line and found that the mysterious guardian was gone.

With a shudder, I turned from the property stone. My fingers had turned white from gripping the rock and I rubbed the color back into them as I returned to the villa.

## XII - *Wolves in the Hills*

The faint sound of a sandaled foot adjusting its position on the ground reached my ears. I delved on with my story, but Aaron held up a large hand to silence me. My captor's eyes narrowed, and with a speed that seemed unbecoming of a man his size, he stood and bounded to the camel skin covering. Jael gasped as Aaron flung the covering aside. "Come inside, daughter," he said gruffly and then marched back to where he had been sitting. Standing this time, he watched Jael slowly enter the room with her head bowed low. She stopped behind him and said nothing, her veiled head still bowed to her chest.

"My apologies, Dismas," he said to me as he continued to glare at Jael, "for it appears as if my daughter as suffered from a bout of foolishness as she thought she could spy on us and hear your coveted tale. This will not be repeated."

"She was there even before I started," I said.

Aaron looked to me. "Yet you continued?"

"The story was for her, as well."

With a grunt, Aaron nodded and walked closer to the bars. He whispered, "It would please me to hear the rest of your tale, thief, but not tonight, for I'm afraid that my daughter's insolence has befouled the night." He gave me a faint smile. "Perhaps tomorrow night. If you are willing."

I nodded and Aaron turned from the bars and walked to stand over Jael. He whispered something in her ear and though her head was bowed I saw her eyes narrow in irritation. He then left the room, leaving Jael standing there, silent and discomfited. After she was sure that her father had fully left the passageway, she raised her head and looked at me. The veil slipped from her nose and this allowed me to see her full lips. She no longer looked angry, but intrigued. "You knew?" she asked softly.

Her voice, not tinted with scorn, was honey to the ears. "Yes," I said. "I know you despise me, and perhaps rightfully so, but I felt that if you heard about my past you might then better under-"

"Understand you? I do not know if that is possible."

"There is more to share with you, if you are willing to listen as you did tonight."

Jael regarded me in silence for a moment. This was the first time I had seen her face when it was not pinched in scorn. My initial assessment on the night of my capture was correct: she was truly beautiful and I wanted to do everything in my power to keep that unbecoming look of derision away from her bronzed face. "The rest of my tale might surprise you," I said in a low voice. "And once again, I am truly sorry for what happened on the night of the storm. I am sorry about your friend Gideon. I'm sure my words mean nothing, but…" I gave a sigh, thinking of the boy Nahum's bereaved eyes. "As I have caused much sorrow, I also know great sorrow."

Her eyes narrowed but her features stayed soft. Without responding to my words, she turned and left the chamber. She had left the lamp, however, and I remained at the bars for a while in its dim light. As I stood there, my thoughts grew dark. I thought not of Jael, Aaron or my imprisonment, but of my ex-master Quintus Flavius.

***

Later that night, close to dawn perhaps, someone entered my chamber and I was woken by the distinct sound of forged steel being lightly tapped against the iron bars. I rolled over in the dark corner of my cell and saw Jaspe's shadowy form at the bars. The lamp's oil had burned very low, but there was enough light to see that my dagger was in his hand.

I started to rise, but he said, "Stay where you are, pagan."

Motionless on the ground, I waited.

"How large was your band?" he asked.

"What do you mean?"

"Your brothers in murder and thievery. How many were there?"

Confused by his question, I mentally counted the members of Obadiah's thieves and said, "The band had a half dozen men."

He glared at me through the bars for a moment and twirled the dagger in his fingers. "You were not part of a larger band? A band of desert marauders?"

I shook my head. "Never." For all my lying, this answer was the truth.

Above his black beard, Jaspe's lips curled back, revealing his long teeth in a venomous leer. His dark eyes continued to pin me to the floor of my cell. "Your lies will throw them out of Eden, rat." He pointed my dagger at me. It was evident from its gleam that he had polished it and cleaned the grime out from its intricate engravings.

96

"You may sway others with your deceit, but your punishment is coming, regardless if these wolves in the hills are here for you or not. Nothing can stop God's judgment."

"What wolves in the hills?" I asked.

He pointed the dagger at me for a few silent seconds then abruptly fled the room, slapping the camel skin away with the blade as if the covering was an enemy.

Despite the dim light of the nearly extinguished lamp, while he had been in the room with me I had seen an emotion on his sullen face that I had not seen before. Fear. Though I did not fully understand why.

*** 

That night, after the distant sound of heated argument, Jael entered with my food. The yellowish light from her fresh lamp danced around the room. Her veil was pulled down to her neck and she moved silently to the bars with a bowl of porridge covered with a piece of unleavened bread. A water-skin was tucked under the arm that held the lamp and she had a small rug, rolled tight, hanging across her back by a leather sling.

I stood and walked to the bars. "Thank you," I said.

Jael nodded as she handed me the food, not dropping it at my feet as she used to. She retrieved the rug from her back and unrolled it at the bars. She put the lamp between us and sat on the rug. This carpet's pattern was an intricate red and white pattern around a black center. Jael's long tunic stretched across her splendid figure as she adjusted herself on the rug. Suddenly, I recalled several passages from Solomon's scripture about love and desire, and I suppressed a smile.

After realizing that I was standing in silence, staring at her, I cleared my throat and also sat down at the bars. I took a long drink of water from the goatskin bag and asked, "You have come to hear more rambling from a prisoner?"

She gave a soft smile – what a gorgeous sight – and said, "Many things are amiss above this chamber. You are lucky to be here, it would seem."

It was my turn to smile. "Let us trade then."

Her smile grew for a moment then vanished quickly as if she realized the expression was taboo. "There are many problems right now," she said, her eyes narrowing to the familiar glare that I did not pine for. "You know about the other thieves?"

I re-fastened the tie around the skin's lip and began eating the porridge. Though it was undignified, I answered her between bites. "Jaspe was in here today. He spoke of 'wolves in the hills'."

She nodded and looked to the lamp between us. "Do you know this band?"

I shook my head. "He said it was a large band of marauders. I have never been part of such a band. I swear this."

Jael sighed and her full lips pursed for a moment in deliberation. "These raiders have been camped in the hills for several days now," she said. "There numbers are very large. We received word from a lone traveler from the south that this band raided another village near the Jabbok." She continued to stare at the lamp as she talked and I saw fear in her golden eyes. "Everyone was killed. The men, I mean. They mostly kept the women and children alive."

Obadiah had told me stories of these armies of zealot-raiders, as he had briefly been a part of a marauding group from Trachonitis, with his brother Lazya. The brothers had moved east, towards Arabia with the band, which numbered nearly sixty men, but Obadiah had found them to be too zealous – too radical. *"War with Rome is foolish,"* he had told me once. *"Even worse, young scion, it is futile and these brigands are not trained well enough to fight a legion of Roman outriders. I am not one for suicide."* Obadiah had split from their company, despite the curses from his maniacal brother Lazya. He had since developed his own smaller band that relied on stealth and speed, as opposed to numbers and ardent zealousness.

"I've heard of these larger groups," I told her. "They are bad men."

"All thieves are bad men," she said, her glare moving from the lamp to me.

"That may be, but raiders such as these are different." These larger bands of marauders had hated everybody, Obadiah had informed me; such bands loathed both Jews and Romans alike. They grew in number in the east and allowed their fury to kindle in the desert before striking at entire settlements, laying waste to everyone they came across and sparing only those they saw fit for the eastern slave trade. They were not as merciful as *Sicarii* zealots, nor as kind as Roman outriders. These marauders were men permanently darkened by the sun, true desert wolves from Arabia and beyond, who despised the inane, bustling life of the west, and all parties influenced by Rome or the Jewish authorities. They peddled in hate and human flesh. "Perhaps they will just move on," I said. "Hopefully your village is large enough to dissuade them."

Jael shook her head. "The other village was even larger than ours. We don't know what they're waiting for."

"They could be part of an even larger group. They could be

99

waiting for the rest of their forces to join them before they attack… or they're just resting before moving on to somewhere else." I knew this last statement was probably not the case. "You should leave."

"My father and I have discussed this," she said quietly. "We have relatives in Jerusalem that some of us could stay with. A wealthy uncle named Rannut. He's a stingy man, but would surely house his own relatives – at least for a while. Others have talked about fleeing to other places as well. Some want to stay and fight."

"I'm sure Jaspe is one who wants to fight."

She made a face. "No. He is one of the cowards who want to flee at night. He offers to lead groups of our women and children away when the night is at its darkest. My father…" She shook her head again as if the weight of this conversation was heavy. She looked at me. "You probably want them to attack us."

"No, I…" Words failed me. I actually had not considered what would become of me if their village was attacked. Would such a band of raiders free me or kill me with the others? From what Obadiah had told me, it could truly go either way. "I'm sure they would probably kill me, too. To be honest, I hope they don't attack. I wouldn't be able to finish the story you came down here to hear."

Jael switched positions again on the rug so that her knees were tucked high under her tunic and she wrapped her arms around them. "It is a welcome escape," she replied, "for nothing is to be done tonight except more argument and uncertainty. Behind those bars, you're probably the safest one in this village now."

"You could always get the key and join me."

Her eyes grew hard for a moment and I knew I had overstepped my bounds with my flippant words. Then her gaze softened and she said, "I think I'll take my chances with the raiders in the hills, thief."

"Call me Dismas. Or Diz, as my friends call me."

"Dismas then." She interlaced her fingers over her knees and was silent.

The moment was awkward, so I resumed my tale...

# XIII - *Tachu Soma*

**T**he youths who were to qualify had to wear *calceus*, a laced shoe fastened with hobnails, as such footwear was mandated for the race itself. Quintus had a crafter make three new fitted pairs for Tarius prior to the qualifications. I was to train barefoot with him, or use my own worn *carbatina*, which were soft leather sandals not well suited for running. The calluses on my feet were thick, however, so I chose to train barefoot with my friend. My speed was still great and long ago I had been given the nick-name of *tachu soma* or "speedy slave" by the other youths of Sychar.

The morning of the qualifications was overcast with clouds, but rain had been limited to an occasional light sprinkling. The ground would be soft. The qualifying circuit was simply a harrowed stretch of field which was straight with no turns, hills, or obstacles. Out of the one hundred and twenty boys standing in this drizzle, only the fastest twenty would go on to the final race. They would have six races of twenty boys along the field, which was flagged with Caesar's portrait at each end. The fastest five of each mini-race would advance to the final qualification.

As it turned out, Tarius had been wrong… he would only have

to be faster than fifteen others, not one hundred and eighty. This first round of games would reap thirty runners. To weed out another ten, this initial group of winners would race the harrowed field again and the rope would be raised across its width after the first twenty youths had passed under Caesar's portrait. This twenty would be the group to race in three weeks in the Great Race, with Publius Gracus hosting.

Now, an hour before the first round of qualifications was to begin, the fields and adjacent road were filled with people, mostly Romans. These were families in prayer, some in the strict act of shaving and sacrificing goats. It was somber really, as if the families were sending their boys off to stand against the Persian hordes at Thermopylae. As I was not racing, I found the whole throng to be rather humorous. Roman families from all over the seaboard had traveled to Sychar for the event to pit their youths against each other.

As Tarius and his parents watched Mesick struggle with shaving their goat's neck for the sacrifice, I walked along the tilled field and found a cluster of young servants I knew from the central part of Sychar. I greeted them by name and stood with them.

"Look at this mess, Diz," a tall youth named Artillus said to me. "Bunch of fools whoring their children out for the masses. We'll all be soaked before mid day."

I grunted and said, "It would be fun though. To run, I mean."

"That's because you're fast."

"Fast but dumb," one of the other youths said. "You'd probably win the whole cursed thing with your speed."

"Maybe," I said with a faint grin. My reputation had grown among the youths during our frolicking games in the hills.

"No," the youth continued, "you'd show these tight-puckered

nobles that speed and courage has nothing to do with birthright. *That,* friend, would be something to see. *Tachu soma.* You should be out there. I'd be out there if my leg weren't sprained up. I may not be the fastest, but my turning is excellent. I've got the reflexes of a panther."

"Yes, Phillip," Artillus said, "but of a dead panther. My baby sister Ashal is faster by a league." He laughed and said to me, "Curse you, Dismas, you should be out there!"

I smiled. "Artillus, believe me, if I had the chance, I'd be out there right now."

"Did Quintus think you'd outshine his little boy?"

"Tarius is fast."

"You're faster."

"But I'm not free."

Artillus looked at his friends in confusion, then back to me. "What's 'free' got to do with it?"

"Only free youths can race. Ah, but if I weren't a slave, boys, I'd be out there. Quintus be damned."

Artillus gave his friends another odd look and then gave me a great smile. "Dismas," he said, beaming, "you don't know, do you?"

"What?"

"Publius has decreed that *any* youth may enter, freed or not, as long as they can speak good Greek and live in the Empire. You didn't know this?"

My heart skipped a beat. "No, I..." Quintus had evidently neglected to tell me of this decree. Tarius surely would have, had he himself known; I was sure he had been kept in the dark as well. "Are you sure?" I asked them.

Artillus gaped at me. "Yes, Diz, we are sure! Maybe there is still time. Go!" He pushed me towards the throng, in the direction of the elected judges, who were posted near the field's eastern opening. "Go, and may the gods be with you on this rainy day!"

The other boys yelled their approval and encouraged me to consult the judges. Quintus himself had been elected a judge, but I would consult another. Regardless, I would have to ask him for his approval, but I wanted the truth before half-truths.

The horde of people did not notice my frantic search as I ran between their wet forms. I did not scan faces, but togas, searching for the red stripe that signified a judge. After a minute's search I spotted two of the toga-sporting judges ambling through the large group of people, calling out greetings and blessings. As I walked towards them, I saw Quintus bound in their direction as well. It was now or never, I thought.

"Master," I called out to Quintus as I neared. He turned to me, as did the other two plebeian nobles. My hope was that he would not lie in front of them. "As all youths may enter, sir, could I by chance have your-"

"Dismas," he said quickly, seeing my intent, "has Tarius been tended to? He was looking for you, boy. I think he's along the fence line with Cornelia. Go to him. The time is drawing near." He pointed towards the fence and then turned away from me to talk with the two robed men.

I would not be so easily swayed. "Sir, pardon," I said, and Quintus looked back to me, a look of irritation on his face. "Please, good master," I asked, "could I have your permission to race, as all youths, free and not, may enter the qualifications?"

His silence complimented the vengeful stare he shone upon me.

There was still a slight sprinkle from the gray clouds above and the small droplets hit my master's rigid face, as if he was a statue – immovable and cold. Before he could reject my plea, one of the plebeian judges, an older white haired man, said, "Ah, one of your slaves, Quintus Flavius? Are you fast, son?"

I nodded and nearly flinched from Quintus' hard stare, but instead moved the wet hair from of my forehead and said, "I would like to partake in the great Publius Gracus' benevolence as he decreed all youths may enter. Not for myself, but to be there with my master Tarius in the Race, to help him win."

The old man nodded and looked to Quintus. "What say you, Quintus, friend? A faithful companion of your son alongside him, encouraging him to be faster and run harder? Not a bad strategy, I think."

The old man gave me a sheltered wink then and in that moment I knew that he had also seen through Quintus' anger and agenda.

"Dismas," Quintus said slowly and I raised my eyes to meet his. "For Tarius," he said. "I'll make the arrangements with the other judges. Find my son and ready yourself. By the spirit of our ancestors, boy, you don't even have sandals."

"I'll find-"

"Just go."

I gave a slight bow. "Thank you, sir."

"Go."

The old man next to him slapped me on the back and gave a hoarse laugh. "Godspeed, young one!"

And I ran to find Tarius, both the rain and Quintus forgotten as I breathed deep the drizzle and excitement.

106

***

The *calceus* were too small for me, as my feet were slightly bigger than Tarius'. They had been fitted smaller still to hug the foot as one ran, offering good grip and no slip on turns. The tight pair which I now wore had served as his first training shoes and they were already worn from our weeks' exercises.

The rain had slackened, but the harrowed field was now littered with puddles and deep footprints in mud. My group was the last to go. Tarius had since raced and placed fourth in his group of twenty. He would move on to the final qualification to eliminate ten more from the winning thirty.

The grim portrayal of Caesar wavered above me in the breeze and I knew I was ready. I was in the middle of the line of twenty young men, and I knew I was faster than any of them – even the youths who were a year or two older than me.

At the starting line, at the field's eastern end, we crouched and waited for Caesar's wavering face to fall, signaling the start of this qualification. All of the citizens and travelers had lined themselves against the width of the field to watch. Now, before the falling of the flag, they were all silent, hands clasped, waiting to yell and cheer for their favored runners. Tarius was somewhere along the fence, as was his mother and Mesick. My mother, Freda and Shara had remained at the villa for chores, and I wished - to all the gods known to me - that she could be here to see her son race, but there was no way she could have known due to Quintus' deception.

My limbs trembled in excitement, and I knew I should be staring at Caesar's face, but I continued to look at all of the faces of the spectators, my eyes moving along the far length of the field. My stare fixed on a man closer to the end of the track. Though there was little wind, his dark cloak fluttered in accord with his wavering black hair; he was like a lone man caught in a tempest. He stared at only one of the runners in line. I felt this intense gaze on me from across the whole field.

Just when I realized that his stare was somehow giving me some sort of fortitude – not fear or misgiving – the flag descended suddenly and the man was gone, as was the distance between us.

The western end of the field – the end of the race – swept under me and I was finished. After slowing myself and putting my hands on my hips to catch more breath, I looked back to the field and saw that no other boy had even been close. After a moment, one boy crossed the end line, then three more behind him; the other fifteen slowed, red faced and fuming. Suddenly, I felt several hands on my back as spectators congratulated me on the win. They guiding me out of the mud and told me how fast I was for a slave.

***

There was a half hour's respite before the last qualifying race and as I looked for Tarius and other friends, I felt a strong hand grip my shoulder and spin me around. It was Quintus. His mouth opened wide as if he were about to yell, but he remembered the mass of people around us and gathered himself before speaking.

"You've won the people's respect now," he said quietly. "That was *your* race and I commend you for it. This next race, Dismas, is my son's. You're out there to help him - not beat him. You're very fast, boy, I'll be honest, but your winning the big race does nothing for the good of our family." He looked around then leaned closer to my ear. "I'll reward you if you help Tarius make it into the twenty. Just keep him ahead of the last ten. Understand?"

I looked at him in silence for a moment then slowly nodded. He leaned back and smiled. "Race well, Dismas. May the gods be with you." With that, he left me.

With muddy shoes in hand, I walked to one of the larger puddles next to the paved road and sat upon a tree stump. As I bent to clean the soles and laces, Artillus and several other slaves ran over to congratulate me. There was much patting on the back and exclamations of my speed. I continued to scrape the mud from the shoes as I made a weak attempt to remain humble.

It was a good moment, just then, and I'll always remember it. The wet earthy smell of rain and mud. The slight drizzle on our faces as they sung my praises.

Tarius joined us and was also congratulated, though not in such a hearty fashion.

"It's nearly time for the last qualification race," he said to me. He grabbed my arm and started pulling me back to the field. "Sorry, boys," he called out to them as he led me away.

We were hustled into position and I stooped to fasten my shoes. The field had been widened for thirty runners and straw had been laid out in the deeper ruts of the muddy track. Tarius had been placed near the left, and I was in the field's center. I looked at all the runners on either side of me and knew, once again, that I could win. Everybody else seemed nervous and fatigued already, shaking in the drizzle.

My thoughts turned to helping Tarius. I honestly did not know if he was faster than at least ten of these other runners. Somehow, I would have to make my way behind him and figure something out. I wanted to win, however, to further impress my friends but the dictating voice of Quintus came back to me and I gave a sigh.

One of the judges, the white haired man who was responsible for my entrance into the race, served as herald and made the crowd hush as he stated the disposition of the race. He then asked the runners, as a whole, if we were ready and a loud cry of consent issued from every throat including mine.

Caesar's face was raised, and this time I stared only at the wavering flag, not bothering to look for the Man of Shadow's steely gaze.

The flag was dropped. The youths ran. The people screamed.

Intentionally, I dropped behind and drifted to the left of the pack, towards Tarius. His pace was good, but perhaps tenth or twelfth from the slowest - not good enough. When I was close to him, I sped up and cut in front of two of the faster runners, causing them to slow and curse me. Tarius trudged on. We crossed the field's center point and I drifted to Tarius' position. "Faster," I hissed into his ear. "Faster, Tarius, faster!"

Tarius' eyes narrowed and he lowered his head to power ahead with greater speed. I turned from him and observed the pack ahead of us. We were still on the threshold of the slower ten, but I could not give an exact count as we ran. One of the youths behind Tarius was gaining on him and as he was about to overtake us, I moved into his path and he cursed me with a winded breath and tried to move around. The rain had picked up and stung my eyes as I sprinted.

The field's end neared and youths were already crossing its line. Five of them finished. Ten. Fifteen. We were in a group of perhaps twelve boys. It was going to be close. There were two men at the field's end, each holding the ends of the rope they would raise after the first twenty had passed over it.

As we neared, I screamed at Tarius to go faster. I looked around us and the other boys were pushing ahead, faster than us, and I knew we weren't going to make it. We were almost to the rope. I drifted behind Tarius and pushed him between the shoulders, in his back, with all my might, and let loose a mighty yell. He yelped and was propelled forward, but was losing his balance. I pushed harder and we both dove to the field's end line, above the rope as it swung upwards. As we tumbled in the muck, leaving bawdy depictions of our sliding bodies in the mud, I looked back and saw two boys hit the rope and the others plowed into their backs with painful looks of defeat on their faces.

We had made it as the last two of the winning twenty.

The crowd screamed in approval of the amusing finish and the rain continued to fall upon us as we lay in the mud. Tarius asked me in a winded breath, "Did we make it?" His answer was the horde of spectators clambering over the fence to pick us up out of the mud and pat our backs and shout their compliments. As we stood up, I saw Quintus and Cornelia run to their son and hug his muddy form. Mesick followed and put a knowing hand on my shoulder and smiled down at me through the rain.

As I stood there, my face streaked with mud, I looked for the Man of Shadow but did not see him amid the masses of people.

Tarius tore away from his father's arms and yelled to me, "Dismas! We're in the Race! We made it!"

I waved an acknowledgment to him and looked down at the filth on my tunic, but thought of my mother, who had missed the qualification races. Perhaps she would be allowed to watch the Great

Race, if black-hearted Quintus allowed it.

And the rain continued to pour down upon the people and the twenty winners were raised up and hailed individually by the white-haired man, who yelled out our names as we each whispered them into his ear. When it was my turn, the old man whispered to me, very quietly, "Win the race, young one. Win the race." He then had two men hoist me upon their shoulders and he acclaimed, "Dismas, servant to the Flavius Menenia family!" And the crowd cheered.

More than anything, I wished my mother could have heard her son's name proclaimed to the crowd by this elder noble.

***

The rain stopped shortly after the races and the evening sky was clear. After a large celebration supper at the villa with several other families, I found my mother outside near the property stone where I usually prayed to my unknown father. The night was cool from the earlier rains and her knotted hair wafted slowly against her back in the light breeze. She looked from the hills, suddenly aware of my presence behind her, and smiled. She held out her hand to me and I walked forward to take it. She looked back to the hills and I wondered if she also used this spot to pray, or if she also saw the same cloaked guardian at different times as I did.

Hand in hand, we stood there watching the wispy clouds stretch across the dark sky.

"I wish I could have seen you today," she said softly.

I sighed and said, "I wish you could have, too. There will be the big race, though. Maybe you can make that one. I'll ask Tarius to talk to his father about it, even though you'll just see me lose as I try to help Tarius win."

My mother squeezed my hand. "I heard about today – from Mesick. Everyone knows you could win, Dismas, but I think you did a good thing. You did what you were told. It was wise."

"Maybe."

"No, it was. Sometimes, as you well know, we must make sacrifices for a greater purpose. You might not be rewarded in this family, or even in this life, but certainly in the next by the gods who see everything. You did a good thing and I'm proud of you as I always have been."

This time I squeezed her hand and I felt the silver bracelet slide further down her wrist. For a moment, I considered asking her about the jewelry's origin, but did not want to ruin this time with talk of the past, which I knew was hard for her. After another minute's silence, I asked, "Why are *you* out here tonight, mother?"

She didn't answer at first, and the silence mounted. Just when I was about to repeat the question, she answered, "I've seen you out here, sometimes. After we serve supper or before bedtime, and in the morning occasionally. You pray, I imagine. Or muse. I just wanted to see what your little place was like out here." She sighed. "You have picked a good spot."

"It can be your spot, too," I said. "From here, you can see outside of the Menenia acreage and the world seems a little brighter – not so confined. When I look to the hills, especially during the sunrise or at dawn, I feel almost... free."

The faraway laugh of a wined plebeian reached our ears and we both chuckled. Back at the villa, Quintus and Cornelia were still hosting their party, in honor of their son. My mother would need to return soon, so Mesick, Freda and Shara would not be alone in attending to the guests. I had helped a great deal earlier, but it was now time for slumber, as Tarius was already in his bed. We were to wake early, before the sun's rise, to train.

My mother turned from the hills and gave me a strong hug. "I'm sorry," she whispered, "that I cannot give you more, Dismas." She sniffed and I knew that she had been crying before I found her.

Wanting to tell her that she had given me a great deal in life, I remained silent, for I feared that my words would be too choked with emotion. I simply tightened my embrace and treasured the end of a day that had been filled with both joy and frustration.

## X I V - *Trust in a Thief*

Jael had somehow moved closer to the bars though her movement had not actually been seen. She stared at me as I spoke, listening intently. She no doubt knew where my tale was going. It was anything but a mystery – no surprise from an unseasoned orator.

A four-legged shadow suddenly ran into the room, ducking under the camel skin and loped over to Jael. It was the same hound I had seen several times before.

"Mathias," Jael said in a surprised voice as she locked her arms around the dog's neck. "Silly dog, you should be in Nahum's room guarding him." She rubbed the dog's ears. The hound dropped his speckled frame next to Jael and sighed in contentment.

"This is Nahum's hound?" I asked.

She nodded. "They're nearly inseparable. All the kids in the village love him. He always repays their innocent torture with a sloppy kiss." She turned to the dog. "Don't you, boy?" The dog wagged its bony tail.

"I've told you much about myself," I said softly, "yet I know nothing of my captors."

She looked from the dog to me, her eyes suddenly cold. "This did not stop you from stealing from us and allowing the murders on that night."

"I would do anything to take it back. There was a man in that band… an evil man named Jaximo. He…"

"The story of your youth intrigues me, thief, as it does my father, but that does not change the fact that I believe all thieves are evil. I believe *you* are evil."

"Men can change."

"A rarity," she countered. "Do you think you've changed?"

I was silent for a moment, thinking of my past and of what my future would be like if I were freed. No, I thought, I was certainly not reformed. But something in my way of seeing things was different. While there was still a prevalent darkness in my spirit – as I knew there always would be – something had certainly been altered. Perhaps it had been looking into Nahum's eyes, I thought. The eyes of a victim. I had never dwelt upon such things before.

After another moment's thought, I said, "Some things have changed."

"I imagine it would be hard to change after a rough life."

"I take it your life has had no rough patches? You won't tell me anything about yourself, so I have no way to compare."

With a sigh, she said, "Everyone's life has rough patches." She then told me about her younger years, before her mother had passed away from disease. Her family, from the Jewish tribe of *Gad-Manasseh*, had traveled extensively throughout the whole region of Ramath-Gilead. When she was five, she lost her mother and her father became chief of their nomadic group. They would settle in one place for a year or so, then move on, always collecting, always bartering, saving for the western markets during Passover. Her mother's death had greatly affected her and she still thought of her often.

"This is a pain that we share," I said when Jael paused to wipe her eyes. "I also lost my mother."

"Her name was Eliza," she said quietly. "Unlike so many of the other families in this tribe, in our faith even, she and my father were actually in love. She was not a simple possession. They showed their love, too. My father cherished her and it nearly killed him when she passed on to be with God. He remained strong though, and it was this strength that propelled him into his position as chief."

With my gentle prodding, Jael went on to tell me about her later youth as a rebellious girl who was constantly chastised by the villagers for unbecoming behavior. Because of this rambunctious attitude, she was shunned by the other girls in the settlements. She was diligent about her chores, but she had a bad habit of neglecting her scriptural readings. Aaron feared she would never marry. To his credit, he refused to accept proposals from eager men and their families. Thinking of the love he had with Jael's mother, Aaron wished for his daughter to choose her own husband.

Jael had grown close to a boy named Gideon, who had fallen ill last year with a disease that the villagers called "old man's bones". Hearing rumors of a Nazarene rabbi who was allegedly a miracle worker, Jael formed a plan to convince her father to make the Passover journey early in hopes of finding this man. Aaron agreed to this and made a special place for Gideon in one of the oxen-driven wagons and sought out two Arabic scouts to guide them through the hills near the Jabbok River.

Gideon, she told me with a cheerless look, was the last remnant of her youth. He was a year younger than her, but his body had withered greatly with his unusual disease, which made even the youthful feel, and sometimes even appear, to be elderly.

As I well knew, they never finished their trip. This last thought made me grimace but I did not offer another half-hearted apology. Instead, I said, "It is odd how people's lives can clash together, both in good fortune and in bad. For the sake of your village, though, I wish our paths had never crossed."

She nodded and stood from the rug. "As do I," she said quietly as she picked up the carpet piece and rolled it up. Mathias rose as well and followed Jael as she walked to the door covering.

"You should flee, Jael," I said to her back. "Take Nahum, and whoever else you can, and flee at night. Do not wait to see if the marauders move on."

Without pausing she left the chamber with Mathias at her heels. The lamp she had left continued to burn though my cell seemed much darker in her absence.

***

The army of raiders did not attack that night, though my sleep was fitful as usual. The morning light from under the camel skin looked bright and I knew the day was sun-filled. By the gods, how I longed to feel the sun's rays! Once again, I took up reading the manuscript and focused on the songs of King David. My search was for an encouraging word – a single phrase or doctrine that would possibly fill me with a newly discovered strength. As the day moved on and as the light eventually faded from the doorway, my unease remained and my search wrought nothing helpful.

That night, it was Aaron who entered the chamber with my

118

food. With his lamp dangling under his arm, he walked to the bars and handed me my supper: a helping of spiced meat, bread and a full wineskin. He was still a large man, but his size had clearly diminished and there were dark circles under his eyes. Regardless, he smiled at me and said, "Wine for you, Dismas. Not water, nor sand."

"My thanks," I said. "What is the occasion?"

"Your last meal. It appears as if things will be changing upon the morning, and I believe it is the custom of the Greeks to sometimes offer a final meal, with wine, to their prisoners before they are executed."

Ignoring the threat, I unfastened the wineskin's lip and took a long swallow. From the tone of his voice, it seemed as if he had already partaken of a good amount of wine.

"It is good, no?" he asked. "From my own reserve in a blessed vessel."

I nodded. "So you are to put me to death tomorrow?"

He leaned against the wall near the cell door. "There is much going on and I believe your time behind these bars, in one fashion or another, will be over very soon. Whether it is by our hand or by the hands of your brothers in the hills, I do believe you will either be killed or released."

"I told you, Aaron... I do not know this band. I'm no desert raider."

He grunted at me and gave a furtive glance behind him to the door covering. Turning back to me, he said, "Do you think you could somehow stop them from attacking us? If you were freed, I mean to say. Would the word of a fellow thief hold any bearing with other such men?"

119

I opened my mouth to inform him that it would be futile, but said nothing for a moment. Was my captor offering me freedom? What would prevent me from simply fleeing to the west once I was free? This man was obviously a fool for even entertaining the idea that I would risk my own life to help his village.

Aaron saw my silent deliberation and gave me a nod. "Something to dwell upon, I suppose, though taking the key from Jaspe would be near impossible." He gave a mirthless laugh. "Even for me, these days." He moved from the wall and stood close to the bars. "May I have the manuscript back, thief? I think you have had ample time to peruse its contents."

I leaned over and picked up the bound scripture, still reeling from the thought of an impending freedom, and I was scared of saying anything that might tear apart such a notion. I handed him the manuscript through the bars and said, "I could do what I can, Aaron, but there's little time. Anything is better than just waiting for wolves to pounce."

He left me without a response and I wondered if his words had been meant to just give me false hope. If they had been, I mused, it was working.

***

Another hour of darkness went by before lamplight once again found its way to my cell. Jael entered the chamber with a clay lamp in one hand and the bound manuscript in the other. The same rolled carpet from the previous night hung from its string at her back. She placed the rug near the bars and sat down. Her golden eyes were aglow with the lamplight. "It is time," she said.

I moved closer to the bars and asked, "Time for what?"

120

Slowly, she placed the manuscript on the ground before her and opened its thick pages, revealing something hidden within that I had thought long lost. In the flickering lamplight, the polished steel of my dagger seemed to come alive.

"It is time for you to tell me about how you won this dagger," she said with a mysterious edge to her voice, "while my father takes care of other things. We only have an hour or two before he comes down to explain our plan. We need to have your trust, Dismas." She took the dagger and plunged the blade into the dirt next to the bars... easily within my reach. "But in the meantime," she continued, "finish your tale."

Despite my urges, I refrained from asking her how she had retrieved my dagger, though I desperately wanted to know. A smile accented my face as I contemplated Jael turning thief, even for a single incident. Had she snuck into Jaspe's tent as he slept, as the peg-wielding Jael of the scriptures had done, or had she plucked it from his person as he stood talking with others in the village?

After an anxious sigh, I said, "Is this why you and your father started talking to me? Why I've been kept alive longer than his 'forty days' and why you seem to have an interest in my past... pretending to almost befriend me, even? You are hoping to put your trust in a thief?"

Her eyes widened for a moment, then narrowed quickly and grew cold. "While I do actually have somewhat of an interest in what you've told me – and as I am curious about how someone could become a thief – you are possibly in a position to help our village. This is a better position than where you were before, no?" Her beautiful eyes remained cold, while I sensed that much of her earlier scorn for me had, in fact, been replaced with something resembling curiosity mixed with a subtle contempt.

With a sudden laugh that seemed to startle her, I said, "Well, since we apparently have some time, do you still care to hear about the dagger?"

She curled her knees up to her chest and nodded. "Proceed, thief."

With a curt shake of my head, I said, "I think you can call me Diz now."

Her smile was slightly more genuine than the ones she had graced me with before tonight. "Alright… Diz. Let us hear about this Great Race and the acquiring of this exquisite dagger."

With a glance to the hilt of my blade, I started to finish the tale of my youth, knowing full well that if they freed me in some outlandish plot to save their village, I would immediately betray them and escape into the hills near the Jabbok. Young Nahum's sorrowful eyes be damned.

## X V - *NON FID*

The day of the Great Race was sun-filled and beautiful. The track had been formed skillfully and I had never seen more people gathered in a single place. It was truly a grand spectacle, with flags and banners everywhere. It was a colorful event and effigies of the eagle of Rome and Caesar's stern profile lingered over the whole city.

The gathered families fiddled with their sacrifices. The runners stretched, prayed or nervously threw up their breakfasts.

As one of the thirty, I had been charged to attend the opening festival on the eve of the race, but Quintus had ordered me to remain at the villa so that no attention would be taken from his son. This may have been the harshest reproof of all, for as I knew that I would not be able to even attempt to win the race, *all* of the runners were honored at this festival – slaves and free youths alike. I had thought of how grand it would be for my mother to see her son attend such a festival as an honored guest and not just a servant. Even the most simple, obligatory dignity had been denied me.

While the family was at the festival, I had finished my evening prayers and had walked back to the villa to find Mesick waiting for me. The family had returned and Tarius was already in bed, per his father's command. Mesick, bless his gruff heart, had convinced Quintus to allow my mother and Freda to watch the big race. This gave me some joy though it was bittersweet. Was it a blessing for my mother to see her son lose a race with not even a single shred of hope at winning it? At least she would see me involved in something great. Even though I would lose, I thought, she would be very proud. I had thanked Mesick profusely for his intercession.

Now, the morning had come. The city was on fire with excitement. Tarius had said his prayers and all of the runners were hastily being shuffled towards the newly constructed track.

That morning, at dawn, before our family left for the city, Quintus had found me praying at the property stone. He no doubt thought that the gods he assumed I was praying to were busy answering his son's prayers and had no ear for those of a slave.

"You know your responsibility," he said, gripping my shoulder firmly. "There is nothing more I have to say, Dismas. Make this happen. You'll be rewarded with far more than great Publius could ever give a slave. Just make this happen."

My answer to him was a single nod and he left me with an anxious look upon his austere face.

The runner's track was multihued, the banners plentiful, and the hundreds - perhaps thousands - of faces were eager for the contest to begin. The air was alive with anticipation; all this was for a minute's worth of sprinting youths.

My mother hugged me tight before I left with the other runners to the track, where white-haired Publius and the judges awaited for the initial appraisals. "You make me proud," she said softly. The crowd was loud, but she spoke close to my ear. "I've always been proud of you. Help your friend and do your duty. But try to have fun, Dismas. Just enjoy being a part of something big." Her embrace grew tighter. "I love you, young one."

"Dismas!" Quintus yelled from the surging mob of people. "Let's go, boy!"

I ignored him and held my mother tightly for another moment before turning to the track. Quintus jostled me towards the starting line where the other runners and their bright outfits stood out from the crowd. I wore a simple white tunic, cut loose at the thighs. The *calceus* on my feet were almost painfully tight. I had not bothered to stretch or limber up in any way. I already knew that I was still faster than Tarius and I also knew that most of the youths in this race where also faster than him. There was no hope for him to win, but I would have to do what I could to help.

The mob grew restless as the revered senator Publius, a white-haired man much shorter and more portly than I had imagined, addressed each runner by name and family. We each bowed when addressed and I looked for my mother in the crowd when the senator called out my name. She was along the track line, with Mesick and Freda, under a bright blue banner. She waved and wiped her eyes as if she was crying. At least, I thought bitterly, she had been graced with hearing a Roman senator speak her son's name.

I was not nervous. I did not shake. Though the world seemed a blur as the pale toga-wearing judges positioned us at the field's starting point. By the overseeing eye of Quintus, I was placed next to Tarius. We would be running in a few minutes. Now was the time for last minute prayers and stretching as Publius gave a lengthy speech about the glory of Rome and the gods' interest in the "triumphant games of mortals".

This moment, just seconds before the actual race, was what changed my life, setting me on a path that would eventually lead me into desert captivity. Just prior to this, I had been fully committed to helping Tarius and my thoughts focused on him and him alone.

This commitment was shattered when Tarius leaned over to me and grabbed my arm. "Dismas," he hissed suddenly, trying to hide his voice from the other runners. He drew me closer. "Win the race. *Win the race.*"

His words shocked me. "What are you talking about?" I whispered.

He gripped my arm tight and said, "You weren't there last night. The prize for us is a trip to Rome, just like we talked about, but for a slave, its freedom. Do you hear me, Diz? *Freedom.* All the masters who had slaves running – only four of them – had to agree to these terms. I heard Publius himself say the words. My father had to agree, though he didn't want you to know about it. Each master had to place their seal on the individual decrees. If a slave wins, the master must take them to Caesarea to stand before a magistrate and have everything legalized with Publius' certificate." He looked around as if searching for his father's discerning eyes. "My father commanded me not to tell you, but I had to. Win the race, Dismas!"

I couldn't speak. Listening to his words, the scenery around me became even more blurred. The maze of faces alongside the track became two large blotches of color on either side of me. The shake of anticipation began in my legs. The track's end, the finishing point, beckoned loudly. I knew the Man of Shadow would be staring at me from the track's end, though I didn't bother to search amid the blurs of color.

"I can't," I sputtered to Tarius as I looked back at him. "I just can't."

He let my arm go. "You can!" he whispered furiously. "You *will!*"

The blotches of color cheered mightily. Publius had finished his speech and was walking to the starting point. I ran both my hands through my hair then looked ahead once more. With a spinning head, I scanned the blurred faces again hoping for a glimpse of my mother or the Man of Shadow; I looked for anyone to give me some sort of unsaid counsel. Only one face stood out however. Quintus' baleful glare tunneled to my very core. He did not nod or open his mouth, only stared at me with a red face as if he knew my thoughts.

Behind him, Publius addressed the crowds again briefly though I could not focus on his words. The portly senator motioned for the two bearers to ready the banners of Caesar in front of us. Once lowered at his signal, we would race.

My heart hammered in my chest and my vision clouded even further. I did not want a choice such as this. The very thought of making a decision like this in mere seconds was torture. I felt as if I might faint. At least that would rid me of the choice. Not even having raced a single pace yet, my breathing was already ragged. I scanned the crowd again but saw only blurred shapes. Though I couldn't be sure of it, at the far end of the field – at the track's end – I thought I could make out a black, billowing shape amid the blurred colors of spectators and banners.

The bearers raised the banners and a great hush ran through the crowd. The runners braced themselves. Not knowing what to do, I mimicking the runners around me as they knelt to a crouch, readying themselves to spring forward.

The bearers wavered slightly as they awaited Publius' command and Caesar's frowning face upon the banners leered above us like twin gods.

This was the moment. I took a deep breath and looked towards the field's end then back to the banners. I held this breath and thought that I might die of uncertainty and fear – or from my pounding heart exploding in my chest. My thoughts were a concoction of so many emotions, voices and urges, yet one particular sentiment grew stronger than the others: *Freedom*.

The banners suddenly dropped and the crowd roared but I did not hear them.

***

To this day, I believe it was my mother who suffered the worst that afternoon. The initial lashing took place after the race, by the property stone that I usually prayed at. The whole family and all of the servants except Mesick – who had been ordered to stay in town because he was the only one with the strength to interfere – were forced to watch. My mother cried aloud. I had never heard her scream before and the sound was worse than the pain of the leather cracking across my back. This was only the first stage of my punishment and things would grow worse.

***

Before the pain, I was a hero.

Quintus had been forgotten in the initial celebration. After winning the race, the crowd had lifted me upon their shoulders and had paraded me around the city, Publius leading the procession. Much like my first qualification round, the race had been over in the blink of an eye. No one had come even close to beating me. I was the fastest boy in the city, perhaps all of Samaria. Surely one of the fastest in the entire empire. I had run like a god, never looking back at the other runners, nor at Tarius or at his father's screaming face.

After the bleary trek around the city, Publius bade the crowd to set me down that he may deliver his address and prize. We had come full circle back to the track and the erected podiums.

"This dagger," he said, withdrawing the blade from his own tunic and with an endearing look on his pudgy face, "was forged by a metal worker in Damascus for Caesar himself. His greatness declined the knife, however, saying it was fit more for a victor in some sort of game. One of the gods' great games." The senator held the blade for all to see. It was beautiful. A work of art made not by some gruff metalworker, but by a true artisan – one who obviously took pride in his craft. The handle was wire wrapped under a curved silver hilt, complimenting the silver pommel which narrowed to a sharp point. The most exquisite feature of the dagger, however, was its blade, made from uniquely tempered steel, forged and folded countless times upon itself forming a unique ladder-like etching across the blade. The razor edge shone bright in the morning sun in such contrast to the smoky hue of the blade's flats.

I've since memorized the patterns of that blade. Every step and column of the folded steel has been committed to memory.

Publius continued, "Caesar bestowed it upon me to offer it as prize to one of the youths in the festival games around the empire." He pointed the dagger at the crowd. "I picked Sychar, for its warmth towards Rome, and its overwhelming hospitality towards myself during my frequent stays here. This is a grand place for a statesman to visit."

He raised his hands in the air. The crowd hollered its consent.

"Come, young Dismas the slave," he said, motioning for me to stand before him. "I understand you have a fitting nickname, do you not? One that alludes to your great speed?"

"*Tachu soma!*" one of the other boys yelled and the spectators echoed this several times before Publius raised a silencing hand.

"Ah," Publius said once the crowd was quiet, putting one of his meaty hands upon my back. "The 'speeding slave'. But no longer, young one. No longer." He turned me so that I faced the crowd. I kept my face lowered, terrified of seeing Quintus. "As his master has made the necessary accords during the festival," he said loudly, "this servant... this slave to the Menenia family is now..." He paused and gave me a warm look. "*Free!*"

The crowd roared again and Publius went on to say how he would make everything official on the next morning with my granting of manumission. If I so desired, I could accompany Publius Gracus and my master to Caesarea where I could be given a formal manumission before a magistrate where I would be granted both freedom and a Roman citizenship. For now, I would have a *manu misit*, the freeing of a slave by his master.

"If good Quintus Flavius would join us up here," Publius called out to the crowd.

I forced myself to look up. He was near the front of the crowd, walking towards us carefully, his chin held high, and his eyes trained directly on mine. The crowd clapped as he strode forward. This had to give him some sort of pleasure, I thought, even though his young servant had betrayed him. Forcing myself to think of all of his

130

cruelties, I raised my own chin high to match his lofty arrogance.

He stopped next to me and put a hand on the back of my neck. To the crowd, it probably looked like the sincere touch of a proud master, but his fingers tightened mightily – a hidden message reserved solely for me, hinting at the pain to come when others were not present.

"What do you say, good Quintus?" Publius said happily. "Is there something you wish to tell this fine young boy? The fastest I've ever seen." He winked at me.

"Yes," my master said coolly. "There is." He looked down at me and managed to force a smile. His teeth shone white. His grip strengthened on my neck, causing me to nearly gasp. "Dismas," he said loudly, "servant to my family, born into the proud Menenia tribe of statesmen... I grant you . . ." His grip continued to increase. ". . . your *manu misit*. You are now *free*." The word came out like a foul utterance, but his piqued emotion was quickly swallowed by the crowd's applause and unified shouts.

With a step to the side, I wrenched free from his grip and took his wrist, shaking it in feigned appreciation. My neck remained tight. He looked down at me, still smiling forcibly; his blue eyes did not hold the warmth of an azure flame, but the coldness of ice.

"And now," Publius called out, holding out the dagger to me, "you may come claim the other part of your reward, young Dismas... the freedman."

I walked past Quintus to accept the dagger.

***

Briefly regaining consciousness, I felt the coldness of the property stone upon my face. My swollen lips brushed against it and I reeled back in pain only to find myself tied against the marker.

Throughout the first part of the flogging, I had forgotten I was tied. The winded jeers of Quintus grew louder as I came out of this stupor, as did the frantic wailings of my mother and Tarius.

Past the stone, I saw that the sun was setting. It might have been beautiful had it not been for the pain. There was nothing in my world but this pain, the mixture of angry curses from behind me and sounds of lament from even further away.

Suddenly, the rope that had been binding me slackened and I was dragged roughly towards the villa by my arms which had long since weakened to the point of immobility. The whole world tilted during my travel and between glimpses of moving dirt and grasses, I saw my mother holding her hands to her mouth with tears streaming down her cheeks. Tarius was behind her, crying as well, and he was shouting something to his father.

Good boy, I thought as I was dragged. You're finally standing up to him.

Quintus hauled me towards the slave quarters, near the back patio of the villa. It was here that Mesick kept the gardening and field tools. There was a fire already burning in the smoke pit at the rear of the house.

White-faced Cornelia stood next to the fire pit, poking at it with an iron. Her face was pinched in great annoyance. "You're sick, Quintus," she said dropping the poker on the stone base of the pit. "I refuse to watch such... a *thing*. You're sick." She walked away, strutting like a peacock.

Quintus dropped me next to the pit, jarring my head against the stones. "I didn't ask you to watch, Cornelia," he said fiercely. He left me and walked to the storage shack where Mesick's tools were.

Surely, he would stop this if he were here.

Frenda's voice came to me then, faint, behind me: "Just leave him, Lucilla," she was saying. "He won't kill him, woman. Let it be! It will be over soon."

Then Tarius, standing above me, said shakily, "Hey, Diz? Can you hear me? I'm so sorry, Diz. I'm so-"

Quintus slapped Tarius on the mouth so hard the boy toppled onto the base of the fire pit and scorched his flailing hands. He retreated from us, shocked and gasping. Quintus sneered and looked behind him. "Frenda! Shut that woman's mouth or she'll get marked like her son!"

There was a great commotion behind me that I could not see. My mother continued to scream but was slowly pulled back by unseen hands.

Quintus bent down and looked at me. He was breathing heavy and sweat rolled down his high forehead. "You want to be unfaithful?" he asked me. "You want to be treated like a dirty mining slave? That's fine, Dismas. That's very fine. I'll get you your formal manumission but until then, you're still nothing more than property. As is your bawling mother. The punishment for a slave's transgression is solely in the hands of his master." He stood and fiddled with one of the smaller branding irons. Its stamp was a single line, a finger's length and the width of a pea. He placed it in the coals.

My mother continued to scream and Quintus shouted angrily at her then strolled out of my vision for a moment. Frantically, I tried to move, but managed only to roll onto my back. My rent skin surged with new pain and I nearly fainted again. I heard my mother cry out in anger and deviance and as I attempted to crane my neck backwards to see her, I could only make out struggling shapes in my peripheral vision.

Quintus was suddenly over me again, bending down to grab a handful of my hair. "Your mother is a tough woman," he hissed between clenched teeth. "She's fighting me over this almost as hard as she did when I exercised my full rights with her long ago. Though she'll never admit to you, whelp, she knows who your true father is. I've denied this for years but in light of today's events, I figured I would just give in. As it turns out," he sneered, "I *did* have a son win the race. A half breed, but a son nonetheless." He stood and pulled me to the pit's fencing by my hair. Using the same rope as with the property stone, he tied my wrists to the spit posts so that I lay on my side and faced away from him with arms and back exposed.

Through the pain I tried to process what he was telling me. I closed my eyes – and in my delirium – I tried to conjure the epic figure of my father but only saw Quintus's scowling face. Was this horrific vision possibly the truth?

"Cornelia always suspected," I heard him say. "It matters not. It was only once, though I think I may partake of such pleasures again." I heard iron sliding against stone. My nose was bleeding from his earlier blows but I still smelled scorched iron and an arid metallic smoke.

"This," he said to my back, "is what happens to unfaithful mining slaves, Dismas… the freedman."

My world was afire again as the brand was pressed against my right arm. He withdrew for a moment then pressed again in a different spot on the same arm. He was trying to write something. The pain, coupled with the revulsion of what he had told me, fully engulfed me and I fainted once more. In this new blackness, the fire on my arm remained.

*** 

My mother stayed with me next to the fire pit the whole night. My head was in her lap and I could feel her cool tears on my face. She sat against the base of the fire pit, stroking my hair gently with a trembling hand. She was still shaking when the morning sun came up over the horizon.

The only words she said from sundown until dawn were, "I'm sorry." She said this over and over in a diluted whisper. "I'm sorry... I'm sorry."

The sunrise was beautiful. Through squinted and swollen eyes, I thought that this was, for a reason unknown to me, the most dazzling sunrise I had ever seen. Despite the horrors of the previous evening, the colors seemed more vibrant and rich than ever before. The coolness of the morning and the dew upon my face seemed to soothe my wounds.

Above me, after nearly an hour's respite from her ceaseless apologies, my mother began to whisper a song. I recognized it as one that she had sung to me as a very young child. *Asphaleia*, she had always called it, which meant "safety for the baby". Many young Greek mothers sang this to their nursing infants, both to sooth them to sleep and as a prayer that the fertility goddess Isis would watch over their young children.

She now sang this to me with a shaky, quiet voice and I finally realized that my choice would not only greatly affect my future, but hers as well. Though flogged and scarred, her son would be free while she would still be bound to the Menenia family forever.

Quintus' terrible revelation had been echoing in my head all night, though I still did not have the will or the strength to ask my mother about its verity. As she sang to me, I looked away from the sunrise and clenched my eyes shut tightly while my head throbbed with the effort.

The sun continued to rise and I eventually opened my eyes again after she had finished her song. The tunic had been ripped from my body and I was naked except for the bloodied pair of runner's *calceus* on my feet. My right arm, a handbreadth above my elbow, was black and scorched from the branding. There was a definite pattern there but I could not discern it through the peeling skin and charred flesh.

"What does it say?" I asked my mother in a croaking voice.

"It doesn't matter," she whispered.

"Just tell me."

She raised a hand to her mouth and sighed. "NON..." she stuttered as she said it, "NON FID..."

Weakly, I shook my head. "I'll burn it off, mother."

She started crying again.

***

That morning, my mother and Frenda helped clean my wounds with boiled fig poultice and sap balm. After applying a light salve to my back, she bandaged me as best she could and gathered my meager possessions from the house, including several tunics, my own walking sandals, a thin cloak and a goatskin bag to carry it all. My newly acquired dagger had been hidden for me after the initial celebration by Tarius, who buried it at the base of our "crucifixion tree" in an oiled cloth.

Half-carrying me the whole way, my mother walked me into town and put me up in the slave quarters of one of her friends' homes. Her friend, a middle-aged Jewish woman named Rathar, gasped when she saw my injuries. She swore to my mother that she'd do her best to watch over me until I was strong enough to leave on my own.

And there I stayed. A week went by and my strength slowly returned, though the pain across my back and right arm seemed to grow as the ragged skin stretched and pinched together into scar tissue. My mother visited me twice that week and on each visit she assured me that Quintus had not laid a hand on her in any way. Each time she visited, I came close to asking her about Quintus' proclamations that day, but did not. I was fearful of her acknowledging it as the truth.

Tarius visited every day. His words were few and he told me of his planned trip to the west. Quintus was going to take his wife, son and servant Shara on a journey west to the capital cities where he would try and further instill himself into the monarchy of the senators. Publius had heard from a secret source – Mesick, perhaps – about my scourging and the senator had apparently reprimanded Quintus fiercely. Publius had one of his own scribes from Caesarea hand deliver to me a formal manumission of freedom which bore the senator's own seal. Though still considered a youth, I was officially a freeman under the Menenia family name. I burned the ornate scroll that very night.

Tarius had retrieved my dagger, which I hid under my bedroll in Rathar's home. Despite the pain it had cost me, the blade was still beautiful and I stared at it for hours when I had no one to talk to, when sleep seemed such a chore.

Rathar fostered me for ten days in her own quarters. No longer a boy, I now possessed enough strength to begin my decided journey as a man.

***

This dawn held storm clouds.

My mother embraced me as we stood near Jacob's well, at the southernmost part of Sychar. My pack was ready, filled with my scanty possessions: my dagger, bread, cheese, two water-skins and a small lambskin sack with fourteen copper *leptons* and eight *denarius*. This was nearly all she had saved in the last year and I protested mightily but she would not relent.

"You'll need money," she told me, still gripping my arms. "The world is run by silver and the stamped face of Caesar."

I sighed and looked behind her, towards Tarius and Mesick who were waiting to say their own goodbyes. "You've given me so much, mother," I said softly. "You've given me all you had when I've only given you strife. You've given me so much love and with this I leave here a rich boy."

"My Dismas, you're wrong. You leave here a man. Just promise to come back at some point and visit me. I'll look forward to hearing of your adventures and of your new free life." She pulled away from me and started to undo the clasp of her silver bracelet.

When I began to protest she shushed me and said, "Long ago, I was in love with a boy – years before your birth – and when Quintus informed us of our impending move to Samaria, I knew I would never see him again. We were meant to be together, but the pleadings of servants mean little to their masters. He gave me this bracelet on that day so long ago." She closed her eyes and fresh tears ran down each of her cheeks. "Years later, when you were born to us in Samaria, I could not give you a proper name as your bloodline entitled, so I thought of

138

my old love's name... which meant 'sunset'. I named you Dismas. While not named for your... father, it is a name belonging to a great love and a happier time." She took my right hand and fastened the bracelet to my wrist. "The leather shows the humble lives we were destined to live, while the silver shows the goodness – the love and rich memories – we would share. Now, you will wear this to remember your poor mother. Don't look at me like that, Dismas. We both know your money will be gone in a flash, your sandals will soon crumble, but this... always keep this on your wrist to remember me."

My own tears began to fall. "It will never come off," I promised her.

She hugged me again and walked to where Mesick was standing at the well. The old servant gave me a single nod and wiped his wrinkled eyes before putting an arm around my mother. This was the perfect goodbye, I thought, knowing that Messik would do everything to watch over my mother and would make sure Quintus did not lay another hand on her.

Tarius walked over to me and took hold of both my shoulders. I searched his face for any similarities to my own face and actually found several. I also knew that whenever I looked into a water's reflection that I would search for Quintus' face.

"I know this isn't the way you wanted it," Tarius said softly, "but we have pretended to be brothers for as long as I can remember. You may be ashamed of this blood, as I am after what happened, but I am happy that we at least share it." He glanced at my mother then embraced me and added, "I'll watch over, brother. My father will not always be the head of our family. Wherever I end up, you will always have a home there."

139

I nodded as fresh tears ran from my eyes. I looked away to the hills that beckoned.

"Do you have any idea where you will go?" he asked.

"No," I answered, looking back towards him. "It doesn't matter really. The horizon has always called to me. At least now I'm free to travel as I please."

Tarius wiped his eyes. "May the gods be with you and may they always watch over you."

"Keep them," I said with a sad smile. "I've never had much use for them."

He nodded and stepped away.

My mother waved again, as did Mesick.

There was a slight breeze in the cool air and I was suddenly thankful for the cloak. I tightened my grip on my shepherd's bag and started walking. Though I had sworn to myself that I wouldn't, I turned around once to see them again. My mother was wiping her eyes and Mesick still had an arm around her. Tarius just stood there silently, a sad look on his face.

That exact moment – the last time I ever saw my mother – will stick with me for the rest of my years and each distinct sensation is still recollected: the new weight of the bracelet on my right wrist, the coldness of the dagger within my belt, the ache of my scarred back and the painful brand on my arm.

Not knowing that this would be my final look at her, I turned and resumed my walk towards the south – towards the sable-cloaked guardian who I had seen waiting patiently in the distant hills to guide me.

# SECOND INTERLUDE

*My visitor Siergo paused in his recollection of Dismas'
narrative and gave me a prying look. "Do you abide in the past,
Marcus, as Dismas did? I do not have to tell you that such musing is-"*

*"Pointless," I finished for him. "I know. But all men focus on
their past at one time or another. Though it may be damaging, I can't
think of a way to fully avoid it. And it sounds as if Dismas has good
reason to dwell upon his own past."*

*Siergo leaned forward and said, "The goal should be to
transcend one's past."*

*I did not attempt to hide the look of confusion from my face as I
asked, "How does one transcend their past?"*

*"Learn from it. Don't dwell on it. Become better than your
past. Transcend it."*

*I nodded at his words and looked past him to the acreage
outside. Though it was an insane thought, I felt as if time had stopped
in a very subtle manner. It had been over an hour since I had last
looked at the sky, and the hooked moon had not traveled any further*

*across the heavens. And then slowly, as if mere thoughts of the phenomenon had ruined it, the familiar sounds of night returned to my ears: insects chirping, nocturnal animals crooning, and the faint breeze through my employer's crop.*

*With a shiver, I wondered if this phenomenon was just the cunning trick of a skilled orator, much like a magician of the theaters, or if it was actually a divine occurrence. My mind could not accept the latter, so I poured another cup of wine and said, "I imagine it would be hard for someone to transcend the memory of their own father disowning and torturing them. Perhaps this is why he became a thief."*

*"One of the reasons," Siergo said. "But anyone can transcend their past."*

*"You're an optimist, my friend. Perhaps you should preach to the masses and earn yourself the credentials of a teacher. Rome is always looking for new lines of thinking and fresh faces to idolize."*

*"The masses are not my calling. I have been charged to console only a few. Besides..." He leaned back in his chair and smiled gently. "I am not one for crowds."*

*"Nor am I," I said with my own smile. "And what of Dismas? I imagine he did not remain behind those bars forever."*

*"Allow me to continue his tale then, for I have to leave at dawn."*

*My eyebrows rose. "What schedule does a drifter keep, Siergo?"*

*"Even drifters are bound to certain rules. If you're tired, then..."*

*"Not tired in the least."*

*After a moment's silence, Siergo continued to recall what*

142

*Dismas had told him. I sagged on my bench and listened intently to both my visitor's words and the faint noises outside that slowly withdrew to the quarters of silence as I had hoped they would.*

## X V I - *Exodus*


The female's scream came from outside the chamber yet it echoed loudly as if the woman had been in the room with us. Amazingly, her wail increased in pitch and other shouts and voices joined hers in terrified alarm.

"*No*," Jael said and quickly stood. We both knew what was happening. There was no time to even begin their futile plan. She moved for the doorway, then stopped and looked at me as I stood up. "Can you help us?" she asked in a trembling voice.

Reaching through the bars, I bent and grabbed hold of my dagger's handle, pulling it from the ground. I looked at her. "Stay here, Jael. Don't go up there."

She turned to the door covering in deliberation. Above us, the sound of steel against steel, steel against bone, and echoing screams continued. A small cloud of dust rained upon me as someone either ran on the ground above or fell to it.

"Don't," I repeated and pointed behind her. "Hide behind the pots, Jael. Don't go up there."

She turned back to me and her large golden eyes were wide with fear. As if remembering something important, they grew even wider. "Nahum," she breathed, and ran to the covering, ignoring my pleas for her to stay. Mathias followed her with ears folded flat against his skull; the hound also sensed the discord above.

All around me, the flickering shadows from the lamp seemed to increase their feverous dancing as if they knew that blood was being spilled above them. Outside the chamber, the terrible chorus of sounds continued and I tried to imagine exactly what was happening in the village. The marauders would most likely kill all of the men – me included – while sparing the more comely women and young children for the slave market. Perhaps they were simply killing everybody and I would be no exception.

With a grunt, I grabbed the iron cell door and started shaking it as hard as I could. This had been tried many times during the early part of my captivity, but I could think of nothing else to do. My sinewy arms strained as I pulled and pushed at the door. More dust fell into my hair and eyes. It mixed with the fresh sweat that had broke out upon my face.

Outside, a battle raged. If I could just be rid of these bars, I thought, I could run out into the night and keep running – run as I had during the Great Race – away from this accursed village.

Over the clamor above, I heard feet slapping in the passageway outside the door covering. I hid the dagger behind my back and moved to the rear of the cell. The camel skin was slapped away and Jael reentered with a small boy I recognized as Nahum. There was blood on the boy's small tunic, and though he was quietly whimpering, he moved as if he had no injury and I wagered the blood had been someone else's. Breathing heavily, Jael ushered him to the wall opposite my cell and pushed the boy into the shadows behind the pots.

"Stay here and be as quiet as you can," she commanded in a shaky voice.

I moved back to the bars and said, "Jael, where's the key? Free me so I can help!"

She moved for the doorway but turned to me. Her eyes were red with tears and still wide with horror. "Watch over him, Dismas," she said. "You owe him this." And she was gone again, the sound of her footfalls fading quickly into the chaotic discord above.

With a curse, I leapt to the cell door again to start prying at the lock with my blade. Any thoughts of marring the beautiful steel was forgotten as more screams from above reverberated into my chamber. Behind the tall pots, Nahum continued to cry between deep sobbing breaths. Just as I inserted the trembling point of my blade into the lock's keyhole, I heard footfalls, heavier and louder than Jael's, just beyond the door covering. The sound of a man's labored breathing reached me and I once again moved from the bars into the deeper shadows of the cell. With a moan, the man flung himself through the camel skin and stumbled into the chamber. Through the sweat matted hair and bloody brow, I saw Jaspe's sharp features pinched in pain. Blood trickled from his scalp into his eyes and he fell to his knees in the center of the room, nearly knocking the clay lamp over. The flame flickered and the shadows seemed to surge in approval. He bent over to cough and I saw the wooden shaft of an arrow jutting from his lower back. The short sword he held loosely in his right hand was clean save a faint layer of rust. He coughed blood onto the carpet piece that Jael had been sitting on and raised his head to look at me. Between ragged breaths, he gasped, "Thief... this is your exodus..."

"Open this door and let me help," I said quickly, ignoring his rambling.

His frantic eyes wandered over me and came to rest on the dagger in my hand. With a surprised grunt, his eyes narrowed to bloody slits and he shuffled to his feet as the arrow shaft wavered behind him. With a gurgling cry, he threw himself at the bars and stuck his sword through them at me. I leapt backwards and my back hit the hardened dirt of the rear wall. Jaspe's blade continued to arc and swing just inches from my face. There was no more room for me to retreat. Behind him, I could hear Nahum bawling. Jaspe was grunting like a dog as he swung the sword at me, his eyes wild with the delirium of one mortally wounded.

There was a fleeting shadow of movement behind him and for a moment I wondered if Nahum had emerged from his perch behind the pots, but the sharpened head of an arrow suddenly sprang out the length of a hand from Jaspe's throat, instantly speckling me with blood. The rusty sword stopped in mid-swing and Jaspe's eyes went wide with newfound pain and confusion. The eyes focused on my face for a second before he slid down the bars and crumbled into a heap upon Jael's rug. Nahum had grown silent and I guessed that the child was equally shocked at what had just happened.

From the folds of the door covering, one of the marauders entered the chamber slowly as if wary of an ambush. He had already nocked another arrow into his long bow and as its point scanned the shadowy corners of the room, I quietly slipped the dagger into the back fold of my tunic. The man was tall and darkened from a lifetime in the deserts of the eastern provinces. His coat was nearly as thick as plate armor and a dirty black beard stretched over it. A blue scarf was wrapped tightly over his brow to keep sweat out of his deep sunk eyes.

At his thick leather belt, a sheathed sword, curved and large, swung with each of his measured steps. Once closer to the bars, he regarded me in silence for a moment but kept the arrow pointed at my chest.

I slowly raised my empty hands, and despite this, the man began to tense as if readying himself to loose another arrow. Thinking quickly, I sputtered, "Thank you, my brother."

He looked from his point of aim – my heaving chest – to my eyes and studied them for a moment. I hoped that maybe a wolf could smell another wolf, and this marauder would know that I was not merely one of the villagers imprisoned for some inner transgression.

"These Jews captured me for robbery," I said weakly, "and they planned to kill me upon the morning. I'm in debt to your group for saving me." I kept my hands raised but forced a smile onto my face. Above us, the screams had started to die down while a great many voices continued to whimper or moan in either pain or beseeching.

The man continued to search my face for a few seconds as if confused, then suddenly whirled around and fired his arrow at the wall of pots behind him. One of the large pots next to where Nahum was hiding shattered loudly and the boy yelped in terror. In the single fluid movement of a seasoned warrior, the man flung the bow over one arm, stringing it across his chest, and drew the curved sword at his belt. Seeing this from the shadows, Nahum hopped over the broken pot and tried to run for the doorway. The man raised his sword to swing at the boy, and for an unknown reason, my instinct for self-preservation fled me at that moment and I leapt forward, reaching my arm quickly through the bars, and grabbed the fabric of the man's outstretched arm. I pulled as hard as my weakened muscles allowed, wrenching the full weight of his body towards the bars. With my other hand, I quickly withdrew the dagger and drove the blade into the upper part of his back. He gasped and struggled to turn but I held onto his coat as hard as I could as I withdrew the dagger from between his shoulders. I stabbed again and again, until he finally dropped the sword and toppled onto the ground over Jaspe's still form.

Nahum had vanished. I stood there for a moment holding the bloody dagger. Knowing my foolish actions had certainly doomed me, I remaining standing there as I shook from spent energy and fear. While I had injured many in my chosen trade, this had been the first time I had ever actually killed someone. I stared at the bodies before me. The blood from both men spread and mingled in the dirt. My fate was now sealed, I realized, and I was no more alive than the dead bodies atop Jael's carpet piece.

Suddenly, as I watched their blood continue to merge, a last gambit game to me – something more ghoulish than I thought I had the strength for. A hoarse victory cry roared from above, and several other guttural voices joined the first. Upon hearing this, I suddenly realized that I would have to quickly attempt my plan – ghoulish or not.

*** 

It took them longer to enter the chamber than I had thought it would, and by that time I had finished wiping the blood from my hands upon the inner folds of Jaspe's cloak. After breaking up one of the bloody arrows and dropping it into my waste-hole, I stood in the rear corner of my cell waiting, trying to make out what the marauders were saying outside over the continued weeping of the spared women and children. I did not bother to wipe the blood from my dagger and I kept it visible in my hand as I stood there.

After another few minutes of waiting, someone finally entered the chamber. Even taller than the first marauder, this man looked at me then at the two bodies intertwined at the bars. His hands were behind his back and I saw the long, curved blade of his sword behind him, the dark point nearly touching the dirt. The figure's cloak was dark and on his broad leather belt, a crimson-stained hide sack had been tied. Its contents were a baleful mystery and the man saw my stare upon the bag.

"Mementos for Caesar," he said in Aramaic. "To one day give to him that he may see the atrocities he has forced his conquered people to commit." His voice was deep, cultured and oddly familiar. His face was long and his gray beard cut short. A peculiar shine within his stubble caught my eyes and I saw that the left tip of his chin had been cleaved off in a past battle, leaving only shiny scar tissue and bone at the point of his jaw. Gray hairs sprouted on either side of the old wound and the man gave a grin, displaying long yellowed teeth.

He took a step towards me, still holding the sword behind him. A small puddle of blood had pooled from its steel onto the dirt floor. I wondered if any of that blood was Aaron's or Jael's.

"A criminal?" the man asked me in his refined voice.

I nodded slowly.

Behind him, another marauder entered the room. He was a shorter, thick-bearded man with a bloody axe. "Sir, Rapha," he said to the tall man, "we've finished the count. Ten women of any worth, with about the same in younglings." He looked to the bodies on the floor and his eyebrows rose. "Is that Hahmet?"

The leader Rapha walked to the bodies and stood over them, regarding them in silence. The tip of Jaspe's sword was sticking into the dead marauder's back, while Jaspe's neck appeared to have been

150

ravaged by a blade. The dead marauder's sword was still clean and devoid of any blood.

"As one of my captors was killing your man," I lied in a soft voice, "I grabbed him through the bars and was able to take a dagger from his belt and kill him. They were planning on killing me in the morning."

The tall man looked up from his study of the bodies and looked to the shorter man. "Is this where the boy came from?" he asked him.

The man with the axe nodded. "Yes, though I cannot believe Hahmet would ever allow someone to stab him in the back like this if he was going sword to sword with someone."

Eyes narrowing, the tall man looked back to the bodies.

"My captor had been shot with an arrow in the back," I said. "He came in here and pretended to be dead as your man walked past him. I shouted a warning, but it was too late." I pointed my bloody dagger at the dead men. "At least I was able to kill him, though I wish I had been faster."

The tall, scarred man sighed and looked to me but spoke to the shorter man, "Did we lose any more, Makir?"

The short raider shook his head and said, "Only Hahmet here. Few of these Jews fought better than children. Only the big, older man gave us any sort of real scrap. His sword claimed two of Voht's fingers and he managed to knick a few of our other brothers before he fell by your hand."

Certain they were talking about Aaron, I felt something akin to grief at the mention of his death. Much like my act of lunacy in saving Nahum from the marauder's sword, this sentiment came from somewhere long thought lost to me. Had my captor ever really befriended me?  Not quite, I reflected, though I still felt some sort of negative pang upon hearing of his death, and likewise felt somehow proud that he had fought with such fierceness.

The tall thief continued to stare at me intently.  There was something oddly familiar about the man's face and voice, but I could not fully discern what.  Not the scar, I thought, but something else entirely.  One would certainly remember that scar.

"What is your name?" he asked me as he fingered the bloody sack on his belt.

As I opened my mouth to answer, I had a dire thought and hesitated.  As it seemed this man hated both Romans and Jews alike, I wondered if I should give the truth about my name or fashion some sort of lie.  I wagered my very life might depend on my title.  My gaze drifted to the blood on his sword.

"Choose a fake name carefully," he said, his lips curling into the slightest of grins, "for we have many different countries and faiths in our brethren.  We have at least two Adams, a Zechariah, Hermes, Ral, Brucius and many others.  The truth should suit you well enough, I think."

"Dismas," I answered after another second's thought.  "Freeman from Sychar, and more recently, from a small band of thieves hailing from Judea."

"A Roman?  A freeman no less."  He moved the sword so that it was perched upon his shoulder, not minding that blood smeared upon his cloak.  Gripping the iron bars of the cell door, he said, "You were in another band of thieves?  What was your leader's name, if you had one?  And how did you end up in a desert peasant's dungeon?"  He started pulling on the door.  It creaked under the new, stronger pressure but remained closed.

I suddenly realized that it was *Protos*-Obadiah's brother who stood before me. Other than the marred chin this man sported proudly, they had the same facial structure and hawk-like nose. However, their eyes were vastly different. Where Obadiah's eyes had always seemed wise and calculating, this man's eyes seemed devoid of any sort of emotion – much like the eyes of a corpse. Obadiah had told me very little of his brother, but I did know that they hated each other greatly.

"Our leader's name was…Tarius," I lied. "Another Roman. Older and bald, but a good thief."

He looked disappointed by this answer and he rubbed his mangled chin in thought, or possibly in remembrance of something. Perhaps he was listening to the whimpering above as the raiders finished their culling of the village.

"My band," I added, "tried to rob these people's caravan closer to the Jabbok forty days ago, during the storms. They kept me imprisoned here this whole time watching me starve to death, feeding me only scraps."

He grunted at this and looked at the dagger in my hand for a moment in silence. He then took a couple of steps away from the bars and said, "The lock, Makir."

The stout marauder with the axe stepped forward, and with one hard swing, shattered the rusted lock, tearing it from the bars. Dust swirled in the lamplight as Makir stepped back. With the sword still leaning against his shoulder, blood slowly dripping down the front of his cloak, the tall man then said, "Come out of there, Dismas, and stand before us."

With a deep breath, I wiped the bloody dagger on the front of my tunic, slid it into the rear fold of my garb and slowly walked to the door. With both hands, I pushed against it. At first it didn't budge, and I thought the men would leave me stuck in there without further help, but the hinges eventually gave a rusty pop and the door slowly opened as I strained against it. It swung outward and I finally stepped out of the cell and into the adjoining chamber. Having not stepped more than two full strides in the last forty days, my legs were shaky and weak. I put a hand on the outside of the bars to steady myself. "It feels good to finally-"

My words were cut short as the tall man's sword swung down from his shoulder and found the hollow of my throat, poking my bearded skin. I backpedaled into the cell as he advanced until my back hit the dirt wall. The blade's point pressed harder into my skin and I held my breath. A warm trickle could be felt running down my chest and I was unsure if it was sweat or blood. How close I had been to freedom, I thought. How horribly close.

"Know this," the man said, twisting the sword against my flesh, "My brethren have rules – laws that must be followed. I am Rapha-Ayzal. You did not know me before this night but from this night forward you are mine. Like a blade, like a sandal, like a simple possession, you are mine."

I needed air but could not draw a breath for fear of the sword's tip poking deeper into my skin. I did not even consider trying to pull the dagger from behind me.

"We are but thirty men," Ayzal continued, "and you can now take the place of Hahmet or we can kill you. The choice is yours. I am in the early stages of a great commission and in this early phase I am building an elite band of men for a special task. These are dire times and a message must be sent to Rome. By pushing us east, to the deserts, Caesar has forced us into raids against *all* of his conquered peoples. He has declared war and I have plagued him along the empire's outskirts for years. I will be the desert rat eating away at his fat hide.

"And you, Dismas," the blade's point bit deeper, "can now be part of this campaign. Consider yourself blessed among men to have an opportunity such as this. Now what is your answer?"

The man's face was vivid with emotion. He truly believed he could burden the territories of Rome with a mere thirty men. I thought this to be madness and though I was a thief, I did not fully understand the notion of pillaging entire villages not controlled by Rome. Despite my inner protests, however, I gave a painful nod and said, "I would be honored."

Rapha-Ayzal finally lowered his sword and held it at his side. "We count our loot and move on in the morning. The city of *Ra' Sahay* is little more than a day's walk and the slave market will be bustling."

He stepped aside and motioned for me to exit the cell which I gladly did. My gait was still unsteady and I walked slowly. As I followed Ayzal out of the room I turned and gave one last glance to the rusted iron bars that had restrained me for so long. The rotten burlap sack, my only possession in captivity, still lay crumpled in the corner of my cell, and I thought of the seemingly countless days lying in the dust as I read Aaron's translated scripture. Much of those passages were committed to memory but as I left the cell I believed I had no further use for Jewish antiquities. My thoughts were, once again, of escape – though this time my impediment was not iron bars, but the insane leader of this murderous band. And I knew that I would be able to break away from this band at the first possible opportunity and travel west to find Obadiah. Any thought of rescuing Jael and Nahum was futile – suicidal, even. Yet the thought lingered as I followed Rapha-Ayzal through the door covering and into a new form of captivity.

# XVII - *A New Man*

Following Rapha-Ayzal, I exited the underground chamber through a short series of stairs and ascended into a mud-brick storage house with more glazed pots and sacks of supplies. Through the abode's doorway, beyond the pillaged village, I saw moonlit desert hills under a clear sky. Behind me, Makir prodded me with the handle of his axe, and I walked through the doorway into the cool night air.

Despite the smell of smoke and blood, and the lingering cries of the survivors, the stars above were a blessed sight after my captivity; the thought of seeing the sun rise in but a few hours seemed nearly too wonderful to swallow at that moment. My gaze returned to earth and I saw that dozens of bodies littered the ground around the village – mostly men with bearded faces, their bloodied tunics fluttering in the breeze. The village had been small, consisting of a dozen large tents, five mud-brick structures and a small bathing pool and well – all within a crumbling, waist high stone wall that curled around the village like a dead snake. The marauders had set several of the village's large goatskin tents on fire and the flames licked northbound with the cool wind. Smoke whorled up and contorted with the wind, creating nefarious shapes above the pillaged settlement.

Rapha-Ayzal stood next to me and he breathed deep the stench of this carnage. "This does not feed me, Dismas," he said in a sad voice. "It pains me. Blame Caesar. Blame his legions and outriders... his taxes and swelling greed have caused this."

The marauders continued to run throughout the burning village making their coated forms looked like hellish figures moving wildly in the firelight. Their laughter could be heard above the crackling flames as they bantered with one another, calling out coy summons to anyone still in hiding. In another section of the village, near the water pool, I saw a group of raiders gathering the captive survivors into a tightly packed cluster. The women and children were crying, and firelight ran over their wretched faces as if they were a newly damned assembly awaiting passage into a fiery hell. These captives were forced to their knees as they were assessed. Squinting through the smoke, I scanned their faces, searching for Jael and Nahum but could not make out their faces among the anguished countenances.

One of the marauders, a portly man leaning against one of the untouched mud structures, did not toil with spoils or captives. He just stood there in silence and stared at me intently. His striped robe stretched over his large stomach. Unlike the others, he had no weapon in his hands, nor one strapped to his belt or back. His face seemed to hold sadness at the massacre before him.

Ayzal led me to a section of the wall, stepping over numerous bodies, and bade me to sit with him. My body was not used to the pressure of stone and I winced as I sat.

Ayzal stared at the flames for a few moments, entranced it seemed, then said, "My brethren are more than a band of simple rebels acting against Rome's taxes, son. We're not the *Sicarii*. The people in

Judea have always been weak, falling to this nation or that nation or almost any force that challenges them. I acknowledge that it is *impossible* to ever defeat the hoards of Rome, though…" He paused as he continued his vigil of the flames and rising smoke. After a few seconds he said, "A small group of smart men, placed in the right cities at the right times, could perhaps cause so much disconcert with assassinations and high profile robberies that even more high ranking Roman officials would be sent to these lands – and in turn, even more would be assassinated. They'll blame and further punish the locals, of course, all while our squads plan more stratagems to bring chaos to Judea, which will bring some small measure of chaos to Rome."

His words trailed off and I found myself staring at the slain men around us. The wind continued to whip at their hair and robes. There were no wounded men – only the dead.

As if the dark raider could read my thoughts, he said, "I've trained my men to kill quickly and leave no surviving men. No wounded are to suffer. The suffering I will bring to the Romans and to the merchants and officials who have made pacts with them. Before my plan can truly unfold…" He swept his arms over the village. "We need these settlements to help us amass money to buy our upcoming secrecies and allies. After we barter in the far eastern market, we'll develop our plan further – split our ranks and journey west to Judea. This will be a war in the shadows, Dismas, and you are now a part of it."

Not fully grasping his madness, I said, "Once again, I am honored to be a part of such a campaign. A force such as Rome can only be brought down with ingenuity and chaos."

Rapha-Ayzal nodded briskly as if pleased with my words and

stood up. He put a long fingered hand on my shoulder and said, "You seem smarter than many in my army. My select group of men would benefit from one such as you. Why don't you clean up a bit at the pool. Find some clothes and maybe a sword to go with that small dagger you seem to have some skill with. I'll spread the word to my men that you are not to be harmed."

***

The heat from the burning tents was great and I walked a clear path around them. Within several of the charred tents I saw more pots, bed rolls and shelves – now all aflame with the goatskin ceiling and walls. The tents were now nothing more than black skeletons. As I passed over bodies, I peered into each one's still face as I looked for Aaron. Nearly all of the men's eyes were open – as were their mouths – as if each one had died with a word of protest or prayer on their lips.

My search did not take long. Aaron lay near one of the burnt tents, on his back. His immense robe was pierced in several different places and its hue had fully changed from blue to a deep purple from all of the blood. His gray beard was also tainted with crimson. In his clenched hand he held the same short sword I had seen him with several times. The Hebrew letters on the blade's flat had been expertly engraved and several of them were now filled with blood. The blade's double edged tip was also bloody and I was silently proud when I saw the raiders' blood. Slowly, I knelt next to his body and gripped the fingers of the hand that held his sword. They were cold and already stiffening in the night air.

I sensed one of the raiders walk over to me and the man said, "He was their leader, you know." He spoke in Greek but possessed a clipped eastern accent.

Moving my fingers to the sword's handle, I looked up at the man. He was the same heavy individual with the striped robe who had stared at me so intently earlier. His gut was tremendous and his half beard was cut close around his wide mouth, while his face held the potential for great joviality under a nearly shorn scalp. He smiled sadly and continued, "He put up the most valiant fight, too – more than any of the others. He was the only one with courage, it seemed. Something to admire."

"I admire his sword," I said, mustering a cold voice. I pried Aaron's fingers away from the ebony wood handle. Once the sword was free, I took the oiled scabbard from his belt. I then stood and cleaned the sword's blade against my ruined tunic and placed it into the sheath.

The man sighed and said, "You *do* belong with Ayzal's band."

"What do you mean?"

"It takes a certain kind of man to do this work. I'm not such. My name is Jamal Raysid Rahan. I am from Damascus but was born in an Arabic city much further east. You are Dismas, no?"

After a pause, I offered a slight nod and asked, "Why are you here, then, if you're not such a man?"

"I possess certain... traits that Ayzal deems necessary to his campaign. I'm familiar with nearly every language of the east and west, every rendition and all idioms. I know of history, current political matters – as of a year ago anyway – and..." Jamal gave a weary grin. "I make the men laugh, as I was once in the Roman Theater as a humorist and soothsayer. Judea's Mecca burns within me though. I follow after the raids, as Ayzal commands. I am no warrior, nor thief, and I am not one for dead bodies."

161

"Then why do you stare at this one?" I asked.

"It was Ayzal, himself, who killed him. This man had already wounded several of his fighters. No one could get past this sword – until Rapha-Ayzal finally struck him down, that is. This Jew never cried out either and he only stopped swinging this sword when his heart stopped."

I nodded, thinking of Aaron's last few moments in this world. "Are you a Jew?"

"I was once," Jamal said with a wide smile. "I have been many things and have worshiped many gods. What about you, Dismas? Whom do you worship?"

"I worship no god," I answered curtly. I walked away from him and began the search for a clean tunic, belt and sandals. To my dismay, the large man followed at my side, still talking about the deities he was currently praying to, which, at this juncture in his life, included Egyptian river gods with animal heads atop the bodies of men. When I finally found a pair of leather sandals that appeared to be a good size for me, I stooped and began untying them from the body.

"I have found this life," Jamal said to my back, "rather dreary and much too grisly. These men have taken a liking to me, though, and Rapha-Ayzal has forbidden me to leave. I believe I am safe from their greed, but regardless..." He pulled apart his big robe and I saw two bejeweled daggers stuck in his belt, one on each side of his large belly. "It is always good," he added, "to be prepared when you sleep among wolves, especially before the cockcrowing hour."

After I finished removing the sandals, I assessed the corpse once more and then removed the leather belt from its tunic.

"Some cultures," Jamal said, "believe that if one robs the dead,

162

then they will be forever haunted by their ghost."

Ignoring him, I opened the man's cloak to see if he had anything else to pilfer.

Jamal gave a grunt. "Apparently you are not of one of these cultures, friend."

"Apparently not," I said under my breath and stood. The other marauders were still milling around the village as well, while some had already laid out bedrolls for a few hours of sleep. Many of these men eyed me suspiciously. Most seemed to be from the eastern deserts – Arabs that called no province home. I paid no heed to their stares and ducked into one of the remaining huts, searching through it until I found a suitable tunic and cloak. I fixed the scabbard to my newly acquired belt and carried my new clothes out of the hut. Jamal was waiting for me, his grin obscure in the starlight.

"Have I yet told you of how I came into this mass of derelicts and deserters?" he asked. "It's quite a story and perhaps to your liking." When I did not answer, he mistook my silence for consent and continued, "I was traveling alone on the Eastern Highway – foolish, I know - and Rapha Ayzal swooped upon me with his then smaller band. He was about to kill me and steal my jewelry, when I fell upon the ground, put my nose to the sand... and started squealing like a swine as loud as I could. I'm not sure why I did it at the time – perhaps terror induced insanity – but Ayzal's eyes went wide and he began to laugh at me. All of his men laughed. I hastily told them my mother had bedded with a hog and that I was a god-child with wonderful soothsaying powers and intellect, but that I smelled vastly better than any pig." Jamal waited for me to laugh, his eyebrows raised and face expectant.

I grunted in feigned amusement and Jamal's face lit up like the sun. "Ah!" he said loudly, pointing a finger at me, "I have prevailed! Your day has been brightened by the ever-winsome Jamal Raysid Rahan. That will be six flecks of silver, thank you. Ha, another jest, friend! My payment is your own amusement, no matter how meager."

"If anyone has actually paid you for your words," I said, tired of his banter, "then you're more of a thief than you know." I walked away from him towards the pool to clean myself. This time, Jamal did not follow.

*\*\**

As the eastern horizon turned from black to gray, I bathed in the pool slowly, and with great pleasure. It was a true labor to ignore the whimpering of the captives so close, but I had not bathed in a long time and the cool water upon my skin felt wonderful. When I finally dried myself and dressed in my new clothes, I took my dagger and shaved my face as best I could. Lifting my still wet hair out of my face, I scanned the group of enslaved villagers again in the growing dawn light.

Forget them, I told myself. You owe them nothing. You saved Nahum from the sword and that is enough - what happens to them is not your concern.

Yet still I stared. Flanked on two sides by guarding raiders, the captives had finally quieted down from exhaustion. Most of the women's veils had been torn from their heads and I could see heaps of dark hair in the morning sun. The women all had their heads bowed to the ground as they gripped each other or children in still shaking arms. Some of these children stared out from their perches between the women with wide, confused eyes that were red-rimmed from crying and smoke. In the group's middle, I finally saw her. Sitting in the

164

sand, a sleeping child huddled in the folds of her robe, Jael stared directly at me. How long she had been looking at me, I did not know. Her eyes were also red but still somehow defiant. She did not scowl at me, but her look held something resembling contempt, though it was also a questioning look. Her lips trembled slightly and I saw another emotion nearly break through her strong façade... deep fear, coupled with the desire to plead, though she remained silent as she returned my stare.

"Find one you like?" one of the guarding raiders asked. I looked at him and saw a bluish wolf's head inked onto the back of his left hand. His beard was braided tightly into a single serpent-like tail of hair.

"Perhaps," I said and turned back to Jael who was now looking down and whispering to the child in her arms.

The marauder added, "Rapha-Ayzal may let you take one into one of the remaining tents for a little relaxation time. But he will have your head if you mark any of them too much."

While such thoughts did not enter my mind, it did give me an idea – another crazy inclination that would probably cost me my life. However, as I had proven to myself nearly my whole life, I was a fool for such plans. When I realized the man was still waiting for a reply, I said, "Not a bad idea."

The thief grunted. "Though our time is short here, there will be more time once we reach *Ra' Sahay*. We will likely have a full night before the markets reopen in the morning. Many of us have already staked claims to most of them." He gave a curt bark of a laugh. "You may only be left with the children, if they have not already been claimed as well."

With a grunt of my own, I looked back to Jael. Once more, she was staring at me, though her eyes had drifted lower. I realized that she was looking at her father's sword upon my belt. Next to me, the marauder moved away to another group of thieves, and when Jael's eyes met mine once more, I gave her the slightest of nods. Not sure myself what the motion was supposed to mean, I waited in silence to see if she would return the nod. Her golden eyes searched my own for a moment before she looked back down to the sand.

"Dismas!" a hoarse voice cried from the other end of the village. I turned and saw Rapha-Ayzal motioning for me to join him near an assembled group of men. With a wary sigh, I walked towards them. About a dozen of the raiders stood around Ayzal. Jamal was among them, hands raised upwards and contorting his fat body as he told them some tale.

"Ah!" Ayzal said with a long toothed smiled as I neared. "You look human again. New clothes, a new sword and a shave – a new man before us. How does freedom feel?"

I nodded. "It feels very good."

The tall thief returned my nod. "We're readying our group for the journey to *Ra' Sahay*. Per his request, I've assigned Jamal to watch over you during our voyage. While we should reach the city by nightfall, it can be a taxing hike and I'm sure you're still very weak from your time in that cell."

Behind him, Jamal was smiling widely, while some of the other marauders glared at me in mistrust. Clearly, they were not pleased that their leader had taken such a blatant liking to their group's newcomer.

Still feigning an interest in Azyal's campaign as I contemplated how to be rid of his army of lunatics, I pointed at Jamal and said, "This is good, as I know that I am still regaining my strength, but are you sure that *he* can make the journey."

Many of the men's scowls disappeared as several of them laughed. Jamal gave an ungainly bow and said, "I will manage fine, thank you."

Ayzal maintained his wolfish grin for a few seconds, allowing the men their laughter, then raised a hand into the air to silence them. "Ready the captives, livestock and plunder for the journey. Pile the bodies into the huts and burn them. Leave nothing unburned." His tone turned commanding as his corpse-like eyes stared out at his ranks. "Work fast, men. I want to be in *Ra' Sahay* before sundown and I want our bartering done at first light so we can move on to the bigger plans we have for the western cities."

Apparently his men were more disciplined then other thieves I've known, for they quickly scattered and began their toiling in the decimated village. Jamal gripped my shoulder and led me away from Ayzal, towards the well at the far corner of village. Surprisingly, he did not open his mouth until we were out of earshot from the other thieves. Once his ample backside was resting against the stones of the well, he let out a great sigh and said, "We have much to discuss during our journey it seems."

Only half listening to him, I looked to the western hills – my true destination that would have to wait until I'd fabricated a plan to flee – and said, "And why is that?"

"Because of all your lies," Jamal said. I turned to him and saw that he was smiling broadly. "And because I believe we are two men who want the same thing though are unsure of how to achieve it." He saw my eyes go wide and his grin grew even bigger.

"Why do you think I've lied?" I asked and looked back to the hills to hide my surprise.

"I am a seasoned reader of men, Dismas," he said as he leaned closer to me. "As are all good soothsayers in the theaters. While I don't see the purity of a baby in your eyes, I don't see the same evil as these men. I see the way you looked at the captives – your alleged former *captors* – and I know that you've lied to Ayzal about much. I recognize such lies because I've had to do the same with him for years. Do not be afraid, for as I said… I think that we want the same thing."

Still trying to process all he had said, I remained looking away from him but asked, "And what is that?"

"To be rid of these cursed wolves and their mad leader."

Finally interested in something Jamal had said, I turned towards him and quietly said, "It appears that we *do* have much to discuss."

His grin widened further to an impossible size and I found my own lips involuntarily curving into a faint smile. Upon seeing this, the large man bellowed with laughter and said, "Finally a smile! Let us hope this will not be the last of them."

Very quickly, however, my smile faded as I thought of Jael and Nahum, and the horrors that awaited them in the squalid trade city of *Ra' Sahay*. Aaron's sword – with its unknown Hebrew etchings – grew heavy upon my stolen belt.

## X V I I I - *Exceptional Thieves*

After setting the rest of the village and bodies afire, we left southbound through the rock hills, adjacent to the Arabic trade route, through the Arabian Desert. Ayzal's men decided to kill all but the four largest animals of the livestock because they preferred to mainly deal in human stock. When we finally left, the sun was high and its warmth grew uncomfortable on my face and arms as I was not used to its rays. Jamal offered me a blue-patterned square of thin fabric which he pulled from his immense cloak. I fashioned a quick headdress to keep some of the heat from my head. The other men in our caravan did not appear to notice this heat.

During the journey, I learned from Jamal that most of these men were Nabataean dregs who had been exiled from their settlements in the Arabian Peninsula for various transgressions including murder, thievery and sins of the flesh. Several of these outcasts had even helped maintain the red-rock city of Petra, which had been built only a few miles off the same trade route that stretched from Aqaba to Philadelphia.

Our procession walked on. My feet grew sore and my legs fatigued quickly. It had been so long since I had undergone any sort of journey. My new sandals remained intact, thankfully, and did not overly blister my feet.

Three hounds followed our ignoble caravan from a distance. Judging from the brown spots along its flank, I recognized one of them to be Nahum's dog, Mathias. The hounds wove through the hills behind us like scavenging jackals.

Our southern trek turned east and our Bedouin trail became much more rocky and steep as it wound around various cliffs and outcrops.

As my pace slowed from weariness I found myself at the very back of the group with Jamal and the two marauders who guarded the villagers from the rear. Jamal and I had started near the pack's center, but from his portly gait and my own weakened stature, we both slumped backwards and were passed by my new compatriots. The women walked silently, dried of tears, carrying the younger children who were wrapped in blankets in protection from the winds. Jael was in the middle of their crammed group, holding Nahum's hand as they trudged onward. While still not sure why I harbored such protective feelings towards them, I knew for certain that I did not want them both sold as stock on one of the slave stones of *Ra' Sahay*.

Just before evening descended upon the desert, when we were still an hour or two away from the desert city, one of the childless women issued a sorrowful scream and ran from the group. From the procession's front, Rapha-Ayzal gave a loud command to his underlings to let the desert claim her. The whole group stopped and watched as she wove around a rock gully and then disappeared into one of the shadowy chasms, tumbling like a snipped flower in the wind.

170

Though fed, the desert was still hungry, as it always would be, and Ayzal gave the order to continue on.

*** 

The winds died down as the sun started to set behind us. Jamal had been talking for most of our journey and the rotund man had been forced to alternate his stories with the upslope of hills as his lungs would not allow both speech and exertion. Finally out of earshot of the other marauders, but still close enough to see the tortured faces of their captives, we spoke of Ayzal and his band.

"Does Ayzal have six fingers on each hand?" I asked him quietly.

He gave a fatigued smile but waited until we had crested our current hill before answering. "You are familiar with the legends of the Jewish histories?"

"There were people – six-fingered giants, even – with the name of Rapha in the scriptures…"

"Rapha-Ayzal is not his birth name, but a chosen name. His birth name from Damascus is Lazya."

"How did he get the scar on his chin?"

Jamal shook his head. "That happened before I was brought into his group. At the time, years ago, he was a part of another marauding brigandage from Trachonitis with his brother. His brother wanted to leave – to seek the company of fewer, less fanatical men, while Ayzal had been awed by the vision of the raiders. One night, they argued and eventually fought over the issue as the rest of the brigands watched. During the battle, his brother had cleaved off the tip of his chin and had let him live like that, scorned in front of the other thieves and disfigured for life." Jamal rubbed his own chin as if

171

thinking about such a wound. "After his brother fled, Ayzal left the band to start his own with new men who knew nothing of the battle. He now claims he received the scar battling Roman outriders at the gate of Jerusalem. Over much wine, he has told me the truth though. Whenever he visits a city or settlement, even when robbing caravans, he'll ask people if they know of a man named Obadiah who speaks like a Roman and has many scars. He has not forgotten his brother and never will."

I thought about this in silence as we continued to walk. Obadiah had told me so little of his past and nothing of this battle. I was told how his brother hated him and that was all.

"He believes your small band's leader was his brother," Jamal huffed as we rounded another mountainous sand dune.

"He is," I said in a surprised voice. "But how would he know this? I lied about this to him after I realized who he was."

"He's not sure, I should say. Ayzal said that you sound like his brother. Apparently his brother, Obadiah, was tutored quite well before fleeing Damascus. Perhaps you have spent enough time with the man that some of his mannerisms have rubbed off on you. Who can say? Either way, he would have killed anyone else for such lying, but he wants to know for sure. If you can eventually lead him to Obadiah, then he will kill him." He turned to me. "And kill you as well, Dismas."

"I'm hoping to be gone long before he has a chance to pry further on the topic. We need to fabricate a plan to leave once we reach *Ra' Sahay*."

Nodding his large head, Jamal said, "The sooner the better. There is much confusion in that city and that will hopefully aid us. I

172

will pray to all of the gods known to me until we get there. But I have another question for you." He stopped for a moment to catch his breath. I stopped as well and took a long swallow from the water skin that hung from my shoulder. When he had rested for a few breaths, we started walking again and he continued, "Will it be just you and me who flees *Ra' Sahay*?"

Looking past the nearest line of marauders in front of us, I saw the captive women and children still huddled together as they shambled towards a life of harsh slavery or forced prostitution. "Perhaps your soothsaying powers are beginning to fail you, Jamal," I said.

Despite his huffing breaths, he smiled. "I think not, friend. You had better have a very clever plan to escape *Ra' Sahay* with your life… towing captives meant for the market. Such a feat seems worthy of Homer. Or of the theater."

My gaze drifted past the captives and past the hoard of marauders in front of them. At the procession's front, standing out against the rocky horizon, a tall figure in a dark cloak had stopped and was staring back at us. While not the Man of Shadow, Rapha-Ayzal seemed nearly as formidable. Fleetingly giving him supernatural attributes I knew he did not possess, I imagined for a moment that the dark thief could hear us from so far away. After a few seconds, Ayzal turned back and continued to lead his men and their catch further into the desert.

"Tell me," Jamal said, "how did you come into the bustling vocation of thievery?"

I sighed despairingly. "I'm tired of telling people of my history."

He was quiet for a moment, breathing heavily, and then said,

"As you explained much with your earlier lies, you explain much with your short, barbed answers."

I remained silent and trudged onward.

"Who did you recently tell of your past?" he asked after nearly a half mile's silence. "The previous owner of the sword on your hip? One of the captive women up there, perhaps?"

"It doesn't matter right now."

"We still have a few hours of walking ahead of us," he said. "Tell me how you became a thief and how you met Ayzal's brother. Ayzal said you are a freed slave. Yet you take your new freedom and become a common thief?"

I smiled. "Obadiah would say that we are *exceptional* thieves."

"In that case," Jamal said, "I would like to hear about how you became an exceptional thief. Your talking will give me a much needed respite."

"Silence is the best respite," I said pointedly.

Raising a thick finger which he wagged in the air, Jamal said, "I have always considered myself silence's stern antagonist."

"I can tell," I said. After a moment's thought, I briefly told him of my days in Sychar, summarizing the fateful race, my branding and my accompanying freedom. Though it may have been simple exhaustion, Jamal seemed to be a rapt listener and seemed sympathetic when he asked clarifying questions, which were few. After my brief telling of my exile from the Menenia family, I told him of how I had met Obadiah and how I had finally found a family in which I belonged.

## X I X - *In the Midst of Vile Men*

The Man of Shadow never lingers for long – and always in the distance – so it had been a lonely journey from Sychar after my sorrowful farewell.

Southwest of Sychar, the mountain of Gerizim jutted from the hills and was not of great height but was very wide. From its rocky base, one could see the bleakness of the coastal plains in the west, which stretched the along the Great Sea's coastline from the port cities of Jamnia, then north to Tyre and Sidon. This was good farmland and I passed several farmers and cordoned fields on my westward trek.

My destination was the port city of Joppa, which was a day's journey south of the much larger city of Caesarea Maritima, the largest Roman trade city and coastal byway. Joppa had many ports, but was much smaller than Caesarea which was a desired quality, for I was not yet ready for a city as bustling as its northern sister. It had always been a dream of mine to see the Great Sea with my own eyes.

A narrow dirt road curved into my path and I followed it southwest. Before entering the coastal plains, I walked through a countryside blanketed with rocky hills and scattered foliage. Numerous other dirt paths and shepherd trails wove into my own road, but I fixed my gaze southwest. Other travelers were scarce in this season, and the ones I came across had no interest in talking to a young man from Samaria.

My bearings became confused at some point, because I walked throughout the evening and the coastal plains – which should have dipped westward towards the Great Sea – became swelling hills once more. Had I fully turned around or had I diverted too far south?

The sun neared the horizon – the same sun I had planned to see setting over the Great Sea – and I set my bearings upon its descent. The shadows grew long across the land. With nothing in sight save hills and the occasional tree, I knew I would have to find some sort of shelter unless I wanted to walk through the night. My still-healing back and arm ached, and I decided to stop at the next tree grove I came across. With the darkness came clouds, and with them, thunder. After another half hour's walk, I spotted a large hill with a great outcropping of boulders embedded in its side. Several large trees stretched out from above the outcropping. As the first drops of rain started to fall, I quickened my pace and veered off my path towards the stony hill.

The boulders loomed before me and I ducked under one of the tree's offshoots into the darkness between two of the larger stones. The fissure continued backward and I saw that it was actually a rather expansive cave that widened under hill. I ducked down and crept into the cave, avoiding the exposed tree roots above me.

As night fully descended and the storm outside strengthened, I found a comfortable roost behind a wide boulder and lay down. Using my traveler's bag as a pillow, I reclined against the cool stone and watched the rain sprinkle across the shadowy hills. This was a good shelter, I mused, and the time in which I came upon it signified good fate. While not usually dwelling upon such superstitious ideas, I drifted off into a content sleep, not realizing that the shadows of my new shelter would host more visitors on that night.

***

Despite the vigilant measures of Roman administration, Obadiah had told me many times, brigands thrived in Judea and her surrounding lands. The greatest asset to thieves in such a country is its geography. With numerous caverns and hiding places to serve as both shelter and sites for ambush, such hill-country is well suited for robbers – even more so than for farmers, it might seem. The area around Jerusalem was especially susceptible in this time, for the authorities were tied up with inward revolt in the city. As Jerusalem was supposedly the highest authority in the land for the Jewish sects, it was important that Rome kept its grip upon her throat both gentle and resolute. Obadiah had knowledge that Herod had recently declared that he would take care of the prevalent bandits by dispatching highly trained outriders into the wilderness on routine patrols. The authorities were also developing a new, separate court system to deal specifically with robbers who plagued the Romanized cities.

The punishments for brigands were also administered more swiftly and in a very public disposition… this was a message to others stalking the roads. Rome loved to crucify and the public loved to watch.

The much acclaimed crucifixion hill was just outside of the Gennath Gate, just north of Jerusalem. Obadiah had ruminated if it had always resembled a skull or if it was simply Rome's dark influence that had further molded it. Either way, it had been named *Golgotha* – the Place of the Skull – for as long as he could remember. It became almost a theater of sorts, as spectators – both Gentile and Jew alike – watched with earnest fascination as criminals were pierced and hung like effigies upon the splintered bars at the hill's summit. It was said by the Romans that mythical Charon, the skull-faced ferryman, was guardian to this knoll and that his spirit was fed with each execution at his semblance, which grinned upwards in the direction of the Gennath Gate. The Jews maintained a less ethereal viewpoint of the hill, but still acknowledged its somber magnitude.

For obvious reasons, Obadiah had told me early on, thieves feared the Skull. If one robbed within Jerusalem's walls or on her flanking roads, they were on the "Path to the Skull". Crucifixion was not a pleasant death and the Praetorian guard was always eager to feed the Skull.

Whether it was from stupidity or simple obstinacy, many thieves continued their business in the cities and on the roads. The hill's grin would always be suppressed in the back of their minds, however, but they would always jaunt the Skull's path - as was the nature of such men.

And like wandering boys on respite from their homeland, such men needed shelter from the elements.

***

The drizzle was short lived. The hills had been quenched.

Sleep was intermittent upon the rocks, though my cloak kept me relatively warm. The wind trilled throughout the cave, through the small cracks and fissures which facilitated the wind like a reed flute.

It started with voices intertwined with the wind's song. The

178

only light in the cavern came from the lone entrance where the faintest amount of starlight shone through the clouds.

Sitting up from my rock bed, I leaned towards the entrance and looked out. As my eyes slowly adjusted, the figures came into focus… six men, some tall, some short, but all were walking directly towards my cave. Even at a distance, I could hear their brash voices. Their forms were dark, but I could still see the grime on their tunics.

Thieves, I thought. Men who would probably kill without the slightest hesitation. Kill you, or worse.

Outside, the voices grew louder, one giving a gruff laugh and two others talking about the night. Clutching my cloak to my chest, I grabbed my traveling bag and moved into the darker recesses of the cave. The rock cavern was much larger than I had imagined and I felt my way over moss covered boulders and around crevices until I could no longer see the grayish light from the cave's entrance. I settled behind one of the larger boulders and crouched atop my cloak. Something furry scurried across my sandaled feet and shrieked its displeasure at my intrusion.

"This will have to do," one of the men said loudly, his voice echoing throughout the cave.

"I'd wager you were born in a cave like this, Mercius," another announced. Other voices laughed mightily, one even sounding like a depraved hyena.

"Better than being born in a waste hole, and left there as dung," the derided man countered, initiating a new surge of laughter.

"Calm yourselves, scions," a strong voice said, silencing their jargon. "I doubt this place is big enough for the usual scrapping, so let's just try and get some rest."

"Should I count the catch, *Protos*?" one asked.

That could only mean their stolen bounty, I thought as I crouched, trembling against the boulder.

"Do you want the flints?" one asked.

"Afraid of the dark, Titus?"

"Hardly. The dark is my ally."

"Ah, mine, as well."

"But only to poke the knave sleeping next to you!" Laughter echoed throughout the cavern.

I noticed a chattering noise coming from somewhere in the cave. After a moment, I realized it coming from my own teeth and I bit down hard to silence them.

"There's room enough for everyone," the leader *Protos* said. "Just space out and find a flat surface. We don't need any flints and the catch can wait until morning. Hand it over, Titus."

"Ah," another gave a wounded sound, "you do not trust me?"

"Would you?"

"Probably not. Here you are, good *Protos*."

Then, after a moment's silence as the thieves settled, another voice – articulate and gravelly, like one whose throat had been cut – issued from the darkness: "We're not alone."

My heart quivered and seemed to stop for a beat.

"He spoke!" another exclaimed. "By the blessed gods, Charon spoke. I didn't see it, but he surely did!"

"Shut up," the leader commanded quickly. "What do you mean, Charon?"

This new speaker with the odd voice whispered something that my ears could not pick up over the wind. My heart resumed its

180

hammering; each beat was a loud stomp within the walls of my chest. It felt as if it were trying to break free through my ribs.

The other men were now whispering and I heard a rustle as if one were fiddling with objects in a bag. Then, clicking noises mixed with the dreaded sound of steel slowly escaping from its leather scabbard. The men were murmuring amongst themselves and shuffling around the cave. Another sound, wood rattling against stone, reached my ears.

The clicking grew more rapid and over the earthy, damp odor of the cave, I smelled smoke. Then finally a faint light grew near the cave's entrance and I could hear several men blowing and whistling, trying to fan the growing flame. They were fastening a torch.

As the firelight grew, I looked around the cavern. I was already as far back as I could possibly go. The chamber was wider than I had imagined, stretching beyond the hill's radius into the damp earth. Scattered bones littered the ground at my feet and I wondered if this was still the home of some vicious wolf or jackal. Regardless, the beast's abode had been overrun with more loathsome, two-legged animals.

Shadows twisted and danced over the cave's walls as the men neared. The shapes resembled demons more so than men. Lowering myself further to the ground beneath me, I peered out from behind the boulder.

Three men, all dirty and bronzed from endless days of trekking under the sun, were crouched down; their various blades were drawn as they inspected the shadows. Behind them, another three men were scattered amid the boulders, also crouching. A short, stocky one held the torch, while another tall one with gray hair – the leader no doubt –

181

had risen and was standing at the mouth of the cave. The tall one's silver hair was long and pulled tight into a braid. His beard still held a generous amount of black within the encroaching silver. His short sword was held at his side.

There was no time to plan an assault. Furthermore, to try and fight them would be suicidal. The dagger in my bag did not beckon to me. Their blades were far too many and I had no experience with combat save the childish battles with wooden swords in my youth. Words would have to be my weapon.

*Courage.* I repeated this several times in my head like a mantra – one that seemed to evade me in my search for it. Despite this, I forced my trembling body to stand. The closest three men had their backs to me as they searched another small alcove of the cavern to my left. The fourth closest man, one with a skull-like face and intense beady eyes, saw me immediately and his expression grew even sharper. Without alerting the others, his hand reached toward his thick belt where he had attached a numerous iron throwing darts. No doubt, this was the same man who had heard me before – Charon – and from his skeletal face I understood why they had named him after the ferryman of the River Styx.

"Greetings," I called out in a shaky voice. The closest men whipped around to see me. The skull-faced man slowly withdrew one of his darts. His position shifted as he moved his right side back, readying for a throw.

My first instinct was to duck back behind the boulder, but I thought of my weak mantra and forced myself to remain standing. "I'm nothing more than a poor traveler and I mean no harm. I can share this cave with you fine pilgrims or I can leave."

182

The silver-haired leader regarded me quizzically for a moment, his sword still relaxed at his thigh. Aside from the whistling wind, the cave was silent for a few heartbeats before the leader ordered in a calm voice, "Grab him." Immediately, the closest thieves loped towards me, ducking under the overhanging rocks.

"Wait!" I shouted. "There's no need for this!" As they continued towards me, grinning and breathing heavily, I cursed and ducked back behind the boulder. I pulled the dagger from my bag and I rose with it, pointing it at the men before me. They stopped when they saw my blade, but their grins did not slacken.

"Oh, he wants to dance," one of them said. His voice was slurred and I could smell the wine on his breath from several paces away. A much-stained wineskin swung from his shoulder. His own dagger wavered in front of him as if he were casting a spell with it. The thief next to him was younger, scarcely older than I, and he seemed more uncertain than the drunkard. He raised the torch he held as if it were a club, its embers snapping and twisting towards the stone floor.

"There's no need for this," I repeated, holding my dagger in front of me, its point trembling. *"Please!* Just leave me be and I'll go!"

"If you wouldn't mind, Charon," the large muscular thief behind their torch bearer said. "Please spear that whelp, since Mercius and Titus seem too shy."

The skull-faced man tensed his shoulders and was about to throw his dart when the leader cried, *"Hold,* Charon! Just wait, all of you." The man walked towards me, sword still held against his leg. He stopped next to the short man with the torch and stared at me intently. His eyes seemed to match the gray of his hair, and I noticed that he was staring at my blade.

"Please," I said softly. "I have nothing to steal and you certainly have nothing to gain from killing an aimless voyager. I'm not even-"

"You have that blade," the drunkard said, "and the silver on your arm catches my eye, as well."

My eyes narrowed. "You may very well take my dagger and the tunic off my back but you will *never* acquire this bracelet. In a rush, you all may overpower me, but I'll kill at least two if you try for this jewelry. I do not joke."

The drunk one scoffed and took a step forward, "I elect to try it, *Protos*."

"Stop," the leader said, still staring at my dagger. To my surprise, his gaze held puzzlement and not greed. "What is your name?" he asked me.

"Dismas," I said slowly, "a freedman from the Flavius family of the Menenia tribe in Sychar. As I said, I'm nothing more than a vagabond looking to chase my fate along the ports of Joppa."

The leader nodded. "And how is it, Dismas, that a former slave has come to procure a uniquely tempered blade such as that?"

This man was observant. He had seen the dark, step-like patterns across the blade, even in the darkness of the cave. "It was a prize," I answered, "for winning the Great Race in Sychar. I also won my freedom that day."

He laughed then and several of the other men smirked. "*You* won the race, huh? Well, why are you not enjoying the comforts of your former master's estate? Was your good Master Flavius not proud of his slave for winning?"

"He was not. He wanted someone else to win."

The man's grin widened. "Ah, I see," he said. "The slave won while the son lost. And what of your bracelet?"

There was no point in lying. "A parting gift from my mother. As I said before, if you want it, it will cost you at least two of your men. Perhaps more."

The man's eyes leapt from my bracelet to my face. "I take what I want, boy. With a snap of my fingers, you'll have two darts in your throat before you can even blink if you threaten me again. Brother Charon never misses, as he is guided by Hades himself."

The dart-wielding man was silent and ready, his right shoulder dropped low as his beady eyes locked on my neck. Somehow, though I had never seen his endeavors, I believed the words spoken about him. "Forgive me," I said softly, noticing the tremble in my voice was greater now. The dagger's point quivered in the torchlight. "But you must understand that this bracelet is worth little in the markets but it is valuable to me alone – priceless to me even. The loss of it would surely cause me to do rash things. I did not mean that as a threat. What is it that you want of me?"

The leader *Protos* eyed my blade for another moment as his fellow thieves offered several suggestions on how to dispatch me. He then held up a hand to silence them, and said, "Let me see your dagger."

No doubt, they would rush me as soon as my blade was gone. They would probably rush me anyway though, and I still felt queasy about the thought of actually trying to kill someone. I would do anything to protect my bracelet, though, but as the silent gods watched this dire scene, I knew that I had little choice but to obey the man.

Slowly, I twisted the dagger in my hand so that the handle faced towards him.  With a matched slowness, he sheathed his sword, took the dagger with a scarred hand and said to his tensing bandits, "Just wait, scions.  Just wait before you act."  The thieves looked to each other and sighed in disappointment.  The one with the torch, however, looked relieved.  He did not appear to be one for violence.

"I used to forge such blades," *Protos* said as he fondled the weapon.  "In Damascus, during the dry season.  My brother and I both worked as blacksmiths before the siege in our town.  The shop was destroyed, but there are still a few blades buoying around out there.  This one is newer, but nearly mirrors the design my brother would always temper into the steel.  We both would spend so long on a single blade, folding the two different types of steel – one hard and bright, the other more flexible and dark – until the pattern was perfect and the steel was stronger than any blade before it.  We worked hard and made little but those were good days."  His deep voice was softer, nearly sad as if he had fallen under some sort of sorcery from looking at the blade.

The other thieves all looked at each other with equally astonished looks on their faces.  Their leader had evidently never spoke about this before.

"When did you leave Damascus?" I asked, trying to fan the embers of his trance.

Running his finger along the flat of the dagger's blade, he sighed and said, "Long ago.  After the siege."  His voice was soft with remembrance.  "My brother and I left Damascus to chase our fates..."  He looked at me.  "Much like you are now."

I nodded with sincerity and asked, "What became of your brother?"  I regretted the question as soon as it came out of my mouth.

186

Most likely – given the life these men led – his brother was dead and the black memory would drive this man out of his spell.

"Let us be realistic," he said, eyes growing narrow. "You care not for my brother, nor for me. As I would, you care for your own skin and nothing more. This," he said, looking again to the dagger, "is a fine blade. It is *your* blade." He then flipped the handle towards me and held it out.

With a trembling hand, I accepted it and kept it lowered at my side. Though obviously displeased with their leader's last action, the other thieves grumbled and finally relaxed. The large, muscular man with curly hair looked particularly upset and set his scowl upon my face with such intensity that I was worried he would still attack me, ignoring any commands from his chief.

The leader folded his arms over his chest and said, "I am *Protos*-Obadiah, once from Damascus, now hailing from this cave. You're in the midst of vile men, Dismas. You may go if you wish, or you may stay in the further recesses of the cave for shelter. Given some of my scion's inclinations though, you might do better to leave."

I looked past him to the wet hills outside the cave. While I was trembling from fear, I was dry and wanted to stay as such. "I'll stay," I said. "In the rear part of the cave. Thank you for your… hospitality."

Obadiah gave me an amused look and then turned away to find bedding closer to the cave's entrance. The other thieves turned as well to lie down and the bulky one said, "I'd sleep with one eye open, boy." He flexed his broad shoulders once then turned to follow his cohorts.

Back in the rear of the cavern, it took me three tries to put my dagger into my bag. Sleep, I thought, would certainly be scarce on this night.

***

The next morning was bright and sun filled, the dawn free of clouds. There was a chill in the air from the night's drizzle and the ground was still damp.

Upon this first light, I had tip-toed past the still sleeping thieves and stood at the hill's opposite end, watching the sunrise.

Towards the west, the hills gave way to the coastal plains. I scanned the horizon. The Man of Shadow was not seen. Was he, I mused, a specter of the gods... a divine wraith sent to steer me out of, or perhaps into, adversity? Or was he just a figment of a bygone child's imagination?

A lone figure emerged from the cave. *Protos*-Obadiah. He called me to his side; his tone was not commanding, but almost cordial. When I neared him, he adjusted his cloak over his shoulders and said, "In my younger years, I tired of others having what I could not have. I tired of so much being denied me because of my status. While not a slave, a poor Jewish boy in Damascus fared little better. When my brother and I finally fled, plain survival forced me steal. When I learned I was good at it, I realized that despite my status in life, I could have whatever I wanted." He reached a hand out and snatched at the empty air. "Anything can be stolen, Dismas. You don't need money to be rich. You don't need a ceremony to be free."

He paused and looked to the setting sun. "We're making our way west," he said after a moment. "Towards the city of Apollonia, and perhaps Joppa after that. The view of the Great Sea from her ports takes one's breath away. Just a subtle proposal, young scion." He then winked above his black and silver beard, below one of the crisscrossed scars on his brow, and returned to the cave.

188

Despite the lingering sense of danger and iniquity, as I looked back to the sunrise, I already knew what my answer to his proposal was.

## X X - *Choose Wisely*

**T**he city of *Ra' Sahay* was still active when we arrived just after sundown, but the slave market was already closed for the evening. The band decided to camp for the night near the city's northern stone wall. Before entering the municipality, which surprisingly lacked much of the ever-present Roman influences of the west, several caravans and slave merchants passed us on the road and informed us the market was good for children and would be open again at dawn. It appeared that most of these men were tall Arabs. They had been informative but strikingly unfriendly. This was not an empathetic borough. However, we need not fear Roman outriders in this land, as this was well outside of their normal patrolling routes.

*Ra' Sahay* is a strange concoction of many different peoples, faiths and eastern cultures. The city is not unlike those found in the Decapolis, with strings of homes sharing a single adobe roof. Many dirt paths weave in between these clusters of homes, but the desert city's main attraction is its slave market, which is little more than a huge stone court in the city's heart. This court is large and runs adjacent to the other markets and smaller vendors of *Ra' Sahay*. Every morning, the market opens and the slave hawkers cry out their prices and physical attributes of their newest fleshy catch. Those wanting to barter on the market must pay the designated hawker a fee, which can be rather steep, depending on recent business.

Entire families are divided, sold and carted away by wealthy merchants. Women are turned into prostitutes, men to chained tillers, and children to whatever the buyer pleases. For one with a weak heart, any such slave bartering is not easy to watch, whether it be the *Delos* market – as I have seen several times in my travels – or the Arabic ones such as in *Ra' Sahay*.

For the Arabs and other desert peoples, slave management was vastly different than that of the Romans. Servants to Roman families were usually treated as valued property – myself being an odious exception – and these slaves, as well as their bloodlines, are seen as heirlooms. For the crueler eastern cultures, slaves are seen as little more than dogs; unless, that is, you possess a comely female, who is kept sustained, but only to please the carnal desires of her master and her master's close friends and brothers.

As we passed the stone slaves' court, Jamal tapped me on the shoulder and whispered, "Do you suppose they know this is where they will be sold?" He nodded towards the shuffling captives.

"As long as Jael and Nahum are not among them," I answered, "I care not."

"I would wager the other women and children care very much."

"They are of no concern to me. It will be difficult enough to save even two." Just because I felt the inane desire to rescue a woman who had always despised me, as well as a young boy who believed that I had killed his father, it did not mean I had to harbor any sentiment for the rest of them. I sighed, thinking about how this newfound empathy of mine would probably be the death of me. Somehow, Jamal and I would have to contact Jael after we had camped for the night. Then if we somehow managed to escape the city, we would have nearly a four day trek back to the Jordan. Angered marauders would likely be snarling at our heels the entire time. Insanity, I thought again. Jamal and I had discussed a hurried plan for our escape, but the added rescue of two captives would be left up to me as soon as we stopped for the night. I had an idea to get Jael, and possibly Nahum, away from the other marauders, though it would take a fine amount of luck... or a divine hand from the gods I loathed. I was already planning on failure, and then flight.

Frowning, I looked away from the slave court to the vendors that lined the central street we were on. When they saw our morose caravan, they hollered and cried out in Aramaic for us to consider their goods.

"Bread of God!" one cried.

"Sandals, daggers and leather!"

"Silver so fine - finest in the east!"

"Vegetables so grand!"

This city, like many large bartering towns, was always loud until the cock-crowing hour, as vendors and beggars would yell until their lungs fatigued. Even then, they would rasp and whistle their pleas for business.

At the group's front, Rapha-Ayzal passed by all of these venders in silence. Further into the city, he suddenly turned between two crumbling buildings and we followed a dirt path into the deeper shadows. This route wove behind the merchant lane into a trash-filled alleyway. We diverted again and found ourselves in another – even

192

darker – alleyway that ran along the city's northern wall. Towards the front of the group, I saw Ayzal's shadowy figure speaking to his men and making motions for them to camp at this location. The captives collapsed in the refuse and dirt, still clinging to the children who had long since stopped their incessant crying. The whole group needed sustenance after their desert trek.

Jamal and I sat upon a heap of timber that had been disregarded by some luckless carpenter, and I watched as Ayzal walked in between the captives. He grabbed their heads – turning them to scout for blemishes that might detract potential buyers. The women cried out upon his touch, but he shushed them gently, like a tender father would a baby. One woman in particular was somewhat elderly and had a red lesion upon her brow; whether it was from hives or was simply a red mark from the desert sun, this mark – along with her age – would surely hinder her from fetching any money on the slave stone.

As the other captives wailed at him, Ayzal grabbed this older woman roughly by the hair and drug her into one of the darker, adjacent alleys. Despite her howls, he calmly drew a curved dagger and knelt over her in the shadows. I turned away as her keening suddenly stopped.

Jamal looked queasy and he stood to enter the market. I gripped his arm and whispered, "Do not forget our plan, Jamal. Give me at least until the night's middle." Without a nod or any other acknowledgement, he left the alley. I turned back to the captives and found Jael staring at me. When she saw my gaze, she quickly looked away towards the alley's dirt floor. Suddenly, Ayzal was next to me, still holding the bloody dagger. My heart stopped for a moment, but he gave a grim smile. "Come, Dismas," he said as he cleaned the blade against the already crimson sack at his belt. "Let us have a talk."

After I stood, I followed him past the dead woman and into the city.

***

*Ra' Sahay* had grown dark quickly. The homes were stacked high upon each other and the shadows from lamplight and trash fires were long. Despite the continued chants and hollering of the merchants who were hoping for credulous night shoppers with coinage to spare, vermin left their crags to feast upon scattered offal along the city streets.

Rapha-Ayzal gripped my arm just under my brand as we walked slowly down the streets, ignoring the vendors and beggars. "You seem to have more strength," he told me. "This is very good. After we sell this pitiful batch of slaves – your former captors – we'll return west. To Judea, I think, to begin the next phase of our plan."

"I am looking forward to it," I said with only a half measure of truth. "Your words inspire, as do your actions. In my travels, few are willing to do the necessary work to make a plan run smoothly. Such as letting the old woman go back there." I nodded back towards the marauder's camp.

Ayzal scratched his mauled chin with the hilt of his dagger. "Was your previous leader not a man of such action?"

I shook my head. "He wasn't even a man of words," I lied. "Every time I tried to bring up a plan to increase our holdings or strike out at bigger merchant groups, he would decline in fear. And when he abandoned me to these desert fleas, I knew that he had always been jealous of my initiative."

Ayzal stared at me for a moment then asked, "What was his

194

name again?" He turned and led me into another alley where the darkness was deep.

Suddenly, I became afraid. Did he mean to dispatch me in the shadows? No, I answered my inner fears. If he had wanted to kill me, a man like Ayzal would do it in plain view to further edify his marauders. "Before answering that question," I said slowly and with a smile, "I have a confession to make to you."

"Oh?" he said softly as if expecting such a statement.

The shadows continued to grow thicker as we stepped over dark piles of trash in the alley.

"Your brother talked of you only on rare occasions," I said carefully. "He told the others in his band that if we ever came across you that you would kill us on sight because you despised organized thievery. He said you were only a barbarian that killed without thought."

Ayzal stopped in the darkness and stared at me. The dagger was still at his side, though the whiteness of his knuckles shone out from the darkness like bone. "My brother?" he asked with a dead-like voice.

I nodded. "Obadiah," I said. "He had commanded us to tell others that his name was Tarius for a reason that still escapes me, but after talking with Jamal, I realized that you were the brother he had spoken of. And I realized that he had always lied about you."

Without another word, he continued down the alley and I followed. We walked along the eastern wall of the city and came to a gate. Once outside the city, Ayzal released my arm and he sat upon one of the wall's larger protruding stones, near its base. I sat across from him, next to the gate, and watched him expertly twirl the dagger

195

in his long fingers.

When Ayzal remained silent, evidently in thought, I added, "If we go west, to Jerusalem and her sisters, I want to kill him if we are able to cross his path." Though I was lying for my own gain, such words made me want to wince. If *Protos*-Obadiah were witness to my speech, I told myself, he would have understood.

Slowly, Ayzal opened his cloak and sheathed his dagger. He looked at me then, his eyes still like those from a corpse, and said, "I pride myself on those I choose for my army. You, Dismas," he pointed one of his long fingers at me and smiled, "are no exception."

I slowly let out a pent up breath and said, "As I said before, I have never had a leader who inspires and dreams of greatness. I look forward to the coming days."

Ayzal seemed to beam in the starlight. "I am a thinker and philosopher," he said. "Never once was I trained in combat. My training is from my own practice and experience. Truthfully, I never believed in any cause enough to join any league or sect. Until now, my friend. We are not some band of worthless rabble as my brother would have preferred. No... I have taught these men to be smart – to use their minds – that we might accomplish great things. It appears that you, too, have a smart mind. Perhaps even more so than the majority of my inner group."

I nodded my gratitude though my thoughts were elsewhere. I hoped that Jamal had made the necessary preparations for our departure. While I was glad that Ayzal's trust in me was quickly growing – which would hopefully make my later actions easier – I could not help but worry about how difficult it would be to follow through with our plan. My main objective was to escape with Jael and

Nahum – securing them at her uncle's home in Jerusalem – and then track down my old band and continue with our *eschatos kleros*.

"I have been looking for smart, resourceful men to help me realize my goals," Ayzal continued. "The men you see back there," he nodded towards the city walls. "There are only a small handful of them that I trust. These ten, maybe twelve men, are of a different bearing than the others. They can imagine *more* than just fleeting spoils. After we've earned enough, hopefully after the morning sales, we will order the others to their own mission in the northern provinces – but they will fail. Brave souls, all of them, but every army needs a front rank willing to die for a cause."

"I take it they don't know of this," I said with a fake smile.

Rapha-Ayzal's grin seemed to glow in the faint starlight. "The true warriors," he said, "including you and my other handpicked group of a dozen or so men, will then begin our new plan in the west. This will be a group of warriors who are also thinkers – soldiers of the mind as well as the blade. We will be the 'Wolves of the Jordan', Dismas."

Rapha-Ayzal was nearly rambling now, and I pretended to listen intently as his voice grew louder and more passionate as he spoke of his new elite group of men. My intent look of understanding further heartened him. He gingerly lifted the crimson bag at his belt and said, "I tell you now, friend, the poor souls that fill this bag will not go unheard."

Not knowing what exactly to say to this madness, I mustered a solemn voice and said, "I believe in your vision. The only thing more important to me than helping you find your brother – so that both of us can take a blade to him – is making this vision a reality."

Ayzal beamed. His teeth were long and yellowed. "You are

much more than a simple freedman, I think. You will certainly be an asset. But I doubt there will be much of my brother left for you when I am through with him." He stood and bade me to stand beside him. He took my wrist and said, "Now, friend... Brother. What is it that I may do for you to make our time in *Ra' Sahay* to your liking? A token of my goodwill – just name it."

Perhaps the gods did favor me at that moment. My plan was falling into place and Ayzal was only helping.

For several long seconds, I pretended to weigh his offer and then said, "A girl from our lot. Just for the night. It's been so long, Sir Rapha. Far too long, I think."

His smile widened. "Done. I will choose a fine one for you." He laughed and gripped my arm tighter.

I smiled warmly but quickly said, "Could I be allowed to choose my own? There was one who caught my eye as we walked from Gilead. She would do very nicely, I think."

He nodded. "Surely. But chose wisely, Dismas. And do not mark her. As unfortunate as this whole business is, I take pride in my stock and I am known for it at this market."

As he turned to lead us back to his camp, I finally spoke words that I actually meant, saying, "I will make sure that she is kept safe."

Ayzal nodded his approval and I followed him back into the shadows of the city.

## XXI - *Under a Crescent Moon*

**D**uring our walk back to the marauders' camp, Ayzal continued to spout nonsense about his war against any and all established authorities in the land east of the Great Sea. Only half listening to him as we walked, I continued to run scenarios through my head in case I should come up with obstacles in my plan's path. While I had the harder part of actually pulling Jael and Nahum both away from the marauders, Jamal's role in our plan was also vitally important, and if he was true to his word, he would be performing that role now… gathering necessities and supplies from the vendor's near *Ra' Sahay's* lower dwellings, near the southern wall.

When Ayzal and I finally reached the back alley, where the rest of his band and the captives were, the raider named Makir strode over to us. He wrinkled his squat nose at me then turned to Ayzal and said, "Sir Rapha, I know you wanted to speak to Jamal, but the boar has left for the markets for food. Many of the others left to see the city and to barter some of their smaller possessions or to steal. I could not stop them, but I did tell them to not raise any stir. Ten of us have remained, and half of those are now asleep. The slaves have quieted down, though."

Ayzal put his arm around Makir. "Very good," he said. "The men need a rest, I think. These slaves barely have the energy to stand, let alone run away. Food would be nice. Hopefully, they will bring some back for the rest."

"Sir, Rapha," Makir said quietly and looked to the dirt between them, "would it be acceptable if some of us – the ones who remained behind, at least – to partake of the…" He didn't finish his sentence, but his motives were clear as he nodded to the captives that huddled together against the stone wall.

Ayzal gave a laugh and said, "Ah, you are famished in that way, as well? Surely, Makir, but I will be letting our new compatriot here pick first." He slapped my shoulder and I withheld a wince. "He has been denied probably much longer than you, and his tastes probably aren't as young as yours anyway."

The short thief glared at me but nodded at his leader.

Ayzal pushed me towards the villagers and said, "Remember my words, Dismas. Choose wisely, for some of these Jewesses have no small amount of fire in them."

The moment had come.

The alley was very dark, so I had to wade through the trembling captives as Makir watched my every move. After turning several heads and looking into several different terrified faces, I found Jael huddled against the stone wall, clutching a child tightly. Her long, black hair spilled over the youth, covering his face. Hopefully, it was Nahum. If not, I would have to just take Jael.

I reached down and brushed a section of her hair away. The child was indeed Nahum. The boy was asleep, his eyes pinched together tightly as if he was enduring a nightmare. Jael's eyes were

200

open but fixed solidly on the ground. I bent down as I pretended to further access her body, and whispered to her in a soft voice the same words she had told me on the previous night, "It is time."

She remained silent, staring at the ground. "Don't let Nahum go, Jael," I whispered. "Whatever happens, do not let go of his hand – drag him if you have to." Holding the back part of her robe, I rose and turned to Ayzal. "This one will please me fine," I said.

"Enjoy yourself," Ayzal said with a smile and walked away towards the remaining men.

I gripped Jael's robe and pulled her off of the trash-covered ground. She resisted at first, clinging to Nahum fiercely. Hopefully, she would understand what my intentions were – how I was trying to save them both.

One of the older marauders behind Makir bellowed at me, "You need help there? She's not going to let that babe go. Ha!"

As I struggled with Jael, I yelled to the man, "Then he can watch."

The man gave another bark of a laugh and turned away.

Finally, Jael rose and slumped against me, still holding Nahum between us. "You must walk, Jael," I whispered, "and do not let him go. Trust me now."

From behind me, Makir's deep voice said, "Leave the boy, freedman. He is mine."

I turned to look at him and his eyes bored into mine in a dead way not unlike Ayzal's. He looked from my eyes to the boy in Jael's arms and I saw a terrible lust amid the numbness.

With a sigh of exasperation that was equal parts disgust and alarm, I pretended to pull Nahum away from Jael's firm grip. Her arms were locked around the boy and following my instruction – or simply from just the strength of her guardian nature – they would not budge.

The same thief behind Makir laughed again and said, "Are you trying to take them both, boy? She's probably as strong as you are from the look of it!" Some of the other men laughed at this.

I ignored them and began to pull Jael, with Nahum still in her arms, into the darkness of the alley. I called over my shoulder to Makir, "The boy is yours, Makir, but she won't release him and I don't want to mark either of them as Sir Rapha instructed us. As I said, he can watch, and you can have him when I'm done with her." I did not wait for a response but continued to shuffle them into the dark alley, moving further from the marauders.

Once through one alley, I led them onto another path, which ran along the western wall of the city. There were other marauders skulking through *Ra' Sahay*, both from Ayzal's band and from other rogue traders, so I would have to be careful. I still had my sword strapped to my belt, as well as my dagger, but I did not want to attempt combat with someone in the shadows. If I was forced to, and if I was physically able, I would not hesitate to kill to achieve my objective.

Now that you've killed once before, I thought, you are so willing to do it again. Perhaps I was no different than Rapha-Ayzal. Or Jaximo, for that matter. We were all kin to Abaddon and Hades. I shivered at the thought – hoping I possessed some sort of virtue or honor that made me unlike them – and continued trudging through the dirt alleys.

As I led them, I spoke to Jael, telling her of our plan of escape to Jerusalem. I told her of Aaron's death, and how he had stood courageously while others had hid. I told her that it was I who had saved Nahum in the chamber by killing the marauder. During my whispered discourse, she remained silent but allowed herself to be led throughout the alleys and shadows of the city.

Once near the southern wall, nearly as far from Ayzal as we could be within the city, I continued to follow the directions that Jamal had given me earlier and turned into another alley which led us to a covered bathing pool and well which had been constructed between two clusters of tall homes. Above the pool, which was exactly where Jamal had said it would be, a pillared stone awning spread over the water. There was a faint shuffling sound outside the walls and I thought I recognized the familiar mewling of camels.

Jamal emerged from the shadows near the stone well, breathing heavily. "Praise every god known to me," he said. He gently helped me lead Jael to the pool and bade her to sit. Nahum remained sleeping in her arms. "Ah, this plan of yours is working, Dismas," Jamal said. "I have fulfilled my end, amen and amen."

I ignored him and knelt in front of Jael. I moved the hair out of her face. "Jael," I said. "This is Jamal. He is a friend and is helping us escape." I nodded towards him.

Jamal gave a great bow and said, "Jamal Raysid Rahan." He then crossed his arms over his immense belly.

I turned back to Jael and whispered, "He's going to help us get back to the Jordan. We can find your uncle Rannut in Jerusalem maybe. Jael, please say something."

A tear rolled down one of her cheeks and she whispered, "They were going to *sell* us…"

"Not anymore. You are both safe."

"The others…" she said in a tortured voice, still looking at the child in her arms.

I shook my head. "There is no way to save the others. It was of great luck to get both you and Nahum away from them. But our time is very short, Jael, and we must leave now." It had been long enough for Makir to realize that I had fled with both of the captives, I thought as I stood. Ayzal would lead his raiders throughout the city in search of us. No fine words or lies would help me to escape his blade this time.

With a shiver, I shook off my premonitions and gently took Nahum from Jael's hesitant grip as Jamal retrieved several bags from behind a cluster of vessels near the pool. They were leather bound and filled with food and water-skins, all purchased with money from his own pocket or stolen in the last hour.

Looking down at Nahum's sleeping form, I said to Jamal, "We won't make the journey on foot, friend."

Jamal slung the bags over his thick shoulder and replied, "As blissful as I am that you called me 'friend', I must also reprimand you for not giving me due credit. There are three camels waiting for us just outside these south walls."

I looked at him and said, "Perhaps you *are* a god-child, Jamal. Rapha-Ayzal will do poorly to be without you."

"Perhaps your band in Judea needs me more," he answered, his jowls held high in pomposity. "Just fulfill your end of our deal once we get them to Jerusalem. I help you get them to this house of Rannut then you find me a place in your band... or a fine theater at the least."

I nodded and gingerly handed Nahum over to him then helped Jael to her feet. We entered the back alley once more, this time headed around the pool, towards the *Makay* Gate, which was where Jamal had tied the camels. As we walked through the shadows once more, Jamal stated that he had actually swindled the camels from one of the vendors to use for one day – a grand lie – and that he had also bribed a young man to watch them at the gate for a couple of hours.

The gate itself was wide enough for three oxen to stroll through, horn to horn, and its stone archway stretched high into the night sky. The crescent moon hung above us like a sideways grin. Or a sideways frown, I thought. Once through the gate, Jamal pointed to his newly acquired camels. The boy he had paid was lying on the ground in the deeper shadows of the wall and looked to be asleep.

"Fool," Jamal muttered as we passed him. I then had Jael lean against the wall, next to the sleeping lookout and I helped Jamal with the camels that had been tied to an iron stake in the ground. With Nahum in one arm, Jamal loaded one camel with the supplies while I hastily fiddled with the second. I turned to Jael, who was staring down at the boy. Her eyes were open much wider and she looked newly stricken. Taking her arm, I guided her to the first camel, the smallest of the three, and helped her climb atop it.

"That boy," she whispered to me. "Dismas, he…"

As I quickly adjusted the bag behind her on the camel's hump, I said, "We must hurry, Jael. Everything will be fine."

In the dim moonlight, I saw she had more tears in her eyes and she glanced back to the city walls. "He's dead," she whispered.

Before mounting the third camel, I looked once more at the hired youth lying in the shadows. Though our time was swiftly running out, something about the tilt of his head made me pause. I stepped into the shadows next to him and saw that the sand under him shone a wet black in the moonlight. The boy's chest did not rise and fall for breath.

"Let us *go*," Jamal murmured from atop his mewling camel.

A furtive movement in the shadows within the gate brought a terrible word to my mind: *ambush*. The word hit me like a slap in the face and the night was suddenly darker. Jamal had been followed. Our plan was known. My ears picked up the sound of running feet and muted breaths drawing near.

"*Go!*" I hissed to Jamal and led Jael's camel to him, handing him the lead. "Your lookout boy has been killed. I'll meet you in Jerusalem. The merchant house of Rannut. Follow the Jabbok. Now *go!*"

"May every god be with you!" he answered and clucked furiously, leading the camels in an ungainly trot into the dark wilderness.

As Jael was led away – her black hair bouncing and fluttering in the air – she looked back at me and I saw her expression change from subdued fear to intense panic as he eyes focused behind me.

I was moving before the attack came. One of the marauders had snuck along the wall and was diving towards me, dagger in hand. Rolling away from his swinging blade, I collided with another thief running through the gate and we both tumbled in the dust. Knowing I needed to draw attention to myself and away from the fleeing camels – but still wanting to survive – I drove an elbow into the man's nose as we grappled and I leapt to my feet. The first attacker jumped over the fallen man and swung at me again.

*Draw your sword!* I heeded my inner voice and yanked the short sword from its scabbard as I jumped backwards to evade the dagger once more. I turned and ran back into the city.

Just as I met the shadows of the nearest alley, another raider suddenly appeared before me. It was Makir, and I saw that the stout thief had not yet drawn his axe. His hands pulled at its handle on his belt as I swung my sword at him with all my strength. My blade hit low, striking the steel axe head and the force of the blow caused Makir to fall back into the alley. I bounded over his cursing form and ran deeper into the alley which curved behind one of the homes and spilled me back into the small courtyard next to the pool.

In the corner of my eye, as I neared the pool, I saw several more men skirt through the shadows. The sound of angered shouting filled the air when they spotted me. Running hard, I curved around the pool and a tall figure suddenly rose from behind its stone base and I collided with him. The man gripped my wrist – the one that held my sword – and my free hand clutched the hilt of his own drawn sword. We struggled there for a moment, thrashing in the moonlight like forlorn dancers.

"Betrayer," the man growled and I saw it was Rapha-Ayzal. He leered at me and his long teeth gleamed in the crescent moon's light. "I'm going to cut you into piecemeal, you traitor... but I'll still cart you around until you lead me to my brother!" He propelled me backwards until my back was against one of the palm trees next to the pool.

The other raiders were nearing; their footfalls echoed loudly against the walls and alleyways. With no other option, I let go of Ayzal's sword and rammed my fist into his neck. He sputtered and loosened his grip, allowing me to pull away from him. As more raiders entered the small courtyard, I realized that I would not be able to make it to one of the other alleys, so I hopped up onto the stone base of the pool and jumped for its awning. Ayzal grabbed me around the waist as I hung there. I kicked my right leg out and connected with his midsection, and the dark thief released me – but not before tearing my dagger from my belt. He swung at me with my own blade, missing my legs by a hair, as I pulled myself onto the tiled canopy.

I continued to climb until I was fully on top of the stone awning, out of his reach. A lower roof of one of the homes was close to the canopy and I wagered if I could get on top of it, I could make my way across the connected homes.

Below, Rapha-Ayzal bellowed orders as the men poured around him. Some plucked rocks from the well's base and threw them at me. One brave marauder started climbing the pool's awning as I had. His fingers suddenly came into view and his head followed. It was Makir, and his face was still pinched in rankle.

"You stole that boy from me," he growled as he tried to hoist himself up.

With a grunt, I swung my sword downwards at his hands and quailed at the harsh jarring against stone. Makir screamed in pain and tumbled backwards in a wake of numerous severed fingers.

As Makir's howls echoed throughout the street, I sheathed my sword, ducking as more rocks flew towards me. Trying to push away thoughts of what would happen if I fell, I ran towards the nearest home and jumped into the night, sailing over a pair of astonished raiders. My hands found the ceiling's edge and I slammed into the mud-brick wall. With a grunt I pulled myself on top of the home as a thrown stone hit my thigh. My jump had briefly silenced all of the raiders except Makir, who continued to wail into the night.

Without taking any time to rest, I scrambled across the first roof and climbed onto one of the higher apartments next to it. I jumped from one series of homes to another, finding myself deeper in the city. I came across several beggars hiding on one roof and they cursed at me as I jumped over them. There was a cloaked figure ahead of me, a dark wraith that I followed desperately.

Other people in the city were starting to yell as well. The marauders were raising quite the ruckus, it seemed. In addition to bloodthirsty thieves chasing me, I would soon have Arabic guardsmen at my heels.

As I neared the now quiet marketplace, I jumped from one home onto a lower building and crashed through the thin ceiling. Darkness and dust engulfed me. I picked myself up from the pile of wood and crumbled mud-bricks, coughing mightily. A woman behind me started screaming. In the dim light from a nearby lamp, I stumbled down a dark series of stairs and suddenly found myself in the street with several people gawking at me. Hastily, I moved back into the darker alleys and wove in and out of different side streets and crooked paths. In the darkness of one alley, I found a large burlap sack. Taking a moment to rest, I drew my sword and cut the sack open down its middle. Though the burlap smelled strongly of urine, I draped its length over my head and shoulders, fashioning it as a makeshift cloak.

After I had caught my breath, I sheathed my sword and fostered a drunken gait through the alley. I had no idea which direction I was facing, but somehow after a good deal of turns, I neared the city walls and found an open gate. There were two guards posted there. Their hands both rested on the handles of the curved swords. They cursed at me in a gruff Arabic language when my smell reached them. Hiding my sword under the burlap, I passed by them and moved into the hills.

I passed several tents and huddled groups of merchants along the street outside the city walls but I did not stop until I was much deeper in the wilderness. Only then, did I finally discard the soiled cloak.

I walked amid the hills and followed the descent of the crescent moon to the west. Eventually, the eastern horizon began to redden and I put this new light to my back as I walked. When I looked back, after nearly an hour of walking, *Ra' Sahay* could no longer be seen.

My journey would be a difficult one without food or water. The desert's maw would be wet with hunger upon seeing my pitiful form enter its realm.

The wind whipped at my hair as I walked away from the dawn, hoping to find those I had lost and vowing to one day retrieve my dagger.

## X X I I - House of Cedar

After the first half day of walking through sand covered hills, I collapsed under the first palm grove I came across and slept in its shade. My dreams were blood-filled and erratic. Having planned to only sleep an hour or two before continuing my journey, I was surprised when I woke up under another crescent moon. Angrily, I got to my feet and began stumbling westward through the dark wilderness again. After the curved moon above had traveled halfway across the sky, I realized that I no longer felt my steps through the sand, nor did I feel the movement of my legs or my swinging arms. I woke again – not knowing I had fallen unconscious – and found myself at the base of a sand dune. It was still night and in the distance I heard the cries of desert jackals. Thinking back to Gaius's corpse and how fervently the jackals descended upon it, I tried to rise but fell back to the sand once I had risen to my knees.

Sprawled out on the ground, I stared at the silver bracelet gleaming on my wrist. Another animal bayed at the dark sky from somewhere in the hills nearby. Little more than fodder for beasts, I lay still on my side as I watched the silver of my bracelet fade with my consciousness.

\*\*\*

The lone beast circled the dune several times before eagerly jaunting towards me. Its breathing was heavy, guttural, as if the animal was incensed. As it neared, the breathing grew louder. It was almost upon me though my mind focused inward.

Pushing thoughts of Gaius's rent body away, I remembered something else from a few days before our ill-fated night hunt. *Thief... You are damned to Hell for this.* The Jew's condemning words, from so long ago it seemed, suddenly came to me. This would be a suitable hell, I mused: starving in the eastern wilderness, parched and exhausted, before being eaten alive by jackals.

The beast was suddenly on top of me and I flailed my weak arms at it. It yelped once but dove in towards me again, licking my face and beating my legs with its wagging tail. In the dim light of an approaching dawn, I regarded my attacker; though ugly, it was not the demon-faced animal I had expected.

"Mathias," I murmured. The hound mewled and attempted to shove his wet nose under my arm. His gaunt, speckled body was ghostly in the starlight, and as he curled against me his skeletal tail wagged furiously in the sand.

\*\*\*

It is a dangerous thing, no doubt, to trust a desert straggler in your home.

The family was kind – a Jewish couple with several young children just old enough to start chores. Their parents made me rest on a bedroll and gave me small amounts of fresh water and food until my body could handle more. Two days I stayed with them, resting on the floor.

Their home was quaint – little more a hut consisting of two main rooms: one for sleeping and grooming, the other for storage and cooking. My bedding was in the storage area. Everything seemed dusty in the house, and the kids were continually charged to brush the floors and walls with a pair of wicker brooms. This was a common practice for those living on the outskirts of a desert.

For two days, Mathias and I had followed the muddy Jabbok River, sleeping in the shade of its leafy banks during the day while traveling at night. Fresh camel tracks appeared and disappeared several times along its banks and I hoped they were Jamal and Jael's. The brown water from the river helped my thirst, but my lack of food drove sharp pains into my stomach and made my head cloudy as I walked. My last night of walking had been a full blur and I had only the vague recollection of collapsing at a wooden door as the morning light rose from the horizon. In and out of consciousness, I had seen a woman standing over me, hand raised to her mouth in uncertainty and fear.

For two days, I partook of their charity. It was nice watching the children – Ira, Rizpah and Sarah – play with Mathias. Their father, Levi, who walked with a noticeable limp, spent much time working outside, while the mother stayed in the house mostly making new tunics and clothing for her family. Her name was Mirza and I learned from Levi that they were of the Dan tribe of the Gilead region. Mirza sang in soft Hebrew as she hemmed her fabrics. Working at her bench, she would offer me the occasional glance of mistrust. For some reason, the children were also frightened of me and glared at me from their numerous hiding spots in the home.

Despite their fear of me, the children were at once taken with

213

Mathias. They played with him outside, throwing sticks and bones for the animal to fetch. Levi did not mind, but did warn the children to keep the mutt away from his caged fowl.

During my first night with them, I could hear the gales of wind whistle through the palms of the nearby oasis.

*** 

On that first evening with the family, as Levi stored my sword behind a line of clay pitchers in the rear of the home, he limped over to my bed and asked in Aramaic, "When did you acquire this?" The lamp light flickered over his bearded features. The rest of his family was already asleep.

Lying on the bedroll, half awake, I said, "Nearly a week ago. It belonged to a... friend of mine. He is dead."

"I'm sorry," Levi said softly.

"So am I."

Levi continued to stare at me for a few minutes and I drifted into slumber. I awoke later and he was still staring at me, his brow creased in thought. "Forgive my ceaseless questions," he said. "But do you know where you are, my friend?"

"Near Amathus?" I answered weakly.

Levi nodded. "Yes, we are just east of Amathus, along the Jabbok's south bank." He continued to stare at me for a silent minute then asked, "Do you know what the symbols on your blade mean?"

"I do not speak good Hebrew. Hardly any at all, really."

"'House of Cedar', it says. Was this man a warrior?"

"A village chief. But he died a warrior's death, I suppose. What does 'House of Cedar' mean?" In my own readings of the scriptures during captivity, I had surely read of this parallel, but my mind was still too tired to search its memories.

"Long ago," Levi began, "our great ancestor David – king of Israel – spoke openly to the Lord through the prophet Nathan. David, in all his passion, wanted desperately to build a 'house of cedar' for God. A great temple. Instead, God said to David, '*The Lord declares to you that the Lord himself will establish a house for you: when your days are over and you rest with your fathers, I will raise up your offspring to succeed you, who will establish his kingdom. He is the one who will build a house for my Name, and I will establish the throne of his kingdom forever*'." Levi smiled and continued, "In God's own perfect wisdom, He elected David's son Solomon to build His temple for Him, though David had wanted the job. Your chief friend, an insightful man, was acknowledging God's perfect will. The house of cedar. We may have our heart set on something – perhaps even something great – but the Lord may want us for another chore. The 'house of cedar' represents our acceptance and obedience to God's perfect will. Let this sword's message guide you, brother."

I closed my eyes and thought of Aaron. This was certainly something he would have dwelled upon: the will of God. My own mind drifted.

Later, I opened my eyes and found that the lamp had burned out and Levi was gone.

***

On my last morning at their abode, I woke late to find the whole family outside, working with their bird cages and cleaning the goat troughs. The children helped grudgingly then played in the mud with Mathias and the other hound near the home's fence. As I watched from the doorway, Levi limped towards one of the cages with a bowl of tar

215

sealant. He gave me a single nod and started smearing the tar along the top of the cage. The fowl inside fluttered and cried at him. When the children saw that I was finally on my feet, they ran to their mother and pointed at me. She whispered to them and they ran to the rear of the house, out of my line of sight with the dogs trailing happily.

I walked around their home to stretch my fatigued muscles. Mirza had left a small pitcher of water and bowl of soup for me on their eating bench, and I quickly consumed both.

After retrieving my sword from behind the pitchers, I lay back down and thought of Jael and Nahum, wondering if Jamal had succeeded in getting them past the Jordan. They had left *Ra' Sahay* nearly four days ago. It was possible they were even in Jerusalem by now, that is, unless Rapha-Ayzal had tracked them westbound and had already crossed paths with them somewhere in the wilderness.

With a shake of my head, I tried to rid myself of such thoughts. As I lay there, I traced my fingers along the Hebrew etchings on the sword's flat, thinking about my own objectives and wondering if the God of the Jews even existed.

Levi entered the home and sat across from me on one of the chairs in the room. He had black tar and mud on his hands which he tried to wipe off with a piece of pale cloth. His feet were bare and equally dirty.

"The radiance of hard work," he said with a smile, holding his soiled hands up. "Feel better, Dismas?"

"When did I tell you my name?" I asked.

"When you first arrived at our door... two evenings ago. You were nearly unconscious but you answered some of our questions. You kept talking about a girl, too. One with golden eyes, I think. We cleaned you and tried to make you comfortable, and we prayed for your health. It seems that our gracious God has answered those prayers."

I nodded and said, "You and your family have my thanks, Levi. If you had not taken me in I surely would have died." If he had known, I thought, what I had done to others who had blessed me with such hospitality he would certainly have let me die at his doorpost. So many times, I had used that generosity to my own sinister gain.

"We did not have much time to talk last night," he said. "You were in and out of sleep – a good thing, for you badly needed rest. Where are you from?"

"I have no home," I answered. "I have been a wanderer for many years, but I was born in Hispania. I am actually a freedman – a former slave from Sychar."

Levi nodded and continued to stare at me. His face held something resembling uncertainty and amusement.

"Why do you stare at me like that?" I asked.

After a long sigh, Levi said, "Do you remember our talk last night about your friend's sword?" He nodded to the blade in my arms, which I was still cradling like an infant.

I nodded.

He smiled. "There is something I want to show you, friend. It may help to explain my look." Levi stood and walked to one of the shelves that lined the room. From a small, ornate box, he withdrew a cloth bundle. He sat back down across from me and looked at the white package in his hands for several seconds in silence. He then nodded to himself and handed me the bundle. "Look inside," he said with a warm smile as if the bundle contained some sort of grand treasure that he was most proud of.

The bundle smelled grainy and I felt something round inside. When I unfolded the cloth, I found a piece of bread, little more than palm-sized and still soft. It smelled freshly baked. "Bread?" I asked in puzzlement, smelling its fresh aroma.

Levi nodded again. "It is simply bread, friend. But so much more. This bread has been stored in this cloth for over a month.

This did not make sense. I sat up from the bedding and looked at the cloth as if it held some magical faculty of preservation. The white cloth looked ordinary enough.

Levi gave a chuckle. "No, the wonder is not in the cloth, but in the bread itself. I acquired it last month in a small town called Bethsaida, during one of my travels west along the Galilean countryside. My cousin and I deal in fowl and tempt our fate to the northern markets this time of year. There, in the hills with many others – thousands even – we were audience to the great teacher, a wondrous man, who spoke to us the whole day. His *words*..." Levi looked away. His eyes were blurry as if he were holding back tears. "His words were of the greatest wisdom, friend. From the *highest* order. We could all feel it."

I rolled the bread in my hand, staring at it. "What about the bread?"

Levi wiped his eyes and continued, "The day had grown long and no one had eaten; the man's words were that powerful. Nobody had even noticed the hour and no one wanted to leave. In those hills, we were too far from the markets and only a handful had any sort of food – just a few pieces of bread and fish. There were, however, thousands to be fed, not even counting the families of the men present. The great teacher took the bread and fish, gave thanks as he looked heavenward, and had his followers pass out pieces." Levi sighed blissfully. "Everyone ate and was satisfied. *Everyone.* There were even several basketfuls left over somehow. Never, my friend, had bread tasted so good – so fresh. I kept this piece, here, so that I could remember this miracle."

The twinkle remained in Levi's eyes as he spoke. He looked from the bread to my face. "I also remember the man's words, and this is why I look at you in such a way, Dismas. I look at you in this way because I forgive you for your transgressions. I only hope you can forgive me mine; the sins of the tongue can stab harder than blows from one's fists. My anger is no longer harbored and I replace it with love - as the teacher instructed on that day."

I did not understand his words. What sin had he committed against me? What transgressions of mine did he speak of? Had I wronged him in the last two days in my tired delirium? I stated this confusion to him and his eyes only grew brighter and his grin wider.

"It can be a precarious thing," he said quietly, "to let a stranger into your home, yet I will always do so if one knocks. May you leave here with strength enough to finish your journey. Remember our words, though." He took the bread from me and tore it in half. He looked at both pieces longingly as if they were gold or silver. "Yours for the journey," he said and handed one to me. "For strength of body and soul. Eat or pass it along, that others may benefit from this spirituous bread."

I looked at the broken piece, which, surprisingly, seemed nearly as large as the original piece, though it may have just been a trick of the home's dim light. The bread's aroma smelled good, as if it had just been baked – an odd occurrence, no doubt. Perhaps Levi was a magician of sorts – an expert of tricks of the eye, with quick fingers and a quick tongue. No, I thought as I smelled the bread and felt its soft texture. No trick. Something curious was at work here and it wasn't mere trickery. Could this teacher he spoke of so reverently be the same rabbi that Aaron and Jael had talked about?

As I continued to feel the bread, it began to slowly harden in my fingers – first the outer shell, then the exposed pith. Suddenly ashamed for an unknown reason, I quickly placed the bread within my shepherd's bag and gave an edgy smile. "Once again," I said, "You have my thanks, Levi. For the bread as well as the hospitality."

Levi nodded and stood. "My wife has prepared two water-skins for your journey and a bag of cheeses." He pointed at the table in the front room and I caught a glimpse of a gold ring on his thumb that had been forged to look like braided rope. "Whenever you are ready, friend. Stay longer or resume your journey. Either way, may you find God in your travels." He touched his forehead with his right hand and limped out of the room. He paused at the doorpost and looked back. Above his slightly crooked nose, his eyes were still bright. "Do not forget about David's house of cedar," he said quietly and left me.

***

The realization hit me like an arrow from Apollo's strong bow, actually snatching the breath from me like a well-aimed lung-shot.

Before the recognition, as I stopped on a hill just outside the small fence around Levi's property – Mathias' new tether in hand – I looked back at the family toiling at the rear of their home. Levi was hard at work dragging a series of empty cages away from the home. His wife Mirza glanced up at me and I sensed the relief in her face from nearly a hundred paces away. The children seemed happier, too, now that I was leaving. The young ones danced around the yard, holding hands as they sang.

At my side, Mathias stared at the cavorting children and let a low whine escape his throat.

"Sorry, boy," I said as I stared back at the family. "You belong to someone else."

Just before I had turned to leave, Levi glanced up at me from the yard and it was then that an awful – and somewhat incredible – realization hit me. From a far away memory, Levi's voice said, *"Thief... You are damned to Hell for this."* After I had ruined his knee and broken his nose, he had looked up at me with a mud streaked face and proclaimed this.

This is why he limped, I thought with shame – why his nose was crooked and his family was terrified of me. They could have drug me back into the wilderness to die or turned me in to the next band of outriders they saw along the road. Levi had shown mercy to me when I had given him none on that cruel evening nearly two months ago. And inexplicably, Levi had wanted *my* forgiveness for his words to me during that encounter.

My free hand found its way to the bag slung over my shoulder and I felt past the small cubes of cheese that Mirza had prepared for me, and past the full water-skin, to the piece of bread Levi had given me. It was soft again.

I looked back to the family and I saw Levi wave to me before turning back to finish his work. With a shaky hand, I waved back though he did not see it. I then took off at a brisk pace westward, dragging Mathias with me. My heart was newly filled with a strange concoction of shame and awe. In the distance, the smoke trails of the Amathus Village could be seen rising in the air over the oasis, and beyond that, the Jordan River and my uncertain providence.

## XXIII - *Bearings in Jericho*

From the fork of the Jabbok, I followed the string of villages and merchant camps along the Jordan River as I walked south. The wilderness was hilly and there was a great deal of lush vegetation along the river banks. Near Alexandrium, many traveling families had erected tents along the river and children swam in the cool muddy water. The youths taunted each other in Aramaic and wrestled in the mud. Mathias struggled to break free of the leash, baying at the children as if he, too, wanted to frolic in the water. Their splashing and laughter reminded me of my own childhood with Tarius – the good times before the race and my exile.

Now, nearly eight years later, I wondered what path Tarius was traversing. On my only trip to Sychar since leaving – after learning of my mother's death from a Samaritan servant on a family errand in Bethel four years ago – I was told by an infirm Mesick that Tarius had set off with a group of young scribes from Tiberias to seek erudition in the port cities of the Great Sea before sailing west to greater Rome. Though I had not seen my old friend in many years, I still wished him well and hoped his dreams had come true. I also hoped that he was nothing like his father. *Our* father, I thought with a grimace.

223

At nightfall, once I reached the city of Archelais – midway between the Jabbok River and Jericho – I stopped and slept in an alleyway between two houses within the city walls. In the morning, after tying Mathias' leash to an ancient tree stump behind a fish merchant's hut, I stole food for myself and the hound. Mirza's bag of cheeses had long since been devoured, though I had refrained from eating the lone piece of bread which I kept cradled at the bottom of my shepherd's bag.

After our pilfered meal of fish and peppered snails, we continued our journey south, but banked west away from the Jordan towards Jericho. In my travels with Obadiah's band, we had frequented Jericho many times and I hoped to find word on their whereabouts.

***

Though I was raised in a Greek family, the Jewish lore of the city of Jericho had reached my ears in Sychar. In my captivity in Gilead, I had learned even more from the Jewish scriptures, which according to the Jews was not fictional lore but the remnants of actual historical records. Supposedly, Joshua – son of Nun, aide of Moses the Deliverer – was ordained by the Jewish God to conquer Jericho for the Israelite people. Joshua sent two spies into Jericho, which was inhabited by the pagan Canaanites, and the men were harbored secretly by a prostitute named Rahab. This woman was later spared as Joshua and his forces marched around the city, blowing their trumpets mightily which made the walls of Jericho collapse. The Israelites then slaughtered all of the Canaanites, young and old alike, sparing only Rahab and her family. The city was plundered and burnt to ash; only the toppled stone of the walls remained.

The scriptures declared that as Joshua stood over the smoking

224

ruins of the besieged city, he pronounced a solemn oath: *"Cursed before the Lord is the man who undertakes to rebuild this city, Jericho - At the cost of his firstborn son will he lay its foundations; at the cost of his youngest will he set up its gates."*

As fortune and greed would have it, Jericho was rebuilt five hundred years later, by the order of the Israelite king Ahab. In this last century, however, when Herod the Great expanded his reign and stocks, he deemed Jericho capital of the kingdom in the unfavorable seasons. The newly fashioned city was heavily fortified and three lavish palaces were built to overshadow the ancient traditions.

It was unknown to me if either Ahab or Herod lost their firstborn sons.

*** 

That afternoon in Jericho was a sun-filled one. I passed through the city gates, rebuilt with large stone columns with a wide base, and shuffled past several gatherings of people who were in an argument over a matter of grain. The color of Jericho was welcomed after being prisoner to the drab eastern wilderness for so long. Rising out of the dusty streets, many of the merchants and city folk had colorful cloaks, sashes, brightly dyed banners and headdresses. Green vinery grew over many of the brick homes, giving even the stones a taste of ornament.

For several hours I wandered the city streets, stealing this and that, developing a respectable sum of coinage and jewelry. My swift hands served me well. My shepherd's bag was growing full and I began selling my stolen sashes and perfumes for more coinage. In exchange for two small baked lamps, a metalworker sharpened my sword's blade. A young woman washed and trimmed my hair for the cost of an ornate cedar box with Jewish scripture burned into its lid.

For the price of a stolen pair of leather cattle whips, the same woman outfitted me with a new tunic and washed my old one while I waited. The woman's younger siblings even bathed Mathias for no extra charge and the hound paid them with contented laps from his tongue.

By mid-afternoon I felt like a new man; I was groomed, clean and not entirely poor.

After my spree of thieving and bartering, I ducked into a familiar fabric shop and allowed my eyes to adjust to the dim cache of rolled textiles and heaps of satin. The store smelled of fresh linen and faded perfumes.

"No hound in here!" a woman's scraggly voice yelled. "Get it *out*!"

I drew Mathias' leash closer to me and squinted into the darkness. The woman was large, middle-aged, and standing near an inner doorway which was blocked by a vibrant red linen door cover. She had a bundle of colorful poplin in her wrinkled arms and her face held a grimace.

"He is fine, woman," I said to her. "I'm just looking for Joab-Seth. You needn't-"

"Get it out!" she repeated hastily and started towards me. "Woe to you if you do not get that hound out of here!" She raised her linens as if she made to smother me with them.

I sighed and pulled Mathias back outside. The sun was still high and I squinted as I searched the bustling streets. "You there!" I called out to a long haired boy carrying a jug of water on his head. He turned carefully and regarded me. After haggling with the boy to watch my hound for the price of five lepton pennies, I stopped to peruse the merchandise of a street-side vender who sold waxed vials of dye. I slipped one of the darker, wire-tied vials into my tunic and quickly held up another vial to the merchant, asking the price. Then feigning disinterest, I replaced the second vial on his wooden spindle and told him it was overpriced. He cursed my back as I left.

Once back in the fabric shop, I raised my empty hands to the thickset woman to show that the hound was outside. She jerked a fat thumb towards the red door covering and I walked past her. As I moved through the doorway I thought of my countless hours of staring at the camel skin door covering of my cell quarters in Gilead. With a shudder, I pushed past the red fabric and into the musty darkness of the back room.

Joab-Seth, a haughty merchant who claimed he was a direct descendent of King David's high priest Zadok, stood at a hanging wicker cage with his back to the doorway. He was surrounded by piles of white linens and other fine textiles.

"I did wonder," he remarked without turning around, "what sort of fool would be arguing with my lovely Abigail." He turned and regarded me sullenly. A quivering sparrow was cupped in his hands. "I now see."

His beard had more gray in it than when I last saw him and I considered asking him if he still wore blocked sandals to enhance his height. Instead, I said, "How have you been, old friend?"

He frowned and sat on a bench at the linen table, still holding the chirping bird. "I am Obadiah's friend, young man, but I've always considered those in his accompaniment fools fit for Herod's theater. Or Jerusalem's Skull, perhaps." In one deft movement, he wrenched the bird's head off and threw it into a basket next to the table. The sparrow's body continued to vibrate in tune with its slowing heart.

Ignoring his insults, I asked, "Have you seen Obadiah in recent days?"

"Perhaps he was here," he said with a grin. "Perhaps he was not. Perhaps I tell you he was here when he wasn't or give you directions to a place I know he is not."

With a sigh, I pulled the vial of dye from my tunic. Wordlessly, I untied the wire and loosened the waxed opening.

"What is that?" Joab-Seth asked, his smile wavering.

I reached my arm out and held the vial over the white linens on the table before me and started to tip the container.

"Wait!" he croaked, dropping the headless bird to the table as he raised his hands. "He was here! Obadiah was here and I know where he's headed."

I held the vial still as the dye nearly tipped out and said, "Speak fast, Joab. You don't have enough time to fashion some sort of lie and I want to see the truth in your eyes."

"Two weeks ago," Joab gasped. He cupped his hands beneath the vial, ready to catch the dye. "He was here two weeks ago just after Purim's feast in the month of *Adar*. He was short-handed if I recall."

I let a single drop of the dye fall to his hands and he flinched but was able to catch the drop. "Where was he headed?" I hissed. "Quickly, Joab!" I started to move the dial over other pale linens on the table.

"Obadiah said he had a contact that was up north," Joab sputtered as his hands followed beneath the moving vial. "One of the coastal cities near the Galilean Sea. This riotous man, Barnacle or Barnabas…"

"Barabbas," I said.

"Yes, he has some information for Obadiah about some sort of deft arrangement in Jerusalem." He flinched as I allowed another drop to fall to his cupped hands. "It is the truth, I swear it!"

Joab's pained face did appear truthful. Obadiah was trying to follow through with his arrangement with Barabbas, which the Gentile rebel had been scheming at for over a year. "Why are they meeting him in Galilee?" I asked. "I thought he hailed from Judea?"

"Yes, but he is at one of the prisons up there."

I shook my head and muttered, "The fool." I had never met Barabbas, but I had heard of his exploits. He had even been kicked out of the newer rebel *Sicarii* group for being too zealous – a feat nearly impossible for the seditious faction was filled with no small number of lunatics.

"Who was with Obadiah?"

"Young Titus. That tall, egg-headed man... Cicero or Syrum... And the large one, Jaximo... ah, I cannot remember all of your fellow buffoons' names. That is all, I think. Obadiah would not tell me what happened to the others."

I tipped the vial back up and lowered it to my side. Joab cursed at his stained hands and bent down to retrieve a discolored cleaning rag from the basket. As he wiped the dye from his hands, he said, "I would not have lied to you, Dismo. I swear it. You thieves are fools to mistrust everyone."

Ignoring his mispronouncing of my name, I said, "You have never been truthful to us, and you only tell half truths to Obadiah. I didn't want to spend weeks or months traveling in the wrong direction only for your impish amusement."

Joab had always been spiteful towards Obadiah's band, treating only Obadiah himself with respect – be it a small measure. They had met decades ago, in Laish, near Mount Hermon in Phoenicia. Joab-Seth enjoyed the company of "those who dwell in the shadows" and he favored Obadiah's stories, but favored his own jests towards our band most of all. The man had always vexed me.

I turned from him and started to refasten the tie on the vial's lid. "My thanks, Joab. I'm glad your overpriced linens are still spotless."

He looked up from cleaning his pudgy hands and glared at me. "They're the nicest materials east of the Great Sea, thief," he said.

"Is there nothing else Obadiah told you?"

. Joab raised a dye stained finger and said, "He also said the strange man – the ugly one with the silly throwing darts – had fallen ill from infection and would remain at Eli's inn for the season."

"Where is this inn?"

"On the west side of town, near Elkanah's Gate." He glared at me and said, "Too bad it wasn't you dying of infection."

"One last question and you'll be rid of me, Joab," I said as I finished refastening the vial's lid. "Do you know of a half-Arab named Jamal? He is a very round man and he may have entered town from the east with a woman and young boy a few days ago. They would have been on camels."

Joab smirked at me and shook his head. "I do not keep records of every poor traveler who enters Jericho. Check the inns." He looked down at my belt. "How did you acquire that ugly Hebrew sword? You must have stolen it, I wager."

"I do not always steal my possessions, Joab."

"I have no faith in that, Dismo. For as your brand suggests… you are *unfaithful*." After this last comment, he gave a curt laugh and leaned back on his bench.

I stood there in silence for a moment, fingering the vial of dye in my hand. Joab's scornful smile remained until I unfastened the vial once more. "You, Joab," I said with my own smile, "are a stain... just like the rags you sell." In an arc, I swung the vial from right to left, flinging its black contests over the bulk of his precious textiles – and into his stricken face.

He squealed like a wounded pig and cried, "The Skull *will* find you, thief! And I will be there to watch you squirm on the crossbeams!"

When I exited the back room, Joab's wife stared at me in wide-eyed horror and I gave her a malicious wink. Joab continued to scream from the back room as he examined his ruined linens and this sound faded as I quickly ducked out of his shop and into the afternoon sun to retrieve my hound.

## XXIV - *Ferryman's Toll*

**Eli**'s Inn was the most repugnant and dustiest of the three lodges in Jericho. It was a large structure with cluttered stables at each of its sagging ends. The oaken beams along the building's walls appeared rotted and eager to collapse while several colorful rugs had been nailed to the higher trestles to cover the more spurious patches of the building's decay. The inn had two levels and I saw movement on top of the roof just over the thin parapets – a fluttering of cloth and tent flaps. Usually, this meant the inn was so full that even the roof space had been rented out. The wind had gathered itself for the evening and I truly feared for the structure's stability and its indwellers.

A large man was carefully lighting two lamps that hung on either side of the inn's front door. When he saw me near, he called out, "Peace be with you, traveler, but we are full. Try west, near the Dumah pool. Perhaps they have room."

"I'm looking for someone inside," I said as I drew Mathias close to me. "A dear cousin."

"I am Simon," the man said with a slight bow. "Son of Eli. I can aid you, perhaps. Who is it that you seek?" Simon was a large man, bearded and thick in the waist. A short sword was strapped to his

232

belt and aside his immense frame it looked like more of a dagger.

"May we speak inside?" I asked him.

He looked me over fully, an uncertain glimmer in his eyes, but he nodded and led me inside the entryway. He made no fuss about Mathias, so I drug the hound in with us.

The entryway to the inn was dark and anything but lavish. Debris had piled in the corners and my sandals made noticeable tracks in the dust. The inn smelled very musty and dank, but the overseers had allowed a great deal of incense to burn in the hallways, masking the odors only partially. Above the entryway beams, several Jewish names had been etched into the wood. Many were crossed out and I wondered if they were the family titles of previous owners.

Simon stopped under a hanging lamp at the mouth of a hallway and nodded for me to speak.

"I'm looking for a sick man," I said quietly. "He would have been dropped off here a week or two ago."

Simon rolled his tongue in his mouth and said, "We have several sick men here. But I believe you are talking about the burned man."

I grimaced as I remembered the heat of the oil lamp bursting upon Charon, and the smell of his scorched hair as he passed by me in the wagon.

"That would be him," I said slowly. "Is he still here?"

Simon nodded. "He is not doing well. I'm no physician, but I believe the fever has spread to his mind. A gray-haired man paid me silver and an armful of linens to tend to him for a few days, or until... he passes on to our father Abraham's bosom. By his look, though, I do not think I will see him there when I pass on."

"Lead me to him, please."

On the second floor, after climbing a very dark, narrow staircase, Simon led me to a corner room and moved the door covering for me to enter. He took hold of my arm as I began to duck inside the room and Mathias gave a protective growl. Simon glanced at the hound, let go of my arm, and whispered, "The money has ran out for this room, good friend, and there are many travelers looking for lodging."

"What are you asking of me?"

"See me after you're though," he said quickly and fled down the stairwell.

The room was small, windowless, and a dusty oil lamp burned next to a frayed bedroll. Charon lay on his back, small beady eyes motionless, staring at the doorway. His hair was gone and his scalp was red and yellow from unhealed burns. Along the right side of his face, a white cloth had been affixed, but the linen was now yellowed from his seeping wounds. Now, more than ever, he looked like the Charon of myth, the skull-faced ferryman of the River Styx. I was amazed he had lasted this long, suffering for nearly two months in agony.

Under the soiled blanket which half covered him, I saw a subtle movement and knew his fingers were wrapped around one of his iron throwing darts. In truth, I do not think he even had the strength to lift one of the darts, let alone throw one. While the fire had taken much of his skin, it had not taken his keenness.

"Charon," I said gently. "It is Dismas. Can you hear me, brother?"

Charon managed to whisper, "*Gergesa.*"

It seemed he was trying to tell me where the others were. His voice had always been grating, but now it sounded like that of one who had been gurgling iron scraps and molten tar. Mathias, who usually jaunted immediately to strangers, remained still, groveling in the room's corner.

"*Dismas,*" Charon sputtered. Though I had moved next to his bedroll, his beady eyes remained fixed on the doorway.

"Yes, Charon. What can I do to help you?"

"*No toll... for the ferryman.*"

I nodded and knelt next to him. There was a terrible mixture of odors coming from him, so I breathed through my mouth as I stared at him. "You will have a toll, Charon-Festus," I said. "The others left for Gergesa?"

"*Yes.*" The word was little more than a hiss. "*The prison... named for the grave in Gergesa. Sheol. They will be there at Jesse's home... waiting to free the lunatic.*" His whitish, scarred eyelids closed and he hissed once again, "*No toll... They will dump me in the alley...*"

"I will take care of your toll, brother. Just rest."

He was silent then and his breathing slowed until I could not see the sheet over him rise and fall for his next breath. When I thought his spirit had left him, he gathered another breath and whispered, "*He will be so happy you're alive... Dismas.*"

Charon breathed no more.

***

Back outside, evening had fully descended on Jericho and I found Simon in one of the stables. He was dragging one of the large oxen yokes out of the stall. Evidently, Eli's son thought he might earn more money by renting out his father's cluttered stables.

"Hold a minute, friend," he grunted to me as he drug the thick yoke in the dirt behind the livery. "We need to get this done before the Sabbath tomorrow."

Mathias continued to whine, even after he was freed from the dusty inn, so I untied his leash and allowed him to roam around the courtyard.

Simon released the yoke, rubbed the sweat from his brow and turned to me. "Is your friend to leave soon?" he asked expectantly.

"He's dead," I said.

Simon's face was suddenly stricken. "You need to take care of him quickly, friend," he said. "My condolences as you grieve, but we cannot have a dead man in that room."

"What would you charge to bury him? I don't want him dumped in the hills or in an alley."

Simon looked to the inn as he considered this and answered, "The price of a week's stay."

My eyebrows rose at the price. I probably had close to that amount in my shepherd's bag but the fee seemed steep for a couple hours of work. "I would imagine," I told him, "that if I just left then it would get done without me paying a single *lepton*."

Simon's eyes narrowed and his stance adjusted the smallest fraction in defense. "*I* would imagine that your, and your late friend's, dealings in Jericho have not been of the legal sort. Perhaps I need to alert the soldiers to make sure there is nothing amiss in all of this. There is usually a garrison passing by here at this time."

I glanced to his short sword. Simon's hand had come to rest on the weapon's hilt. "The price of one night's stay," I said sternly. "That is all I have."

With a grunt, Simon slung the flails over his shoulder and began to drag a brushwood harrow from the stable. Over the grinding sound, he said loudly, "One night's pay and I keep his belt and throwing irons to trade. For that, I'll have my two nephews move the body now and have it buried in the hills by midnight. The cemetery will cost you more though for they'll require a formal notice."

I agreed to the hills and whistled for Mathias to return to me. After fishing out Simon's money from my bag, I handed it to him and quietly said, "If I gave you two leptons, could your nephews be trusted to put them over his eyes as they bury him?"

He looked up from counting the coinage with incensed eyes. "We will not be collaborators in a pagan burial," he said austerely.

I sighed and left Simon standing in the darkness of the stable and led Mathias into the growing shadows of Jericho.

## X X V - *Prayer Room*


**It** pained me to walk north into the windy night, away from Jerusalem. Having just traveled from the north, I felt as if I were walking in circles and chasing at shadows. Part of me wanted to simply walk the five hours south to Jerusalem and see if I could locate the House of Rannut – to find Jael and Nahum and see if they were safe – while the other part of me yearned to be back with my band and to continue with the risky plan for our final catch. This plan would lead me back to Jerusalem shortly, so I hoped to accomplish both in the coming days.

I walked for half the night then slept huddled next to Mathias under a tree near the small town of Archelais. When the sun rose, I walked into the town and stole a meal for both myself and the hound. The next two days were spent walking north along the lush Jordan River. North of where the Jordan fed into the Jabbok, massive amounts of greenery had sprung up along the river's banks and generous shade trees and palms shielded us from the sun as we traveled. We passed many groups of fisherman toiling in the waters with sodden flax nets. The area's economy was dictated by the fishing market and certain sections of water were leased or bid to hired fishermen or fishing families who knew no other trade.

It was late afternoon, near the tenth hour of my third day of walking, when I finally saw the Sea of Galilee. The Tiberias Sea, as the Romans called it, lay deep in an immense valley that was lush with trees and greenery. The Jordan River met the sea near the city of Philoteria. Gergesa was another few hours away along the sea's eastern coast. Philoteria was a small port town, a hub city that served as a way station for the many fisherman, traders and boat-makers. While small, the city gave me a grand view of the sea, which sparkled brightly under the late afternoon sun in a seemingly endless array of light-filled ripples and waves that stretched towards a horizon filled with more green hills. Dozens of boats could be seen on the water as the fishermen toiled at their craft.

I neared the shoreline which lapped onto the beach in small brown waves. I paid one of the locals a stolen denarius to sail me north to Gergesa. The man, a Gentile named Felix, talked ceaselessly about the miracle-working rabbi who had recently traveled among the port cities of Galilee. I ignored much of this man's rambling as I stared at the sea's beautiful vista. Evening came over the water quickly and the gently lapping water was peaceful despite Felix's incessant talk of rumors such as the rabbi calming a great storm or pulling demons from the possessed.

I turned from the water and looked at Felix. "Did this man also make bread and fish multiply?" I asked, thinking about what Levi had told me.

With an energetic nod, Felix said, "Yes, yes! Sadly, I was not in Bethsaida when it happened but my cousins were. It truly happened. They saw it with their own eyes!"

I thought of the piece of bread in my bag.  Grand trickery, I thought with a smile.  Cleverness of mouth and sleight of hand.  This man who everyone spoke of was apparently a skilled master at this.  Though I'm sure Felix had said it a dozen or more times in the last hour, I asked, "What is this man's name?"

He was exasperated that I had not been listening to him but Felix smiled at me.  "Jesus," he said as he beamed.  "His name is Jesus."

Felix shared my silence for a few seconds.  I then asked, "Tell me, Felix... do you think this Jesus can multiply silver as well?"  I grinned at him.

He frowned at my joke, but said, "He is the Christ.  He can do all things."

Still smiling, I shook my head and turned back to the beautiful sunset before me.

***

The sun had dipped down to the sea's western bank when we finally arrived at Gergesa's ports.   The wind had picked up considerably, making our final half hour's journey slightly tumultuous.  Trying not to vomit over my shaky legs, I led a trembling Mathias from the boat after paying Felix his sum.  Gergesa was too small to deny the man his fee – his uproar would wake the whole town – and as I placed the coin in his palm I took comfort in the thought that it had been stolen and that I would surely steal more.

The trees and long flute-like ferns rustled in the wind as I walked along the shoreline.  As the sound of lapping waves slowly faded along with my queasiness, I passed through the city gates behind a number of fishermen who were retiring for the night.  The city was dark, but dozens of lamp lights speckled its interior. As I walked, I heard scattered din issuing from the homes: arguments, children crying, the mewling of chained animals. Numerous tendrils of gray smoke drifted from the open ceilings of the homes and were seized by the wind. Accompanying this smoke, I smelled the pleasant aroma of cooking meat and hearth wood. Mathias whined in hunger at my heels.

After a half hour of searching, I found the home I was looking for wedged between two crumbling apartments in the east end of the city. There was no stone marking or family etching upon the wood lintel and my search was based solely on memory from nearly four years ago, as Obadiah had taken us to Gergesa to see an old friend of his for word of his family. Jesse and his sons were accustomed to making a trip to Damascus several times a year, while Obadiah refused to journey back to the city of his youth.

After four solid raps on the worn door, a young man answered and peered at me from the lamp-lit entry. "Peace, friend," he said hesitantly, searching my face. He was no more than fourteen years of age and had a wispy beard at his chin.

"Friend," I said warmly, "I am Dismas, nephew to Obadiah of Damascus. I am a friend of your father, Jesse. Is he here and is he well?"

The young man regarded me for a moment then his eyes seemed to open a little wider with recognition. "Diz?"

I nodded. "Yes. Caleb, is it? Jesse's youngest steed. You've grown taller than I almost, boy."

Caleb stepped aside and said, "Yes, come in, friend. It has been a few years, hasn't it? Come in, please."

Jesse's home was warm and well lit with hanging bowl lamps

and a smoldering brazier in the center of the main room. This small fire was surrounded by goat-hair carpets and colorful rugs. Several sleeping mats had been rolled up neatly and were stacked inside one of the carved storage niches in one of the walls behind a wooden table and bench. They were burning animal dung and the smell was mild but grew stronger as I neared the fire.

One of Caleb's older brothers was in the corner of the room and he nodded to me as he continued to hang sheaves of drying raisins and aromatic herbs from one of the support beams near the side wall.

"Father," Caleb called into the darkness of the home's rear hallway. "You have a visitor."

Jesse came out from the hall and his bronzed face lit up merrily when he saw me. "Ah, young Dismas!" he exclaimed and moved forward to embrace me. "Returned from the grave and spared death's sting!" He was a tall, lanky man with a gray beard and strong sinewy forearms. His hair was wildish as was his manner. Jesse was quick to love, slow to hate and always dwelt in the highest of spirits. He had no business being kind to thieves, I thought as he embraced me with the strength of someone half his age. His eyes held the vigor of a child.

"You look somehow younger," I said to him with a grin. "Surely, Miriam has been fixing heathen potions for you to drink to stay so young."

Jesse gave me a weak punch to the shoulder with his wrinkled fist. "Ah, you've found my secret, my boy. Perhaps you should try some of her brew, for your face seems almost as old as mine now. You've had a hard journey, no? You look... wizened but still strong." He gripped my head and turned it, pretending to examine me like a battlefield surgeon. "Yes, a definite change in your eyes, even. Your face is sharper while your eyes are softer. But softer is a good thing, no doubt." He gave a quick bark of a laugh, and then grew serious. "Like our good scripture says, '*Though you have made me see troubles, many and bitter, you will restore my life again-*'

"'*From the depths of the earth you will again bring me up,*'" I finished for him, thinking back to my compulsory studies of the Jewish scriptures.

His grip on my neck slackened in surprise. "That's right," he said slowly. "I am glad you are restored, Dismas. And I am glad your eyes are softer." He released me and looked at Mathias, who had been waiting patiently behind me. Obviously sensing a kind man, the hound started to briskly wag his tail.

"You've brought me another friend, Diz," Jesse said as he bent down and took the dog's head in both his hands. He rubbed the animal's ears vigorously.

"This is Mathias," I said. "My compatriot and guide."

Jesse laughed and Mathias gave a pleasured whine from the massage.

"Jesse," I said, as I lowered my shepherd's bag to the floor. "I do not mean to intrude on your night, and I know it is rather late, but I've-"

"You search for Obadiah," he said before I could finish. He released the hound and stood.

"Have you seen him, Jesse? I was hoping they were still here."

Jesse gripped my shoulder. "They were here, but have left already. My heartiness may have driven them away, it seems. They stayed for one night only. We talked about the prison I deliver food to and about a particularly foul prisoner we call Barby. Why Obadiah would associate with one like him is a mystery to me."

My heart sunk. "When, Jesse? When did they leave?"

His face continued to shine while my insides seemed to unravel. "Do not concern yourself with this right now," he said, making a dismissive gesture with a wrinkled hand. "Why don't you go to the roof and fetch me a jar of oil." He pushed me towards the hall. "Just through there – you know where you're going – up the stairs and against the west parapet. I'll make you a fine meal and we'll talk more then. Miriam is with her sister in Bethsaida, so it is to your delight that I'll be fixing dinner tonight. Baked desert hound. Ha!" He turned back to Mathias and said, "Just a jest, my four-legged friend. But I will have a fine stew brewing when you get back down, Dismas."

With forlorn thoughts and shuffling steps, I made my way to the hall and turned right into a dark passage that led to a series of rickety steps. The wind howled in the darkness above and I could barely make out the curve of the steps as they fanned out onto the home's tar-sealed roof. Halfway up the stairs, I stopped and put my head against the cool mud brick and let the draft wash across me like a cleansing fountain. I was sick of walking, tired of the last week of journeying and searching. After a moment's deliberation on what my new course should be to find my band, I pulled away from the wall, rubbed the stubble of my face, and continued up the stairs.

I emerged at one corner of the tar-covered roof, near a parapet wall, and immediately heard nearby whispering intermingled with the night wind. To my left, I saw Jesse's upper prayer room – its latticed windows were illuminated with lamplight. Shadows twisted inside the room. Dust from the neighboring rooftops stung my eyes, and I raised a hand to block my face as I continued to stare at the prayer room.

Someone was in there, I realized. The wind abated for a moment and I was able to hear distinct voices... in Greek. They sounded rough yet jovial.

In one slow, silent movement, I drew my sword and walked to the open doorway of this upper room. The voices continued, not knowing they were not alone on the roof.

Suddenly, I understood why Jesse had asked me to go to the roof to fetch him a vessel of oil. So typical of Jesse, I thought. He was infamous for his good-natured pranks and jests.

After taking a deep breath of dust-filled air, I opened the prayer room's thin door and found myself bathed in yellow lamplight. The talking stopped, though the flickering shadows continued to dance on the inner walls of the room. Five faces stared at me, each with their own unique emotion. One was of awe, two were of befuddlement, one was of thanksgiving, and one held intense anger. All shared a portion of great surprise.

## X X V I - *No Embellishment*

Silence reigned for a number of seconds. It was Titus who finally spoke; he was still pock-marked and rotund, with warm eyes that were wider at that moment than I had ever seen them before.

"*Diz...*" It was a light whisper that seemed to blend with the breeze outside. My old friend uttered my name like it was the title of one of his favored Greek gods. His mouth then hung open slightly as he stared at me. His was the look of awe. *Adelphos* in life. *Adelphos* in death.

The one who looked somewhat befuddled was Cyrus. His thin lips moved slowly, speaking my name in silence, as if he was not entirely sure what was transpiring. The thoughts moved slowly in his smallish bald head.

Behind Cyrus, a stranger – a new addition to the band – shared his look of confusion. He was a small man with a thick curly beard and receding mop of dark reddish hair. His eyes trailed from my face to the drawn sword in my hand.

Jaximo's look was of anger, but also of disappointment. Like his manner, his eyes were still black and cold under his curly hair. His great heaps of muscle gave a spasm as he sat on the floor glaring at me.

Seeing my sword, his thick hand slowly moved from his belt and he produced a curved dagger in one large hand.

I suddenly remembered the night of the terrible storm again… Jamimo bellowing like an ox and hacking away at the man under him. That man, I thought, was Nahum's father.

The last face – the one of thanksgiving – stared up at me with eyes that seemed suddenly off balance. While always wise and in control, Obadiah seemed astonished and wordless. Above his silver beard, his eyes were wide.

"*Protos*," I said to him, trusting my voice little. The sword nearly fell from my hand as I felt suddenly staggered with relief.

"Young scion," Obadiah said in a soft tone. Without taking his eyes away from me, he slowly stood and walked towards me. He stopped in front of me and looked me up and down – from sandaled feet to sun-darkened face. "You're *alive*," he whispered. His eyes still held the intense look of thanksgiving. I knew this was no act, but a true sentiment and the knowledge made my eyes suddenly burn.

"Barely," I said, and dropped the sword when he suddenly embraced me.

\*\*\*

There was a series of awkward greetings in the prayer room after the initial flurry of emotion. During this, Jaximo remained sitting with the newcomer, Rufus, who I learned was a thieving poet from the north lands. They had acquired him recently near Tyre, half-drowned in the Litani River after a botched robbery attempt. Obadiah was at once taken with Rufus' musings and verses, and the red-headed thief was quickly absorbed by the rest of the band.

"A fabled hero returns to his family," Rufus told me with a

slight bow that revealed a growing patch of hairless scalp. The little man had a small, ornate box tied around his neck; it swung under his left arm like a traveler's bag. "Your tales marvel those of Hercules, bold Dismas. Danger, bravery, and a pinch of recklessness – a fine recipe for the heartiest saga."

"Perhaps," I told him, "but you may find yourself disappointed with the truth."

He beamed. "Then *embellish*, friend. The key to all good poetry. Embellishment: a subtle act that has helped forge nearly every good work whether Herculean or not." Rufus tucked his strange tethered box behind him with an impish grin.

The prayer room was filled with the stink of wine and sweat. Two empty wineskins lay strewn on the brown tiled floor of the room. Obadiah suddenly produced a third one, full and nearly bursting. "Scion," he said, gripping my shoulder. "Let us walk a bit."

Titus slapped me on the back as I passed by him. "Don't get captured again, Diz," he said with a smile. I winced at this joke but stated I would try my best to honor his request.

Outside, the breeze continued to whimper through the city streets. Obadiah gripped my arm as we walked towards the parapet to stare out over Gergesa. A dark shape suddenly burst from the stairwell and huffed over to my side.

"Mathias," I told Obadiah. "He is part of my story."

"You have much to tell me," Obadiah said. "And hopefully with none of Rufus' embellishment. Let us escape down the rear ladder and walk the shoreline. I have a feeling there will be little sleep tonight, though there is much to accomplish tomorrow."

After pushing Mathias back down the stairs to Jesse's quarters,

248

we descended the wooden ladder carefully and wove our way through the dark city streets towards the docks.

"Mercius is dead," I told him as we walked.

Obadiah gently squeezed my arm. "I figured. Thought the same of you."

We stopped at one of the smaller docks and sat on the wooden bench at its side. The Sea of Galilee was a flat scintillating disk that seemed to disappear into the night's darkness. The wind had died down a little, and the sound of calm, lapping waves against the shadowy beach was welcomed. Reflections of the brighter stars dotted and wavered on the water's black surface.

We passed the wineskin back and forth for a few moments in silence. There was so much to tell him that I did not know where to begin. After several long swallows of wine, I took a deep breath and began with what happened after my capture. I told him about my forty days in captivity and about Aaron's reserved mercy. I told him about Jael and Nahum, and then about the attack on their village by the raiders. He became rigid when I described the leader of the marauders.

"Lazya," he said darkly.

"Yes," I answered. "He calls himself Rapha-Ayzal now."

"A very backwards man, always." Obadiah was silent for a moment then said, "He is truly possessed, you know. Not simply a mind disease, but *infested* with demons. I've believed this for years."

I nodded, thinking of Ayzal's hollow eyes. "He remembers you, *Protos*."

"I'm sure he does. One does not forget a… wound such as his." Obadiah reached up and touched his chin carefully as he delved into his own memories.

249

"He'll be in Jerusalem," I told him. "He wants to cause all sorts of chaos in Judea. But he'll also be looking for you."

Obadiah took a long swallow of the wine then said, "Let him come."

I finished my story, telling him of *Ra' Sahay*, our escape with Jamal and the loss of my prized dagger. His dark mood was momentarily broken when I told him about my encounter with Joab-Seth. Charon's death did not surprise him, but Obadiah was grateful I had paid to have him buried.

"When our journey leads us to Jerusalem," I said. "I will find her uncle's house and see if Jamal was able to get them there safely. The hound belongs with them."

"That hound," Obadiah said, "is an ugly one. But from your tone I take it the girl is beautiful."

I nodded. "Very."

He gave a gruff laugh. "All this time I was torturing myself thinking of you being executed... and you were just busy falling in love with one of your captors!"

"I'm not in love," I said sharply, taking the wineskin from his hands. "I just..."

"Don't fret, young scion," Obadiah said, still smiling. "With all the hate in your life, you would do well to have a little love in it. A Jewish captor, though?"

He laughed again and I hoped the shadows made it impossible for him to see my face turn a deep crimson.

\*\*\*

Obadiah and I walked back to Jesse's home after the wineskin was empty. I stopped near the dark mouth of an alleyway and looked at him. *"Protos,"* I said carefully but firmly, "I have journeyed long and far to find you, but I do not see a place for myself in this band if Jaximo remains in it. He is a reckless menace and I truly believe he will slit my throat as soon as I shut my eyes for sleep."

"You have always vexed each other," Obadiah answered. "Let us not forget your own reckless nature."

I nodded. "But he kills people for no good reason... bringing more attention to us than is needed. How many more people has he sent to the grave since the oasis?"

Obadiah's eyes narrowed as he stared at me. "You *have* changed," he said. His eyes peered into mine, searching thoroughly.

With a sigh, I looked away from him and said, "I just see no reason for more death. And I value my own life above anything, which Jax will certainly try to steal from me."

"When did you start caring about those you've hurt – crippled, even – and for nothing greater than a couple of pieces of silver or maybe a woven tunic that caught your eye?"

Still looking away, I suddenly thought of Levi's wet face, fraught with pain, staring up at me into the rain.

*Damned to Hell for this...*

And there had been many others I had hurt in such a way – even worse than Levi.

I moved the hair from my eyes and said, "I would not say I am fully changed, but I only think of that line you spoke of when we were in the oasis. Do you remember?"

Obadiah slung the empty wineskin over his shoulder by its goatskin tie and said, "I have not forgotten." He turned to me and gripped both of my shoulders. "I want no part of someone who behaves in a manner like my brother, but I leave Jaximo up to you. You may get rid of him as you like. In truth – to answer your question – he has grown even worse since that night. But he knows of our plan... our *eschatos kleros*. If he was simply banished, he could ruin the whole thing for us."

"He'll kill everyone in the homes, *Protos*. Entire families. We'll be hunted more vigorously than any criminals before us and we will never find rest if he does that. Does he know which homes in Jerusalem are planned for the *kleros*?"

"*I* don't even know the names. Which brings me to our plan for tomorrow." He leaned closer as his voice grew even quieter. "When Jesse works at the prison the locals call *Sheol*, he meets with our contact Barabbas through a wooden door. They call him Barby in the prison. He has been there for a few months now, but he still refuses to give Jesse any information about the *kleros*." Obadiah frowned. "Stubborn man, he is. He knows that information is like gold. Regardless, he is being transported by boat to Magdala tomorrow – at noon. He and several other prisoners. Barabbas is to be tried for riotous crimes in Magdala, as he started some sort of tax rebellion last season. Most likely, he will be executed. His coveted information will follow him to the grave."

Obadiah paused for a moment, rubbing his hands together before continuing, "In payment for his hospitality, Jesse has given me a letter to deliver to our shared friend Blind Abner in Caesarea. After we release Barby, we'll be making a fast trip to the Great Sea before Jerusalem."

He turned from me and stared into the shadows of the dark city. "Jesse told me that this has been a strange time for Gergesa," he said.

"There was a man here a couple of months ago, a teacher from Nazareth, who preformed magic just outside of town. Foolish tales, all of them, but they are to our advantage in getting Barabbas out of prison."

"I've heard of this man," I said. "Do you think there is any truth to these yarns?"

Obadiah shrugged. "Probably just a lunatic stretching out his neck for Rome's sword."

"Regardless, you mean to free Barabbas tomorrow at noon?" I asked.

"In a matter of speaking."

"How many Roman guards will be escorting the prisoners? Surely a good number."

Obadiah's grin returned. "That is where our new brother Rufus enters this discussion."

My eye brows arched. "Rufus? The little poet?"

Obadiah nodded and whispered, "Like this rabbi that everyone speaks of, our new friend Rufus also knows magic."

# XXVII - *Sorcerer's Box*

In the cloudless light of the early morning, Rufus' silver-rimmed box seemed to twinkle as if it had been forged from a piece of the moon.  From the rib bone of a god, Titus announced as he regarded the box.  Or perhaps, he had mused, the ornament had been chiseled from the sky god Jupiter's *Fulgur Divom* stone... seared by lightning and godly radiance.

"Wrong, all of you," Rufus said, letting the box swing from its leather cord around his neck.  The small man made a show of standing still while the box swung back and forth across his chest, in a nearly hypnotic way.  He was careful not to step on the diagram that had been drawn in the dust of the prayer room's floor at his feet.  There were ocean-smoothed rocks strategically placed throughout the diagram to show the guards and the prisoners' paths through the western part of the city near the docks.

"Then where is it from?" Titus asked him.

"I acquired both the box and its contents near the Rhine River," Rufus said, "at the empire's northern border.  They were given to me as a gift from a sorcerer in the darkest forests of the northlands after I saved a young boy's life in their village.  The whelp fell through some ice on the river and I pulled him out – only to discover that he was the son of this enchanted forest inhabitant. This sorcerer bade me to enter his underground home and taught me some of his strange arts – just a fraction, but enough. He then gave me this box to hold the magic substances that bring forth a wondrous yet horrible power."

Cyrus sucked in air and said, "That's amazing." He seemed truly taken with the poet's words.

Titus said, "That's camel dung."

With a look of pain, Rufus declared otherwise, "You'll see, Cretan. Just wait until noon."

Obadiah smiled and said, "As long as you can make the guards *think* it's magic, it doesn't matter if it's real or not."

Jesse poked his head into the tent and smiled at us. "Greeting, my leprous friends," he declared. "I leave you now to your fates. To *Sheol* I go – to Gergesa's prison – to feed the needy and impoverished. May God be with you and may He bless your plan, which is sure to fail." He then threw a great heap of manure-stained cloaks into our midst.

We all cursed him in unison but his smile never faded. He then knelt by Obadiah and handed him a small rolled manuscript, bound tightly with a leather braid. Our leader slipped this letter into his own bag and gripped Jesse's wrist, whispering something that I could not fully hear, but I knew the letter was for their old friend Blind Abner in Caesarea.

"Why do you call us lepers?" Cyrus asked Jesse, his nose wrinkling from the stench of the vile garments.

My palms began to tingle in anticipation as Obadiah explained.

*** 

255

The noon sun became hot and the sky cloudless as our plan began. Titus and I stood behind a seaside net merchant's building, which was along the city's western path which led to the piers. The shop was open in the front and its back storage yard was cluttered with worn boats and heaps of wood and iron. The eastern path was no longer crowded as it had been that morning, when the fisherman and traders had untied their boats from the docks and descended upon the sea in great masses, filling the horizon with yellowed sails. The shoreline was also filled with people casting nets in the waist deep water, aiming for schools of smaller fish.

"This is insane," Titus whispered to me as we stood in the shadow of one of the trees behind the net merchant's shop. Our dirty leper cloaks lay piled at our feet, the sullied aroma wafting upwards to our noses. Next to the cloaks lay four separate vials of powder – two of blue and two of red: magic from Rufus' much-disputed box.

I rubbed my palms together and said, "Unquestionably insane."

"Then why are we here? I can't believe that *Protos* trusts in Rufus – in his silly little magic box that will probably get us killed or crucified." He pointed to the vials. "We didn't even get a chance to test this muck. Magic dust? I've never heard of anything so stupid."

"What happened to your great optimism, Titus? Things have changed since I was captured."

Titus hesitated for a moment then quietly said, "In Phoenix, my brothers told me to never trust a redhead. Too much blood in their heads from drinking it. You think there's any truth to that, Diz?"

"Probably," I answered and winked to him before turning away to watch the road.

This plan of ours *was* rather daunting, I thought. In my travels I had seen sickly looking magicians – self-proclaimed "sorcerers" – doing magic tricks in city streets and parlors. They could seemingly make coins disappear, reappear and do the same with live doves and pull endless colored rope out of their mouths. Some could swallow swords and eat fire. Silly tricks, all of them, and certainly not interesting enough to make several armed Roman guards run away in fear.

From across the road, I heard three quick, birdlike chirps – the signal that the prisoners were in view.

I peered out from behind the rear wall of the shop and saw a train of men walking down the west trail. Four soldiers and double that in ragged prisoners. The hands of the criminals were bound in front of them with chains. The soldiers did not have their plate armor on – probably because of the heat – but the plumes of their tall helmets still stood up straight as if demanding respect. Two of the soldiers marched in front of the prisoners while the other two marched behind.

Even from a distance, it was obvious who our contact was amid the shabby group of criminals. Though I had never met Barabbas, I had heard stories of his wild eyes, expressive face and untamed hair. He was wiry, with veins sticking out of his skin like a multitude of reeds trapped under a thin fabric. His face was red like a beet, with eyes wide and staring down the path as his glance darted every which way but forward. His hair was a mess and had been spiked upwards as if it were an iron battle helmet.

I turned back to Titus and asked, "Are you ready?" He nodded weakly and I draped one of the rank cloaks over my shoulders and head. I gagged as the odor hit me like a harlot's ring-fingered slap. After composing myself, I picked up two of the vials, one red and one blue. Magic dust, I thought. Rufus had explained how to use the powder and had austerely declared its infallibility, but I had known Rufus for less than twelve hours and he had yet to prove his own infallibility.

"I can't believe we're doing this," Titus whispered, picking up the other cloak and remaining two vials. With a grunt, he heaved the cloak around his body and immediately made a choking noise. Jesse had outdone himself with the soiling of the cloaks.

The sound of clinking chains and sandaled footfalls reached us and then one of the soldiers cried out, "Lepers! Get out of here! Back away from us or feel our swords!"

Titus and I looked out from behind the shop and saw that three cloaked forms were already shambling towards the group of men. One was too tall for the cloak; Cyrus' feet and ankles were fully visible under the dirty fabric. His partners, Obadiah and Rufus, moaned for coinage as they neared the front soldiers. Jaximo, much too large to be seen as a wasted leper, was waiting near docks as he readied a stolen boat for our escape. Mathias was tied to the dock behind him and our bags and possessions were hidden in the shrubbery near his tether.

"Here we go," I said and pulled Titus out from the shadows, and we began a shambling gait towards the soldiers and prisoners. Titus and I moaned loudly as we neared the guards, which had already begun pushing Obadiah and Cyrus away with their scabbards.

One of the guards drew his sword and pointed it at me as he shakily ordered us away. These men did not fear battle or any sort of warfare, but contracting leprosy was a shared fear by all of them. Such a disease meant definite banishment, humiliation and a lonely death.

The locals on the road had since moved as far from this

escalating scene as they could, yet still watched from doorways and transoms.

Within the folds of my dark cloak, I opened one of the vials with sweaty fingers and applied the powder to my right hand. Within the horrid stench of my cloak, I thought I smelled incense. The contents of the second vial went on my left hand, just as Rufus had instructed. This stuff was clumpy and smelled somewhat like smoke.

The procession of men had halted and the soldiers all withdrew towards the back of the group in attempt to push the prisoners on through the lepers. As he had been told to do so by Jesse, Barabbas took up the challenge and stepped among us, chained hands held high over his head, a crazed gleam in his eyes. "Peace, friends!" he shouted over our moans, silencing us. "What is it you need?"

"Cleansing!" Rufus shouted. "We want the messiah to make us clean!"

The soldiers began ordering us to disperse again, but Barabbas shouted all the louder, "I can make you clean! I am the messiah! Come to me." His eyes were wide and the whites had long since yellowed from ill diet. The prisoner smiled and suddenly his wrists were free from their bonds. How he had accomplished this was a mystery to me, and I could only imagine that Jesse had somehow given him the necessary tools in his cell to loosen his shackles. The guards shouted and moved forward, but Barabbas had already embraced Titus and started to chant wildly. Within his tunic, Titus' was hopefully rubbing his hands together quickly – mixing the "magic dust" given to us by Rufus.

One of the braver guards stepped towards Barabbas with arms outstretched to apprehend the freed prisoner and declared, "That is *enough!*"

The melee started with a sudden crackling noise, followed by a very real scream by Titus. It looked as if a storm of fireflies suddenly buzzed and snapped out of his cloak; small twirling lights whirled out from his sleeves and around his face. The guard fell backwards, tripped over his own feet and pitched himself away from the screaming cloaked form.

Only Barabbas remained calm, raising his hands yet again, announcing to all, "You are now clean, my child!" The lights crackled and hissed around his extended arms.

The other prisoners screamed and toppled over each other, trying to get away from the spectacle before them. My feigned moans had stopped and I saw that Obadiah and Cyrus were still as well, transfixed by the unbelievable sight. Rufus moved towards the crazed prisoner, yelling, "Make me clean, Lord! Cleanse me, too!"

Barabbas moved from Titus who was spinning in circles trying to rid himself of the fading and crackling lights. The prisoner placed his hands on Rufus' cloaked head and began his wild chant. Suddenly, the same flurry of spinning lights and smoke unfurled out from Rufus' cloak. The red-haired poet threw back the rags over his face, showing clean skin and bright eyes. One of the soldiers dropped their sword, its steel ringing on the stony path. The other guards were silent but all were moving backwards in fear. The remaining prisoners scrabbled on their knees away from us.

"I am clean!" Rufus declared, repeating it over and over again.

Obadiah looked to me and I nodded. We both neared Barabbas, rubbing our hands together in unison as he raised his arms towards us. It was as if the tingling of anticipation in my palms rose to a greater level with a sudden new warmth in my cloak. The light burst from my hood in three separate streams, rising upwards towards the overhanging trees. It was frightening, but I stood standing, moaning in apprehension. The light manifested into sparking whiffs of smoke, twirling around us like flickering spirit-forms, unable to fully enter our physical world. Though it was only an odd chemical reaction of the powders, it was still a startling effect.

When the lights suddenly faded away and the bizarre warmth was gone from my hands, I removed the hood of my cloak and knelt in front of Barabbas with a clean face. Obadiah and Titus were already kneeling in front of the wild-haired prisoner. Cyrus' tall form fled towards the docks in unfeigned terror.

The soldiers were dumb-founded with a combination of awe and horror, and the other prisoners cowered beneath them. Some even held onto the guards' legs as if they were hairy, life-saving pillars.

Among our group, only Rufus remained standing as he touched his clean face. "*Bonus Eventus,*" he called out, "By Castor and Pollux and their merciful twins the Alci – I am clean!" He was thanking the Germanic gods of the north but was paying no such homage to Barabbas, which signaled the final part of our plan.

Barabbas grew suddenly angry. "You refuse to thank *me*, foul transgressor?" he asked Rufus who looked to the prisoner in phony contrition. "You will now witness my darker powers for your lack of thanksgiving." He waved his hands over Rufus and began a new chant of intense utterances.

Rufus began to scream as he started to spin in circles. Smoke suddenly started to billow from his hood and sleeves. He screamed louder and suddenly the cloak was aflame. Barabbas cackled like one possessed. I was forced to roll away from Rufus' spinning, flaming body as he ran wildly around us, screaming hideously.

Over the wails, Barabbas shouted, "See what happens to those who dishonor me!" His veined arms were open wide as if he could cause the whole city to suddenly catch fire.

Fully engulfed in flames, Rufus shuffled towards the tremulous soldiers and slowly removed his hood. To my great and true surprise, the poet's face was aflame, and his screams were of torturous agony. He spit up a long, streaming geyser of blue liquid flame which landed near the guards and crackled wetly on the stone path. They stumbled backwards over the groveling prisoners as the blazing specter neared them. Any semblance of duty was forgotten. Finally finding their feet, the soldiers ran back up the stone path into the city. The prisoners either followed or ran in their own directions away from the street.

Rufus continued screaming until the guards hastily made the turn through the city gates and were out of sight. Several wayfarers stared at us from a distance, holding their chests as if they might faint. The burning figure turned to me and I saw Rufus give an exaggerated wink through the coiling flames. He then pulled the fiery cloak over his head, extinguishing the flames in one expert move. His face was waxen and dripping with some sort of oily moisture. Rufus rubbed his slightly singed beard and giggled. Barabbas gave a hyena-like howl and immediately knelt down in front of the poet, bowing in mock homage to him.

"Spared by Neptune's seawater," Rufus declared, gripping Barabbas' arms to pull him up. "But let Mercury give us the speed to run, friends!" And the wild pair took off running west along the path towards the docks.

With a grunt, I flung the dirty cloak away from me and followed them. My mind was still trying to comprehend what I had just witnessed. Several locals jumped away from us as we neared them. Some cursed us while others still held shocked faces of trepidation. It was hard not to laugh at their sundry faces as we ran, but Barabbas did so with several mocking gestures.

At the docks, Jaximo was trying to make Cyrus stop screaming in true fear. The large thief had pulled a stolen fishing boat to the nearest dock and stood next to it as he repeatedly slapped Cyrus in hopes of shutting him up.

After grabbing our bags from the bush, Obadiah untied Mathias and hopped into the boat with the hound. "Let's make haste," he said, "for the horse-hairs will surely return once their heads clear and they realize what just happened. Outriders will be hunting us along the entire coastline."

The rest of us waded into the water to help shove the boat past the shallows. We pushed aside tall brown reeds which jutted from the water like spears.

Some of the fisherman by the piers, started shouting at us to halt. We quickened our pace alongside the boat. Jaximo moved to the boat's rear, pushing it with both hands on either side of the rudder. His broad back trembled and flexed with the effort.

My next action – planned since the early morning hours, though not discussed with the rest of the band – required no hesitation and a very sure hand. Slowly drawing my sword – the House of Cedar – as we trudged through the muddy water, I moved towards Jaximo's exposed back, towards his rippling muscles as he pushed. It would be beneficial to have a scapegoat, I thought in justification, to take the fall for us when the Romans began their foreseeable hunt.

When I was finally a sword swing away, the burly thief seemed to sense my malicious intent and he started to turn from the boat as his hand reached into his tunic for his knife. His forethought was impressive though not fast enough. I swung the flat of my sword's blade at his head as hard as I could. The sound of steel against his skull rang out over the water and Jaximo stumbled in the water but did not fall. Amazingly, and in a daze, he started to rise, his hand lifting with the curved knife. "Dismas!" Titus yelled at me in confusion. "What…"

I jumped upwards and swung the pommel of my sword down upon Jaximo's brow, and the large thief finally splashed noisily into the water unconscious.

I turned back to the boat. The other thieves were staring at me in horror, while Obadiah barked orders at them to leave things be and get in the boat. I sheathed my sword and pulled myself over the wooden transom as Obadiah readied the sail. Turning back to the water, I held out my hand to help Titus into the boat. He looked at me in disgust, ignored my hand, and pulled himself in.

"And I thought I was finicky," Barabbas said with an uneasy grin as he lay in the middle of the boat breathing heavily.

Ignoring him, I looked back to the shallows as the wind caught our sail and we started moving with speed into the deeper water. Several onlookers were wading towards Jaximo's floating body. They pulled his face from the water and began pulling him to the shore.

"He could be dead, Diz," Titus said between breaths. "What possessed you?"

Without looking at him, I thought of Nahum's sad eyes and

264

said, "Him or me, Titus."

The sail grew taut with the afternoon breeze and we chased the eastern horizon as the shouts of angry Galilean locals faded into silence and memory.

## XXVIII - *Blind Abner*

Two hours later, we ran aground between Magdala and Tiberias. Knowing that Roman soldiers were surely on the water in pursuit – probably no more than an hour behind us – we immediately began traveling southwest through the forest. We skirted around the Galil mountains and continued our journey through green valleys and rocky hills. We avoided the larger city of Nazareth, but camped for the night in an open tomb that was probably being readied for a burial upon the morning.

Before dawn, we continued southwest through the Plain of Esdraelon. Staying off of the main roads as much as possible, we passed by Capercotnei and twice saw Roman outrider legions pounding the roads from atop their steeds. Whether or not they had been informed about the incident in Gergesa or if they simply were on normal patrol was a mystery. We camped once more in the plains near Caesarea. Our plan was to enter the city the following afternoon, stay with Blind Abner for a night and then trek south to Jerusalem to begin our plan in earnest.

The next day, our feet found a paved Roman road and we

finally saw a dark sliver of scintillating black across the western horizon: the Great Sea. The water stretched forever it seemed, and I had been told that the sea actually stretched west into the heavens. The buildings of Caesarea Maritima rose from the shoreline like ramparts. Our group split up into pairs and merged with other caravans and traveling merchants who were also nearing the city. Obadiah and I moved from the others and tried to strike up conversations with the strangers that would help serve as our unwitting partners into the city.

The seaside *horrea* warehouses were plentiful along the coastline near the city's vast docking harbor, but the great temple, theaters and hippodrome stood out highest among the columned buildings; each were dedicated by Herod to Augustus Caesar. Throughout the great city, Herod proclaimed his ability to govern the peoples as well as nature. His artificial harbor, breakwaters and spring-promoted aqueduct gave Caesarea the innate benefits it did not possess before Herod's construction efforts.

If the construction along the shoreline could be thought of as ingenious, the city itself could be thought of as elegant. Marbled columns and walls. Streets of mosaic floors. Frescoed walls lined with molded plaster. Caesarea was a chunk of finer Rome in its eastern lands. Every dock and anchoring point along the coast was committed to a different Greek god so that the large trading city might flourish forever – carried by the wings of the divinities.

We continued towards the city gates, passing by colorful sectioned fields of wheat, fruits and every sort of vegetable which could thrive in the briny air.

Our grouping of a dozen random travelers was stopped by four spear-toting soldiers at the east gate. When they started letting people in after a brief assessment, Obadiah declared to them that we were nothing more sinister than scribes sent to deliver a family message to one of the city's inhabitants. They glared at our dirty tunics and speckled hound but allowed us through the gates.

* * *

We regrouped behind the tent of a hollering street merchant. Rufus explained how the soldiers thought they recognized Barabbas from his wild hair, but the rebel had feigned confusion by speaking only Old Hebrew – most of which he made up as gibberish.

"Your cursed hair," Obadiah declared, giving Barabbas a tired look. "Perhaps you could mat it down a bit with water or something."

The wild eyed criminal winked at Obadiah and said, "The deadliest of weapons, though, my friends." He then lowered his spike-tipped head and rushed at Titus who pushed him away with a curse.

The lanky tent merchant squinted at us and called out in Latin, "If you don't plan on buying one of the finest tents along the Great Sea, then at least pay me for my shade. A lepton each, I think."

"I think there is better shade to be had," Obadiah told him. He then motioned for us to follow him into the crowded street.

A half hour later, Obadiah found a string of wealthy homes in the more Jewish part of the city and bade us to wait in the shade of a small covered pool between two marble tiled wells. He told us to wash our faces and clean ourselves from the journey before he walked to the large oaken door of one of these homes.

After cleansing ourselves in the cool water, we reclined in the shade and waited. After a few moments, Obadiah returned and told us to mind our tongues and follow him.

Like Joab-Seth of Jericho, Blind Abner was an old friend of

Obadiah's from Damascus, though certainly more hospitable. Protos had explained to me how in his younger days, Abner had been a great spiritual rebel in the city, challenging the Pharisees and the elected Jewish council. It was this spiritually mutinous behavior that caused Abner's blindness. The more zealous teachers of the Law detained Abner one evening after he insulted a visiting Pharisee from Jerusalem and blinded him with burning ash.

After this torture, Abner left with his young wife Rachel and traveled south to Caesarea, where he continued to teach. His children grew and eventually became very wealthy in the shipping business. The family acquired an expansive home in Caesarea – ironically the former house of a Jewish Pharisee.

Obadiah had told me that Abner, though blind, saw much and was very wise.

We walked across the street to the home and a plump servant nodded to us as we entered the wide, arched doorway of the vestibule and walked into the courtyard. A woman about sixty years of age strode to Obadiah and bowed before him with a beautiful smile that shone brightly through her smoke-thin veil, which she deftly removed from her face as she rose.

"It is I who should bow to you, Rachel," Obadiah said, taking her hand and gripping it lightly. "The lady of the house."

Rachel shook her head, but continued to offer her buoyant smile. "Nonsense," she said in a cultured voice which bore little accent of her Damascene descent. "I only hope Abner returns from Bethany before nightfall, that he might visit with his old friend. Perhaps you could stay for *Pesach.*" Her smile faltered some when she regarded his soiled clothing.

269

"We've been traveling hard for three days," Obadiah informed her. "It seemed we could only find shelter in the mud and it shames me to have you see us in such a fashion."

"Nonsense yet again," Rachel said and motioned the portly servant to her side. "Philo, fetch clean tunics for our guests, every size and color, cloaks too, and have Tabitha ready dinner."

"Just one night, good woman," Obadiah told her and squeezed her hand again. "We've journeyed from Jesse's in Gergesa and he gave me a letter for Abner. You'll have to suffer the fusses of Passover without me."

"Is Jesse well? I'm sure he still acts as if he's a tenth his true age."

Obadiah nodded and said, "He's still as wily as ever." He then introduced each of us to Rachel and we in turn offered our gratitude for her hospitality. Barabbas remained cordially silent and for this, we were thankful.

After our greetings, we fully bathed in private in the family's bathing pool just behind the walled garden. To Obadiah's dismay, Barabbas was careful not to submerge his barbed hair to the scented waters.

According to Rachel, her husband Abner had journeyed with his oldest son to Bethany two weeks ago to see a sick friend. Abner was supposed to return at sundown on this night, so our timing was fortunate.

After we bathed, Rachel's servant Philo gave us new tunics and took our old ones to wash. We then reclined on cushions in the courtyard's upper balcony and watched the colorful sunset over the vast expanse of the Great Sea as we drank wine from glazed cups. Rachel served us a fine dinner of cooked fish – a reddish meat under the striking blue scales – complimented with several kinds of fruit, simmering snails and fresh bread. Before we dined, I tied Mathias to one of the courtyard's small pistachio trees and gave him a bowl of water and a portion of meat which he turned on excitedly as if it were still alive.

Smelling the freshly baked bread made me think of the strange piece of bread Levi had given me near the Jabbok River. If I plucked it from my bag now, I wondered, would it be soft or hard? I neglected to find out and told myself it was because I did not believe in real sorcery – though it was actually because I feared finding it hard as stone.

After dinner, we continued to drink wine and watch the sun meld into the folds of the ocean. Philo, his wife and another servant named Tabitha lit numerous lamps around the courtyard for our benefit and struck up the patio's central hearth pit.

When the sun was hardly more than a sliver over the horizon, and after Rachel informed us that she was going to turn in for the night, a shout filled the air and someone pounded on the courtyard doors.

Our band was instantly on our feet. The splendidly aged wine and beautiful vista were quickly forgotten as we contemplated an escape from the soldiers we were sure had tracked us to Abner's home.

"Husband!" Rachel cried out with glee as Philo unlocked the door's cedar latch and let two men into the courtyard. We relaxed but remained standing at the balcony as we watched the reunion before us. One of the men was older, with a speckled gray beard and short hair. The other – clearly Abner's son – was clean shaven and grinning wildly; the tears in his eyes gleamed in the lamplight. There were also tears in the older man's eyes as he looked at his wife.

Rachel suddenly fell on the ground at Abner's feet, weeping and unable to talk. Philo staggered against the door in shock, holding a plump hand to his mouth.

Next to me, Obadiah sagged against the balcony's iron parapet. I was about to ask him what was happening but remained silent when I saw how white his knuckles were on the railing. I turned back to the courtyard before us and when I saw Abner reach down to pick his wife up from the ground I suddenly understood what had happened. My own knees were suddenly weak.

Abner was seeing his younger children and servants for the first time. He was also seeing his wife for the first time in over thirty years.

Abner was *seeing*.

The man of the house cried out in happiness, pulled his wife to her feet and embraced her with a furious passion that sent a shiver of emotion through me. Caught up in their joy, I gripped Obadiah's shoulder and asked, "How is this possible?" Part of me already knew the answer.

From the courtyard, Abner turned from his trembling wife and looked up at us, his smile still wide. He waved to Obadiah and then led Rachel carefully to the landscaped garden.

"That teacher," Obadiah whispered to me.

"What teacher?" Titus said, still not understanding what had transpired in the courtyard.

"The miracle-worker," our leader said softly. "The teacher from Nazareth has healed him."

I looked back over the balcony and gave a sigh. "Jesus," I said slowly. "The man's name is Jesus."

The sound of joyous weeping carried upwards from the garden

and Obadiah looked towards the Great Sea which had fully swallowed the sun. "Jesus," he said softly. We then waited to greet his friend Blind Abner who was no longer blind.

## XXIX - *Do You Believe*

For the better part of an hour, Abner remained downstairs with his family and servants, telling them of what happened in Bethany and trying to quell his wife's confusion with no short amount of embraces. Our band stayed on the balcony and we were mostly silent, trying to become recaptured by the city's beautiful nightscape before us. Every one of us, however, yearned to hear of Abner's tale, but we understood his need to first be with his family.

Eventually, Abner parted with them and bounded up the balcony stairs to greet us with a large pitcher of wine in his hands sloshing its dark liquid over its rim to the wood below as he moved. He handed the pitcher to a confused Barabbas and embraced Obadiah with a loud kiss to his cheek. "My brother!" he exclaimed, newly healed eyes still red from crying. "So long it has been. Even longer since I've seen your face. Who would have thought we would each have so much silver in our beards, ha! Rachel was kind enough not to tell me of this." He rubbed his chin and chuckled.

Obadiah was quiet and seemingly unsure of what to say. He simply held his old friend's arms and nodded.

"You want to hear of Bethany, no?" Abner said with a widening smile. "You *need* to hear of it."

Our leader cleared his throat and said, "It might help a mite, good friend. Be slow in speech, though, for just seeing your clear eyes is hard to digest."

Abner nodded and regarded the rest of us. "Your pilgrims, I take it?" He began chuckling again and motioned for Obadiah to sit with him on the cushions. Our host took a generous sip of wine, looked heavenwards in gratitude – for the wine or his restored sight, I did not know – and began his story.

Abner had traveled to Bethany with his oldest son to comfort a sickly friend named Lazarus. When Abner had arrived, all of Bethany was in celebration at Mary's house, who was the sister of Lazarus. The villagers told Abner about a great teacher, a good friend of the sick man, and how Lazarus had indeed perished from this illness but had been brought back to life by the miracle-working teacher.

He was the messiah, they told Abner. The son of both man and God, named Jesus.

An elderly man from Jericho named Timaeus led Abner and his son to the house and talked about how this mysterious traveler had also healed his son Bartimaeus from blindness while in Jericho. Timaeus had quieted when he saw Abner's own blindness then insisted that he fetch the teacher to see them.

Abner took another sip of wine and continued, telling us about his talk with the allegedly resurrected Lazarus in their oval courtyard. Suddenly, as if his hearing had matched the extinction of his sight, the room had grown deathly silent. Abner asked what was wrong and he then heard someone's footsteps walking towards him on the patio stones. Slow footsteps – unhurried but purposeful.

*"Do you believe?"* a man's voice had asked quietly in his ear. The voice was gently robust, spoken with authority but in a low tone meant only for Abner.

When no one else answered the question, Abner nodded to the man he could not see and said, "I believe." Emotion had suddenly filled him then, and he wept for reasons he could not quite explain. His eyes had burned with each sprung tear from his insolvent eyes.

The callused hands were warm on his face and Abner had flinched for a brief moment before surrendering to the gyration of the moving fingers. The unseen man felt Abner's hot tears and traced them towards his ruined eyes.

In his blindness, Abner was accustomed to seeing the mere fragment of bright light through his eyelids, as one does when they close their eyes and stare up at the sun. For Abner, this image was changing as the burning tears became cool – like dew – and the infringing light was soft and welcomed. The man gently pulled back Abner's crusted eyelids and looked into his eyes.

And Abner looked back.

"What did he look like?" Titus asked. His own wide eyes were riveted to Abner's.

Abner smiled warmly and said, "He looked no more unique than you or I, but his was the first face I had seen in so long." He paused and wiped his eyes. "So very long."

Obadiah put a hand on Abner's shoulder. "The darkness is over, old friend."

"Surely," Abner said with a sigh. "But not forgotten."

He went on to tell us about the healer: a man tanned by the sun from traveling, hands rough from woodwork and labor. The teacher's eyes were as normal as any man's but there was something else in them that Abner could not quite explain. Not just compassion, but as if the man's eyes were where compassion had begun. Not merely power, but as if the supremacy of *everything* could be found just behind this gaze. What Abner saw, he decided, was a great love in those eyes.

The crowd in Mary's house had begun their celebration anew and everyone had pulled Abner away from Jesus so that they could look into his healed eyes and dance with him in the courtyard.

"I never saw Him again after that moment," Abner said sadly. "The crowds told me He left with His companions to travel to Jerusalem, despite the warnings of the teachers." He shook his head and allowed a frown to steal its way across his face. "They want to kill Him, you know. Kill the Son of God... if you can believe it. Perhaps if they go through with it, the Lord will cover the whole world in ash, just as they stuffed it in my eyes so long ago."

Abner turned back to Obadiah and looked him deep in the eyes. "Our paths, my brother, are along vastly different currents," he said as his smile returned. "But you must see this man, Obadiah. It is never too late to change... to find a different path."

Obadiah gave a single grunt of laughter which was more disbelief than humor. He then stood and walked away from the band to the stairs of the balcony. In the lamplight his face was almost sickly.

Abner called out to him, "Forget Damascus, my friend. Leave it to the wind, as I have."

Without a response to Abner's appeal, Obadiah descended the stairs and walked across the courtyard to the vestibule.

With a curse, I stood to follow him. Abner also stood and gripped my arm gently. "Young brother," he said, "pull Obadiah from this life of hurt and darkness. In his youth, he used to be there alongside me, preaching of a coming change. All this was before he became overcome with hatred and resentment." His eyes narrowed as he stared at my face. "There is something changed in your own eyes, friend. Perhaps you've been witness to your own miracle?"

Pulling away from him, I said, "I don't believe in miracles."

With a troubled sigh, Titus put down his cup and followed me as I neared the stairs. As we descended into the courtyard, Abner's voice called out from the balcony, "I think your *Protos* now believes."

***

In silence, we walked the streets of Caesarea with Obadiah leading. He led us south to the great hippodrome which stood out from the dark streets like a shadow-cloaked mountain. Its columns stretched high and curved around the theater's front perimeter. Our leader continued into the structure, stepping over several sleeping forms at the gate.

From his unhesitant gait, I figured he had been there before.

We had to climb a short wall to get into the theater itself and I found myself following Obadiah up stone steps to the highest benches of the hippodrome. There were several huge rolls of *velum* coverings bunched at the base of the cedar poles which stretched over the spectator benches for use when the weather was foul. Obadiah finally stopped and sat upon one of these bunches of thick fabric. Titus and I sat on the nearest bench and waited for him to talk first.

After several minutes of silent thought, Obadiah cleared his throat and said, "There is much to be found in Jerusalem." His voice was soft and was still tinged with unease. I knew that he had long ago forsaken the Jewish god, so to see his friend Abner healed was surely

278

difficult to process.

"Jael and young Nahum," I said. "I need to see if they made it there safely."

Titus nodded and added, "The *eschatos kleros*. Perhaps after Jerusalem we will be so rich we can give up thievery and then seek this man known as Jesus. Surely, he must be in league with the grand spirit Roma and her deities."

Obadiah's figure was as still as a statue as he stared out across the Great Sea. After a moment, he looked away from the massive harbors and sparkling waves. He turned his gaze to the southeast and looked towards Jerusalem. "My brother," he said gravely. "He, too, will be in Jerusalem during this Passover season. I feel it."

"What do you think of this Jesus?" I asked him though I knew this was the exact question he did not want asked at that moment.

Obadiah exhaled a weary breath and said, "Who can say, scions. If we do happen upon this man – this healer they call the Son of God – then I have something I would ask of him. Perhaps he could give me an answer to something that has troubled me for a long time." In the moonlight, I saw his frown deepen as he continued to stare southeast. "Perhaps not."

"What would you ask the Son of God?" I asked in jest.

He looked at me for a moment, his face hidden in shadow, then grunted and looked back to the dark horizon.

From my perch far above the streets of Caesarea, I followed his gaze and looked towards the southeast as I thought of our path. Thinking of Jerusalem, I did not dwell upon its great temple, the massive walls, or the city's many springs. Nor did I think of my greed or my mounting desire to see Jael again. It was the thought of a hill that entered my mind – a raised mound just outside Jerusalem's northern gate that appeared to form a terrible shape when the sun struck it just right.

*Golgotha.*

The Skull.

Though Obadiah had always preached against it, we would be walking along the path to the Skull during the archaic city's most frenzied Passover season.

# THIRD INTERLUDE

*We broke again for a moment – Siergo from his imparting and I from my listening.*

*The silence slowly receded and the night resumed its pace, noises and all. I stretched on my bench as Siergo remained silent with his hands folded on the table.*

*"Have you, traveler, been to Jerusalem?" I asked him. I, myself, had been to Jerusalem twice during my travels, though the time Siergo spoke of was vastly different. My visits were after the city's great siege, which took place six years after my birth.*

*"Many times," he answered, his voice displaying the same melancholy as when I'd mentioned the Great Fire. "A city once great, now reduced to rubble and chaos. Regardless, God's prophets have seen future visions of Jerusalem and it is always paramount in the inner workings of this world's end."*

*"This world's end?" I asked with wide eyes. "The destruction of the entire world?"*

*"The end of it, at least. Much has been foretold."*

*"I've heard talk of these 'end days' during my own travels but never really paid attention to such proclamations. These prophets hold*

281

that Jerusalem, and the Israelites, play a role in all of that?"

"A vast role. God does not proclaim a city His cherished capital and then abandon it on a whim like a child tired of an old toy. Jerusalem has always been a very important place... and always will be."

There was another matter that had been biting at me as my visitor told his narrative. "Where, exactly," I asked slowly, "did this thief Dismas impart his tale to you? From the times and rulers you've mentioned, it must have been nearly a..." After a moment's thought, I continued, "...a half century ago?"

Siergo's eyes glittered in the lamplight. "Towards the end," he answered.

"'Towards the end'," I repeated. Most likely as Dismas was dying from old age, Siergo had visited with him. However, I still wondered where he had first met Dismas and I asked him this.

His reply was calm, spoken in a voice hinting at amusement... but just a hint: "Towards the beginning."

Though I did not understand this at all, I nodded and told Siergo to tell me of Jerusalem and of his cherished cast of bandits that jaunted on the path to the Skull.

## XXX - *The Lower City*

*If I forget you, O Jerusalem, may my right hand forget its skill.*
*May my tongue cling to the roof of my mouth if I do not remember*
*you, if I do not consider Jerusalem my highest joy.*

Past Antipatris, south along the Plain of Sharon and over the twin creeks of Elihu – comforter of Job the oppressed – our band found our way to Jerusalem. Under the shadow of the Mount of Olives, the great temple rose from the eastern part of the city and lent itself to our view. As we neared from the northern wilderness, we spied hundreds of travelers along the roads leading to the city. On any given day – with the exception of Jewish festivals and holidays – twenty-five thousand people would fill the city walls. However, during the spring festival of Passover, this number would swell three fold.

Within Herod's pale gray outer defense walls, the string of three towers near the north Gennath Gate – the towers of Phasael, Mariamne and Hippicus – protruded skyward near Herod's palace as if reaching for the heavens. One would think if man did reach high enough into the heavens to proclaim his own divinity, the true gods – if they existed – would smite him back to the hard earth in jealousy. As all knew, however, man would never stop reaching – at least Roman man – and

Herod's occupied cities were evidence of this.

Jerusalem was still overflowing with the spirit of Hellenism. The theater routinely housed stage acts while the hippodrome near the lower city exhibited chariot races and wild game hunting. This Roman influence brought prominent visitors of every nationality to Jerusalem, and despite its Jewish origins, the city had become an influx of many different cultures.

Twice on our trek to the city, travelers warned us of murderous thieves prowling the Jordan River and the wilderness near the Mount of Olives. "The Wolves of the Jordan", the men whispered to us in passing. They said that the Wolves' grizzled leader had a face like a crescent moon with a terrible scar on his chin. Glancing at Obadiah after this, I saw my leader's brow crease in disconcert. We were also told that in recent days Governor Pilate had assured the wealthier Jewish houses that the Skull would feed on any who threatened the inviolability of their festival. This Passover, he had declared, would be the most protected festival in the city's history. Soldiers would vigorously patrol the city streets and alleyways of the upper and lower cities, as well as the paved Roman roads around Jerusalem. Though the Jewish Passover was a celebration in part against bondage – including that of the Romans – Herod and Pilate knew that if the eastern part of the empire was to flourish and grow, the Jews would need to be kept safe and relatively happy.

Even more controversial than the murdering band of thieves circling Jerusalem was the ever-growing talk of the Messiah, who was alleged to be near Jerusalem despite death threats from the upper tiers of the law sects. A generous amount of travelers stated this much to us; some even carted along sick children or lame relatives for the teacher to heal.

When we finally neared the city we split our band up again – as we did to enter Caesarea – and Obadiah led Barabbas and I to the northern Gennath Gate.  Titus, Rufus and Cyrus journeyed further south along the great wall to the colossal Herodian aqueduct, to enter one of the southern gates.  We would meet again in the lower city at the Pool of Siloam, in the southernmost portion of the oldest part of Jerusalem.

Heaving at the tether in my hand, Mathias lurched towards the large gate as a procession of merchants led their livestock and wagonloads of caged fowl into the city.

"Wait," Obadiah said, his eyes drifting east towards the rock quarry which ran along the city's northern wall.  "There is time to spare," he whispered and led us out of line along the wall through the rock hills.

With the afternoon wind beating against our hair and tunics, we continued past the quarry and came to a larger hill that was surrounded by tall weeds that poked out of the stony earth.  This area appeared untouched by the masses of travelers.  At first glance, I thought the area might be good for a camp location despite the numerous, staked prayer flags trembling in the wind at the hill's base.  As we neared, however, I saw the row of tombs that had been cut into the hills beyond the stony mound, and I realized what exactly I was looking at.  My stomach tightened involuntarily.

"The Skull," Barabbas said in mock reverence as if he were impervious to its grasp.  He stared upwards at the dark hill, hands on his hips.  "Why are we here, *Protos*?  To hear the spirits wail?"

Obadiah kept his eyes on the mound and said, "So we might not come here again. I've seen men writhe up there on those beams – men I knew – nailed and tied to a crossbeam which they had to carry across their flogged back all the way from the city's praetorium. Never, scions… never in all my travels have I seen men suffer in such a way as they do upon the cross." He turned as the breeze blew his silver hair into his face.

"It doesn't really look much like a skull," Barabbas said loudly over the wind.

Moving his hair out of his face, Obadiah turned to him and said, "Just watch your backs within the city walls and be careful. Be wary of soldiers and don't do anything to bring attention to us."

"More like a swine's head," the rebel muttered, still staring at the hill. He knelt at the first line of prayer flags and plucked one at random from the hard earth. He removed the small stake and unrolled the flag gingerly. "'For Artirus,'" he read. "'A good husband and good father who has at last found peace.'" He released the rolled cloth and let the wind carry it into the wilderness.

I pulled Mathias close to me and looked past the hill into the distant wilderness. I noticed someone standing out there amid the knolls. The figure's dark cloak fluttered madly in the wind. Even from such a distance, I felt the Man of Shadow's strong gaze boring into me.

Looking away quickly, I bent down and stroked Mathias' ears with shaking fingers. "Let us leave this place," I said.

Ignoring my plea, Obadiah rummaged in his traveler's bag and withdrew a water-skin which he tossed to Barabbas. He then said in an unyielding voice, "Mat your hair down, Barby, or we'll hold you to the stones and do it for you. If you're as well known as you proclaim, then I don't want any problems at the gate."

Barabbas glared at the water-skin in silence for a moment then began the arduous task of wetting and pushing his spiked hair down. Rivulets of brown water, dirtied from his encrusted hair, ran down into his equally dirty beard. The wind took these drops and scattered them across the base of the crucifixion hill. When I looked past the hill again, the cloaked enigma was gone.

***

Obadiah led us quickly through the upper city, past Herod's massive palace and past the great theater. Every wealthy home we passed caught my eye and I found myself wondering which one was the house of Rannut. Whenever I saw a veiled woman near one of these homes, I looked for the telltale golden eyes but did not see any gaze that was as striking as Jael's. After we were settled, I thought, I would make a more in-depth search.

We slipped into the bustling lower city's market through an open gate in the Herodian separation wall. To appease the complaints of the wealthier Jewish and Roman homes, Herod had built a large stone wall to separate the affluent upper city from the shabbier district of the lower city, but there were still numerous gates and tunnels that allowed one to pass between both vicinities.

Once in the lower city, the change in scenery was immediate as we moved between a grouping of older connected apartments and into a packed street brimming with travelers and color. The roads and alleys were full of jostling people and many kinds of animals. Fully armored, red-plumed soldiers stood watch at street corners near the market. Their iron spear points hovered above them as they talked amongst themselves but still scrutinized the crowd with hard eyes.

We waded through the markets until our view of the temple was no longer obstructed by the huge hippodrome and the lofty apartments around it.

"It never fails to impress me," Obadiah said with genuine reverence.

From our vantage near a withered olive tree, the white and gold sanctuary stood out from the immense hills. It nearly resembled a hillside fortress or even a city in itself. The red roof of the Royal Porch stood out brightly; from such a distance, countless money changers and temple vendors could be seen bartering with pilgrims. A massive columned stairway led from the lower city to the common level of the temple.

As all knew, many of the city's visitors were those seeking enlightenment and education from the teachers of the law who operated out of the great temple. The presence of the Jewish God was said to be within the Temple, and those who prayed at the temple – or even at its base – believed that their words went directly to the ear of God. This was the cornerstone of the city, where people completed their vows, offered sacrifices, delivered their first fruits and offered their ever-increasing temple tax.

Obadiah pointed further east, past the Temple itself to another outsized stone-columned building and said, "That's the Antonia Fortress, where the soldiers are housed. From there, they'll be changing shifts every ten hours or so. It would do us well to watch their movements."

We continued south through the central markets towards the southern Essenes Gate and then followed a line of cluttered apartments east to the Pool of Siloam. The tiled court around the pool was lined with tall palm trees and at each tree's base a heap of sickly beggars lay awaiting their turn to touch their fingers in the pool. The pool itself had a column-lined covering and I could see the mouth of a tunnel which curved downwards into darkness at the pool's western end. As I had been told by Obadiah, this tunnel led to the Gihon Spring which was outside the city walls in the Kidron Valley. This made it possible for the city to have a steady water supply even during times of siege.

"Poor fools still think the water will heal them," Obadiah said as we stopped under the pool's overhanging canopy. "The sick and poor come here at all hours of the day, usually at morning for it is said that the first ones to enter the water when the morning sun hits them will be healed of any ailment."

With a sneer, Barabbas said, "Rufus' magic box would probably serve them better."

At our feet, a ragged form rolled over and stared at us with narrowed eyes above a rotted nose. Leprous sores crept their way over the man's forehead but he said in a strong voice, "There is a line, travelers." He pointed a black-spotted hand to the pool's western end where a mass of cloaked skeletons were kneeling patiently. "You may have my spot, though, for a tithe."

"Is your health not worth more than silver?" I asked him.

The man smiled up at me with yellowed teeth. "You must be a traveler from afar. Most of us just come here to wash our hair and faces. This water heals nobody. There are no healers left in the world."

"What of the Nazarene?" Obadiah asked him.

The man rose to his elbows. "Ah, the teacher called the Son of God," he quipped. "You would take me to this man?"

Mathias' leash tugged in my hand as the hound tried to duck his snout into the brown water to drink. I pulled him back, afraid of any diseases he would contract from even a single sip.

The man at Obadiah's feet ignored my struggle with the hound as he waited for a response to his request.

"Find your own way to him," Obadiah said flatly and walked to the pool's opposite end.

The sickly man looked up at me and smiled again. "Woe to the city of David and all within her walls," he said in a mock prophetic tone. "The stones will crumble again and this pool will be no more. Even the temple will be no more. I only ask that I live to see its destruction. And beware even this pool, for at night one can hear the cries of a demon from its inner bowels." The man then chuckled and rolled over on his other side.

We left him man laying there and followed Obadiah to a line of tents posted for travelers at the base of the defense wall. We sat and waited for the rest of the band.

Obadiah stretched and said, "Unless Herod has renovated every nook of this city, I think I may know of a good place to hide out. We'll have to steal some food, though. Soon, if possible, for my stomach sounds like a drunken festival choir."

Before us, the sick and the poor groveled around the Pool of Siloam, coughing and chattering in the universal language of the desperate.

# XXXI - *Under the Wall*

After the rest of the band met us at the pool, we reentered the main part of the lower city. Obadiah led us through the crowds to the great stone Hippodrome. As we neared, Rufus joked that we were going to watch the latest hunting spectacle but Obadiah merely smiled and guided us behind the Hippodrome where a line of dense myrtle trees paralleled a section of ancient defense wall that appeared to have been reconstructed numerous times. This partition now partially served as the southernmost courtyard wall of the arena. In a feeble attempt to remedy the crumbling wall, scraps of cedar had been piled against part of the more decrepit sections.

Obadiah stopped at this stack of wood and regarded it for a moment. "Herod has become a bit stingy with his renovations," he said. "For us, this is a good thing." He then moved some of the planks and squeezed into a ragged hole in the stone wall that was invisible from the street. As he disappeared into the musty darkness a small specter of dust floated outward from the fissure.

"In there?" Cyrus asked with trepidation.

Obadiah coughed from within the hidden chamber then poked his head out and said, "Ready a lamp, Titus." He cleared his throat and turned to the rest of us. "This is part of the olden wall from King David's City, and there is a generous space between the old stone and the new. More than enough room for even a dozen men to camp. I've used this space many a time."

Once Titus had lit the clay lamp from his bag, we took turns squeezing into the hole. When it was my turn, I had to pick up Mathias and pass him to an equally hesitant Cyrus. When the last of us had entered the chamber, Obadiah moved back to the opening, reached through and pulled a section of the cedar over the hole to cover the entrance. Though the entry itself was narrow, the chamber dipped downward and widened under the old wall forming a long chamber of sorts. The lamp light illuminated numerous spider webs and loose stones. Rusted iron guide rods jutted from the stone of the low ceiling and it was hard to tell where the new wall began and the old wall ended.

Titus hung the lamp from one of the iron rods and we each cleared a space for ourselves among the cluttered stones to store our possessions and rest. Mathias sniffed every corner of the chamber and was shooed away by the other band members before settling next to me.

When our meager camp was made, and when the dust of our intrusion had settled, I left with Titus and Cyrus to pilfer food and water-skins while the others remained in the chamber to rest from the journey. Mathias was already fast asleep in my cleared spot when I left.

Evening was beginning to fall upon Jerusalem but the city was still bustling. We moved south towards the markets where the familiar drone of merchants and vendors rose over the crowds in competing yells. At the corner of several of the streets, soldiers stood guard and scanned the crowds. They talked to their partners or leaned against their spears. As the hour grew late, I realized that they were probably nearing the end of their shift. The soldiers were likely eager to journey back to the Antonia Fortress for a respite from the day's clamor. Others would replace them for the night, though probably in fewer numbers.

We avoided the drained gazes of the soldiers and set out into the markets to steal quietly. Titus and I used our common distraction technique and filled our traveler's bags with bread, dried fish, dates, bottled oils, and strips of dried lamb. Cyrus, ungainly in everything except his ghostly-quick hands, stumbled through the markets, feigning dizziness, snatching water-skins, perfumes and lamp oil. Titus took the perfumes from Cyrus and traded them to a merchant for an ornate map of the city which was painted onto a tanned goat hide. Cyrus then stole the perfumes back from the man while I bartered with him for a new leash for Mathias.

At several of the more prosperous looking vendors, I inquired about the house of Rannut which I assumed was north in the upper city. Most of these merchants expressed disinterest while others said they could give me the information I sought for silver. After bartering with one of these men using stolen items from his own cart, he informed me that he knew of a Rannut that lived in the far northeast part of the city, just west of the temple gardens. With a heavy accent, he tried to explain how the home was near a fountain surrounded by stone "*dayags*". When I told him I didn't know what this Hebrew word was, he made a flipping motion with his hands as if mimicking fish. I took this to mean that the fountain had carved, leaping fish around it.

293

The rest of our band expected us back shortly with food, so a lengthy trip into the upper city would have to wait until nightfall.

Many of the conversations we heard in passing concerned the terrible band of raiders known as the 'Wolves of the Jordan' which was surely Rapha-Ayzal's bandits. His gang, cut to a more maneuverable size just as he had spoken of, had found their way to Jerusalem shortly after I fled them. In the last week, the handpicked group of ten raiders had followed the Jordan south towards the Dead Sea, killing and thieving with near legendary brutality, before breaking west towards Jerusalem. Though few, a handful of survivors described the leader as a giant – no less than eight feet tall – with a horrific mauled face. His chin, they testified, was splayed open from an old wound and one could see the yellowish bone gleaming in the moonlight before he struck. His bandits, they said, usually attacked at night and they had reached Jerusalem several days ago. Many thought the band was hiding somewhere within the city while others believed they remained in the wilderness to prowl outside the walls.

When I heard the merchants and travelers speak of these dark thieves, my thoughts turned to my prized Damascene dagger. While tall, Rapha-Ayzal was no giant and I knew from experience that he could be hurt like any other man. If our paths crossed again, I thought, I would find a way to retrieve my dagger. My biggest worry, however, was that Ayzal had caught up with Jamal, Jael and Nahum. Hopefully, I would be able to find out for sure after dinner.

"I wonder if stealing in Rome would be this easy," Titus asked me as we walked the streets, eyeing merchant tables for our next catch. The sun was dipping lower and some of the vendors had lit their own lamps at their carts or hung them from walking sticks next to their tents. The lamps swayed with the evening wind and small curls of dust danced off of the rooftops above us. The chants of bartering still rang out over the streets as each merchant vied for a few more swindles before nightfall.

"Probably not," I answered. "Surely things are different in Rome. Perhaps after this week we will not have to steal anymore."

"Wishful thinking."

I turned to him. "You're supposed to be the great optimist, friend. Do you not trust our plan?"

"I don't trust Barabbas."

"Neither do I, but I trust *Protos* and he seems to have faith in this thing. That's enough for me."

Titus stopped and turned to me. "That surprises me, Diz," he said quietly, "I mean, after what happened in Gilead."

"I cannot blame *Protos* for that," I said earnestly. "I wanted that catch more than any of us. Perhaps Mercius and Charon are floating in the Black River because of me... because of my stupidity."

"Don't say that," Titus whispered. "Surely, our friends are sharing wine with the splendid spirits of Roma and are enveloped in eternal happiness. It does me poorly to think of them any other way. Perhaps I will ask this Jesus about our friends, and maybe about my grandfather, too. Maybe he can give them a message for me."

I smiled and patted his back. "Now, that's the kind of foolish talk I'm used to hearing from you."

He pushed my hand away roughly and said, "You mongrel, I'm serious about that! I guess you haven't been paying attention but half of these travelers and vendors have been talking about this teacher and how he is still near the city. Make no mistake, my lot is for the *eschatos kleros* but I also want to find this man."

Still smiling, I said, "If our plan goes well, Titus, you can buy a whole league of sorcerers."

He laughed and adjusted the traveler's bag on his shoulder.

"Does that map you acquired show the city's fountains?" I asked, pointing to his bag.

"The man told me it included nearly every home, alley and permanent stores." He withdrew the rolled map and handed it to me. I scanned the section that contained the northeast part of the city. Sure enough, a small fountain had been drawn in blue ink. Several tiny fish had been illustrated around the water to signify the statues. Four or five squares were tightly clustered around this fountain and I wagered that they were the homes the man had mentioned.

"Can I keep this for the night?" I asked.

Titus shrugged. "I'd like it back whenever you're done with whatever foolishness you'll use it for."

I smiled as I placed the map in my own bag. "Let's find Cyrus and get back to our hole for dinner."

We walked back along the main vendor street and eventually found Cyrus with his traveler's bag bulging with merchandise.

*** 

That night, after we ate and drank stolen wine by lamplight, Barabbas finally divulged information about the coming plan. With an animated look under newly spiked hair, Barabbas brushed a limestone boulder clean and used a stolen ink vial to draw a diagram with his finger of the first home we would strike. Though his illustration was crude, I could recognize what appeared to be a very large dwelling with many rooms and vestibules.

"Two years ago," Barabbas explained to us, "I pretended to be a traveling scribe from Tyre with a friend of mine from the *Sicarii* crusaders. We were introduced to several higher tier Jews with political ties to the Romans – those ties being silver and gold, men. My friend, who has since been captured and killed by Herod, told these Jews that there was a new way of cleaning and sorting treasures through prayer to God above and by several polishing techniques known only by Caesar's own treasury assistants and ourselves. This technique was even said to make treasures multiply, through the graces of God. We quoted various Jewish scriptures about their great Ark and so forth." Barabbas took a small coin from his own bag and rubbed it between thumb and forefinger. "This was a lie, of course. But after we produced forged letters of reference from other well-known priests and nobles, they showed us their caches of treasure and asked our price for these skills. They truly believed us to be purist pilgrims, indifferent to the potent gleam of silver and gold. I tell you now, my fellow brigands, that these nobles have been hoarding for *years* from sacrifices, tithes and sullied money. I'm sure that much of that gold was red with blood. Each of the three houses had its own secret hoard of wealth. *Thousands* of *talents*. More money that I have even dreamed of."

He paused and let this information sink in. Everyone remained silent, waiting for him to continue.

"My friend and I discussed bringing the rest of the *Sicarii* into this," he continued, "but decided it would be best if we took the matter into our own hands. We devised a plan to steal the treasure ourselves. All of it in one night... from all three homes." He smiled and his wild eyes flashed greedily in the lamplight. His lunatic gaze then drifted to that of sadness and he added, "My friend was captured in a riot before we could attempt this, however. Regardless, I came to realize that this plan would take more than just two men and that is when I journeyed north to locate Obadiah. We discussed the best time to try for it and agreed upon the next Passover festival. After a few ruts in our path... here we are."

In the lamplight, Obadiah's face held no emotion as the shadows danced across his hawk nose and beard. He nodded and said, "How many servants to each house? What kind of tools will we need?"

Barabbas pointed at the uppermost room of his diagram. "Two servants for the first home. A wife – probably still ugly – and three children. There is a hidden floor cache at the base of one of the wall pillars in the hearth room's southern end. If we move their long sitting chair, a piece of the mosaic can be removed and there is a large wooden box that was completely filled."

"It could be empty now," I said staring at the sketch on the boulder.

"It could be more full," Rufus countered giving me a wily glance.

Barabbas smiled and said, "I can assure you that it will be filled. This man, Jashobeam, had lots of goals for the future and all involved retaining more money for himself. If it is empty, we'll pilfer the house goods and go on to the next house. Even one such box would allow all of us to retire in any fashion we like."

Obadiah leaned forward and said, "This brings us to our most important matter: how do we keep the family and servants quiet and compliant for the whole night? If we hold them at bay with our swords, they'll scream brigandage as soon as we're gone. The whole city will be in an uproar after the first home."

"I'm not killing anyone," Titus said as he stared at the dusty floor.

Rufus nodded and said, "Surely, by the end of such a blood drenched night, our own spirits would be in contention with that of Hades and all his vile wraiths. There must be some other avenue to jaunt than that of death." The poet's face was rigid with emotion for a few seconds. He then smiled and added, "I have an idea, but I'll have to do some shopping around tomorrow to see if it is even possible."

As we continued to discuss our plan, a scripture from wise King Solomon came to me:

*Do not lie in wait like an outlaw against a righteous man's house, do not raid his dwelling place; for though a righteous man falls seven times, he rises again, but the wicked are brought down by calamity.*

Hopefully, I thought in earnest, these nobles were not the "righteous" ones King Solomon had been thinking about.

# XXXII - *Wrong House*


**At** night, the smells of the city were vibrant: incense, cooking meat, fermented drink, and always smoke – rising from the iron flues of Jerusalem's lower city.

When I finally reached the Herodian wall, I slipped in between two pillars and found myself in a small grove of fig trees behind someone's expansive stucco villa. The night breeze rustled the tops of the trees and the occasional upraised voice or laugh carried to me from the upper city.

After silently regarding the map in the light of a nearby window, I skulked further north through the larger, cleaner city streets and then moved east towards the temple gardens. These avenues were much less crowded and quiet compared to those of the lower city, where travelers slept at every street corner and in every alley. Eventually, after backtracking twice through the dark streets, I came to a grouping of wealthy homes that encircled a large fountain. In the moonlight, pale stone fish could be seen in a frozen dance around the pool. There were no beggars or travelers camped in this intersection, and I wagered that any night wayfarers would be dispersed by soldiers if prompted by the nearby homeowners. I kept to the shadows of the nearest alley as I regarded the cluster of five homes around the fountain. Four appeared to be completely dark, while only one was lit from within. This home was nearly a palace; it was surely fit for one of the city's more prosperous merchants or perhaps a temple priest. Scroll columns adorned the home's upper corners and I could see the outstretched trees and plants of an expansive garden just over the wall that surrounded the property. The home seemed to spread out over the street and it nearly encroached on the two homes on either side of it. The property lines had obviously been pushed back to allow more area for the garden and the home itself.

I cursed myself for not leaving the hideout earlier. With the other homes dark, it would be impossible to pinpoint which home belonged to Jael's uncle. Unless, I thought, it was actually the immense home that was still lit by lamps.

After a few minutes of frustrated deliberation in the shadows, I cursed under my breath and moved swiftly to the home's southern wall. This partition, which was nearly as tall as I, stretched to the back of the property which could not be fully seen from the street. Several dark fern bushes had to be avoided as I walked through the shadows. Once I was closer to the rear of the home, I faced the wall and gingerly hopped upwards to catch a glimpse of the dwelling. The gardens appeared empty, though there were two windows at the rear of the home and lamplight flickered from between their open wooden shutters. Over the breeze, I could hear voices coming from within the house.

The wind changed direction for a moment and the sound of sandals on gravel reached my ears. I ducked down and hid behind one of the fern bushes next to the wall. Squinting in the shadows, I saw a dark figure walk pass the fountain at a brisk pace. He looked over his shoulder as if afraid of being followed. The man then disappeared from my view as he neared the front of the lit home. After waiting for nearly a minute behind the ferns, I decided that I could at least rule this home out as that of Rannut by looking through the windows and seeing if any of the occupants was Jael, Nahum or even Jamal. The other homes could be scrutinized upon the morning.

As quietly as possible, I climbed the wall and dropped into the landscaped garden. I moved past a small pond to an ornamental tree that offered cover close to the nearest window. When my breathing had slowed, I peered through the leaves and into the window.

The room was beautiful. Ornate rugs covered much of the tiled floor and a long ivory lined table sat in the center of the room. Silk draperies adorned the walls and several golden lamps hung from wall mounts. Men were seated around the table – nearly a half dozen of them – and most of them wore elaborate robes. There was wine and bread on the table but it appeared untouched, as if it was just a decoration. A row of empty, ornate goblets extended out from the bowls of wine.

Beyond the table, in the room's far corner, two armed men stood on either side of a large wooden door. Their beards were long and they were obviously not Roman soldiers of any sort. Based on what Obadiah had told me of the officers of the Temple Guard, I assumed that these two men were part of this group. Those at the table looked like temple priests.

"Moments such as those are few," one of the men whose back was to me said. "Not saying so few as to call this endeavor impossible, but certainly fewer than not. The fewer people around when this happens, the better. Whom should I contact when the time is opportune?" His voice sounded nervous. The back of his head and part of his gray cloak could be seen past his chair's back.

One of the robed individuals, an older man with a complicated headdress, answered in an aged voice, "Go to my son-in-law's servant. You'll be given brisk audience and we'll dispatch some of the Guard." He paused and regarded the man sitting across from him. "Will any of his group try to defend him by force?"

The man thought for a moment then said, "There is one who might. I'm not really sure. But the teacher has spoken against any sort of violence…"

"Either way, the Guard will be able to handle it, I'm sure." The old man smiled then asked, "You are from Kerioth Hezron, are you not?"

The man nodded. "As is my father, Simon Iscariot."

"His line has many blemishes, Annas," one of the other robed men said.

The older man, Annas, was silent for a moment then turned to the other robed man and said, "Do not forget that this good follower has come to us, Jehoiada." Annas put his hands over his face for a moment as if fatigued. From behind his wrinkled hands, he said, "I can speak for my son-in-law when I say that in the fifteen years since he was appointed by Valerius Gratus we have never had so much trouble with a single aspirant liberator. They pop up every now and then, but this…" He lowered his hands and sighed. "The sheep are always eager to flock, I suppose, but the temple holdings are suffering… everything is suffering from one rogue liar. It's long past time they returned to the true teachers of the Law."

Annas paused for a moment and looked down at the table. He

then continued, "I've heard much of this man, my fellow servants of God. The true son of our Lord Almighty would not have hands callused from woodwork. The evidence against him is even in his hands. Is it not, son of Simon Iscariot?"

The man with his back to me nodded and said, "His hands are indeed callused. He has always preferred to work among his brothers and lend a hand whenever possible."

Annas scoffed. "What sort of... *messiah* toils in the dirt with men?"

The son of Simon Iscariot remained silent.

With grim curiosity, I wondered if they were talking about the miracle-working Nazarene that we had heard so much about. If so, then some sort of plot to have the man arrested or killed was being discussed before me. While I was now sure that this was not the home of Jael's wealthy uncle, I remained as still as possible and continued to watch them.

As lamplight flickered over Annas' face, he regarded the other robed men around him in silence for a moment and then turned back to the unseen man. He lowered his voice and said, "When you are with him, what are your thoughts? Answer in honesty."

After a few seconds of silence, the man said, "Such a question... I have not the words to answer but only think of your son-in-law's prophesy. My teacher must die for the whole of our nation. He was not the sword against Rome I believed him to be."

Annas shook his head. "You people should learn to work with Rome and not against her. There are many privileges to be had from it. It was the Romans, after all, who appointed my son-in-law." Annas gave a thin smile. "Sometimes, young follower, it can be the Romans

304

who serve as the sword of *our* nation."

The man across from him cleared his throat and said, "What are you willing to give me if I hand him over to you?"

Annas' smile grew. "We finally come down to it," he said. "If you are able to accomplish this you will redeem much with your vigilance." He made a motion with his hand and one of the temple guardsmen withdrew a small money bag from his cloak, walked over to Annas and handed it to him. The old man placed the bag on the table next to the bread. He then broke off a piece of the bread, dipped it in oil and held it out to the son of Simon Iscariot, who leaned forward to accept it with a trembling hand.

As the man ate the bread, Annas poured a cup of wine which he also held out to him. "Fifteen pieces now," Annas said when the man had drunk the wine. "Fifteen more when the arrest has been made. Does this seem fair to you?"

Clumsily, as if drunken from the single cup of wine, the man stood and bowed before them. "Your son-in-law will hear from me when the time is right," he said in a weak voice.

Annas smiled again, picked up the money bag and held it out to him. "Sooner rather than later would be ideal, good follower."

The man nodded quickly and fled the table. I caught a glimpse of his face as he turned. He appeared to be an ordinary commoner though his face seemed to be drawn in anguish. Clearly, this betrayal was affecting the man, and the money did little to give him peace. The coinage had to be silver, I thought, for blood money was rarely a lesser metal.

The temple guardsmen moved from the room's door and let him pass by.

In a few moments, I realized, there would be a lone man on the dark streets with fifteen pieces of silver in his possession. Perhaps if he was relieved of his blood money, I thought, he would not feel so guilty.

In the room, Annas said, "If he actually delivers him to us, I would have paid five times that amount. Ten times, even." Several of the other robed men laughed at this.

Their laughter slowly faded as I backed away from the tree and moved to the wall.

\*\*\*

The night wind had started to strengthen as it blew through the streets and over the rooftops. It was hard to keep up with the man as he twisted through the city alleys at a hurried pace. Much like a thief, he kept mostly to the shadows, straying from the main avenues and sticking to the alleys. His gray cloak billowed behind him as he strode through the darkness.

Hand on my sword, I matched his pace, but remained silent as I slowly neared him. While our band was in Jerusalem for a much larger catch – three actually – I could not pass up an opportunity as easy as this. Fifteen pieces of silver taken from a betrayer. As I followed the man's form through the alleys, I thought of my brief time with Abner and what he had told us of the Nazarene teacher. Could he really work miracles? Did the law sects really want him arrested? The astounded face of Obadiah came to me. The amazed cries of Rachel, Abner's wife, had not seemed feigned. And now, this healer was going to be taken into custody for such marvels.

*Kill him*, a voice whispered to me from the shadows of my baser consciousness. Truly, it would be an act of charity towards a man many believed was the Son of God.

I am a thief, I answered inwardly. Not a murderer.

Ahead, the man curved behind a string of large merchant stores as he continued his spindly trek west through the upper city. As he was out of my view for a brief moment, I quietly ran up to the mouth of this new alley to catch up to him. Drawing my sword, I rounded the corner swiftly and prepared myself to confront the man in but a few seconds.

A cloaked man stood no more than a few paces away from me in the dense shadows. Even though the darkness was thick behind the stores, I could tell this was not the man I had been following. This figure was much taller and for a brief moment I thought I was looking at Rapha-Ayzal's sinister form. Despite the shadows, however, I could see the man's bearded chin was not horribly scarred from battle. Though the wind was almost non-existent in the narrow alley, the figure's hair and cloak seemed to move as if he were trapped in his own private storm. There was no noise however – no rustle of fabric or silky flutter of hair.

I took a step backwards into the street. Looking past the Man of Shadow, I saw the betrayer's dim figure continue into the deeper part of the alley and merge fully with the darkness. I looked back to the mysterious guardian and found that he was little more than shadow; his wraith-like presence was scarcely a blur among the alley's gloom. And then his image was gone – as if he had never been more than smoke – and this caused me to worry about my own mental faculties nearly as much as the fifteen pieces of silver that had just vanished into the night.

## XXXIII - *Rightful Owners*

The interminable calls of the merchants and vendors served as our multi-voiced rooster at dawn and the sun's red light filtered through the open crack of our hideout's entrance making the floating dust in the air look crimson.  Most of the band was groggy from drinking too much wine the previous night, but the strong curses of Obadiah brought them to their feet in the cavern.

I had yet to tell anyone of what had transpired during my ill-fated scouting trip, and had only told them upon my return that I had been unable to locate the home I was looking for.  I was unsure how to explain exactly what I had witnessed at the noble's house.

Later that morning, after we shared a quick breakfast in the hideout, the whole band set out into the city to view the three homes we were to raid during the *kleros*.  Barabbas led the way north through the lower city towards the Herodian wall, cursing at beseeching street vendors and reaching beggars.  Jubilant to be out of the musty cavern, Mathias pulled against his leash with a newfound fervor.  If the day's fortune was good, I would return Mathias to his rightful owners on this day. But hopefully, I thought, I would not find myself privy to any more fiendish plots involving betrayal, messiahs and priests.

Embarrassingly, the thought of seeing Jael again made my stomach flutter as if I had ingested a live swallow. Perhaps Obadiah had been right in saying that I had fallen in love with one of my captors.

Once we entered the upper city, which was still busy but not nearly as much as its lower half, Obadiah ordered us to cease our curses and jests and appear – once again – as humble pilgrims. After twenty minutes of searching, Barabbas took us into the shade of a grove of palm trees next to a stone well at the far west end of the upper city. We were close to the great aqueduct and nearly a stone's throw from the striking Roman Theater, from which a chorus of laughs and applause could be heard intermittently.

"Our first tier of the *kleros*," Barabbas said quietly with a nod to a large house across the street.

Our eyes fixed upon the largest home on the corner – not quite as large as the palace from last night, but obviously the home of a wealthy priest or merchant. The courtyard garden was small but elaborate and a lone tree stretched out over its small wall. The head of a single servant could be seen walking back and forth from the larger plants as he probably watered them with a clay pitcher.

"The house of Jashobeam," Barabbas whispered, looking back to the well. "Do not stare, friends. He is an impious man given to paranoia and widespread misgivings. He would have soldiers dispatched in a hair if he saw the likes of us staring at his property." He started fiddling with one of the buckets and began lowering it into the well for water.

I rubbed the stubble at my chin and said, "His is first then?"

"Yes, tomorrow night," he answered with one of his wild-eyed looks. "Tomorrow night... tomorrow night." He quietly sung the words as if they were the lyrics to a song. His sinewy arms flexed as he pulled the full bucket up from the well.

"How do we get inside?" Obadiah asked him.

Rufus ran both of his hands through his red hair and said, "We need seven blessed cloaks of invisibility, handed down from Mt. Olympus, sewn by Minerva herself."

Barabbas smiled. "No Trojan horse or stupid invisible cloaks. In the rear of the house, near the servants' quarters, there is a large window. Its shutters are merely tied together by twine – easily cut with a thin dagger from the outside." He took a long drink from the bucket.

Obadiah sighed. "That was over a year ago, Barby. Those shutters could be iron now."

"Trust in the gods, *Protos*," Barabbas exclaimed. "Or in this suspected child of the Jewish god. Find faith somewhere, old friend... it matters not where. If all fails with the window we can always knock, asking Jashobeam for a night tonic or pinch of incense to cure a foul slumber. Let us now find our plan's second bastion." Out of spite for the rich, he then detached the bucket from the rope and dropped it into the well.

***

Ten minutes later, after traveling further east near the Mariamne Tower, I regarded another regal house which mirrored the home of Jashobeam's elegance. This dwelling seemed taller though, and from our vantage, I could see a large porch-style opening on the second floor which surely offered a breathtaking view of the great Temple and the

310

multihued markets. The home's stucco walls had been recently whitewashed and an elaborate garden flanked the home's entryway.

"The house of Obil," Barabbas declared. "Wealthiest of the three, but also the stingiest. There is a side door on the home's eastern side that is as thin as papyrus. A child could force it open, and that will be our entry."

As we stood there, Titus drew our fastest and most covert paths on his city map using a bright red ink. He included possible escape routes in case our plan ran afoul. He continued to scribble on the map as we followed Barabbas to the third home. We refined our plan for the next night as we walked, agreeing that we would wait for the middle of the night before striking Jashobeam's home quickly. We would first subdue the inhabitants – binding and gagging them strongly enough to allow us time for our second and third catches at the other homes. After Jashobeam's, two of us would be charged with hauling our amassed riches to a meeting point somewhere outside the city walls while the rest of the band would make a silent run through the night to the house of Obil where we would repeat our binding and thieving. The two haulers would return for the second catch's money, and then again for the third. As this would be a very high-profile crime – if not the most prolific in the city's history – we would quickly regroup after the final home and flee Jerusalem before dawn. Depending on how long our victim's bindings and gags lasted, we would hopefully be granted a generous head start on ardent soldiers who would first attempt to round up any suspicious looking wayfarers still walking the city streets. We would be hours vanished by then, on our way to the Dead Sea, where we would split our riches and hide out for a few weeks near the coastal towns such as En Gedi.

We continued east through the upper city until we came to a large stone fountain surrounded by expertly carved fishermen. These marble fishermen held real rope nets in various poses. Several large homes were clustered around this fountain, much like the homes from last night had been. Barabbas stopped at the fountain – under one of the stately fishermen – and leaned against its marble feet as he splashed water onto his head. When we were all grouped around him, he began spiking his wet hair and he nodded past the fountain. "The house of Rannut," he said.

While the rest of the group continued looking at the home, I looked to him and said, "That's impossible."

Everyone turned back to look at me. Barabbas stopped messing with his hair and said, "What do you mean?"

"The people I'm looking for… they are supposed to be at the house of Rannut, and their home is next to a fountain surrounded by leaping fish. Not fisherman. This can't be the home…"

"You know these people?" Barabbas asked with both surprise and irritation in his voice.

"No, I…" Perplexed but suddenly excited, I looked to the home, a dwelling as big and affluent-looking as the previous two. This home's garden was the most expansive of the three, hinting at a large populace of servants. Northwest of the home, the Gennath Gate loomed at the street's end and just beyond that, the rock quarries and place of the Skull.

"Scion?" Obadiah prompted me.

"I don't know him directly," I said, "but I have friends who are possibly staying with him. Yesterday, a merchant told me that this home was near a fountain surrounded by fish. He used the Hebrew word *Dayag*, so maybe it is a different Rannut."

Obadiah shook his head and said, "The word for fish is *Dag*. *Dayag* means fishermen." He turned to Barabbas and said, "It looks like we may have a problem."

As Barabbas grew red with irritation and began to rant about how horrible of a man Rannut was, Mathias pulled against the leash with such force towards the home that I had to pull him back with both hands. Once he was reigned in, I regarded the home once more. Three young children were in the garden, tilling at the soil around one of the date trees. The children were small, much too young for such physical labor. Though we were close to fifty paces away, I thought one of them was a boy, perhaps five years of age, while the other two were girls slightly older. Rannut wouldn't have Nahum slaving away in his garden, I thought as I squinted in the afternoon sun. The boy had his back to me as he plunged a small iron stake into the earth, readying the soil for either flowers or more colorful shrubbery.

Mathias stared at the home intently as well and started to whine urgently. The speckled hound strained mightily against the leash until his front paws were nearly off of the ground. His rear claws dug furrows in the dirt next to the fountain.

There were other servants outside the home by a small, marble well on the street's opposite side. Four women, all veiled and dressed in gray, long sleeved tunics, moved about the well and conversed quietly among each other in hushed voices befitting servants. Knowing that Jael was surely not among the lowly servant women, I swept my gaze back to the home.

"Either way," Obadiah was saying, "we shouldn't linger here for too long."

As if immediately proving his point, a group of robed men frowned at us as they walked past the fountain. Despite our newly stolen tunics and sandals, we could never pass for refined pilgrims.

"I'll come back later in the afternoon or evening," I said in a dejected voice. "I don't even know what I would say if-"

Mathias suddenly jerked against the leash again, and this time, I wasn't able to hold onto it. The hound shot across the street like a loosed arrow, heading for the home's garden. Under the legs of a mewling donkey, and past another group of robed men, Mathias raced across the street and flew through the open gate of the home. He barked as he reached the children in the garden. The young girls screamed in fright, while the younger boy turned just as the hound reached him. The boy tried to ward off the speckled hound for a moment in fear, then gave a shout of delight and yelled, "Mathias!"

"Nahum," I whispered as I watched the spectacle unfold before me.

One of the servant women stepped towards the garden and removed her veil as she watched the hound nuzzle against the boy. She then turned to the fountain in search of the hound's deliverer. The sun hit her full in the face and the gold shine of her eyes locked upon mine. She raised a slender hand to her lips and I saw her mouth move and I knew – *knew* – that she spoke my name.

"We need to get out of here," Barabbas hissed though his voice seemed far away. "I didn't know about this and it's anything but good."

Obadiah grabbed my shoulder and said, "He's right, scion. We'll be waiting for you in the last alley we were in. Take your time but watch what you say." He gave my shoulder a hard squeeze. "Did you hear me?"

I nodded and started across the street. The sunlight continued to hit Jael's beautiful face and as I parted through the street's travelers I saw her golden eyes were shiny with newly sprung tears. Despite these tears, she was smiling at me.

I stopped a few feet from her. Her eyes glimmered and tears ran down her high cheek bones, though her smile remained and her face held both awe and subdued emotion.

Behind her, the sound of Mathias' playful barking and Nahum's shouts of glee washed over us and added to the already poignant moment.

"Dismas," she breathed as she stared at me.

I gave her a large smile and said, "You made it."

She took a step towards me. "Only because of you. You saved our lives…"

I was aware of other people on the street watching us. The other servants at the well murmured amongst themselves. Despite this, I answered, "You saved my life first."

She blinked and more tears ran down her face. As I stared past her at the house of Rannut, I saw that Nahum had finally noticed us and was walking the frolicking hound towards us with a look of hesitation in his young face.

"What has happened, Jael?" I asked her, looking at her plain tunic. "This is your uncle's house, is it not?"

She sniffed and looked to the ground between us. "It is," she whispered.

"Then why are you…" I tried to think of the right way to ask her why she was dressed like a common servant but nothing tactful came to mind.

She looked up at me – her gold eyes red with tears – and said, "Things are not how I thought they would be, Dismas. We weren't given the reception that I-"

A sudden commotion came from the home behind her and a small, wiry man strode out of the house with a purple robe fluttering behind him like dyed wings. He stopped when he saw us standing together. The two young servant girls were behind him, heads bowed to the ground in fear. "*Girl!*" he shrieked in a high-pitched voice. "By God above, get away from him!"

Jael winced and I gaped at the man behind her. Surely, this was Rannut, but I could not understand why he would scream at his niece in such a way.

As Rannut continued his yelling, Jael leaned forward and whispered in my ear, "Find Jamal. He'll be at the theater now... in the upper balcony. He'll explain. I'm sorry, but I must go." She hastily wiped the tears from her eyes and turned away.

"Wait," I said and moved forward to take her arm. Rannut screamed even louder and ran over to us. He grabbed Jael by the back of her tunic and pushed her roughly through the gate. I yelled at him to stop but he ignored me and grabbed a whimpering Nahum by the collar of his sleeveless tunic and hauled him through the gate as well. When Mathias snarled at him, he kicked at the hound which produced a bite on the man's calf. Rannut screamed in pain and anger.

I moved forward to seize the man when I felt a strong hand on the back of my own tunic. Obadiah said in my ear, "Soldiers are around the corner, Dismas. We must go."

I turned and saw a group of horse-mounted soldiers strolling

316

through the street towards the commotion at Rannut's home. They galloped quickly from the west. When Rannut saw them, he squealed all the louder and pointed at us.

"Brigands!" he yelled in earnest. "Brigands! Enemies of Zion and Caesar!" Once Jael and Nahum were within the garden, he pulled the iron gate shut and continued yelling.

With a grunt, I wrenched free from Obadiah and moved forward to grab Mathias' leash. Obadiah seized my arm once more and pulled me away from the gate as the soldiers neared the fountain. We ran hard to the nearest alley where I saw the rest of the band backing further behind the homes. Barabbas was the closest one to us and he beckoned madly for us to hurry. His eyes were wide with fear.

Behind us, a soldier cried out, "Barabbas!"

The first arrow whistled over our heads and skimmed the bald head of a robed traveler that was passing in front of the alley, tearing a pink line across the man's scalp. The others on the street started to scream.

Obadiah and I shoved past the man and entered the alley as more arrows shot past us. One punched a clean hole through my tunic – just under my armpit – forcing me to jump over the arrow when it impaled the ground in front of me.

"Nobody goes to our hole yet," Obadiah commanded as we followed the alley behind the home and onto a different street. "Meet there at nightfall! Split up... now!"

Behind me, I could hear the clomping of horse hooves in the alley and I knew the soldiers would be upon us in an instant. We each scattered different directions in the street, looking to disappear into other alleys or through merchant stores. I let Mathias' leash go and the hound took off down the street, disappearing among the street goers. As I ran under a series of wooden scaffolds that paralleled a half-renovated home, I looked back and saw Barabbas continue down the street with a frantic look in his eye. In the alley we had just come from, two soldiers on horseback entered the street and hollered for assistance. I dove behind a line of tall clay vessels at the rear of a home. Coming out of my roll, I peeked between two of the vessels and saw Barabbas topple over a goat that had burst from its feeble corral during the commotion. He toppled end-over-end and hit the street hard. I watched as the rebel quickly got to his feet. He stood there in silence for a moment, looking in the direction he had been running. Other people hollered and ran around him, though he remained still.

There must be soldiers at the opposite end of the street, I thought. After his costly deliberation, Barabbas turned in a circle and ducked as another arrow skimmed his spiked hair. He pushed past a confused group of travelers and his eyes found my hiding spot behind the clay vessels. He ran towards me.

*He's going to get us both captured*, I thought as I made to stand. I rose to my knees and was about ready to flee from the home's rear when Barabbas suddenly gave a loud scream. I turned back to him and saw him fall to street. The arrow in his shoulder caught the road's hard dirt, cracking the shaft and twisting the iron tip deeper into his flesh. With a horrific shriek, Barabbas finished his roll and came to rest face down. He continued to mewl in pain as he began to crawl towards the fissure where I hid.

This part of the street had mostly emptied and the two soldiers on horseback trotted over to Barabbas' writhing form. They swiftly dismounted and I saw that one had a readied bow while the other had

318

drawn his sword. When Barabbas was no more than ten paces away from me, the soldier with the sword walked over to him and placed a sandaled foot on his back – just under the broken arrow shaft. The rebel cried out and stopped crawling.

Three other soldiers entered this part of the street from the home's other end and joined the first two. They swarmed Barabbas like hungry jackals.

"Whose shot was this?" the tall soldier with the sword asked. He was breathing heavy from his ride through the alley and crowds. "A half-day's respite for the man."

"Mine, surely," two of the bow carrying soldiers declared in unison and a grand argument ensued.

"Liars, both of you," the first soldier said. He sheathed his gleaming *xiphos* sword and pointed upwards and past them. "It was probably from our men on the archway there. I'll inquire of them."

On the ground at his feet, Barabbas moaned and said, "Wait for me..." He moved his spiked head and looked towards the cleft where I hid behind the vessels. I held my breath. The corner behind me was not the entrance to an alley and two homes pinched together sealing me into the cranny without anywhere to flee. I would have to wait for the soldiers to leave.

"What's he saying?" one soldier asked and notched an arrow in his bow. He then walked over to Barabbas and pressed his foot against the back of his head, pushing it to the dust of the ground, but not before my eyes met those of the fallen rioter for an instant. Barabbas was nearly delirious and I worried that he would give away my position. The soldier drew his cat-gut string back with a squeak and pointed the arrow at the back of Barabbas' neck. The honed iron tip glittered like a diamond in the afternoon light. "Well, there will be no argument as to *this* loosing," the soldier said and held a breath to release his arrow.

Face to the ground, Barabbas mumbled, "Wait for me. *Wait…*"

"Hold," the tall soldier said. "This is a grand catch. The people know of this fool; Herod's advisors will be very pleased if we drag the whelp to General Ulpius. This one's a murderer as well as a rioter." He looked at the man with the readied bow. "Relax those fingers, Donatus, and let's get him tied."

The young soldier named Donatus removed his foot from Barabbas' head. The rebel then slowly lifted his face from the dirt and looked to me again. He started to raise a trembling finger towards me. His dirt-streaked face seemed accusatory as he tried to point me out to the soldiers. He opened his mouth to speak – to surely announce my presence to the soldiers – but Donatus said, "I hate having to run in this armor." The soldier then gave a fierce kick to the side of Barabbas' head. The rebel melded fully to the ground; his hand lay slack in the dust while his accusatory finger remained pointing at me.

The tall soldier said, "That's enough, Donatus." He sheathed his sword and pointed at the unconscious rebel. "Bind him now, and do it well for I hear he's a wily one." The tall soldier suddenly looked up towards the vessels and for a terrifying moment I thought his vigilant eyes met mine, but he merely said, "Keep an eye at the ready for the dogs that were with him." He then turned briskly as the other soldiers tied Barabbas' hands together behind his back. The arrow shaft in his shoulder wavered as they toiled with the rope.

Eventually, the soldiers left and the streets refilled with locals and travelers. I emerged from behind the vessels, and walked to the spot where Barabbas had fallen. In the afternoon light, the rebel's blood seemed thick and dark with dust, almost like tar. Several flies had already found this decadent pool and were feasting greedily despite my shadow over them.

# X X X I V - *Fate's Orator*

The white-faced performers groveled about the granite stage of the *odeum* theater. Standing above them, a crimson-robed actor recited a poem that was anything but Homeric. Despite this, the theater seats were nearly full with both loud drunkards and silent critics. Servants – both petite females and young men who were made to look like girls – moved wistfully around the benches of the colonnaded gallery near the top rows of seats. From my lower seat, I saw that each pillar of the prestigious upper balcony area had a different carved wooden façade tied around it – signifying the many different cultures occupied by Rome.

Around me, spectators squinted at the stage, talked or filled their mouths with food and wine. My eyes searched among them for a face more rotund than normal… one darkened by the sun from travel. The balcony was off limits to most; its entrance was guarded by a lax soldier who also drank wine from a large cup. His eyes met mine as I tried to stare up into the balcony and I looked away with a curse. Jael had said that I would find Jamal in the upper balcony, but getting past the guard would be impossible. In frustration I turned to the stage and glared at the white-faced actor as I thought about how everything that I had hoped for in Jerusalem was falling apart. Even Mathias had been lost during the day's events.

*"Dismas of Sebaste!"*

The coarse shout came from high above me, and for one horrifying moment I thought that it had come from the soldier. The voice had been artistically deep – a low rumble designed for the theater and for deep-bellied laughter – and I realized that it had been familiar.

Turning slowly on the bench, I looked to the balcony's entrance and saw Jamal Raysid Rahan clad in actor's robes and pasty makeup as he stood next to the guard. He smiled bountifully and leapt down the limestone stairs towards me. I rose quickly just as Jamal rammed his considerable bulk against me. Before his belly could catapult me towards the stage, his arms gripped me in a strong embrace, keeping me aground. "Dismas!" he exclaimed again when he finally released me. He looked me up and down. "You've gained some weight, I think."

"We need to find a place to talk," I said quietly.

"Ah, but I am to take stage next, good brother," he said. He gave a giggle and added, "An epic I wrote myself about our adventure together in the desert of the Arabs. There is a bit more swordplay on my part than actually occurred, but I've taken much-"

*"Friend,"* I said in a low but firm voice. "I need your help now. Please lend me your time for a few minutes. It cannot wait. This concerns Jael and Nahum, and you might not see me again after this day."

Jamal stared at me in silence for a moment, his smile wavering. "Yes, of course," he finally said. He put a large brown hand on my shoulder and added, "For a friend." He then led me up the stairs

323

towards the column-lined balcony.

"A fellow performer?" the soldier said as Jamal stopped in front of him.

"From his majesty's own court in *Sebaste*," Jamal said with a nod.

The soldier stared at me intently and said, "He looks like a beggar."

"Well of course he does! This garb is part of his act. By the gods, Decimus, you act as if I bring a damnable thief into the balcony."

The soldier whom Jamal knew as Decimus gave a bark of a laugh and stepped aside.

Jamal led me through the crowded balcony as he greeted those we passed by name or nickname. "Why, beautiful Claudia..." he said to one middle-aged woman with fake gold snakes intertwined in her hair. "There you are, Brosis!" to a large man stuffing his face with meat from a large chicken leg. "Hello, hello, Vibius," as he passed an elderly man with a young servant girl on each arm.

We continued past this affluent spectacle and Jamal walked me through a rear door that led to secluded patio that overlooked the upper city. Though my thoughts were dark, I noticed that the view of the Great Temple and the Mount of Olives was magnificent in the afternoon light.

"Ah, the life of an actor and soothsayer," Jamal remarked once we were alone. With the corners of his robe, he wiped his wide face free of paint.

"Seems as if you've been busy," I said as I stared out over the city. My eyes searched the walls and homes, searching for the house of Rannut and its troubles.

324

"That I have," he said quietly. He then lowered the folds of his robe, cleared his throat and said, "As you well know, things are not how they were supposed to be here though."

"At least you're doing very well."

He scoffed and said, "It may appear that way to you... and to those socialites in there." He jutted a fat thumb towards the balcony. "Things are not exactly how they seem, Dismas."

I turned to him. "Either way, Jamal, you were able to accomplish all that I asked of you. You got Jael and Nahum to their uncle's home."

"Their *uncle*," he exclaimed and spit on the ground. "A nasty brood of serpents that man is."

"Tell me what happened."

Jamal sighed and leaned against the stone railing of the porch. "Ours was not an easy trip into Judea," he said. "We made haste until we entered Zion's gate. There were always shadows on the eastern horizon – following us like hungry wolves."

I nodded and said, "Rapha-Ayzal is here."

"I know," Jamal said with a grimace. "I've heard of his... exploits."

"What happened at Jael's uncle's?"

Jamal gave another sigh and said, "I don't know what I expected when we finally found the home. Singers and tambourine players, perhaps, or full-bosomed servant girls with wine and fine cheeses. As you surely know by now, Dismas, this Rannut is anything but hospitable. My services needed no payment, though I did expect to see Jael and Nahum cared for in a befitting manner. On our trip, Jael talked to me a great deal about her father and, of course, you.

"When I announced us at his gate, the mousy little man was fetched by a servant. When he emerged, Rannut regarded us with an upturned nose as if he were viewing heaps of dung in the street. Jael greeted him cordially and told him that a horrible thing had happened to his family in the east. He didn't seem too concerned about this news but he eventually allowed her and Nahum inside. He made me wait outside that evening without even a bowl of water. I slept on the street corner that night. Our camels had since been bartered for money, food and new clothing."

"Rannut did not fetch you the whole night?" I asked, my anger building again.

"Nor the next morning. When I called on him from the gate, he threatened to have soldiers dispatched as he was not fond of 'rabble from the east lands'. I camped in the alley across from the house and eventually met with Jael as she exited the house for water early one morning. I was nearly sick with hunger at that point but I remember her words to me. She said that as her father Aaron had died, his rights and responsibilities under the Law were transferred to Rannut, who demanded that she stay with him in Jerusalem as a house servant. It appears as if Rannut and her father Aaron were never in accord with each other."

"What of Nahum?" I asked slowly, breathing deep to control my anger.

"The boy will either be sold or he will grow up a servant at Rannut's house, as he is not a direct relative of the family." He paused and then added, "I have strayed by the house nearly every day and sometimes, if the hour is right, I am able to talk to Jael." Jamal suddenly hit his large fist into his open palm and cursed. "I am truly sorry, Dismas. If only I would have known…"

"There was nothing else you could do," I said. "You've done your best and I've expected no more. Jael and Nahum would be used driftwood if you hadn't helped us. This is better than a servitude life in the east."

Jamal suddenly turned to face me and he looked to the camel-skin flap of the doorway to make sure we were truly alone. The crowd outside was laughing at something done on stage. "But you're not going to let them stay there, are you?" he asked.

"What do you mean?"

He gave a gruff laugh and said, "You risked the wrath of Rapha-Ayzal and his wolves in one of the most dangerous cities in the east lands for that woman and child. I don't believe you would let an impish fool like that Rannut undo what you've accomplished. I don't believe that for a second." He joined me at the railing, put a hand on my shoulder and said, "So, my friend… what sort of plan are you thinking of."

Though I didn't meet his gaze, I smiled. "Do you believe in fate, Jamal?"

"Fate? Of course. It is prevalent in all my poems and acts. I have considered myself the official orator of both fate and destiny. The gods have their hands in everything we do."

"Which gods?"

"All of them. Roman, Jewish, Egyptian… I would rather believe in all of them than only put my faith in one and have it be the wrong one."

From my readings of the Jewish scripture, I knew that the God of Abraham and Jerusalem would not approve of such a sentiment, but

327

Jamal's multiple faiths mattered not to me. "As fate's orator," I said, "you don't strike me as someone in need of money right now."

When I turned to him I saw his bushy eyebrows rise. "What do you mean?" he asked.

I held my hands out and turned, gesturing to the balcony outside the porch. "You must be doing pretty well to know all these people by name. Which fine palace have you been staying at here?"

He gave a smile and nodded his head towards the baying crowd in the balcony. "To my moneyed associates in there," he said, "I have been staying as a guest in the wonderful home of Spurius-Manius, herald and news bearer to Herod himself." His smile wavered. "Be it forever unknown to my newly made, wealthy friends, I actually sleep in the streets very near to this theater. I've made my bed under a weathered palm behind the home of a rich merchant who just happens to be blind. They rarely pay for reciting poems – no matter how well written and eloquent – but I've been able to eat and drink my fill, all while pretending I'm as rich as any of them."

"How much money would you need to live the life you want here?"

He regarded me quizzically. "I don't know. To rent a fine room in the upper city would be expensive, even for only a month. I would have to make any money I amass grow."

"Is that something you're good at?"

"There is no one better at both investing and swindling than I, Dismas. I could turn ten pieces of bronze into one hundred pieces of silver. I just need to have the bronze first."

I nodded and looked back to the city. "How would like to help my band with a plan tonight that would see Jael and Nahum freed from

328

Rannut's hold… and render Rannut penniless, with much of that money in your own pocket?"

His smile stretched so far across his wide face that I thought the skin would split. "That sounds like something I would very much like to be a part of."

"But it will likely be even more dangerous than our escape from *Ra' Sahay*. And after this plan is complete, you will never see me again."

His smile faded and he looked to the ground for a moment, rubbing his chin. When he finally looked up at me, his grin had returned though a little more subdued. "I was looking for a new epic to compose anyway," he said. "And the true ones are always better than fiction… once heavily overstated, at least."

My grin matched his as I slapped him on the back.

With an exaggerated actor's bow, he said, "Let us bundle a great deal of this free food in our cloaks and retire to a more private setting for further discussion." With a dramatic whip of his robe, he turned and strode to the doorway.

# X X X V - *Wind-Harried*

Once the shadows of evening had started their crawl over Jerusalem, I led Jamal into the lower city to my band's underground encampment. I was overjoyed to find that all remaining band members had escaped from the upper city – except for Barabbas, of course. As I had told Obadiah nearly everything of my time in Gilead – and of Jamal's great help in *Ra' Sahay* – my leader was very pleased to finally lay eyes on the large performer. Titus and Cyrus remained indifferent to Jamal, while Rufus immediately engaged him in several discussions concerning the arts, sorcery, prophesy and the gods. I informed Obadiah that I alone would pay Jamal out of my cut for his services, which could prove invaluable.

Despite the loss of Barabbas, we decided to continue with our plan but we chose to initiate it on that very night instead of waiting until the following night as originally discussed. We all agreed that Barabbas would not inform the soldiers of his true purpose in Jerusalem, but we also knew that torture could make even the strongest of men chatter like a gossiping servant girl. The locations of each home, the quickest routes, and even notes as to where Barabbas had said each hidden stash of treasure was, had been notated on Titus' map.

After acquiring a group of travel-ready camels, Jamal would set up a small camp outside the city walls, near the south gate. We agreed to a location near a withered fig tree which was easily found near the road to the Dead Sea. After each plunder, we would send one or two of our men back – depending on the amount of loot – to this meeting place and Jamal would divide the riches into the different satchels on the camels. Once all three houses were plundered and Jael and Nahum were safely outside the city walls, we would hastily set out on the camels. As rich men, we would head south, while Jamal would quietly reenter Jerusalem with his portion of my loot.

When Obadiah pulled me aside to ask if Jamal could be trusted with our riches, I swore to him that Jamal would do anything in his power to help us. Not just for some of my share, I told him, but because friendship was the most important thing in the world to him. My own sentiment towards Jamal made me truly wonder if others in my band would have abandoned Jael and Nahum for greater speed after fleeing *Ra' Sahay*. Jamal had not, and for this he had earned my full trust.

***

Just before we set out for our night's plan, as our band readied themselves in our hidden encampment, I sat in the chamber's corner and went through my meager belongings. In the lamplight, the silver of my worn bracelet seemed to glow. In my traveler's bag, the piece of bread Levi had given me had grown harder, though it was still much softer than its age should have allowed. I was still greatly confounded by this phenomenon and I remembered Levi's story of where he had acquired it. *"I kept this piece, here, so that I could remember this man's deeds."*

The bread also retained its faint warmth and fresh, grainy smell, as if it had been recently baked.

After putting the bread back in my bag, I motioned for Jamal to visit with me outside of the cavern. The night was wind-harried and we found a quiet place to talk at the wall's curve near the western part of the Hippodrome.

"This *eschatos kleros* proves to me that your bravery exceeds your common sense," Jamal said to me with a wide smile as we stood alone in the shadows. "This makes your friendship much more interesting, though, and I'd have it no other way."

"You must promise me something," I told him, trying to ignore the ceaseless tingling of anticipation in my palms. "When this is over, Jamal, settle down after you've established yourself somewhere – whether that be Jerusalem or even Rome. Find a fat woman and have lots of fat babies. Promise me this."

Jamal beamed and said, "In good time, friend. I have yet to find this Jesus and that will probably be my next aspiration, for I have much to inquire of him. The fat babies can wait."

I nodded and withdrew the piece of bread from my bag and felt it in my hand. It seemed even softer than before. Remembering Levi's words, I handed the bread to Jamal and said, "This might help you with that aspiration."

Raising his bushy eyebrows, Jamal regarded the bread in confusion. He sniffed it and then asked, "Stolen from the markets today?"

"Not quite," I said. "I'll tell you this bread's story when we meet again tonight. You'll find it of interest."

"And if you don't return," he asked. His smile was gone and

his face serious.

I thought back to what Eli had told me to do with the bread. With a grin, I shrugged and said, "Eat it."

Jamal nodded and then embraced me. "Return, my friend," he said. "We'll then share it together over your story."

***

The wind continued to strengthen; its gusts whistled through the city streets, between alleyways, around the stone walls before washing over the great temple.

It was a woeful song, I thought as I set out with the rest of my band. Obadiah weaved a silent path north through the shadows towards the upper city. The contents of Rufus' large goatskin bag gave the occasional clink of metal as we moved. My right hand seemed permanently affixed to the handle of my sword. I was sure that its previous owner had never imagined that the House of Cedar would be used in such a way... wielded in a series of robberies by a lowly thief.

As we coupled with the darkness of Jerusalem's upper city where our target homes lie in wait, the gales seemed to increase as if incensed by our plan. The wind disheveled my hair and unfurled our cloaks as we walked. The ebony handle of my sword was already slick with sweat.

We aimed our shadowy train west, curled past the silent theater and found ourselves in the small grove near the well, directly across the street from the House of Jashobeam. There was no lamplight visible from the home's windows.

As the palms wavered above us, I stared at the house and wondered if any other band of thieves in the city's history – even as far back as King David's reign – had attempted such a bold act of brigandage. If this plan worked, and if we remained uncaught, our band would ascend to a near mythical status.

Obadiah gathered us in the deeper darkness of the grove and whispered, "Rufus, you stay by the front and make sure no one is able to slip past us out of the house."

The poet cringed. "And if they do, *Protos*?" he asked with a slight quaver in his voice.

Obadiah sighed and nodded to Cyrus. "Stay with him at the front, Cyrus. If they flee, stop them. Have your swords drawn in advance."

"I have no sword," Rufus professed, "only divine wit and heavenly verse."

Obadiah withdrew a long dagger from the inner folds of his cloak and held the handle out to Rufus. "Do you care to tell us what you have in that big bag, Rufus?" he asked quietly. "Its contents have been jingling around loud enough to wake even Herod within his palace."

Rufus hefted his mysterious large bag in front of him and untied its leather clasp. "In the markets yesterday," he said, "I was able to convince a young soldier that I was a historian from Tyre and was trying to compile a small collection of military helmets from different soldiering groups around the conquered world for display. Using the last of my stolen coinage, I was able to make a purchase from him that may aid us tonight." He withdrew a round object from the bag that seized some of the starlight and glimmered in the darkness of the grove.

"Helmets?" Titus asked as he peered over the poet's cloaked shoulder.

Rufus nodded and handed Obadiah the first helmet and

withdrew another. "Roman legionnaire helmets, nearly a century old, lying useless in the storage barracks at the Fortress Antonia. Old as they are, I still believe they can aid us in our initial assault. They'll buy us enough time to bind the families at least, before they realize that we're not actually Caesar's elite."

He handed me a helmet, which appeared to be little more than a shined bowl with a horribly frayed plum at its top. Its worn leather chin strap was brittle with age.

Once the ancient helmets were handed out, Rufus started pulling out sections of red cloth from the bottom of his bag and stated they would serve as crimson capes to cover our plain tunics.

In the dim starlight, we transformed from thieves into Roman soldiers – though shabby ones which Herod would certainly not be proud to exhibit among his ranks.

"Two servants," Obadiah said, "Three children and Jashobeam, along with his wife. We will need rope for seven bindings. Bring enough for ten, Titus."

Titus gave a nod and rechecked the loops of rope within his bag.

"This needs to be done fast and smooth," Obadiah whispered. "We worry about the inhabitants first – get them bound and gagged in one of the lower rooms – and then make our search. Barabbas will not be here to show us the exact locations of the caches, but we have the general locations marked on our map."

With a nod, I said, "I've been thinking about what Barabbas said, *Protos*. If so much of this amassed treasure is from ill gain, then the families might withhold information from Herod and his advisors about the robberies. In truth, these three nobles may even wait to discuss the incident together before contacting the authorities.

However, if they are dead..." I paused as I looked to the silent and beckoning house across the street. "If they're dead, then whoever finds them will immediately notify soldiers."

Obadiah gave his own nod. "Kill no one," he said.

"What if we're befallen by soldiers?" Cyrus asked.

"Kill as many as you can."

We all smiled at this though surely none of us felt like dueling with trained soldiers.

"I lead to the rear of the home," Obadiah added, "followed by Dismas. We scale the back wall silently. Titus, have the axe ready and watch the streets for any late night journeyers. Cyrus and Rufus, place yourselves in the darkness in the south alley. If you see anything of grave importance, save a wandering drunk or star-loving pilgrim, dispatch Rufus to enter the home and warn us." He paused for a moment, staring at the dark home before us. "If this goes bad, scions – if a number of us are captured or killed – do not flee to the camp by the fig tree. Wait until morning and we will meet there. Do not forget the escape routes we've gone over."

Above us, the wind agitated the palms and scared a wisp of dust off the top of the building behind us.

Obadiah clasped my shoulder and that of Titus. He regarded our shadowed faces under our helmets and said, "Are we ready for riches, soldiers?"

Everyone nodded and we moved hastily but silently across the street towards the grand house of Jashobeam.

## X X X V I - *Danger Among Darkness*

From the impermeable darkness of the home's rear alleyway, we climbed over the stone wall. My first impression of the home had been that the front garden was rather small – and in this I had been correct – but the rear garden was very large and dipped down toward the alley in a series of limestone terraces.

Obadiah leading, we moved up through the garden, weaving through the trees and hanging plants until we were at the rear of the home, near the servants' quarters. The helmet kept dipping over my eyes, as the leather chin strap was too brittle to fasten. After pushing the helmet up from my brow for the fourth time since donning it, I saw an ornate rear door which led to the home's atrium and another smaller door which surely led to the living chamber for the servants. In between these doors, there was a large window; its dark wood shutters were closed to the night.

Obadiah moved towards the window and withdrew another long dagger. Once we were all pressed against the back of the house, he slid the dagger in between the shutters, searching for the string that Barabbas had mentioned. There was a faint creak and the shutters wavered when Obadiah's knuckles made contact with them. He withdrew his dagger and slowly opened the shutters. There had been no string to cut.

The inside of the home was exceptionally dark, though there was a reddish glow from some inner chamber, suggesting that a dying fire was still clinging to its embers. The window allowed us immediate access to the rear kitchen area of the home.

Obadiah placed a hand on Titus' shoulder and guided him towards the window. He then pointed at me and held up two fingers, meaning I would go in second. I answered this with a nod.

Titus slowly climbed through the window and disappeared inside. I sheathed my sword, took a deep breath, and followed him through. Once inside the home, I immediately smelled a vast assortment of spices in the kitchen area and the aroma of burning cedar deeper in the house. Titus had his axe at the ready and I drew my sword slowly, listening to the quiet serpentine hiss as it came free of its scabbard. Obadiah came next, slower than Titus or I, but managed himself through the window quietly.

In the darkness of the kitchen area, Obadiah pointed at Titus, signaling for the lamps. Titus knelt quietly and readied two of the lamps he had brought. He lit one expertly with only three whispered strokes of the flints and handed it to Obadiah. The second, he kept for himself after lighting it.

Obadiah moved past us into the home's atrium quickly. He sniffed the air, stopped at an open doorway to the right, listened for a moment then whispered to us, "The servants should be in there. Find them and bind them quietly, Titus. Allow not a peep from their lips. Lead them to the hearth room." He then withdrew six pieces of rope and six cloth pieces from Titus' bag. "Follow me, Dismas," he whispered and motioned for me to follow him deeper into the home while Titus moved into the servants' quarters.

Obadiah exited the inner residence through a wide arched hallway and moved through the spacious inner courtyard, past a trickling fountain surrounded by stone benches. The wind whistled overhead and the scattered clouds persisted in their frantic race across the sky.

The firelight came from within the north room, just beyond the courtyard. Obadiah moved quickly through the open stone doorway and we found ourselves in a very large hearth room with lime-colored tile floors and elaborate rugs beneath the spaced furniture. There were two gold hanging lamps that stretched down from the intricate stucco ceiling. They were unlit, as were several tall, bronze lamp stands elsewhere in the room.

I recalled the greed-tinted words of Barabbas two nights ago: *There is a hidden floor panel at the base of one of the wall pillars on the hearth room's southern end. If we move their long sitting chair, a piece of the mosaic can be removed and there is a large wooden box that was completely filled.* Filled with riches, I thought as my eyes scanned the south corner of the room.

There was a stone set of stairs which Obadiah immediately followed upwards from the hearth room. The upper hall branched into two rooms and I moved with Obadiah into the first one. His lamp illuminated a large sleeping room with two separate beds upon the floor with a large heaping of colorful pillows on each bed sheet. A sleeping form was curled upon each of the plush bedrolls.

Obadiah handed me the lamp and knelt over the first figure. I saw it was an overweight man who was snoring softly. With a deep breath and a quick glance at the rotund female sleeping upon the other bedroll, Obadiah firmly covered Jashobeam's mouth with his hand and shook the man awake. The wealthy merchant's eyes went wide and he grunted loudly through Obadiah's fingers. Jashobeam's wife stirred on the floor next to us. I quickly placed the lamp on the marble table near the wall and knelt next to the woman. I covered her mouth with my hand and she shot instantly awake and pulled from my grasp. Her mouth opened wide for a horrified scream, but Obadiah reached with his free hand and slapped her across the face with such force that the woman collapsed back to the bed in a nearly unconscious shock.

Obadiah then lowered his face inches away from the now fully awake Jashobeam, put his dagger to the man's fat jowls and said, "Scream and you'll be imprisoned for life. We are soldiers of Caesar. Nod if you understand."

Eyes still wide with fear, the man nodded.

"Good," Obadiah said and removed his hand from the man's mouth. "We're a *skotia* troop, dispatched by Herod, sent in the interest of the high priest Caiaphas to investigate illegal caches of monies stolen from the temple. You, Jashobeam, are a suspect at present."

The man suddenly thrashed under Obadiah and my leader was forced to push his dagger point a fraction into the man's jowls, which silenced him. A line of red ran down from the man's thick neck onto his bedroll.

"You will be given ample opportunity to answer to this offense," Obadiah said calmly, "but not at this direct moment. Now roll over."

After a moment's deliberation, Jashobeam rolled over and consented to having his wrists bound tightly together behind his back.

340

Obadiah then gagged the man and bade him to stand up, while I bound and gagged his semi-conscious wife. She stood groggily and Obadiah said, "I'll lead them downstairs to the hearth room. Find the children and meet us by the fire."

At the sleeping room's doorway, Jashobeam said something through his gag. Obadiah undid the cloth around the man's face and Jashobeam said, "Our children are gone for the season, studying in Damascus. Now please, if you'd just allow me to-" Obadiah quickly refastened the gag before the man could say more.

We led the pair downstairs after I checked the remaining rooms on the second floor to see if he had told the truth. The hearth room was brighter than before and I was thankful to see that Titus was already there with two bound female servants at his feet. Titus was poking at the rekindled fire with an iron rod.

I led Jashobeam's wife to the floor next to the servants and helped her lay down beside them. I averted my face from the gagged servants. They each had dark hair and looked somewhat like my mother had years ago. Or like Jael, perhaps. Their tears gave me a sudden burst of shame.

"Have you explained to the servants what is occurring on this night?" Obadiah asked Titus.

The thickset thief shook his head solemnly.

Obadiah bent down to the women and said, "Your master has been hoarding money from the temple for many long years and Herod has agreed to aid the high priest in this matter by sending a *skotia* troop to investigate. This affair does not concern you, so make no motion to interfere. Nod if you understand."

The servants nodded and did not seem overly surprised.

341

Obadiah stood and walked over to Jashobeam, who was kneeling on the marble floor near an ornate stone vessel which stretched upwards nearly half way to the stucco ceiling. He withdrew Jashobeam's gag and asked, "Still under the loose set of tiles under the sitting chair, Jashobeam?" Obadiah pointed to the room's southern end, where a long sitting chair beckoned from the wall.

Jashobeam was silent and looked to the floor.

Obadiah grunted and replaced the man's gag before pushing him to the floor. Without waiting for the order, Titus moved to the sitting chair and pushed it across the tiles near the corner. He lowered his lamp and began examining the floor.

As Obadiah and I waited over our bound captives, Titus gave an un-soldierly whoop of discovery and I heard the scrape of tiles being moved. I made a move to help him and to see what treasure we had uncovered but Obadiah firmly said, "Hold." I stopped and remained next to the bound family. I adjusted my helmet again and watched Titus work in the room's corner, behind the oblong sitting chair.

After another minute of exertion, Titus stood slowly and moved back into the light of the hearth. Straining with both strong arms, he carried a large strongbox carefully to the middle of the room and set it on the floor in front of Obadiah with a grunt.

"How much?" Obadiah asked in a measured voice that seemed difficult – even for him – to maintain.

Titus beamed and said, "Full to the brim with gold and silver." He then gave a somber frown and said, "My lord." Titus opened the chest and lowered the lamplight to show off our bounty.

My heart missed a beat and seemed to take a great deal of time in its recovery. The chest was indeed full of amassed gold and silver coins, exotic stones and varied jewelry. It was a fortune – enough for twenty men to live off of for the rest of their lives. It would divide quite nicely five ways. Jashobeam truly had been hoarding for many years.

The plan was working! Suppressing a smile, I realized that the first tier of the *eschatos kleros* was nearly complete. My thoughts relocated to a seaside villa under a beautiful sunset. Jael and Nahum would live with me. We would enjoy bowls of splendidly aged wine, livestock, my own servants... No, I thought. I would not have any servants. I still remembered the pains of servitude. I could manage my own house with a fine wife. However, perhaps a gardener or...

"Soldier," Obadiah said to me gruffly and I realized this was his second attempt to draw me from my reverie. When I faced him, he said, "Take three burlap sacks from our bag and start filling them."

I cleared my throat and withdrew the thick sacks from Titus' bag. The helmeted thief bent over to aid me and after several minutes we had emptied the strongbox and each sailcloth sack was half-full of loot. I tied one of the sacks closed and hefted it over my shoulder with a grunt. There was no way I would be able to take all three back to our encampment.

Titus gathered two sacks and started for the back door. Obadiah nodded to me and I followed my friend across the hearth room. As I passed by Jashobeam, he wrenched his lips away from his gag and sputtered, "You're not soldiers." His eyes were angry and he glared at me. "You're lying thieves and Herod will have you executed in the streets." He spit on the tiled floor in front of me.

Obadiah walked over to the bound noble, stopped over him and said, "If we're not soldiers, then perhaps you should be more afraid than you are. You've heard tales of us in the streets and in the markets, no?" Obadiah gave a wolfish grin and for its duration he looked eerily similar to his brother.

Jashobeam gulped and lowered his gaze to the floor.

Obadiah turned to me and said, "Meet me outside at the rear door. I'll bind them all together and tighten all their gags so they'll last the rest of the night."

I nodded and lugged the bag out through the inner courtyard, towards the rear door where Titus was waiting. He grinned at me in the darkness and said, "I'm going to build a palace in Rome, Diz. In the shape of a winged god to thank the spirits for their good fortune."

"Do not thank them until this night is over, friend," I whispered as I unlocked the door and exited the home.

***

After shedding our quasi-soldier garb, Titus and I met Jamal back at his camp outside the city walls. I dropped my heavy bag next to the line of camels he had readied. Jamal informed us that he had seen a band of soldiers earlier in the night running full gallop through the street towards the western walls.

"Ayzal has attacked again," Jamal said quietly and started to untie one of our bags. "His blood-thirst will never be satisfied." He looked in the bag and his eyes went wide.

"As long as the soldiers stay away from the upper city," I said as I bent and retied my sandals. "Be careful as you ready all of this," I told Jamal. "If the soldiers are about in these hills, it would not do you well to be seen with such loot."

I patted Jamal's shoulder and moved with Titus back to the city walls to finish our *eschatos kleros*. Obadiah, Cyrus and Rufus would be waiting for us in the alley across the street from our second target: the house of Obil. Newly energized by seeing the riches again, we hastened through the south gate and merged with the shadows of the city.

***

Outside the house of Obil, in the darkness of his expansive front garden, I waited while the rest of the band attempted to enter the home through the side door. Rufus had stated that he wanted to tempt his fate "in the dire heat of the siege" and I volunteered to watch the front of Obil's home alone.

The home's windows were barred and narrow, too high to climb through, so the task of entry was left to Titus' axe blade. The three quick axe blows against the door's hinges were sharp in the night, though the wind covered much of the noise. From my perch under a large full-bloomed myrtle, I saw the band push through the door and enter quickly with lamps and blades at the ready.

What was possibly the muted sound of a woman's cry reached me, though I could not fully distinguish it from the wind. I looked out over the garden's wall to see if anybody had exited their home to see what the commotion was. The street corner was abandoned. If anybody had been camping on the street near the home, the stone walls around the garden had fully concealed our dealings. The wind whistled through the garden and continued to offer its angry reproach.

My eyes continued to roam the street while my ears attempted to pick up the hushed tones from inside the home. The tall Mariamne Tower stretched upwards towards the racing gray clouds from the wall just past the line of homes across the street. Our theft was taking place very close to Herod's own palace, which meant that a great number of soldiers were mere seconds away.

Several minutes later, as I continued to scan the street, I saw a furtive movement past the darkness of the road, in the alleyway between two homes. It was a large shape – a man, no doubt – and it had withdrawn into deeper shadows when I turned my head to focus on it.

Soldiers, I thought warily. Preparing to make their ambush as soon as we left the home.

Before I could run inside to warn the band, I heard a noise from the side of the house. I turned and saw that the band was already exiting the home with two cloth sacks that appeared quite full. Obadiah led the band towards me and stopped when he saw the expression on my face. "Is all well, scion?" he whispered.

Before I could profess my worries to him, Titus and Cyrus scrambled over the side wall and disappeared into the back alleys, headed towards our camp to deliver the second catch of riches.

"Dismas?" Obadiah inquired and laid a hand on my shoulder.

I shook my head and turned back to the street. "I thought I saw someone out there in the far alley, watching us," I said quietly. "They're gone now."

Obadiah grunted and joined my vigil of the street. The wind fluttered our red capes.

"Probably just a wandering drunk or beggar," Obadiah whispered after a moment. "More than likely he didn't even see you. If he did, it's just Caesar's business and he'd want nothing to do with it." He tapped my helmet and grinned. "Another wonderful catch, scion. Hidden behind wine vessels in the lower storage chamber. The wife told us. She still thinks we're actually soldiers."

Rufus stopped next to me and asked in a hushed tone, "An ailment, brothers?"

"No," I said quickly. "My eyes are just looking for danger among darkness."

With one more unfruitful glance at the shadows past the street corner, I followed them over the garden's north wall into the adjacent alley. Keeping to the darkness, I moved with Obadiah and Rufus towards the eastern portion of the upper city… to the house of Rannut, where more riches – as well as Jael and Nahum's exodus from servitude – awaited us.

Dawn's red light was less than three hours away, and though I didn't know it at the time, some of our band members would never see that light again.

## XXXVII - *Prints of Mud*

Looking back on that night, I know that we should have seen the signs of a coming danger. If Charon had still been alive and with us, he surely would have picked up on them – those subtle hints of warning that not one member of our band had taken the time to notice. Rannut's front door had been slightly open and we made entry at that point instead of our planned ingress at the back door. A man such as Rannut would never leave his front door unlocked, never mind cracked ajar. And there had been streaks of mud on his floors; grimy footprints littered the marble floors though the ground outside was dry. This would make sense to me much later.

Cyrus waited outside in the home's garden as we slipped through the front door into the darkness of Rannut's house – Obadiah first with a lamp, followed by myself, Titus and Rufus. I was anxious to see Jael, to tell her that her days of servitude were over. Eagerly, I moved to the front of our silent procession and whispered to Obadiah, "I'm going to the servant quarters."

Obadiah nodded and moved towards the home's inner atriums. Most likely, Rannut and his wife would be on the second level, deep in the throes of sleep. Titus handed me his own lamp and followed

Obadiah while Rufus took a nervous breath and followed my lamplight.

Not bothering to draw my sword, I slipped past the long kitchen area and went down a small series of stairs which led to the back portion of the home. In the dim lamplight, I saw that the servant quarters were empty.

"The floor," Rufus whispered, pointing the dagger at his feet.

I bent with the lamp and saw that several muddy footprints could be seen spaced out on the floor of this room. They were from large sandals. At least two or three different sets of feet. One of the servants' bedrolls had been pulled away from the wall and was crumpled against the floor.

With an uneasy feeling growing in my stomach, I motioned for Rufus to follow me back through the kitchen and into the home's main living chambers. The lamplight cast ghostly shadows on the plastered walls of the home as I moved through the house. Every piece of furniture and luxurious adornment seemed suddenly animate and threatening. I drew my sword quietly and moved to the upper stairway, where the rest of the band had halted. They, too, had not found anyone on the first level.

While Titus' eyes remained fixed on the darkness of the stairway and the uncertain shadows beyond, Obadiah drew me near to him and whispered in my ear, "You did not find the servants and your woman Jael?"

I shook my head. "Just prints of mud and a scattered bedroll."

In the dim lamplight, I saw his frown deepen. He then patted Titus on the shoulder and the thief started up the stone steps. Titus held his axe over his shoulder, muscles bunched and ready to swing if necessary.

The stairway led us into a short hallway which branched off into two dark bedrooms, which we cautiously searched first. Like the entire first floor, they proved empty, save more mud streaks on the floor.

At the hallway's end, there was a very large sitting room with tiled floors and a high vaulted ceiling. There were numerous hanging lamps and the walls were decorated with ornate carvings. Various pieces of furniture sat both inside this dark sitting room and outside on the open porch which offered an expansive view of the dark city.

Moving deeper into the huge room, I saw a dark figure sitting silently in a chair near the room's unlit hearth. Obadiah broke from our group and moved slowly through the room's center towards the sitting person, while I moved to the left. Titus followed me, while Rufus remained at the door. Once again, I noticed several muddy footprints on the floor between me and the chair.

Lamplight cavorted off of the decorated walls and furniture, causing the shadows to twist and move about the large room as if revealing half-hidden wraiths.

When he was in front of the chair, Obadiah stopped and I saw his helmeted form visibly tense. I moved behind him and looked past his shoulder.

Rannut stared back at me from his roost in the chair, though I knew he couldn't see me. His once white robe was now a deep crimson and I knew from the dripping sound beneath his chair that he had not been dead for long. The rich merchant's mouth was open in a silent plea, as was his opened neck.

*Ambush.*

Before this thought could process itself fully into my limbs, I looked past the dead man and saw the shadows among the other furniture continue to shift menacingly. These man-like forms seemed to rise from behind other sitting chairs and tables, and I then realized that these multiplying shadows were more real than simple tricks of light and darkness.

The largest of these forms moved closer to us, and from behind him another man removed a small candle he had been covering. He then lit one of the large hanging lamps next to him. Yellow light chased the shadows away and we finally saw our adversaries.

"*Protos*," Jaximo said with a mock bow. His axe was glistening with blood. Behind him, another bloodied body lay on the floor – a woman I assumed was Rannut's wife. Standing behind her body were several other men; among them, a tall figure seemed to loom even higher than Jaximo. Rapha-Ayzal stepped over the body to stand next to the axe-wielding thief as more raiders emerged from different corners of the room. Ayzal's mangled chin shined in the lamplight like burnished iron. In his hand he hefted a long curved sword.

"Brother," Ayzal said softly as he rubbed the marred flesh of his chin. He then used this hand to produce a dagger from his cloak – my own prized blade – which also gleamed in the lamplight.

Obadiah was silent as he regarded the pair before him. The other raiders continued to space out around the room, cutting off our path to the doorway. Rufus gave a whimper and moved to the room's center next to Titus. Despite my building terror, I noticed that all of the raiders' feet and legs were speckled with mud and this made me wonder how this was possible when it had not rained in many days. I also wondered how Jaximo had fallen into league with Ayzal's band, and how they had known where we would be on this night.

Such questioning thoughts were quickly replaced by a rising

panic as the band of raiders started towards us.

Obadiah was the first of us to act, throwing his lamp at his approaching brother. The clay light shattered against the hilt of Ayzal's raised sword but did not explode. Ayzal gave a hoarse cry and bounded forward as he swung his curved sword towards my leader. Obadiah's sword met his with a resounding clang. To my right, Titus rolled sideways to escape two of the charging raiders and he found himself at the feet of Jaximo, who was already swinging his axe downwards towards my friend. Raising my sword to ward off a blow from one of the other raiders, I screamed a warning to Titus, knowing it was too late. The axe blade drove through the old Roman helmet loudly and blood erupted from either side of the blade. My cry turned into a scream of rage as I swung my sword at the raider in front of me, striking his blade with a ring. I recognized this man as Makir – the raider who had coveted young Nahum. He pushed forward and I found myself swinging above him as I was propelled backwards to the outer porch. Still screaming, I kicked out at Makir's knee under our merged blades and felt it buckle for a moment. I used this momentum to swing my own lamp at his face and it shattered against the side of his head, immediately catching his longish hair on fire. Head fully engulfed in flames, he dropped to his knees and began to scream as he swatted his hair furiously with a three fingered hand. I thrust my sword between his arms and felt it sink deep into his throat.

To my left, another raider swung a short sword at me and I wrenched my blade free from Makir and blocked the blow. Pivoting away from him, I saw Obadiah still in combat with Ayzal, while Rufus was trying to pull away from the grasp of another raider – his short dagger forgotten in his fear. On his way towards me, Jaximo swung his axe at Rufus, lopping off the top of the poet's head at the brow. The other raider before me kept swinging his sword, advancing towards me, causing me to backpedal onto the windy balcony. He was suddenly knocked aside by a crazed Jaximo who bounded towards me with his bloody axe held high. I dove aside as his first blow struck the stone parapet of the balcony causing a small explosion of stone chips and dust to fly from the wall. Getting to my knees, I raised my short sword in a feeble attempt to dodge his second blow – knowing full well that my blade would not stop the force of his axe. Obadiah suddenly appeared next to him, swinging his sword with a bloodied arm at the large thief. Jaximo turned from me and blocked my leader's strike.

With a grunt, I rose to my feet as Rapha-Ayzal flung himself onto the balcony and into our midst. His face was bloodied yet still savage as he raised his sword. Hollering a curse over the howling wind, I tore the helmet from my head and threw it at him, striking him in the chest. He fell back a step, and as I rose against the parapet to continue the fight I felt a strong hand grip my red cape from behind. Turning to swing my sword at my unseen attacker, I saw it was Cyrus; the lanky thief had climbed up the latticework to reach the balcony.

"Jump down, Diz!" he yelled, still trying to pull me over the balcony with him. Turning, I saw another two raiders spill onto the balcony past Ayzal, one wildly swinging a curved sword. Obadiah pushed away from Jaximo as the large thief swung his axe at him in a broad sweeping motion. My leader ducked and the axe blade caught one of the other raider's in the face, knocking him backwards into Ayzal. The wind sprayed the man's warm blood over us.

With his own curse, Obadiah threw his helmet at the still off balance Jaximo, hitting him in his crooked nose which caused him to fall to one knee.

Behind me, Cyrus threw his dagger into the group of advancing raiders in the sitting room and then grabbed my cape yet again and pulled. In front of me, Obadiah turned and flung himself over the parapet as I turned and tumbled over the wall myself. My vision beheld a rotating scene of wall, sky and earth before I finally landed in a line of landscaped shrubbery. The wind was knocked from my lungs and before I could find my next labored breath, Obadiah was pulling me to my feet.

"Come on, scion!" he hissed at me.

When I finally stood, I saw one pursuing raider land next to the shrubs and then hastily try and stand to impede us. As we passed him, Obadiah slashed at the man with his sword, cutting deeply into the raider's chest. The man howled in chorus with the wind.

We ran through the garden and quickly climbed the stone wall which led to the street. I heard shouts from the other homes and a woman screaming, "Brigands!" Once on the street, we passed by several locals who had emerged from their homes to see what the commotion was about. They scattered fearfully upon seeing our bloodied weapons.

Behind us, from the balcony over Rannut's garden, Rapha-Ayzal screamed, "*Obadiah!*"

We ran south, finding the nearest alley and continued on as fast as possible towards the lower city. The wind's gales lashed through the alley and the blood on my face was suddenly cool. The sound of other footfalls and shouts could be heard in various parts of the upper city.

After untold minutes of running through the darkness – twisting and curving through different shadowy routes with no real direction other than scared desperation – we finally slowed and hid ourselves behind a line of merchant tents near the lower market. The darkness there was nearly complete. Still breathing heavily, I closed my eyes and listened to the gales whistle over us. Without seeing the restful blackness I had hoped for, my mind only conjured the repeated image of an axe smashing through my friend's skull. My sword slipped from my fingers and dropped to the dusty ground.

Opening my eyes, I leaned forward out of the shadows and was sick on the street. Neither Obadiah nor Cyrus attempted to pull me back into the hiding spot as they too seemed beaten down from fatigue and shock.

The thought of Jael and Nahum reduced once more to Rapha-Ayzal's captives made me heave again into the wind.

After my retching became dry and pitiful, I stumbled back to the tents and collapsed against the rear wall of the apartments behind us. I slid down the wall and curled into a ball in the darkness as I tried to keep my eyes from closing – fearful of what horrors I would relive if they shut. Obadiah rocked against the tent, holding his injured arm. Cyrus glared into the darkness, his smallish eyes narrowed in anger and confusion. I angled my body away from them and stared at the blood-spattered bracelet at my wrist. Thinking of how all my dreams had been lost at the house of Rannut, I tried to summon the courage to stand but found none.

"We need to get to Jamal," Obadiah whispered more to himself than to anyone else.

To me, the riches from the first two homes seemed little better than sand as I tried to understand how we had been ambushed by both Jaximo and Ayzal. Where had they taken Jael, Nahum and the other servants, and why had the raiders all been dirtied by mud when the whole city was dry? Little made sense at that moment other than my grief.

Above us, the wind howled its agreement.

# FOURTH INTERLUDE

"*It appears as if all is lost for Dismas,*" *I declared sadly.*

*The traveler shook his head and said,* "*It is impossible to have 'all lost', Marcus.*"

"*The woman he's grown to love is either held captive once more or dead and half of his hand has been killed. No doubt, their riches are gone, as well.*"

"*You're suggesting his tale has a sad ending?*"

"*No, though I do know that Dismas will survive his time in Jerusalem.*"

"*You know this for sure?*"

"*Well, it's obvious, since he was able to meet with you at some point to tell his tale, correct?*"

"*All things are possible with God, Marcus. And with Him, all can never be lost.*"

*Looking to the night outside briefly before turning back to Siergo, I said,* "*I'm not going to ask any further questions so that you may continue the tale. And because I feel that any more of your answers would only serve to confuse this rustic even more.*"

*Siergo smiled and unfolded his hands from the table to take a* sip of wine from his cup. "Some of the most wonderful truths are hidden in enigmas and parables," he said. "This man's story and its telling are no different."

"You say 'story' like this is a fictional account."

His eyes narrowed a little. "It is very real, I assure you. I am incapable of lies."

"Oh, I believe you, Siergo. It just seems... well, this whole night seems fit for a great fiction, though it is real. Perhaps the best word to describe this night would be 'surreal'. Would that offend you?"

Siergo dwelled upon this for a moment, then said, "Not in the least." He paused and regarded me for a moment in silence before saying, "You remind me of Dismas in some ways. You are both humble and respect your abilities, even though he was a bad man for so long and you have surely maintained a much better nature in your years thus far."

"If this is a compliment, then you have my thanks."

"It is, brother."

Before I could offer another bemused comment, the traveler continued the tale.

## XXXVIII - *Tsinnor – Water Course*

The red dawn held no beauty on that morning; its redness only reminded me of Titus' blood being spilt over tiled floors. With the sunrise, the wind did not cease its pitch, but seemed to grow even stronger. The early morning vendors talked of an approaching sandstorm from the wilderness. Tent cloth was unfurled and eyes remained squinted as clouds of dust prowled the streets. Yet the vendors began their calls and the beggars resumed their imploring.

This same red light bathed the hills outside of Jerusalem and put a scarlet hue on the ruined camp near the fig tree. The riches were gone, the camels slaughtered to spite us and Jamal had been left alive but gravely injured. He lay next to the dead body of one of the raiders under the tree, coughing up blood as he tried to stand when he saw us.

I rushed to his side and made sure he didn't try to rise again. "Jamal!" I cried out. "Where are you hurt?"

He coughed again and more blood speckled his robe. "Everywhere, friend…" he sputtered. "I'm so sorry, Dismas. They took everything. But at least…" He winced and pointed a bloody hand to the dead raider next to him. "At least I was able to send one of them to the grave."

I nodded and said, "What can we do for you? We can fetch a physician or..."

"Don't bother, my friend. Their blades had much bulk to get through on this body, but they were eventually successful in finding my inner workings..." With another wince, he looked up to the clouds and I saw tears in his eyes.

"How did they find us, Jamal?" Obadiah asked softly.

Still looking at the clouds above, Jamal said, "Ayzal was not among them but I recognized several of his men. One mentioned something about a new addition to their band – one of your former band mates."

"Jaximo," I said over the wind.

With a curse, Cyrus stalked away from us and sat next to the dead camels as he looked back to the city.

Jamal looked back to me. "After falling in league with Ayzal, this new raider happened to see us together in the city while we were scouting the..." He coughed again and closed his eyes with a grimace.

"He didn't know which homes we'd be at for the *kleros*," Obadiah said with a scowl, "but he knew to look for us in the upper city. They must have had someone – probably several of them – watching for us yesterday."

"I should have killed him in Gergesa," I said.

Jamal opened his eyes and I saw fresh tears against his dark cheeks. "What of Jael and Nahum?" he asked.

"They're fine," I lied with a forced smile. "They're both safe, my friend."

He nodded and gave his own weak smile. "At least there is

that…" He held out his left hand which was cut and bruised yet still holding something. "And there is this, Dismas. Your gift. They thought it was more riches… but they couldn't pry it from my fingers." He opened the bloody hand and I saw the piece of bread I had given him before we began our ill-fated plan. "Something tells me this bread's story is more valuable than any riches… You know, my friend, I never really believed in miracles. Until now…"

Jamal then smiled, closed his eyes and breathed no more.

I continued to kneel over him for a while, feeling my own tears move across my cheeks. Slowly, I closed his bloody fingers back over the bread, but not before feeling its new stone hardness.

With a hand on my shoulder, Obadiah said, "I'm sorry, scion, but we must go. Soldiers will probably be scouring these hills at any moment."

"Where do we even go?" Cyrus asked dejectedly.

After wiping my eyes, I stood and said, "Back to the city. I'm going to find where they're hiding Jael and Nahum. The raiders are still in the city for some reason. They would have kept the camels if they'd left. I'm sure they'll stay hidden until tonight, and then flee the city when it's dark."

"And we'll kill both Jaximo and Ayzal," Obadiah said with a nod.

Cyrus stood from his perch and added, "And get our riches back. But where do we even start looking, *protos*?"

Obadiah looked back to the city. "After last night – after seeing the raiders – I have a good idea where to begin our search."

"The mud on their feet?" I asked.

With another nod, Obadiah started for the city gate and we

followed.

***

We found ourselves at a small pool near the temple, at the market's north end, where a multitude of sickly beggars fought to be first in the water as the sun continued to rise over the Mount of Olives. The Temple looked like a white fortress in the dawn's light.

Once the beggars and sick had their fill – some feigning to be healed while others cursed the impotent water – we bathed ourselves, washing away the sticky blood of the night's terrible battle.         We had been much closer to the Pool of Siloam once entering the city and I asked Obadiah why we had not bathed there.

.     "Just like real wolves," he whispered with a voice that was barely audible over the wind, "Ayzal and his raiders need a lair within the city."

"But where is this lair?" I asked.

"I wondered where such a number of rough men might hide in the city and not be found suspicious by merchants or soldiers. It ate at me, for the back of my mind knew the answer but would not allow the front to know. And then last night…"

"The mud on their feet," Cyrus said slowly, obviously as confused as I.

Obadiah nodded. "They were not hiding in the city but *under* the city. Even the lame knew before we did."

"What do you mean, *Protos*?" I asked.

"Do you not remember when we heard the beggar at the Siloam pool talk about the 'cries of a demon' from the inner bowls of the tunnels? And now, days later, the pool isn't nearly as full as it usually is… for the beggars know what lies within the tunnels." Obadiah then

362

looked at me and asked, "During your captive studies of the Jewish histories, Dismas, do you recall how King David was able to seize this city?"

I thought back to those long days of scripture reading. The story of David had been one of the more stirring tales of the whole manuscript and I had read it many times. "The Jebusites," I said, "told David that even the blind and sick could ward him off. David told his men they would have to use the..." I tried to recall the word from memory. "*Tsinnor*," I finished. "Whatever that was."

Obadiah nodded and said, "Water course."

At that moment, I suddenly realized what he meant. The raiders had all been wet and muddy, especially beneath the knees from trudging through a watercourse. A *tsinnor*, as the Jews called it.

"The Pool of Siloam," Obadiah explained, "has a tunnel at its back that leads down into the earth and under the old city wall into a vertical shaft that serves as a stone well, of sorts. The Siloam Tunnel has stairs that are easily accessed from the pool. The shaft leads south, underground, outside of the city to the Gihon Spring in the Kidron Valley. David knew of this shaft and he led his men through these tunnels into the heart of the old city and attacked from within. This was how he seized Jerusalem from the Jebusites."

After a moment's thought I asked, "So it is still accessible?"

"Years after David's reign, King Hezekiah made a new tunnel further underground and sealed old ones that the same stratagem might not be used against them."

"So where is Rapha-Ayzal then?" I asked. "Just hiding in the tunnels."

"There are a series of experimental shafts," Obadiah said, "as the workers had tried numerous times to connect two tunnels – one from the city and the other from the spring. There are various shafts and caves that were cut the wrong way or were used as resting quarters for the Jewish workers. My brother…" He paused as a grimace unfolded on his face. "Ayzal is probably hiding Jaximo and the remainder of their band in these experimental shafts and caves, deep underground."

I nodded. "Would they not be seen though?"

My leader shrugged. "The tunnels are deep and if they only emerged at night to conduct their affairs the only people who would see them would be the sickly beggars who slept by the pool."

Looking towards the market in the direction of where the Pool of Siloam was, I said, "That is where Jael and Nahum will be."

"The raiders are now rich and have several new future slaves in their possession," Obadiah said. "Most likely, they will rest through the day and then escape the city under the cover of darkness. The outriders will be out in force on this day and they surely know about the massacre at Rannut's home. Soldiers will scour the roads to and from Jerusalem."

Something inside me gave a twinge of fear but I quickly swallowed it as I thought of Jael and Nahum shivering in some underground cavern while the foul raiders enveloped them like a brutal fog. "Then that is where we will go," I declared. "Right now, while the thieves sleep and dream of how to spend their riches."

Obadiah looked at my face and I saw the same grim resolution behind his own eyes. He nodded to me slowly and we both looked at Cyrus.

After a silent moment of thought, the small-headed thief asked a question of more worth than his usual utterances: "When we are only three, how do we accomplish this?"

"We need a very brilliant plan, indeed," Obadiah said. "Or Rufus' magic box."

"We could just tell the soldiers where the wolves of the Jordan are," I offered. "They would capture or kill the raiders and then free the servants."

Obadiah shook his head. "It would certainly be a battle," he said, "but your woman and the other captives would probably be killed by Ayzal... or Jaximo. The treasure would be seized by the soldiers and all would be a loss."

"The treasure means nothing to me," I said.

A stern look suddenly came across his face. "It should, scion," he said gruffly. "Our friends died for those riches. We've planned this final *kleros* for over a year and its path has ultimately cost us everyone but us three. We will never abandon its path. Not until I'm dead or being strung up on the Skull."

"And of the line you spoke of back in the oasis?" I said.

He glared at me over his silver beard. "That line – and its bearer – can be addressed after my sword is buried to the hilt in my brother's heart."

"And mine in Jaximo's heart," I responded.

Cyrus remained silent but was visibly frustrated as he did not know the names of any other raiders to threaten.

"Either way," Obadiah continued, "I don't think a frontal approach to the Siloam pool will be wise. Ayzal will have sentries posted at their tunnel opening. We'll have to enter from the Gihon Spring, outside the city walls."

"From what you've told me," I said, "the tunnel is underwater for at least forty feet. Maybe more."

"It may be the only way. Attack them from the rear where they don't expect it... from Hezekiah's tunnel. That is the *only* way it will work: surprise. Half of his men will have to be dead before the other half even knows we're among them."

Cyrus' frustration had turned to fear and he said, "Protos, I don't know if I can swim underwater. What if I drown? The beggars will then barter with my bones when they're later found in the pool."

Obadiah put a hand on the bald thief's shoulder. "No one will barter your bones, Cyrus," he said softly. "And you won't drown." He turned to me. "Did we manage to salvage any of Titus' rope?"

"No," I answered with a sigh as I thought of my friend's death. "His whole bag is gone. Why?"

"I'll swim first, taking a line of rope with me. You and Cyrus can follow the rope. It will work. After we get what we need from the markets, that is."

Cyrus shrugged off Obadiah's hand and began to rub his head with a shaking hand. "I am not able to swim," he stuttered, "let alone hold my breath for that long. Never have been able to."

I grinned at him and said, "Today, you learn."

***

Thankfully, there were no travelers near the rocky Gihon Spring, though a herd of sacrificial sheep fed on the vegetation near its base. All around us, the hot wind blew heavily and dust seemed more plentiful than clear air. Though the spring was enclosed by a double rock formation, its surface rippled from the wind. Further back, within the rocks, the dark mouth of the tunnel loomed. The surface disappeared against the tunnel's ceiling nearly eight feet into the void.

Obadiah cut one short length of rope and tied his sheathed sword to his back. He then placed his daggers, dry rope – which he had knotted every three feet before fastening a heavy three-pronged hook to its end – torches and flints inside a waxed sheep bladder and sealed the package with a leather tie which he fastened to his belt.

"Now, the daunting part," he said and began tying the remaining length of long rope around one of his sandaled ankles. He stood, handed me the other end of the rope and walked into the water until it was up to his waist. "Keep feeding the rope," he said between deep breaths. "Only stop when it's gone. If you feel me yank three hard times after the general towing stops, start pulling me back. If you feel me pull six times, then I've made it. Then you may follow."

"Lunatic," Cyrus muttered as he looked back to the valley to make sure nobody was spying on us.

"Lunacy can win battles," Obadiah said. "Even a battle among thieves." He continued to take deep breaths, expanding his lungs with each of them. When he seemed satisfied with this, he moved into the deeper water and swam towards the tunnel opening. After one more loud breath, he disappeared into the blackness of the water. A line of bubbles sprung up where his head had been. The rope slowly fed through my hands.

We waited in silence. The wind whipped through my hair and I nearly toppled into the water with the gust. My palms tingled and I was shaking from anticipation. I was more scared to feel six pulls rather than three, knowing six would signal my turn to descend into the tunnel. The darkness of the water course looked harrowing.

Cyrus walked down the rocky slope and stood next to me. "If

he needs it, I'll help pull," he said quietly as he stared into the dark water. "Part of me hopes he doesn't make it and we have-"

Suddenly the rope lurched in my hand once. Twice... three times, as if I were fishing in the Great Sea for some monstrous leviathan. I readied myself to start pulling him back – something had surely gone wrong – when the rope was pulled three more times. In my confusion, I was still. Then the rope was pulled six more times in obvious succession.

"Lunacy wins battles," I said with a wry grin and handed Cyrus the rope. "After I'm through, either stake this or tie it good to one of the rocks."

"I don't know if I can do this," Cyrus said weakly.

I looked up at him. "Cyrus, did you not brave Rufus' scary magic powder?"

After a moment's thought, he answered, "I suppose so."

"And who was it who saved Obadiah and I on the balcony last night?"

"Well…"

I patted his shoulder. "Perhaps you are the bravest one of all of us, friend." I started to take deep breaths. Between them, I said, "If my passage is really easy and fast… I'll pull seven times on the rope so you know it's easy, okay?"

He nodded and said, "Seven times if it is easy. But don't lie, Dismas."

As I continued to draw in huge lungfuls of air, I waded out into the deeper pitch of the spring, towards the dark opening of the underwater tunnel. The water was surprisingly cool. I waited a few seconds near the opening for any sudden bursts of courage – and waited out of resigned fear, too – and when none came, I thought of Jael and Nahum, took a final breath and dove underwater with my hands gripping the rope as if it were my life's dear cord.

## X X X I X - *Hezekiah's Tunnel*


**H**and over hand, I pulled myself through the blackness of the tunnel. Terrible visions flashed through my mind as I struggled further and further through the narrow underwater passage: the faces of my dead friends, blood over marble floors, more blood on my face and hands. If I were to survive this final gambit, I wondered fearfully, would I ever be able to close my eyes without be tormented so?

On either side of me, the rock tunnel seemed to close in, scraping against my shoulders. More than once I bumped my head into a protruding stone. My lungs started to burn and my heart began to hammer so loudly in my ears I felt as if it might burst within me. Yet I continued on, hand over hand, forcing myself to replace the images of violence with the untarnished faces of Jael and Nahum.

The darkness was absolute in the underwater tunnel. My lungs began to scream and it reminded me of how my throat felt when I inhaled fiery smoke on that night in the oasis, just before my capture by Aaron's caravan.

The darkness of the water tunnel, even behind my closed eyes, grew even darker. It was total, utter blackness, and I realized that I was losing consciousness. I felt as if I was falling into the current of the mythical River Styx and the hands of my fallen brothers were clutching at my tunic, dragging me deeper into the blackness. The rope was gone; my hands fumbled weakly against those of my fiendish assailants.

"Breathe, you suckling," one of the ghosts said. I felt a cold hand slap my face. "There's a ridge here. Move your body this way and stop that wheezing or you'll get us killed, scion."

Suddenly, I felt stone under my legs and I collapsed against it as the water continued to lap at my chest. After slowing my breathing, I opened my eyes but continued to see only blackness intermingled with dancing specks of light. I found that someone had placed a sheep's bladder bag in my trembling hands.

"He's not coming," Obadiah hissed. "What's he doing out there?"

"Seven," I sputtered.

"What?"

"I told him I would pull the rope seven times for him... if it was easy. To encourage him to follow us. He was so scared..."

Obadiah whispered a curse and I felt him yank the rope next to me seven times in the water.

I was suddenly mindful of a faint light above us and I craned my head upward. As my eyes adjusted and the spots of light receded, I saw that we were at the bottom of a vertical shaft and the dim light was coming from somewhere beyond the shaft's summit. Obadiah's form was little more than a dim shadow, but I saw him holding the rope tightly as it strained with Cyrus' weight.

A few moments later, there was a splash and frantic sputtering as Cyrus reached the surface. As Obadiah calmed him, I moved further

371

up the stones with the bag and waited.

"Lie…" Cyrus stammered. He coughed up water and added, "You lied to me…"

I gave a tired smile in the darkness and whispered, "You didn't think it was easy?"

The bald thief's only response was the chattering of his teeth.

In the dim light, I saw Obadiah look upwards at the vertical shaft. His own breathing had calmed as he weighed our options. "Hand me the bag," he said after a moment. As my eyes continued to adjust, I thrust the bag towards him. There was the quiet sound of him rustling in the sheep bladder and he then said, "We're going up, scions. I hoped you've rested enough."

Before Cyrus could protest otherwise, Obadiah grunted and I heard him throw the three pronged hook, attached to the rope, upwards towards the lip of the shaft. Steel clanged against stone. Obadiah waited a moment after the sound and then started pulling on the rope. The hooks must have taken hold of something sturdy over the rim of the shaft, for the rope held taunt. Obadiah slung the bag over his shoulder and started to climb towards the dim light.

"I can't do that either," Cyrus whispered as he watched our leader climb over the shaft's rim and disappear.

"Fine," I said. "You'll have to go back the way we came in then."

Cyrus looked at the dark water and shivered.

With a tired sigh, I stood on the ridge and took hold of the rope. I placed both my feet on the wall of the shaft and started climbing upwards, hand over hand once more. Towards the top, my forearms became extremely cramped but I was too close to give up. Obadiah was only a few feet away. He reached down and helped me over the lip.

I tumbled against a pile of stones and came to rest on the limestone floor next to the shaft. The light was coming from beyond the curve of the dry tunnel which led further into the Siloam tunnel system.

Obadiah struggled with the rope, trying to help pull Cyrus' weight. I stood and helped him with the rope. We braced our feet against the lip of the shaft and pulled a few inches more with every breath. My forearms began to cramp again mightily and it felt as if the tendons within were going to pop and unravel down to my elbow.

Finally, Cyrus' hands reached the lip of the shaft and he pulled himself out, collapsing on the floor next to a pile of ancient buckets at the opposite end of the shaft's mouth. With a grunt, I sat next to him and rubbed my forearms.

"Rest for a few moments," Obadiah whispered as he pulled his sword free of its scabbard. He held it over his knees as he joined us in our rest.

Deep within the tunnels, I thought I heard the sound of someone laughing; it was a man's deep voice, echoing off of the stone walls. The laughter was not repeated, but a few seconds after it stopped the sound of a child's crying reached my ears. Nahum! I thought, pushing myself up from the lip of the shaft to stand. I drew my sword.

Obadiah stood next to me and stretched his arms and legs, readying himself for the fight to come. "Let us finish this," he said softly and offered Cyrus his hand to help him stand. Cyrus tried to make a show of standing on his own. Once on his feet, he drew a dagger from his belt and nodded to me.

Deep within the tunnels, the child cried out again.

\*\*\*

The tunnel dipped back down and then widened to a small cavern. From the growing light, it was evident that someone had fastened a torch to one of the cave walls. Obadiah stopped shy of the cavern opening, hugged the stone wall and peered within. He then leaned back to us and whispered, "This cavern looks empty but there are numerous sacks piled in one of its corners. I think it might be the riches from the *kleros*. Let's move in slow with blades ready."

We crept into the first cavern and I saw a nearly extinguished torch wedged into a large crack between two massive boulders. Half a dozen sailcloth bags had been stacked in a line against the far wall, next to another tunnel which curved into darkness. Other than the bags, the chamber was empty save more old buckets and a dusty stack of rotting wood.

Standing over the bags, Cyrus nudged one with his foot and we all heard the faint jingle of coinage. Our riches were right at our feet – there for the taking with no one to guard them. The raiders had evidently not thought anyone would brave the water course to enter their lair from the rear.

"We could take as many bags as possible and try to go back through the *tisinnor*," Obadiah whispered.

"Wouldn't we sink, Protos?" Cyrus asked.

"Then we'd simply tie the bags to the rope and drag them back through after-"

"What of the captives?" I hissed. "You're suggesting we just leave them with the raiders?"

After staring at me for a long time, Obadiah looked back to the

374

bagged sum of our previous night's plan and said, "Are we thieves or saviors, Dismas?"

Before I could respond, a female's terrified cry echoed into the chamber from deeper in the tunnels. Without another word, I started for the second tunnel's entrance.

"Scion, wait," Obadiah said, grabbing my arm. "We'll go together and get them, but we're taking some of this loot. Remember my words from before... I would rather die than not see our *kleros* through to the end."

We bent to the bags and emptied enough of the riches to the dusty floor to allow us to easily carry two bags apiece on our belts. Though I'm sure it pained both Obadiah and Cyrus to do this, our selected portions would still be enough to make us all rich men.

"Let's hurry," I whispered at them once we were done. "Don't let these cursed bags jingle too much on our hips."

After redrawing our blades, we continued through the other tunnel, moving up into the limestone earth towards another ring of torchlight. There was a faint whimpering coming from the next cavern. The captives were close.

At the tunnel's curve, just before it widened into the light, we stopped and both Obadiah and I peered around. Though we could not see the back half of the cavern, it appeared to be of good size: at least twenty feet wide and maybe thirty-five long. There were a series of boulders in the cavern, cut away from the wall and piled against each other, which blocked our view of the chamber's rear half.

A male voice came from the cavern: "Hold still, precious..." The voice was slightly slurred from drink and the whimpering grew louder. There was the sound of fabric scuffle and skin against skin.

375

Suddenly filled with rage, I emerged from the tunnel's bend and moved swiftly into the chamber. To my right, two huddled forms – a woman and child – were curled up against the wall; a raider stood over them, whispering to them drunkenly. At the chamber's opposite end, slightly closer to me, I saw two struggling forms behind the boulders. The top figure was a raider, and kept trying to push another female to the ground. In my fury, I could not tell of this crying woman was Jael or another captive servant yet I moved towards them swiftly. At the sound of my footfalls the man turned towards me with an annoyed look on his face that quickly turned to one of alarm. I swung the sword at his neck as hard as I could – did not even feel the resistance of his flesh – and watched his head spin away from his body in a spray of dark blood. Off balance, I turned as fast as possible to go after the other raider, but saw Obadiah stab the man through the throat while Cyrus' blade pierced his heart.

Both kills had been quiet enough – surely no louder than the cries of the female had been – but I knew we still needed to hurry. With any luck, the rest of the raiders would be sleeping elsewhere in the tunnel system, and we'd have enough time to plan our escape.

I knelt next to the female who lay curled beside the headless raider. It was not Jael, but I bent towards her and offered my hand. "We're friends," I said in a trembling voice. "We're here to get you out of here."

The girl slowly took my hand and rose to her feet. She tried to adjust her long tunic but recoiled from it when she found it splattered with the raider's blood. Turning from her, I moved to the other captives and looked at them in the torchlight. The woman stood from the floor and cringed away from the dead raider as she knelt to pick up the child beside her.

"Jael," I said softly. When she rose with Nahum in her arms, I saw that her eyes appeared to have lost some of their unique glimmer; some of that gold had been tarnished, I thought as I watched her squint at me in the torchlight. "It's alright now," I added. "We've come to rescue you."

Slowly, she moved towards me. When she was little more than an arm's length away, she started to cry. With my free hand – the one not holding the bloody sword – I reached out and slowly gripped her shoulder above Nahum's sleeping head.

"You came for me," she whispered.

"I always have," I said with a strained grin.

Obadiah moved next to me, gave the captives a singular look and said, "We'll have to move through one of these tunnels, scion. Your guess is as good as mine." He nodded to the two stone openings. "Unless one of the captives knows the fastest way out."

Jael looked at him and shook her head. "I was half-unconscious when they carried me down here," she said softly and shuddered as she put her head against Nahum's.

Obadiah nodded, moved past Cyrus and entered the nearest tunnel in silence with his sword held before him. "This larger one is Hezekiah's main tunnel. We'll start with this one and move slow."

Our measured path through the tunnel started an upward trek towards the surface. We passed by another fork that branched to a smaller tunnel where numerous voices were heard. This was likely where most of the other raiders were hiding, and we all held our breath as we moved past this secondary tunnel. The main tunnel dipped down once more and we were forced to quietly slosh through knee deep water and dark mud.  It then continued upward past two separate series of stone stairs and we finally saw a dim illumination near the end of the rising passageway that was too sallow to be torchlight.

Obadiah stopped suddenly and we all followed his example, ears perked for the faintest sound.  We were so close to the Siloam Pool that even the smells of the street wafted down the tunnel towards us: baking bread, incense, frying fish and perfumes.  Even the sounds of the city drifted down the narrow staircase.

Gripping my tunic to pull me closer to him, Obadiah whispered, "I think I hear voices up ahead, but it's obvious we're nearing the entrance to the pool.  There is probably going to be one – possibly two – raiders acting as lookouts at the pool's access."

Behind me, I felt a slender hand find my own in the shadows.  I turned and saw Jael move her body towards me as she pressed her arm and Nahum against my back.  Whether this was for warmth, thanksgiving or adoration, I did not know – but I knew I felt all three from it.

"Lure them down to the tunnel's curve," Cyrus said as he readjusted the tied sacks at his belt.

Nodding, I pulled away from Jael and moved to Obadiah.  "Let me try something," I whispered.  "Be ready when they come and keep the captives behind you."

He nodded as I slowly moved to the tunnel's curve and peered around the side.  The remainder of the narrow tunnel sloped upwards and I was able to make out the outline of two raiders standing guard at the low entrance to the pool.  I quietly cleared my throat, summoned a deeper voice than my own, and said, "Look lively, fools.  Ayzal said the boy is missing and he wants everyone down to the main chamber *now.*"

After a unified curse, the men could be heard moving hurriedly towards the tunnel's curve – towards us. Obadiah and Cyrus had merged together behind me, and when the first raider rounded the corner, I struck him in the head with the flat of my sword. The second raider toppled over the first with a yelp and was quickly overtaken by both Obadiah and Cyrus, who repeatedly stabbed both men into silence.

Sheathing my sword, I moved back into the tunnel's shadows and grabbed Jael's free hand. "Let's go," I whispered and pulled her past the still-twitching raiders. While carrying Nahum against her chest with her other hand, she allowed the female servant to hang on to the rear of her long tunic.

We rounded the corner and started our trek upwards towards the Siloam Pool. The tunnel leveled out and we were forced to descend a single step into knee deep water that sparkled from the reflecting light beyond the low ceiling. Just before ducking under this wall – and finally reaching the relative freedom of the pool and lower city – an unbearably loud scream traveled from the bowels of the tunnels and washed over us like an icy wind. It was a man's enraged cry, full of wrath and violent promise. This howl was surely heard by any who were near the pool and its adjoined market. After the cry tapered off, we heard other raised voices from below – and all of them seemed to be growing louder as they followed.

Ducking under the stone wall, we thrashed through the water and found ourselves suddenly bathed in the bright noon sun.

## X X X X - *Dust and Blood*

The bright sunlight coupled with the harsh wind felt like a physical slap to the face as we began sloshing through the Siloam Pool to its closest wall near the market. To the beggars and assorted travelers near the water, we must have been a ragged sight: three blood-spattered men bearing swords, two haggard looking females and one whimpering child. Those nearest to us scattered as we hastily climbed out of the pool.

At the line of palms just west of the pool, I looked back towards the tunnel's low entrance and saw several figures scrambling under the stone entry. Rapha-Ayzal emerged first, standing tall with an angry red face and drawn sword. On either side of him, four more raiders – Jaximo among them – poured out from the tunnel and stopped next to their dark leader; all of them searched the crowds hungrily for us.

I pulled Jael further into the market, handed her one of the sacks of treasure, and said, "Head north through the streets and don't stop running until you find a group of soldiers. Just wait near them, as out of sight from the streets as possible, until nightfall."

"How do we find you again?" she asked breathlessly.

Before I could think of a suitable place, Obadiah pushed me in the back and hissed between clenched teeth, "They're coming, scion… Move!"

Turning, I saw Rapha-Ayzal leading the charge towards us; his long legs kicked up splashes of water as he trudged through the pool with his raiders in tow.

"The Gennath Gate," I said to Jael. "At nightfall. Now go!"

And with that she was gone, running through the residential district with Nahum still cradled in her arms. The young servant girl followed them.

"We must lead the raiders away from them," I said, already turning to run west into the markets away from Jael's path. With a deep breath, I bounded out from the line of palms above us and entered the busy marketplace with Obadiah and Cyrus following. The remaining sacks of riches bounced at my hips. Running swiftly, I turned again and saw Rapha-Ayzal exit the pool and cut through a beggar who had blocked his passage with eager cupped hands. Blood – startling red in the noon light – jetted over the stones causing the locals nearby to scream. Two of the faster raiders had already sped past Ayzal and were little more than thirty paces behind us. Their faces were determined, vengeful and eager for blood. Inciting a violent scene during the day was not beyond them.

Turning back to my route through the market, I lowered my head and pumped my legs harder, hoping that Obadiah and Cyrus would be able to keep up. Many screamed at us as we ran past them and I was forced to shove several street-goers aside into racks of displayed merchandise. Some hollered for soldiers and others for God's curse upon us. Their screams turned more frantic when Ayzal's raiders entered the market.

I turned northwest and headed away from the bustling market into the residential street that bordered the Herodian wall. Behind me, Obadiah and Cyrus panted with exertion. Obadiah's breaths were coming in throaty gasps and I knew that neither one of them would be able to run much longer at this pace.

There were more shouts from the street corners as the red-plumed soldiers finally caught on that something criminal had escalated in the streets of the lower city and was in danger of spilling into the affluent upper city. As I ran, I looked upward and saw a soldier on the great wall blow a ram's horn signal; the cry for more soldiers rung out over the entire city. With another glance upward I saw the same soldier grapple a long arrow into his bow and release it towards us. The arrow whistled over my head and sank deep into one of the mud-brick walls above us.

To my side, I saw more distinct red plumes bobbing within the crowds, moving parallel with us through the street. Another arrow hissed over my head and struck a traveler in the shoulder. Screams followed our path like fluttering banners.

Two mounted outriders in full armor seemed to explode from the street corner in front of us, knocking over two vendors and collapsing a merchant's large, gray goatskin tent. Merchandise clattered to the ground. With a shout, the soldiers wheeled their horses towards us and lowered their spears to charge. The horses snorted angrily as if they, too, wanted us dead. The soldiers looked monstrous atop the steeds, like war titans that were neither man nor beast, but of the same flesh. The ground shook with their charge.

"Alley!" Obadiah cried out and yanked on the back of my tunic, sending me careening north in between two buildings. I chanced a look behind us, certain that I would see the spear-wielding beasts at my back, but only saw the crowd swell and howl as the first two pursuing raiders collided with the outriders. Turning back to the narrow alley, I saw it terminate at the large wall that separated the upper and lower cities. The two residential buildings had been built up against the massive stone wall. We were trapped.

Obadiah put his hands on his knees and struggled for air. Cyrus started turning in frantic circles, unsure of what to do next.

Near the street we had just come from, the screaming continued and I knew our time was limited as other soldiers would eventually enter the alley. I searched the buildings for any doorways or windows we could enter and my eyes focused on an old ladder close to the dividing wall that was attached to the tallest building.

Cursing after seeing we had no better options, I called out, "To the roof!"

"The archers, Diz…" Cyrus breathed. "We'll be easy targets!"

"No choice," I said as I gripped the ladder and started climbing.

When I was half way up the building's side, I looked to the alley's opening just as several of the raiders managed to push their way through the crowds into the alleyway. Rapha-Ayzal was at their forefront. Jaximo and one other followed – their blades all bloody. Just past the advancing raiders, I saw that both of the horses had been struck down and that a new detachment of soldiers was still doing battle with the remaining raiders.

Once at the top of the ladder, I pulled myself onto the roof and helped both Obadiah and Cyrus over its low wall. The wind was fierce in the open air and the city's mingling scents were quickly taken in by my quick breaths. Dust from the roof swirled around us and was flung into the streets below.

Alongside the roof, the great wall stretched high. On the wall's east end, near the massive stone causeway that led to the temple, two soldiers armed with bows ran towards us.

This line of residential buildings ran along the wall's length, and as I scanned their tops for any sort of escape route I saw several other groupings of people on the roofs watching the spectacle unfold on the streets below. Past them, at the furthest building – the one closest to the temple's causeway – a lone figure stood on its roof staring at us. Staring at *me*, I realized when I saw the black cloak fluttering in a different direction then the winds.

"Follow me," I said as I started across the first roof. Without hesitation, I jumped through the wind-torn air over the alleyway. Landing with a grunt, I paused as Obadiah and Cyrus completed the first jump. The tar-covered ceiling had bent just a fraction upon my landing, but held for all of us. Behind them, the heads of Rapha-Ayzal and Jaximo became visible from the first home's side wall as they reached the top of the ladder.

We continued our trek over the building tops, running eastbound towards the causeway. We passed by several people on the roofs who yelled curses at us or fled in fear through the exterior doors. The two archers were nearing us along the wall and they suddenly stopped and readied their bows. More archers ran towards them from both ends of the wall.

"Where are you *going*?" Obadiah breathed behind me.

"The Man of Shadows," I said, not knowing how else to answer.

"*What?*" he asked.

Before I could offer an explanation which would surely make little sense to him, an arrow ripped past me and stuck into the tar in front of me. A second arrow skimmed my shoulder as I was in mid-jump over another alleyway. The force of the arrow caused me to turn in the air and I landed in a roll on the next rooftop. Cyrus helped me quickly to my feet and we dodged another arrow which flew between our heads.

My confidence was fading quickly. I looked to the east and saw that the Man of Shadows was no longer on the last rooftop of this line of buildings. Regardless, I continued running as the raiders shouted their indignation behind us.

This last rooftop was higher than any before it yet I ran as hard as I could and jumped towards it; sailing over the alley, I struck the wall at my chest but was able to still hang on to the roof's edge. My hands grappled for leverage and I pulled myself up next to a grouping of clay water vessels. A second later, Obadiah's body slammed into the wall and he started to climb next to me. I helped him to his feet as Cyrus made the jump, his long arms pulling himself up the steep wall. I looked past them and saw the raiders had already made it to the previous rooftop and were accelerating for their own jump.

Two arrows whistled past and struck the tar next to us. We ran to the upper storage room of this home, feeling the thin wooden roof flex and shake with our steps. We collapsed next to a small pile of fist-sized rocks that had been chiseled from the storage unit's base. There was a thick wooden door at the unit's end that would lead down into the home itself, but I watched in frustration as Obadiah struggled with the locked door to no avail. It had been securely latched from the inner room. A safeguard against thieves.

Obadiah leaned against the wall next to me and sighed with exhaustion. His silver hair fluttered in the wind. "Dismas..." he wheezed. "There's something..."

"Save your breath, *Protos*," I said. "We'll have time enough to talk later once we've escaped this mess."

Faces were appearing over the curve of the wall; dirty hands grappled for purchase on the roof's end. Ayzal sneered when he saw us hiding behind the storage unit. Arrows stuck into the ground on either side of the dark raider as he pulled himself up and knelt behind the tall clay vessels. Next to him, Jaximo slid over the roof's edge and rose to his knees behind the containers. The last raider – a long haired man with a braided beard – pulled himself up to join the first two behind the vessels but only served to crowd the small area of cover. With a thick arm, Jaximo pushed the raider out from behind the vessels as another volley of arrows descended from the wall. The bearded raider was struck in the shoulder and then twice in the chest. He fell with a gasp to the center of the roof which shook with his weight. The whole roof seemed to tremble for a moment before relaxing. The bearded raider tried to rise but another arrow whistled through the air and struck him in the side of the head. The man collapsed to the roof once more.

Next to me, Cyrus took a deep breath then untied both money sacks from his belt and dropped them to the ground before us. He then gripped both Obadiah's shoulder and my own. "Escape and enjoy the *kleros*, my brothers," he said as he gave our shoulders a squeeze. He then stood and closed his eyes.

"Cyrus, don't," Obadiah whispered.

The bald thief opened his eyes and I saw tears there that had nothing to do with the wind. Cyrus turned and ran out into the open directly towards the kneeling figures of Jaximo and Ayzal. With a war cry that could have come from the heartiest soldier, Cyrus plunged towards the raiders in hopes of knocking them over the roof's edge – but was stopped by another barrage of arrows. The feather tipped shafts seemed to appear magically all over his lurching body and with a final cry that was more sorrow than courage, Cyrus fell to the roof over the dead raider at his feet. The roof seemed to surge with the stress of his fall.

With a sad groan, I rose to my feet and drew my sword. Obadiah stood next to me.

"Brother!" a deep voice bellowed from behind the vessels. "Face me, brother! Let us finish what we started long ago under this pleasant rain!" Rapha-Ayzal's voice seemed nearly mad with bloodlust. Peering out from behind the storage shed, I saw that Jaximo was crouched next to Ayzal, hiding his bulk behind the thick clay vessels. The iron-tipped arrows broke off small pieces of the vessels, but did not have enough force to fully penetrate them.

Another arrow clanked off the vessel and Ayzal flinched, but his wolfish smile remained.

My sandaled feet bumped into the pile of stones next to the storage unit and I suddenly had an idea. "Aim for the clay vessels, *Protos*," I said and reached down to pick up several of the fist-sized stones.

Even before I threw the first rock at the vessels, I saw Rapha-Ayzal's face shudder in angst when he saw the stones in my hands. The first one crashed into the closest vessel, breaking it in half. Ayzal moved down the line behind the intact vessels. Obadiah and I threw again and again, breaking the vessels apart with much greater force than the small arrows. The vessels exploded under our forcefully thrown stones. Ayzal and Jaximo both screamed in rage as they jostled closer to each other for safety behind their diminishing cover. Arrows started to rain down upon the vessels again.

Suddenly, the storage room next to us shuddered from a commotion within and the locked wooden door started to splinter from a steady banging from within. Angered Roman voices from inside the room found their way to my ears and I realized with a sick dread that more soldiers were trying to enter the roof from the home beneath us, using the inner stairway which led to the storage unit.

The firing of the arrows from above had tapered off as it seemed the soldiers on the wall had nearly run out of them. Ayzal snarled as he leapt to his feet. Jaximo rose behind him and both started across the roof with blades drawn. Obadiah and I moved out from the shadow of the storage room to confront them.

At that moment, many things happened at once. The wind had strengthened and a fresh wave of dust whipped between us and our adversaries as we closed the gap between us with swords raised high. The storage room's door splintered open as soldiers spilled out on the roof behind us with round battle shields held before them. The coupled weight of both the soldiers and the thieves caused the whole roof to rumble under our sandaled feet. Everyone on the roof stopped and stood still as the roof's dust seemed to dance upwards; the entire top floor of the building shook as if one possessed. Too much weight had been distributed over the old roof.

As Ayzal howled with rage before charging at us again, the entire roof collapsed inward with an explosion of brown dust; thieves, raiders and soldiers plummeted into a chaos-filled darkness.

I awoke to total darkness and screams which seemed far away. My limbs felt as if they were stone as I gasped in the dust-filled air. In truth, I could not tell where my arms and legs ended and the rumble around me began. The darkness seemed to shift before me, yet I remained blinded by the dust cloud.

"Brother!" a rasping voice cried out. My mind was a jumble as I tried to recognize the voice. "Brother Obadiah! Where are you?" The sounds of wood scraping and stone shifting also reached my ears and I realized that someone was moving towards me in the rubble. Other voices whimpered near me.

"Osteo!" a commanding voice yelled from somewhere outside the house. "We cannot breech the door, there is too much rubble! Are you alright, soldiers? Speak to me, damn you!"

The cloud of dust was beginning to diminish and I saw that sunlight was beginning to spear its way through the dust from the open roof.

"Answer me, soldiers!" the first voice said again outside the door. "Work on this door, men. Fetch axes, anything!"

Where was my sword? My trembling hands started to shift through the rubble around me, but I could not find the House of Cedar among the pieces of mud-brick and wood. My leg started to throb with pain and I realized that I would not be walking out of this crumbled dwelling. My shoulder had been sliced open from the arrow and the blood mingled with the dust making my crawl across the rubble a sticky one.

"I'm coming for you brother!" Ayzal's ragged voice yelled. "Coming to finish what we started!" The sound of shifting rubble was coming closer to me in the dark cloud.

As I slowly crawled away from the voice, my fingers closed over a sandaled foot. The toes twitched in my hand and the owner of the foot groaned. Gingerly, as Ayzal continued his ranting behind me, I moved up the still body and felt the face. Bristly beard. Hawk nose slick with blood.

"*Protos*," I whispered. The figure beneath me stirred in the darkness as I gently patted his chest. "Come on, Obadiah," I said softly. "Wake up."

The frantic rustling of Ayzal stopped and I imagined his ears perked upwards like a wolf's as he tried to hone in on where my voice had come from. "Yes, brother," the dark raider whispered venomously. "I'm coming for you. Coming for you, now…" His crawling resumed in our direction.

"Dismas," Obadiah whispered to me as I squinted in the dust cloud to see the approaching raider. "There is something I have to…"

"*Coming for you…*" the voice hissed right in front of me as a faint specter emerged from the dust. Ayzal had my prized dagger in his hand and he was sweeping it from side to side in the dust before him.

Though I had little strength left, I reached out and grabbed the hand that held my dagger and pulled myself towards its wielder. We tumbled in the wreckage of the dwelling and I landed on top of him, still holding his wrist. He lunged upwards and snapped his teeth at me like a crazed animal. With my free hand, I started hammering my fist into his face; I felt my already sore knuckles rake against his mangled chin yet I continuing punching him as hard as I could. Eventually, his hand released the dagger and I pulled it from his fingers with a cry of triumph. I then plunged the dagger into his chest – all the way to the hilt, as Obadiah had declared – and then twisted the blade fiercely. In my clenched hand, I felt the dagger tremble in time with Ayzal's ruined heart and I only released it when this fading tremble stopped.

Leaving the dagger in the raider's chest, I crawled back towards Obadiah as the shouts from outside the dwelling increased. Someone had started chopping at one of the blocked entry ways with an axe.

"*Protos*," I whispered in a shaky voice. "I… Ayzal is dead."

Obadiah stirred next to me and his shaking hands found my own. His grip was cold and had little strength. "Ah… Dismas," he said weakly. "Something I must ask of you…"

I squeezed his hand and said, "Anything." Outside of the cavernous pit, soldiers were screaming as they tried to breech their way into the room. Somebody else in the rubble had started to moan in pain as they came to. The sound of axe blows continued to echo through the dwelling.

"When you escape," he said – an incredulous thought that made my bloody lips crack into a weak smile, "I want you to ask that teacher Jesus for something. Could you… do this, scion?" His voice was fading.

Tears now mixed with the dust which caked my cheeks and I nodded. "What would I ask him for, *Protos*?"

Obadiah shuddered fiercely then lay still again before giving my hand one final squeeze. He then whispered, "Forgiveness." And he breathed no more.

For a long moment, I continued to hold the cold hand in silence as I pondered Obadiah's last words. With a quiet sob, I embraced his body to mine. The man I had upheld as my leader, my friend and my father was dead – a casualty of this cursed battle of thieves.

391

The sounds of splintering wood drug me out of my pained trance. I looked back and saw that the dust cloud was continuing to fade. A few dim bodies could be seen among scattered timbers, brick piles and ruined furniture.

No escape, I thought. My path would end in the ruins of this building when the soldiers entered and saw a living thief among dead soldiers.

*Dead soldiers.*

In attempt to gather my wits for one final gambit, I shook the dust from my head. Releasing Obadiah's body, I started crawling through the rubble towards the nearest unmoving soldier.

\*\*\*

*Keep the darkness away at all costs*, I commanded myself as the armored men gingerly carried me out from the ruined home. *Keep your wits about you and don't fall unconscious.*

The soldiers cleared a path through the crowds with threats and shoves, and lay me in the shade next to an expansive pool which was directly under the great archway.

"Herod will surely honor you, Praetorian," one of the young soldiers said to me in Latin and patted my stolen breastplate gently as he left to tend to the rest of his wounded or dead fellow soldiers.

I slowly moved the helmet further up on my forehead and watched the crowds continue to swarm around the half-collapsed building. Struggling into a sitting position, I looked behind the ornate pool and saw an opening between one of the causeway's pillars and the adjacent merchant's shop. If I could only stand, I'd make my way through that gap and find some place to shed my stolen armor before hiding in one of the alleys of the upper city until nightfall. Then, Jael could care for my wounds and we could finally escape Jerusalem. The tied money sack was still attached to my inner belt. We could buy camels, food and drink for travel, and set off to wherever we fancied.

If I could only stand. Gripping the pool's edge next to me, I slowly pulled myself to my knees, gasping at the pain in my leg and cut shoulder.

There was a loud scream from the crowd and as I turned, I saw the soldiers drag a bound and bleeding Jaximo from the ruined building. The large thief had been taken alive. He howled his indignation and spit at his captors, only to be granted a generous amount of fist-strikes for the effort.

*Stand up*, I commanded myself as I tried to push myself to my feet.

"Samaritan!" Jaximo screamed with a fiendish conviction. I turned and saw that the hulking thief had been pinned to the ground by four of the soldiers. He pointed his rope-bound hands towards me. "Dismas! He's a thief! Right *there*, in the armor... one of us! A thief!" Bloody spittle flew from his mouth as he yelled.

Several of the soldiers started to strike their captive again, but a few more insightful ones started gazing out into the crowd with inquisitive eyes.

Before the soldiers could figure out how they had been fooled, I pulled myself over the pool and into the cool water. The last thing I heard was Jaximo's deep voice yelling, "The soldier in the *pool!*"

While submerged fully in the shallow pool, I looked up and saw the sun shining down through the water which clouded quickly from dust and blood. The sun streamed through this murk and as my consciousness ebbed I thought it was a beautiful sight. A figure above the water suddenly blocked the sun and through my stinging eyes, I saw that the Man of Shadows was staring down at me. His cloaked form reached down into the water, extending a hand towards me.

Knowing he would help me complete my escape – despite any odds – I reached upwards to the hand and grasped it. I was pulled up through the water and as my face broke the surface I saw that the Man of Shadows was gone. The same soldier who had patted my breastplate in comradery was glaring down at me with a grim face. Other uniformed figures appeared beside him, and as I was flung out of the pool and onto the street, the darkness finally prevailed.

## X X X X I - *Wayfarer*

**W**hen I awoke, I found myself being eaten.

Crawling over my legs and arms as they offered blood-drawing nips, the zealous rats made their rounds. Moving slower than I would have liked, I sat up and brushed the vermin away as they nipped at my fingers and squealed in irritation at having their meal interrupted. I must have had dozens of bite marks on my uncovered skin, and each one felt like a small fiery brand; it felt like *thousands* of bites.

I gave a forlorn glance to the wooden door of my cell. The squirming floor was cloaked in complete darkness, while the faint yellowish light of a torch peeked in through the food-slot in the fortified door's center. The walls were dark stone and the floor was sticky with both rat and human excrement.

My head was ringing loudly and after close to an hour of shivering in the cell's corner – fending off hungry rats with my bleeding fingers – I realized that this ringing was actually a never-ending chorus of squeals from the vermin. The cut on my arm ached fiercely and I knew it was probably infected. My right ankle was swollen with a bad sprain and though I couldn't actually see it amid the dark vista of shadows and scuttling shapes, I imagined it to be purple. It *felt* purple, if not black.

Even if Caesar himself opened my cell door with a rusty squeak and granted me clemency for my actions, I would surely die of some rat-abetted disease before the week's end.

Hours turned into what had to be days. Captivity in Aaron's village was a veritable paradise compared to this, I thought.

And the rats continued their siege upon my flesh.

***

After what I believed to be several days – though it could have only been hours or even weeks – a pair of soldiers ordered the jailer to open the thick wooden door of my cell. One of the soldiers, the taller of two, ducked into the small chamber with a torch and immediately covered his mouth with the back of his free hand and made a retching sound. It was then – with the first true light I had seen in days – that I finally gazed upon the flesh of my legs and arms and saw the hundreds of red and yellowed bite marks that littered my skin. My ankle was indeed purple, but various hues of yellow and green also tinged the royal shade. Dark feces, both from my own body and from those of my devourers, was caked upon my legs and smeared into the fang-torn skin.

I moaned. The soldier gagged once more and then backed out of the cell. Behind him, I saw a heavyset jailer and another soldier who sported the distinct helmet of the Praetorian Guard. This man's torch was pointed at me and he said, "Thirty-nine will surely kill this one."

"Twenty-nine then, lord?" the jailer asked. "Or less?"

"No. Thirty-nine. And another for Osteo."

396

"As you command," the jailer said and slowly donned a pair of heavy leather gloves that appeared stiffened with unknown dried fluids.

"I've prayed to Jupiter that he makes it to the Skull," the tall soldier said. "But death from the tails will be adequate, as long as his screams are loud."

The fat man smiled at the soldier, displaying a haphazard row of browned teeth. He then bounded into the cell with surprising speed, stomped on two rats with an echoing crunch and cursed the remainders of the hairy platoon away from me. One encrusted, gloved hand clamped onto my hair with great strength and the other hand gripped the back of my tunic. With a piggish grunt, he drew me to my knees and dragged me out of the cell.

*** 

They wanted my screams more than anything else. So much of my character had broken – courage, faithfulness, and wit had all been lost to fear and pain. Despite such losses, however, as they shackled my wrists to the base of the hewed torture block and pressed my weakened chest to the rough stone, I clung to the one lasting trait that I had always possessed: stubbornness. Friend of the fallen soldier Osteo or not, I vowed that this tall Praetorian would not hear a scream from me.

To my credit, I did not scream until the jailer bellowed "Three!" The other thirty-seven lashes went unfelt as I fell unconscious. They were heartily felt, however, when I woke up an untold time later, with the tall soldier standing over me with a look of naked contempt on his face. "Your weakness has robbed me of much of my pleasure," he whispered in my ear. "I'll hear more of your screams at the Skull, though. Everyone else may be watching the Jew King, but I'll be watching *you* as you're nailed and hung, you lowly dog."

He then patted my head in what seemed to be an almost affectionate manner before driving the heel of his sandaled foot into my temple. As I tumbled into pain-filled darkness yet again, I wondered who he had meant by the "Jew King".

***

After waking, I found myself lying on my stomach in a different cell; this one was devoid of rats and much brighter as sunlight shone in from a horizontal slit near the roof of the compartment. Through the thick, iron barred door, I saw other holding cells and glimpsed a room at the end of the stone hallway that was filled with soldiers who were in various states of undress. Their battle tunics, worn armor and nicked helmets were replaced with ceremonial attire. Uniforms suited for a trial.

Slowly, with enough pain to make my eyes close fully in a tight grimace, I rolled to my side and sat up. The floor of the holding cell was splattered with fresh blood and I saw a crimson trail leading from my cell into the hallway where they had dragged me.

There were scores of hasty scrawls and etchings on the stone walls of the cell. Most were names, both Jewish and Roman. There were quotations of Jewish scripture, single-lined prayers to Roman gods, as well as odious curses concerning the Romans and gouged pictures of a leering skull. One of the faded writings declared, 'Caesar will burn on a cross'. Another stated, 'Juni lost his courage at the block'.

There was a sudden flurry from the end of the hallway and I saw the men in the soldier's quarters suddenly stand upright in rigid salute to someone who had entered from beyond my vantage. Two members of the Praetorian Guard exited the room, followed by an ornately robed man and what appeared to be two scribes. The soldiers led them towards the line of cells. They stopped and peered into the cell next to mine, whose inhabitant I could not see.

One of the soldiers rapped on the bars loudly with the scabbard of his sword as if attempting to wake someone from sleep. They moved aside and allowed the stately looking man to step forward. "Wayfarer," he said to the unseen prisoner, "your trial is waived based on accounts. You stand convicted of brigandage in the empire and murder of Caesar's own soldiers. Your death will come in but a few hours at Golgotha." The man peered into the cell as if searching. "A word from the convicted, perhaps?"

After a few seconds of silence, the robed man nodded and moved to my cell. I swallowed and attempted to stand. After a moment's struggle, in which I missed the first half of the man's discourse, I rose to my feet.

"...of soldiers of Caesar. You will be executed at Golgotha by the light of this sun. Is there a word from the convicted?" The middle-aged man looked at my battered form and his nose gave a subtle wrinkle. Behind him, the young scribes stopped writing on their clay tablets and both looked at me expectantly.

I stepped forward to the bars, leaned my body against the cool iron, and said in a shaky voice, "I murdered no one, save one of these thieves you mention. And I, myself, stole nothing." I took a deep breath, winced at the pain and continued, "How is it, sir, that I find myself flogged and sentenced to death?"

The man rubbed his shaven chin and said, "Your comrade next to you has already given you up as one of his fellow thieves. If, wayfarer, you are innocent of all of these charges, why would you steal armor from a murdered soldier and don it to aid in your escape? This was witnessed by nearly a dozen soldiers and twice that in citizens. In my experience as governor of Judea, I would consider these accounts 'damning evidence', as would any educated man. Your band, these 'Wolves of the Jordan', have terrorized Judea long enough, I think, poor wayfarer."

The governor's scribes scratched his immortal words upon the clay.

"Why do you call me 'wayfarer'?" I asked. "My name is Dismas, a freedman from the Flavius family of the Menenia tribe in Sychar. I am a citizen, deemed free by Publius Gracus after I won a-"

The governor's nose twitched again and he raised a hand to silence me. "Where are your manumission papers, Dismas?"

I shook my head and muttered, "They... they were lost." My thoughts were jumbled as I vaguely remembered burning the papers long ago.

The governor smiled at me. "No man would squander a citizenship such as you have, and Publius died three years ago. I call you a wayfarer because that is what you are. A vagabond who has left the correct course – a journeyman who has forsaken the path of righteousness to tread upon sin. All who have sat in these cells have left the correct course, just as all who have walked to the hill have forsaken the course. You strike me as no different... though perhaps more articulate than your other light-fingered predecessors. The slave-mark on your arm tells a wholly different tale of your past and I question if we should not add a charge of slave-flight to your sign, in addition to robbery and murder."

I looked down to the frayed fabric at my arm and winced when I saw the brand was fully visible for all to see.

"As your brand suggests, you have been unfaithful to our laws," he declared and waited a few beats for his scribes to catch up. "May the god of Judea forgive you, wayfarer." He then smiled to himself and added, "Perhaps you'll be meeting him sooner than you think with today's procession, if the crowds have their way." One of the soldiers gave a half-stifled laugh and the group then returned to the room at the end of the hallway.

After standing at the bars for another minute, staring at the troubled dust where my sentencing group had stood, I moved back to the rear stone wall and sat down carefully. My entire body throbbed with pain and I felt suddenly nauseous with fear.

You're going to die, I thought. Painfully. These Romans will stretch it out for days if they can.

After a while, a man wearing a dirty tunic entered the hallway with three long contrivances and stuck the first into the ground in front of the cell next to me. He then moved in front of my cell, gave me a malicious wink and shoved the second device into the dirt directly in front of my bars. It was a sign-post for accused criminals – little more than a hastily carved notice. Mine read 'Robbery and Murder' in Greek, Latin and Hebrew.

The man sneered and said, "The Skull will be fed well today, convict." His snickering faded down the hall as he left.

Turning, I placed my head on the cool stone wall and agonized over the coming hours. Later, when I opened my eyes to the wall, I saw a thin scratching in stone directly in front of my face. It was a piece of scripture from the Jewish writings which read, '*What man can live and not see death, or save himself from the power of the grave?'*

No man can, I thought, and certainly not I. Putting my forehead on this etching, I wept against the stone.

# X X X X I I - *The Skull*

The day of my crucifixion was hot and windy.

An army of dust specters made a hasty patrol through the city streets, heralded only by their ghostly howl through the stone alcoves of the city. An unruly mob had filled the north courtyard of the Antonia Fortress and the shouts of angry men merged with that of the wind. Spectators young and old had managed to fill every nook in and around the courtyard, sitting atop walls, perched within dank crevices, roosting within tree branches; all of them were vying for a view of the trial.

My own vantage offered no great view and my eyes were too clouded with dust and sweat to see anything past my outstretched hand, which appeared blurry as well. The only thing that remained in focus was a pair of worn military sandals a foot away from my face that shifted in and out of focus as I lay in the dust of the courtyard. The soldier's feet moved occasionally, always in time with the surge of the crowd. Squinting in the sun, I glanced upward and saw the soldier was carrying my *tittulus* sign-post which displayed my charges. With a grimace, I closed my eyes and lay back in the dust.

The sun was hot upon my scourged back and the occasional

trickle of blood down my lower back made me shudder. The smell of sweat and blood was overpowering.

A loud voice, presumably that of Governor Pilate, pled to the crowd in words that were lost among the mob's echoing screams. The violent discourse went back and forth for a while and I wondered if this trial was for me.

Then, building quickly like a brushfire, a chant arose from the group: "Release to us Barabbas! Release to us Barabbas!"

For a few painful moments, the name flittered across my mind and I knew it was a name I recognized. Barabbas... the rebel who had given us the information about the *eschatos kleros*.

And now, I mused with puzzlement, the crowds wanted this zealot – imprisoned for murder and rebellion – to be released. As all knew, it was the occasional custom for a prisoner to be released to the crowd on the day of a feast – if the crowd so pressed – but why would they attempt to free a man such as Barabbas?

The horde's chant died down as another loud voice from the front yelled to Pilate, "This man is not our king! Herod is our king! Crucify him!" He repeated the last two words several times and a new chant began; this one was even louder than the previous one.

The refined, and now thinly strung, voice of Governor Pilate rose above the chant: "I have examined him in your presence! Verily, I find no basis for charges against him. Herod has sent him back to us, and as I conclude, he has done nothing deserving of death!"

The mob's vocal outrage filled the courtyard. The chanting continued after the initial chorus of screams. Crucify him! Crucify him!

Pilate, his voice now angry, shouted, "I will have him punished

404

and then release him!"

Like a ravenous pack of animals, the crowd howled their dissent. One angry spectator yelled, "If you release him, you are no friend of Caesar's! Any man who claims to be a king or divinity opposes Caesar!" The crowd screamed its concurrence.

I craned my head upwards and looked past the soldier's feet. Behind the governor, a prisoner was held upright between two soldiers. His head was hung low and his face was obscured by shadow and sodden hair. The man was of average height – as tall as the two soldiers – and as my vision continued to clear, it appeared as if the man had been dressed in a large purple robe. A dark, twisted garland of sorts adorned the man's lowered head. My eyes continued to sort distortion from reality and I saw that the garland was actually a crudely made crown of thorns that had been pressed onto the man's scalp and over his forehead. The man's hair, black with blood and sweat, hung over his eyes.

Slowly, I craned my neck to the left and saw another prisoner – this one half-naked like myself. He was large and muscular – also bloody and trembling. The man's hair was short and curly and when he looked up from his study of the bloodied sand at his feet, I recognized his crooked nose and dark eyes as those of Jaximo.

We would die together, I thought, my enemy and I.

As the crowd continued to bay at the governor, I lay my head back on the ground and allowed my consciousness to drift away. I thought of Jael and Nahum. Were they finally safe? Had they fled the city or were they watching this screaming horde?

I then attempted to imagine a better time and place: my younger childhood in Sychar, playing with Tarius near Jacob's Well. The smell of blossoms around our hill. Before the cursed race and my exile from the family, a majestic red sunset splayed over our childhood kingdom...

The soldier next to me struck me in the shoulder with the *tittulus* sign and said, "Watch, thief. No miracles today, I suppose." He then laughed and those spectators around him also laughed at his joke. Following his orders, I looked back up to the stage.

The robed prisoner was being flogged. When the count reached thirty-nine, the crowd chanted, "Thirty-eight!" The soldier looked to Pilate as if caught in a mistake and the crowd laughed their jollity, hoping to induce the soldier into giving an extra lash. Governor Pilate shook his head solemnly and nodded to the group of soldiers near the entrance to the fortress. They parted as two guards led a dirty looking man towards the governor. The man was of a slight build and his hair was spiked into a strange array of odd angles.

Barabbas was smiling as one of the soldiers brandished a dagger to cut his rope bindings. Even from this distance and through my blurred vision I recognized the blade as my prized dagger that I had left in Rapha-Ayzal's chest. The rebel's eyes met mine as his binds were cut and his fanatical smile widened even further. He raised his hand towards me, which was still wrapped with frayed rope, and pointed his accusatory finger at me, just as he did during his capture. He then laughed and took a sauntering step into the crowd who had forgotten him as soon as he had been freed.

The soldiers surrounding the stage unshackled the robed prisoner and drug him to the crowd who immediately seized him in such murderous haste I wondered if they were cannibals hungry for flesh. I watched as two soldiers carried a thick cedar crossbeam, nearly six feet in length, and dropped it near the prisoner. Two more beams were carried from the side of the fortress and the crowd started to part in two directions, allowing a path towards Jaximo and another path towards me.

My heart started to pound in my chest. The walk north through the city was next, and quite abruptly I found myself terrified of death – the terrible pain to come and then the unknown. My breaths came in ragged gasps. I longed for the darkness of unconsciousness.

The soldier next to me seized my arm and pulled me to my knees with a strong grip. "Here it comes, thief," he said in a mocking voice just loud enough for me to hear over the jeering of the crowd. "Your own wooden pack to carry on your journey. Can't forget your traveler's pack."

Another soldier was suddenly next to me, holding my other arm as the wicked looking crossbeam neared me, moving through the parting crowd like wooden royalty. Some of the spectators reached out and allowed their hands to brush against the beam in culpable reverence.

Sychar, I thought, closing my eyes. The fresh smell of the fields. The laughter of Tarius as we defended our hill from scores of imagined enemies. My mother's dear face, wishing me good fortune on my journey away from home…

The soldiers on either side of me pushed the crossbeam against my back but would not allow me to fall. Splinters dug into my already ripped skin and I gasped with the new pain and weight.

"A gift from our fallen soldiers to you, murdering filth," one of the soldiers whispered in my ear.

"Come now," someone griped. "Be a man about it and accept

your burden."

A leather whip suddenly opened the skin of my right calf and I cried out in pain.

"Raise yourself and walk," one said, "or I'll skin your face with this leather."

My heart pounding, I remained kneeling and stared at the bloody ground beneath me. The weight of the crossbeam was already pressing the air from my lungs.

The crack of the whip sounded again and my left calf erupted in hot pain. Wincing, I lifted my head and saw the robed prisoner already carrying his crossbeam past me, head lowered in exertion. His face was hidden from my view as he passed. The trail of blood he left was quickly trampled into a sticky red dust by the mass of followers.

"The Jew King has taken his cross," the soldier said into my ear. "Be a good boy and follow him." The whip explored the flesh beneath my skin once more, this time at my thigh.

Slowly, I stood. It was not the sting of the whip or the threats from the soldiers next to me that gave me such compulsion. It was the generous trail of blood I saw in the first prisoner's wake. He had not doted or straggled in his inevitable burden, but had taken it willingly without a grudge. In his slow stride, I detected some sort of courage. He was *ready* for the cross. Head lowered, he carried the damnable crossbeam on his freshly ruined back without words of spite as if it had been his charge his whole life.

This – not the whip's forages into my flesh nor the cruel taunts – gave me strength to rise, keeping the heavy crossbeam across the breadth of my shoulders. The oaken burden slid for a moment, driving myriad splinters into my back, but I kept my footing despite my swollen ankle. I adjusted the crossbeam with a grimace and followed the first prisoner's crimson trail.

***

Step by step, as my own drops of blood merged with those of the prisoner I followed, we were led and jostled north through the streets towards the Gennath Gate. And beyond that, just outside the city walls, the stone quarry and Golgotha waited, surely as hungry for blood as the spectators.

Twice before the gate, I had fallen and had been unable to rise without help, despite numerous lashes from the whip. On the second time, one of the spectators was pulled from the crowd and forced to help me with my burden as the soldiers were tired of helping me with their own splintered hands.

With this new help, I was able to turn and glance behind me. I saw Jaximo moving up the street towards me with a red face. The anger was still in his eyes, while my own fury had been forgotten long before our northbound walk through the city.

As we slowly neared the stone arch of the Gennath Gate, I looked up and saw that the crowd in front of me had stopped. The robed prisoner had evidently fallen. I stood there trembling beside the stranger next to me as my blood collected on the dirt at our feet.

There was a chorus of lashes from the soldiers near the prisoner and after a few moments – when the prisoner did not rise – the soldiers picked out a traveler from random in the crowd and forced him to take up the crossbeam on his own back. Fearing much more than a verbal lashing, the stranger complied and struggled with the beam for a moment before moving through the gate. The prisoner was then forced to his feet and he continued walking, this time without the burden.

409

We continued onward, through the gate and into the windy hills outside the city walls.

In front of me, a heap of veiled women had pressed towards the bloodied prisoner, wailing in earnest. I saw the prisoner turn to them and address them in a weak voice I could barely hear over the wind and jeers. I only heard the proclamation's end as the man said, "For if men do these things when the tree is green... what will happen when it is dry?" The women were then pushed aside by the soldiers and we moved on through the stone quarry.

As I looked over the heads of those in front of me, I saw the road dip past the quarry where dozens of tombs had been cut into the rock wall. The crowd continued onward, past the tombs to the hill beyond.

To the Skull, I thought with a shudder.

As it did when Obadiah took us there days previous, it appeared to be a mere hill – in no way resembling a skull from my vantage. Three tall, vertical beams had been raised from their fissures and were laid out along the ground by soldiers who waited with jaded faces. Behind the hill, a large trash heap smoldered; its gray smoke curled north with the wind.

The first prisoner ascended the hill, a soldier at each of his arms. When he reached the hill's apex, the soldiers stripped the robe from his body. The man's torn back was muscled from hard labor and I wondered what his trade had been. While not overly long, his dripping hair hung over the back of his neck and covered his forehead and ears. Facing away from me, he was moved to the center beam and then forced to his knees. The man charged with carrying his crossbeam hefted it up the hill after the prisoner. The traveler's face was tight with exhaustion and he was no doubt glad to have finally reached the hill – whereas the prisoner surely wasn't.

As the wind continued its howl around us, I fell with a gasp at the hill's base. The man who helped me with the crossbeam was forced to his knees at my sudden collapse. Those around me laughed in delight at my obvious fear.

After being drug by the soldiers to the top of the hill, I was dropped next to one of the beams on the ground. Much of this wood was dented and gouged, and I saw that it had been permanently stained a reddish-brown color. It would receive another coating on this day, I mused fearfully.

The soldiers near the first prisoner were fixing the man's crossbeam into the horizontal recess of the vertical beam. The crossbeam slid into place with an oaken thud and the soldiers began hammering thick, foot-long nails into the crossbeam to hold it firmly into its niche within the vertical beam. Two nails on each side. The hollow blows from the large iron hammer echoed against the city walls and voyaged throughout the windy quarry.

The prisoner was then guided onto the center cross, his back against the vertical beam while his arms were stretched out against the crossbeam he had just been forced to carry through Jerusalem. The hammer-toting soldier stood over the right arm, waiting as two other soldiers tied the man's forearms to the crossbeam to prevent the prisoner's weight from tearing through the nail. The rope was double-knotted and tight, probably even strong enough to support the prisoner without aid of nails.

The round-faced soldier with the hammer then brushed aside the other two soldiers with his knee as he withdrew one of the long, rusted nails from the bag around his shoulder and knelt next to the man's right hand. He looked at the prisoner's crown of thorns and was about to deliver some sort of snide remark, but faltered. His mouth opened and closed several times, but no sound came out or if one did it was swallowed by the wind. One of the standing soldiers blocked my view of the prisoner's face.

The prisoner, from his bed upon the cross, could be heard whispering something to the soldier then, and after a long sigh, the soldier gave a sad nod and placed the tip of the nail in the palm of the prisoner's hand. The fingers of the prisoner were trembling and I also saw that the nail trembled, though not from the prisoner's shaking but from the soldier's. After a few more seconds of hesitation, the round-faced soldier raised his iron hammer to deliver the first blow. I looked away just as he brought it down upon the nail's head with great force.

The prisoner gasped but did not scream. He gave a low moan through nearly a dozen more hammer strikes. I gave another look to the center cross and saw that they had also nailed the inside of the prisoner's ankles – just above the heel – against the dented bump of wood that served as a diminutive footrest at the sides of the vertical beam. The same small man I had seen in the hallway outside the soldier's barracks proudly displayed the *tittulus* sign over the prisoner's head at the top of the cross. *King of the Jews*, it read, though I was still greatly confused as to whom this prisoner was.

The soldiers then fiddled with my own crossbeam and nailed it into its place within the fold of the vertical beam. A separate group of soldiers fastened rope around the top of the center cross with the crowned prisoner nailed upon it. They then guided the base of the vertical beam against the stone lined hole and started raising the top of

412

the cross upwards by pulling the thick rope down the hill. When it was nearly vertical, the crowd hushed, waiting for the beam to drop its measured distance into the fissure. When it finally did drop with a loud crack, many of the spectators cheered. The prisoner gasped with the pain of his tearing joints and lack of air. His breathing was ragged and tinted with quick pants as he rose up on weak, nailed feet.

I was then forced by several pairs of hands to lie down upon the wood of my own cross. I closed my eyes as my sore back touched the wood. My head met the vertical beam and my hands were grudgingly stretched out across the crossbeam. They quickly and expertly tied my arms to the wood. Gasping for air, my heart pounding, I forced myself to open my eyes and confront the soldier with the hammer. His eyes were blurry from tears as he knelt over my right hand. He placed the tip of the massive nail against my palm and raised the hammer.

"What…" I sputtered, "…did he say to you?"

The man hesitated another second and a wind-claimed tear flew from his cheek and struck me in the chest. He took a deep breath and swung the hammer down against the nail's head with distraught force. The pain was sharply immense and I screamed out as the Praetorian soldier from hours ago had hoped I would. Amazingly, the pain grew in its intensity as they continued with my other hand as warm blood rushed out from around the nails.

Above my screaming and pitiful form, the small man with the signs bent down and started to fasten my *tittulus* at the top of my cross. Robbery and Murder.

My rat-bitten feet were then jostled against the wooden bump in the sides of the vertical beam. Nails were placed against the soft tendon, just above my heel and the hammering began again. This time, as the rusty iron pierced my flesh, scraped against my bone and affixed me to the cross, I gasped mightily for air as if one drowning. I closed my eyes and panted in more air as they finished with my second foot.

When the echoing blows stopped ringing through my head, I opened my eyes and saw the blue sky. Clouds moved hastily across the clear expanse as if fleeing something sinister. My whole body throbbed and the pain in my hands and feet grew to a maddening level. My breathing continued to come in ragged, throaty gasps and I suddenly tasted hot bile as my gorge rose. I started to choke. More vomit came up and with a sputtering satisfaction I realized I might die quickly from choking.

My view of the sky suddenly jerked downwards as the cross was hefted by the ropes. The upper part of my cross rose slowly. First, the towers near Herod's palace came into view, followed by the city walls. Then the crowd came into view: a few hundred faces ravenous for death.

When I was nearly vertical, I coughed the vomit from my lungs and breathed deeply of the coarse wind.

With a sudden lurch downwards, the vertical beam fell into its hole and the nails tore into my hands and feet with an audible rip. Yet my flesh held fast to the nails and the ropes around my arms did their duty. The breath was instantly taken from my lungs and I was forced to press upward against the iron in my ankles to take a breath. *The pain...* Through my worst nightmares – through my days of imagining this moment – I had not adequately prepared myself for this. Such a preparation was an impossible feat.

The wind caused my cross to sway in its hole, rattling the wood against the stone base. No one had cheered for my crucifixion.

Each breath was agony. Despite any supposed effort to refrain from breathing – to reach the end more quickly – my body continued its jerky motion in rising upward for air. The nails continued their slow tear through my flesh yet they never actually tore completely through my extremities but kept my hands and feet fastened to the rough wood. The Romans, as all knew, were experts in the trade of suffering.

I turned my head and saw the first prisoner, the alleged King of the Jews, suffering on his own cross, rising intermittently for breaths. His face remained downcast, awash in blood and dust. Blood from his pierced hands and feet continued to dribble from the nails and were claimed by the wind to spatter against the stones and ferns below.

The sound of hammering started again and this time it was accompanied by screaming. Jaximo howled like an animal as he was nailed to his cross. Intermingled with his shrieks of pain were vile curses and impotent declarations. When the hammering was done, his cross was slowly raised alongside ours. The large thief screamed the entire time as if on fire.

Beneath us, some of the robed locals raised their fists at the center cross and hurled insults at the prisoner. "You who were going to destroy the temple and rebuild it!" one shouted. "Come down from there and save yourself!"

This invigorated some of the other spectators and they joined in with their own affronts, yelling, "You saved others! Great King, save yourself and we will believe in you! If not, you are nothing but a common fool!"

The center prisoner rose up for air, looked upwards to the blue sky, and said, "Father, forgive them…" He gasped for air and finished, "…for they know not what they do."

415

The few people in the crowd who heard this statement made as if they were tearing their robes in indignation as they spread the man's words out to the rest of the horde.

I turned away and stared out into the hills. In the south, dark clouds loomed against the horizon. My eyes blurred with new tears as my body struggled to survive despite my bested spirit.

***

Hours.

Nailed to a wooden cross.

Thirsty, bleeding out from my hands and feet.

Twice more, bile came up into my throat and I was forced to cough it out over my chin. My lungs felt as if they would burst. My knees ached from the constant rising motion my legs forced upon themselves. The scores of infected rat bites yearned to be scratched.

The black clouds – like the sable cloak of the absent Man of Shadow – had nearly completed their pursuit towards Jerusalem. The wind strengthened and a rumble of luminance peppered the dark mountain of clouds. A brutal storm was nearing but no one on the ground seemed to notice.

I watched the heckling of the center prisoner for a while, felt the now cool wind on my face and listened to the constant groans from Jaximo. Blood pounded loudly throughout my body in time with my slowly dying heart.

Quite suddenly, the black clouds were over the hill. The darkness swept over the city like a dark wave from the River Styx. Thunder rumbled throughout the land.

Next to me, the center prisoner cried out in a loud voice, "My God, my God, why have you forsaken me?" His voice held an infinite amount of despair. His words were familiar and I knew they were an echo from Jewish scripture.

Despite the disconcerting shadow across the land, the crowd continued to insult the man on the center cross and some more spirited men even threw the occasional stone at his rigid form. "He called to Elijah," one said. Several of the spectators then fixed a sponge upon a long stalk of hyssop, doused it with vinegar and gall, and raised it to the prisoner's lips for him to drink. Once he caught a whiff of the sponge, he gagged and the crowd laughed at him as they dabbed the sponge all over his face and neck so the potent liquid would run into his wounds.

"Perhaps Elijah will come from this darkness and save him now!" someone yelled and those around him laughed uneasily.

Why did they hate him so? I wondered, despite my pain. Who was this 'King of the Jews'?

Below the center prisoner, at the bloodied base of his cross, a gathering of soldiers knelt over the stones, tossing rocks in lot for the man's possessions.

Each of our crosses rattled in their holes with the stark wind. A few sprinkles of rain could be felt whisking from the darkening sky.

I gazed out amidst the crowd, searching for Jael but the men and women were blurred together. All I saw were masks of anger.

Jaximo's wheezing cries were suddenly directed towards me. "Dismas!" he wailed between breaths. "I'll find you in Hell, Dismas!"

As the wind whipped my hair in front of my eyes, I turned slowly and stared at the prisoner next to me, ignoring Jaximo's words.

*Father, forgive them... for they know not what they do.*

With another gasp, this time fueled by an anguish that had nothing to do with my physical pain, I realized who was crucified next

417

to me. I turned to face the crowd and tried to listen more intently to their jeers.

"Come now, Christ," one yelled with an upraised fist. "Save yourself!"

I looked back to the prisoner, the miracle worker Jesus, and started crying again, this time in shame. I thought of Blind Abner, who had been healed simply by this man's touch. I thought of the mysteriously soft bread that Levi had given me.

*When you escape...* Obadiah had whispered in the dust-filled rubble. *I want you to ask that teacher Jesus something for me. Could you... do this, scion?*

What would I ask him for, *Protos*?

*Forgiveness.* The last words of a dying thief.

The sprinkling grew in temper and thunder rumbled overhead within the black clouds. The crowd murmured amongst themselves in hushed tones, as if the darkness where a bad omen. Some had already left the quarry, while others were slowly moving away from the hill. In such contrast from their journey to the hill, their faces now displayed indignity.

I stared at the man next to me on the cross. He stared downward, away from the darkness, and under the bloody mess of thorns pushing against His scalp, I saw a great sadness in His eyes. Almost a look of pity. Already, this man – this divine Son of God – had forgiven those who had drug Him to the Skull. He raised His broken body for a weak breath, pushing against the nails within His feet.

*Forgiveness.*

On Jesus' left side, Jaximo cursed the clouds, groaned in pain and then fixed his stare at the figure upon the central cross. "You!" he spat from his rigid posture upon his own beam. "Are you not the Christ?" He gasped for another breath, rose again and yelled, "Save yourself and us!"

Jaximo was still blind to the truth – something I found myself accepting as I stared at the innocent man dying next to me. "Don't you fear God," I yelled to Jaximo, "since you are under the same sentence." I gathered another thin breath. "We are punished justly... for we are getting what our deeds deserve. But this man... has done *nothing* wrong."

Jaximo turned away, spat at the crowd and offered another painful moan.

The rain had picked up fully now, carried forcefully by the wind.

Turning from Jaximo, I looked at Jesus, who was staring at me with warm yet pained eyes. "Jesus," I said softly, reverently. "Remember me when you come into your kingdom." Obadiah's request went unsaid. It had already been granted. This I felt and knew.

With a nod of His thorn-crowned head, Jesus answered, "I tell you the truth... today you will be with me in paradise."

Despite the pain, I smiled as the rain beat down upon us. I would not feel the Black River's current on this day. After the last several hours – the last several years – paradise sounded more than nice. In a way, I thought wearily, I had managed to escape as Obadiah had said I would.

My body rose painfully for another breath – one of my last – and I looked down at the dwindling crowd. Instantly, through the blur of faces, I saw Jael near the back of the horde. Nahum was in her arms.

They both turned from their gaze upon the center cross and met my eyes with tearful expressions. Amazingly – *impossibly* – the hound Mathias was at their feet. The desert mutt was also looking up at the three crosses.

Behind them, standing taller than the other men, the cloaked Man of Shadow stared at me with a warm smile. Though it had meant my death, I had been guided to this hill to witness this horrible and wonderful moment. This, I realized, had been my charge: to die next to the Son of God – to find redemption at the very end. My own personal miracle.

Next to me, Jesus took a deep breath and said, "Father… into your hands… I commit my spirit." And, slumping against the cross, He breathed no more.

Thunder rumbled again, though this time it sounded as if the very earth had cried its lament.

It was, I thought, the sound of a Father losing his Son.

The wind roared through the hills and the walls of the city seemed to groan in fear of reprisal. Below me, one of the centurions leaned against the center cross, bloodying his hands, and said in a reverent voice, "Surely this man was the Son of God."

My own pain had numbed to such a degree that my only labor was rising for intermittent breaths.

Below me, the soldiers stirred in vexation, evidently wanting to be done on the hill Golgotha. A young soldier with meaty arms now wielded the iron hammer – I do not know where the round-faced soldier had fled to – and he went to Jaximo's legs and smashed the iron head against the bones under his knees. Jaximo's scream slowly diminished as he found he could not rise again for a breath. He started to gasp and sputter. The last words on his lips were a curse towards me.

My legs were broken next, though I felt only happiness as the bones were shattered. The last of the air drained from my worn lungs as I watched the soldiers take a spear and pierce the side of Jesus to see if He was still alive. He did not move as blood and water flowed over the spear's shaft. The soldiers stood in silence as the mixture fused with the rain and was taken by the wind.

My lungs burned horribly as my legs subconsciously tried to push against the shards of broken bone to raise me up for air. It mattered not.

As blackness started to converge at the corners of my vision, I looked up to the wall of shadowy clouds above. They stirred, moving in anger as they showed hints of emotion in their churning swath.

When the blackness had fully consumed me, a light suddenly pierced through this veil – delicately at first before spreading over the entire dark vista before me. The darkness was fully consumed and only a brilliant light remained. Emerging from this light, Jesus stopped in front of me and I saw that He was no longer bloodied and spent. He wore a white robe which matched the brilliance of the light around Him and a new crown – one made of light and not thorns. He reached His hand down to me, and with a warm smile, said, *"Come with me, friend."*

Bound by the nails no longer – nor by heartache, sin nor strife – I reached out and took His hand.

EPILOGUE - *Transcending*

*The tale of Dismas was finished.*

*Over Siergo's shoulder, through the open stone doorway of the watchtower, the vineyard was aglow with the dawn's subtle light. The night was fully spent and the shadows retreated to their refuges. The moon was but a memory beyond the horizon and the stars had faded with the red and purple light.*

*Staring at the traveler before me, my eyes shiny with tears, I asked, "How did he tell you the whole tale, Siergo? How could he tell you its end?"*

*Across from me, he was silent.*

*"I didn't know it had been like that," I then said. "The stories... they had always been different, I suppose. Impersonal. I..." I swallowed and looked to the table. "No one had ever told me of that day. Not like that, I mean to say."*

*"It was a hard day," Siergo admitted sadly. His own eyes seemed suddenly clouded with emotion. "Wonderful and terrible at the same time."*

*"But how..." I started, thinking of how to word my question. "When did Dismas impart this tale to you?"*

*Despite my inquiries, I already knew the answer. Somewhere, deep inside my mind – my heart, really – I knew exactly who sat before me in the watchtower. If true, the questions certainly multiplied; the implications were too fantastic to fully comprehend.*

*Siergo nodded, met my eyes with his fierce blue gaze and said, "In shadow, I was with him through it all, from Sychar to the cross... and even after the cross, I was there with him. My appointed charge."*

*My mouth opened to form another question, but the words would not come. The Man of Shadow's hair, once a sable black, was now a brazen white so many years after the events in Judea. I had initially thought this to be from disease, but now knew it was from his own preference and could probably be changed at will.*

*So many questions... My mind blurred as I opened my mouth yet again and still nothing came out. This man had advanced out of the setting sun like a mirage that refused to dissolve. He had no need of water or food – not even rest. It was* my *need he had come to slake.*

*The divine guardian across from me stood suddenly, gave a look over his shoulder to the breaking dawn behind him, and said, "Once again, Marcus, your hospitality is appreciated. You bless yourself by listening to this tale, but do not let it end with the absence of a lowly attendant. Keep the tale alive. Remember the Skull and the One who died there. It is important to know of this pain – to know what was undergone for each of us." His strong face was joyful as he spoke. "It is never too late for redemption. Never too late for forgiveness. Dismas found his at the very end. Yours has come in the middle of your life's journey. Transcend, Marcus."*

*And with a warm nod, he left the watchtower and entered the bright vineyard.*

"Wait!" I cried out, suddenly finding my stricken voice. Standing, I followed the mysterious guardian outside, into the rising column of light that traversed the vineyard. The hills outside the Apostello acreage were ablaze with color and cool mist.

As Siergo continued to walk eastbound, towards the blinding light, I said, "There is still so much that..." My voice faltered with emotion.

Little more than a half-faded silhouette amid the rays of white luminance, Siergo turned and said, "Transcend, Marcus Athleo. Despite every darkness or affliction... transcend."

And the light closed over him. I squinted into the rising sun but could no longer see the traveler. Untold minutes, I stood there, searing my eyes as I squinted into the sunrise, hoping for one final glimpse of him. Eventually, the sun was high enough from the horizon to offer a view of the brightly lit, rolling hills beneath the blinding orb. There was no receding figure among the green knolls.

With the setting sun he had arrived, I pondered, and with the rising sun he had departed.

My mind still fresh with the images of suffering upon the cross atop the Skull, I wiped the tears from my face and started back to the watchtower to ready myself for the day... and for the rest of my life, which had surely changed with the knowledge of Dismas' tale.

*** 

So many years later, the metallic scent of rain is in the evening air and I'm hoping it will bring a guardian back.

Thirty years have passed since that night in the vineyard, and I've told Dismas' tale to many though most have cast it aside as mere fable. Such conclusions hurt my esteem and worst of all, give me cause to wonder about that night so long ago near Hispania, when I toiled in the dirt as a vineyard watchman.

Twice more, in the last thirty years, I have seen Siergo. Once, in a radiant snowstorm north of Thessalonica – a mere shadow in the white crested hills. The black-cloaked phantom said not a word but raised a single hand into the falling snow towards me, as if to say, 'Be at peace, Marcus. Transcend...' My own thoughts at the time, before I saw Siergo that evening, had been terribly forlorn, as I had just walked out of a tavern, half-drunk and contemplating the end of all things, including my life. The snow fell so heavily that Siergo's form was lost in the sallow blizzard. Once more, my fortitude was restored.

The second time – little more than a decade ago – having been terribly ill for a time while staying as a guest in a villa on the east shore of the island of Sicily, Siergo approached me once more from the dazzling rays of the setting sun. We spoke for a great while that suspended night and he imparted another epic tale of a different charge of his. This tale was even more harrowing and laudable than that of Dismas and I find it to be a pity that I have not shared this new story with but a handful of close friends on the island.

That night in Sicily, my body was healed from the telling of this new tale. Siergo then disappeared into the rising sun, walking towards the beach – unafraid of the dark waves. As in the vineyard so many years ago, I wept aloud at his departure. I have since deduced that while not currently appointed to a charge, his coming and going can only take place during a change – an alteration of some sort – such as the rising or setting sun, or perhaps a storm or spectacle of falling stars or snow. This thought was furthered during my later readings of the Jewish scriptures when I read about an angel of God – or perhaps an incarnate version of God himself – confronting Jacob before they wrestled through the night. Towards the end of this match, this heavenly being told Jacob, "Let me go, for it is daybreak." Supported even by scripture, this time seems special to those who walk between the realms.

The sand in my glass has run low, baring only a fine line that I watch evaporate with each passing season. Often, I wonder if Siergo will come to me at the end as he did for Dismas. My end, which will have nothing of such drama, will be slow and expected. When I think of meeting the bronze-faced guardian yet again in this life, before I pass on to a place where I can speak freely with him, a smile comes across my wrinkled face.

Surely, he will be there at the end. He and his Lord and Commander, for whom I have yet to face but am most eager to do so.

In my lonely cottage, paid for by a lifetime of savings and odd jobs, a quiet rain has begun to fall during the sunset and I pray that such a display will bring Siergo into my presence. This is a common prayer.

As the rain falls above and as the sun sets in the west – giving a gentle purple hue to the falling drops – I await the end... always transcending.

# AUTHOR'S NOTE

While this is a work of fiction, the brief but wonderful exchange between the unnamed criminals and Jesus, while the three were being crucified, can be found in the Bible – in the twenty-third chapter of Luke. Different Christian traditions have assigned various names to this thief – commonly referred to as "the penitent thief" – though he is most widely known as Dismas, which stemmed from the apocryphal work, the *Gospel of Nicodemus*. Other than a small handful of minor stories in different traditions, there is no historical information about the thieves crucified alongside Jesus of Nazareth.

www.ingramcontent.com/pod-product-compliance
Lightning Source LLC
Chambersburg PA
CBHW071217250626
47163CB00001B/23